Praise for Linda Winfree's *Anything But Mine*

"Ms. Winfree has taken romantic suspense to a whole new level... an exceptional read that leaves you with a lasting impression... She's a star of the genre and I won't even be reading the blurbs anymore; if her name's on the cover, I'm buying it."

~ *Rachel C., Fallen Angel Reviews*

"Anything But Mine is an emotional minefield... I can't recommend Anything But Mine and the rest of Linda Winfree's Hearts of the South Series highly enough."

~ *Melissa, Joyfully Reviewed*

"Stanton and Autry... are fully developed and likable individuals, real flesh and blood characters... If you are a fan of romantic suspense, ANYTHING BUT MINE by Linda Winfree is well worth the time and money spent."

~ *Scarlet, Romance Junkies*

"Ms Winfree manages to put everything together along with the romance to make this one a gripping and emotionally-charged read."

~ *Mrs. Giggles*

"Winfree ties it all up nicely, with a believable romance and tremendous skill at creating suspense...This complicated tale is a great read."

~ *Literary Nymphs Reviews*

Look for these titles by
Linda Winfree

Now Available:

What Mattered Most

Hearts of the South Series
Truth and Consequences (Book 1)
His Ordinary Life (Book 2)
Hold On to Me (Book 3)
Anything But Mine (Book 4)
Memories of Us (Book 5)
Hearts Awakened (Book 6)
Fall Into Me (Book 7)

Coming Soon:

Hearts of the South Series
Facing It (Book 8)

Anything But Mine

Linda Winfree

A SAMHAIN PUBLISHING, LTD. publication.

Samhain Publishing, Ltd.
577 Mulberry Street, Suite 1520
Macon, GA 31201
www.samhainpublishing.com

Anything But Mine
Copyright © 2009 by Linda Winfree
Print ISBN: 978-1-60504-084-4
Digital ISBN: 1-59998-891-7

Editing by Anne Scott
Cover by Anne Cain

First Samhain Publishing, Ltd. electronic publication: March 2008
First Samhain Publishing, Ltd. print publication: January 2009

Dedication

The Class of 2008: Although you tried to keep it a secret by not signing the card, good deeds always come out. You will never know what a blessing you were to me that day or even over the five years you have been in my life. About all of you, I can never say that you are "anything but mine" because, as the kids I've taught the longest and loved the most, you are mine in my heart.

Even when I despaired that you'd ever learn how to use a comma or master sentence structure, when all you wanted to do was cut up, when you didn't want to write another essay or read *The Scarlet Letter*...you were special to me. You were my ninth graders, my sophomores, my juniors, my seniors.

So one last time... "All right, y'all, listen up. We've got things to do. This is important. *Focus!*"

I love you all very much and wish you the best in all you undertake.

Ms. Winfree's Favorite Students Ever: Ashby, Bryant, Brent, Whitney, Chelsea, Keke, Anna, Alex, Jordan, McLeod, Kaleb, Carrie, Kaley, Matt, Lindsey, Brittany, Amanda, Ashley, Vance, Emili, Layne, Preston, Danielle, Holly, April, Jennifer, Oliver, Michele, Ashton, Jay, Justin...and Jakie.

Chapter One

She wasn't going to die. It just felt like she was.

And right now, she really, really wanted to.

Autry Holton rested her forehead against the cool wood of the vanity. The orange-scented cleaner she used wafted from the floor, and nausea churned in her stomach again. Whoever had coined the term "morning sickness" was an idiot. It was more like morning, noon and night sickness, and anyone who said it didn't last beyond the third month needed a mental health check too. Tonight, she'd be willing to bet labor pains wouldn't feel like menstrual cramps, either.

Holding the vanity for support, she pushed to her feet. Her knees trembled, and she rested for a minute, breathing through her nose. Avoiding her reflection, she reached for her toothbrush and toothpaste. She didn't have to look to know her eyes were red and watery, her hair stringy, her skin pasty.

Yes, she had that pregnant-woman glow people raved about.

The mint cleansed the awful taste and left her feeling somewhat refreshed. She spit and rinsed her mouth. This constant nausea couldn't last five more months, could it? At least, if nothing else, it would go away when she had the baby. Stress. It had to be the unremitting stress. If she could just relax—

A high-pitched whine rent the air, and she dropped the cup, ceramic shards flying everywhere, plinking off the tile, hitting the wall with soft thumps. Her heart thudded, tempo picking up to an uncomfortable race. Oh God. He'd come for her, just as he'd said he would. Her stomach pitched again, and she wrapped her arms across the small bulge of her baby. She couldn't let him hurt the baby.

Think, Autry. She slammed the door closed and threw the lock, hitting the panic button next to the light switch. In the bedroom, the phone rang. She took a step back, and pain sliced into her foot. The broken cup. Just a cut. She could handle that. She could handle anything as long as *he* didn't get through the bathroom door.

The phone continued to ring, and she strained to hear other noises—splintering doors, shattering glass, footsteps. Nothing. Simply the harsh whine of the alarm and the phone's shrill ring mingling with the roar of her pulse and her own rough breathing.

In her stomach, the baby fluttered, the low, soft movement she'd only noticed in the last few days. "It's all right," she whispered, the sound of her shaky voice too loud in the bathroom. She slid down to sit on the floor again, blood oozing from her foot to pool on the white tile.

"It's all right, baby," she said again, rubbing a palm over the soft mound. Maybe she should have gone for the phone, but that meant crossing the bedroom to get the cordless from her desk and she'd already been here, in the safe room with the panic button. Besides, if she didn't answer, the monitoring company would automatically call the sheriff's department. Help should be on the way. Everything would be fine. She just had to keep telling herself that. Help would arrive soon.

The lights went out. The alarm ceased its wild squeal in an instant. A neighbor's dog barked in a wild frenzy.

Autry screamed.

Stanton Reed slid from the patrol car and left the door slightly ajar. Sound traveled farther during the quietness of night and he didn't want the snick of a closing door to alert anyone to his presence. Darkness shrouded the neighborhood, punctuated only by pools of blue from security and street lights. Welcoming the shadows, he slipped into them, using the dark for cover. He jogged across a damp lawn, eyeing the street as he went. No one moving about, no one hiding under vehicles.

With each step, Autry's name beat in his head. Hard to

convince himself this was any routine call, when it was Autry's house, Autry's alarm, *Autry* not answering the phone.

Dogs barked in the distance, a wild chorus, but the alarm remained silent. A lawn away, he could see her house sitting, completely dark, even the outside lights extinguished. Foreboding shivered over him. Had someone cut the power, silencing the alarm before the neighbors awoke?

Why didn't she answer the damn phone?

Dread lay like a lump in his gut. Four minutes since dispatch had received the call from her alarm company, another two minutes before that between the initial alarm and the call to dispatch. A lot could happen in six minutes.

A person could die.

No. Damn it, he couldn't let anything happen to her. As he reached Autry's dark yard, one of the shadows to his right moved, morphed into the running form of Tick Calvert, his lead investigator. Any other time, he and Tick both would have been home in bed this time of night, but tonight, Stanton was thankful for the flu that had more than half of his deputies incapacitated. Autry deserved the best his department could offer. He might not have been the right man for her personally, but he and Tick were the best cops to respond to her call.

"See anything?" Tick whispered as he reached Stanton's side. He had the entry ram slung over his shoulder, flashlight off but ready in his hand.

Stanton shook his head, trying to still the nervous pulsing under his skin. No noises came from the house. He closed his eyes for a brief moment. God, let her be okay. Don't let him be too late. "You?"

"Nothing." Tick tilted his head toward the house. "Ready?"

"Yeah." With the well-oiled timing of a long partnership, they circled the house, Tick moving right, Stanton moving left, so they met up at the back door.

"Looks clear," Tick said, his voice a mere breath. He lowered the entry ram and stepped back. "Ready to do this?"

He'd been ready four minutes ago. "Just do it."

Seconds later, the steelcore door swung inward with a deafening bang. The sound echoed in the still night, and the dogs barked again, wilder this time. The door hung on its hinges at a drunken angle, and Tick laid the ram aside. Stanton eased his gun from its holster, aware of the hushed slide of Tick's Glock leaving its leather case as well. On either side of the doorway, they made eye contact using the dim illumination cast by a neighbor's security light. Both eased to a crouch.

Stanton hefted his flashlight, rubbing his thumb over the switch, prepared to perform a "flashlight roll". The house remained dark and silent, but they couldn't take a chance it was empty. For all they knew, a suspect waited, set to ambush them at the first opportunity. The glow behind them would serve to silhouette them as they moved through the door, so a low-profile entry was key.

He strained his ears, listening for any sound that would alert him to Autry's presence. Where was she? What was going on?

With a soft click, he depressed the flashlight switch. Brightness burst into the kitchen, and he let the cylinder flow from his fingers, rolling across the doorway to rest near Tick's waiting hand. Nothing moved in the light.

"Same as always?" Tick murmured. Stanton nodded. He lifted his gun, offering cover while Tick slipped into the room. Grabbing his flashlight, the beam extinguished again, Stanton followed. In the dark, his senses seemed heightened. The silence pulsed with a noise of its own, a heaviness against his ears. The familiar smell of the house, a blend of orange cleaner and the cinnamon potpourri Autry loved, surrounded him. The urge to cry out her name gripped him, and he shoved it down. The training had to win over instinct.

Progress through the house was torturous. Each room required a cautious approach and thorough check, with the dark serving to underscore the tension. At least he knew the house, which saved them minutes, but his foreboding grew as they neared Autry's bedroom. He'd heard nothing to let him know she was in the house, that she was okay, and he dreaded what they might find once they crossed that threshold.

The bedroom door stood open, and once more, they repeated the flashlight roll and covered entry. The room was empty, the bed rumpled. The scent was different here, the unique smell he associated with Autry, her body wash and the pure sweetness of her skin filling his senses. An image flashed through Stanton's head, of those same sheets wrapped around his and Autry's sated bodies, of her soft touch and softer sighs. He shook away the memory.

Where was she?

Tick checked the closet and nodded toward the shut bathroom door. Stanton closed his eyes. The safe room. The panic button was in the bathroom. He crossed to the door, crouched, and reached up to turn the knob. Locked. A tendril of relief snaked through him.

"Autry?" His voice sounded more like a strangled croak.

"Stanton?" Through the door, she sounded small and frightened. Scared, but okay. He closed his eyes, gripping the doorknob, his knees going weak.

"Yeah, baby, it's me. Can you open up?"

"Yes...just...a second." Her voice sounded muffled now.

Stanton straightened. What was she doing? "Autry. Come on. Open the door."

The latch clicked and the door swung inward. Tick flicked on his flashlight, the beam bouncing around the room, dancing off a small puddle of blood on the floor. Stanton's stomach dropped, but before he could take in the ramifications, Autry flung herself into his arms, her slender body trembling. She gasped against his chest, a rough sobbing that tore at him.

Gun in hand, he held her the best he could and stroked her back, her bulky robe soft under his palm. A hint of toothpaste wafted to him. "Honey, what happened?"

She shuddered, her face buried against his chest. "The alarm went off and I thought it was him. I closed the door, and then the lights died. I was so scared, Stan."

He groaned. "Why didn't you answer the phone? If we'd known no one was in the house yet—"

"I was already in the bathroom." She stiffened and pulled away. The loss sank in immediately, his arms curiously empty, the way they'd been the last four months. "For all I knew, he was in the house."

"You said you thought it was him," Tick said, his voice quiet. "Like you knew who it was."

"I don't..." Even in the dim reflection of light from Tick's flashlight, Stanton could see the tension tightening Autry's face. She shook her head and took a cautious step back, arms crossed over her midriff. "I just meant…"

Stanton watched her. She wouldn't meet his gaze, looking everywhere but at him. What was she hiding? "Tick, do me a favor, would you? Check the breaker box, call this in, and take a look around outside."

"Sure thing."

With Tick's departure, the room plunged into darkness once more. Stanton pulled his flashlight from his belt. Light bounced around the area, and he shone it over the bathroom floor. The blood glistened, wet and crimson. Autry's blood. His stomach rolled.

"Are you all right? What—"

"I dropped the cup and cut my foot." Her voice steadied, the panic gone. She sounded more like the competent attorney now, less the frightened woman. The walls, the ones she'd begun erecting even before he'd told her it was over, rose higher. "It's fine."

"Let me take a look. You might need stitches."

"I said it's fine." She stepped farther away, and in the uneven light, he could tell she watched him with a wariness that tugged at his heart.

No, not his heart. He felt guilty, maybe, for ending what had been between them, for hurting her, but that was all. He'd been worried about her tonight, but no more than he'd have worried for anyone else he knew. She didn't have his heart.

And he damn sure didn't have hers.

The lights clicked on, brightness flowing out of the bathroom. The alarm chirped once and fell silent. Her digital clock flashed 12:00 over and over. Stanton blinked, glanced at her, and did a double take. Her hair fell about a too-pale face, her blue eyes big and smudged with exhaustion.

He dropped his gaze to the foot she favored, a slow trickle of blood dripping onto the tile. "Let's do something about that."

"I've got it," she said, a hint of testiness in the words. She edged away from him, grabbing a hand towel and sitting on the toilet to wrap the terrycloth around her foot.

Stanton sighed. "What's going on, Autry?"

Her fingers trembled, but she shrugged. "I don't know. The alarm—"

"Autry. Don't lie. What's going on? And does it have anything to do with Schaefer?"

Her head jerked up. "Everything with us always comes back to him, doesn't it?"

"It's a valid question. Lots of people are upset that you're defending him."

She lifted her chin. "I'm doing my *job*. If people can't understand that the system works for everyone, not just for those who are obviously innocent, then they'll have to get used to it."

Stanton shoved his flashlight into its loop with a tight, tense movement. "He's about as far from obviously innocent as somebody can get."

Her jaw went taut. "He hasn't been tried yet. Remember that whole thing about 'innocent until proven guilty'?"

The old anger flashed through him. "I don't understand you. Tick's one of your oldest friends and you're defending the guy who tried to kill him—"

"It's my job," she said, her voice subdued, all the fight draining from her face. She rubbed her arms, exhaustion coloring her movements and posture, and guilt curled in Stanton's gut. She'd been through hell tonight and he was adding to it. "I took an oath, Stan. I thought you of all people would understand that."

"If it were any other case, I could." Weariness tugged at his soul. Why was he pushing this? He hadn't been able to change her mind at the beginning and he sure as hell wasn't going to do it tonight. What he needed to do was pull his act together, treat this like any other call and get back out on patrol. Quit worrying about what shouldn't have been in the first place.

A sheriff involved with the public defender.

Could anyone define "political suicide"?

They stared at each other a moment, the silence and intimacy, with all its memories, pressing in around them. That last weekend before everything had gone to hell...Stanton rubbed a hand over his nape. Focus. He needed focus.

He dropped his gaze to her foot, red seeping through the hand towel. "You said 'him'. Who did you think 'him' was?"

Her body stiffened. "I told you, no one. I thought someone was trying to get in. The first logical—"

"Main breaker was switched off." Tick's voice filled the small space. He leaned against the doorjamb opposite Stanton. "Footprints under the box, around the side of the house. Looks like someone tried to jimmy the dining-room window. Neighbor's dog may have scared him off."

Autry's face paled further. She swallowed, the muscles in her slender throat spasming. "There was really someone trying to get in."

She seemed to crumple, folding in on herself, knuckles whitening as she clutched the towel closer around her foot. Stanton's chest tightened, a combination of protectiveness and anger. The idea of what could have happened coated his mouth with a foul taste. Her very real fear raised his instincts to their highest level.

And a matching fear kicked off low in his gut. "Autry. Come on. Tell us what's going on."

She massaged her forehead, rumpled chestnut hair falling forward to shield her face. "My briefcase is by the armoire. The letters are in there."

Letters? The dread turning icy, Stanton glanced at Tick. He nodded and slipped into the bedroom, returning in moments with a short stack of lined notepaper in his gloved hand. Stanton took them and unfolded the topmost. Careful block lettering filled the page, line after line of filthy names, filthier threats. And the stack in his hand held at least ten of the notes. Bile rose in his throat, mixing with the anger and apprehension.

He swallowed hard and handed the letters to Tick. "We'll need a bag for those."

Tick lifted an eyebrow, but didn't demur at being dismissed. "I'll just..." He cast a glance between Stanton and Autry. "Run back to the car."

"Thanks." Stanton let him clear the room before opening his mouth again. He cleared his throat, attempted to pitch his voice to a gentle tone and not let his alarm show. "Autry?"

A visible shudder ran over her body, huddled still on the toilet, arms clutching her midriff.

"I thought it was nothing," she said, her voice small and shaky in the bathroom.

Watching her and keeping his movements slow, Stanton hunched down and picked up the shards of ceramic littering the floor. "It. The letters?"

She shrugged, a stiff uncomfortable gesture, and fiddled with the hem of her robe. "I had some late night calls, just breathing. He didn't say anything. I-I had the number changed, left it unlisted, and the calls stopped. I didn't...I never thought he'd really come after me, Stan."

Her voice broke and he fought an impulse to sweep her up, hold her close and soothe the fear and the bad memories away. Instead he dropped the pieces from the broken cup in the wastebasket. He glanced up at her face. She bit her lower lip, but her chin trembled anyway.

"Why didn't you tell me sooner?" He focused on keeping his voice even. "I could have set up a detail, offered you some protection—"

"No." A wistful expression chased some of the terror from her eyes. A tremulous smile twisted her mouth and she clutched the robe tighter, elbows on knees, her entire posture closed to him. "Not you. I thought about talking to Tick, but it was just a few letters. I had the security system and I've been careful."

"Not careful enough. What if the guy hadn't gotten scared? What if he decides to come back?" The worry-induced anger threatened his professional control and he pulled it back in, the same way he'd smothered the spurt of hurt that she'd considered calling Tick, but not him. Rising, he rested his hands at his gun belt. She didn't look up at him, but he hadn't missed the flash of dread in her eyes. "Autry, keeping this to yourself was not smart. Did you at least mention it to your dad?"

She reacted then, posture straightening, narrowed gaze flying to his. "No, I didn't, and you'd better not."

"What is with you?" This time, he let the frustration leak into his words. "What's more important, your safety or your pride?"

Slumping again, she opened her mouth, closed it, and shook her head. She pressed her fingers to her forehead. "What am I going to do?"

Her voice trembled and tore at him again. "Tonight, you're going to find somewhere else to stay."

She nodded, a hint of relief in her expression. "You're probably right. I don't think I'd get any sleep if I stayed here." She grimaced. "Like I will anyway."

"Want to call your parents?"

She pulled at the ends of her hair, the chestnut mass tumbling around her shoulders. "Mama's not feeling well lately. I really don't want to bother them—"

"You can go to my place," Tick said, and Stanton jumped at his deep drawl. With his normal loose-limbed posture, Tick leaned in the bedroom doorway. "I dusted the window and the fuse box. No prints on the window. Got a thumb and a smudged partial. Those will probably turn out to belong to a Georgia Power employee. I'm about to cast the footprints."

Autry pulled her feet up to rest on the toilet's edge, knees tucked to her chest. "You don't think Cait would mind me crashing at your place?"

Tick lifted an eyebrow in an exaggerated grimace. "Why would she?"

Stanton shifted, bothered by the exchange without being sure why. Probably because Autry trusted Tick so easily. And why not? She'd known him all her life, spent her early teenage years tagging behind him in a blend of hero worship and puppy love. The two of them still laughed and teased over that crush fifteen years later.

"Why don't I give you a ride over there?" Stanton ran a thumb along the vanity's cool edge.

Her gaze darted to his, none of the easy trust present. Instead, wariness lurked in the blue depths. "I can drive."

"Not until we have a chance to check out your car. No telling what this guy could have done." Visions of bombs wired to ignitions, rattlesnakes under front seats and other memories from his days with the FBI's Organized Crime Division danced in his head. He wasn't taking any chances with her safety.

18

Autry blanched. "You think—"

"You can't be too careful, Autry," Tick said. "Let Stan take you. I'm going to be a while, processing the scene."

She nodded, a slow, tentative movement, and picked at her hem. "I need to get dressed."

"I'll be right outside with Tick," Stanton said, wanting to reassure her. "Let me know when you're ready."

She didn't look up, but he caught the quick flash of white teeth sinking into her full lower lip. At the door, he glanced back. She'd wrapped her arms around her knees, forehead buried in the fold of her elbows. Every inch of her body screamed of tension, fear, dejection. He steeled himself against the wave of protectiveness. She wasn't his to comfort. She was anything but.

Clad in loose sweats and the bulkiest jacket she owned, Autry huddled against the patrol car door. Fearful thoughts bumped and tumbled around her mind, a jumbled montage of what could have happened and the unknown threats around her. Under it all lay the secret she kept from the silent man in the driver's seat.

The baby fluttering in her stomach, hidden by the Mercer sweatshirt and battered denim jacket, was his. She was four months pregnant with Stanton Reed's child, and she had yet to breathe a word to him. As far as lies of omission went, this one was a whopper. Shame burned her cheeks.

She studied him, his strong features highlighted by passing streetlights. During the long nights without him, she'd lain awake, wondering if her baby would share his high cheekbones, the rugged point of his chin, his dark hair. Maybe even those weird elfin-pointed ears of his too. If she bore him a son, he would probably look as much like Stanton as his two sons did. Half-brothers. Her baby would have siblings, cousins, a grandmother on Stanton's side. A whole family. How much longer could she justify keeping a secret of this magnitude?

Tears, something she'd never shed easily until her pregnancy, stung her eyes, and she blinked until the passing landscape of empty parking lots and vacant businesses cleared. She'd wanted to tell him, as soon as the home pregnancy test

19

stick turned blue, but knowing how strongly he *didn't* want another child made keeping this particular secret too easy. The awareness of how much he despised her for defending Jeff Schaefer made it that much easier. Even if Stanton wanted to embark on fatherhood again, she was the last woman he'd want bearing his child.

Depression pressed her deeper in the seat. Stanton glanced her way. "Autry? You feeling all right?"

She kept her gaze trained on the road in front of the windshield, the town behind them, the darkness of the country spreading around them now. "I'm fine."

"You look...a little under the weather."

Diplomatic bastard. She smothered a spurt of anger. If she looked a little under the weather, it was because his offspring, his *spawn*, refused to play the pregnancy game by the book. The damned nausea was *supposed* to have disappeared by month three.

She dug her nails into the car seat. "I think I've got a touch of that flu going around. I promise not to breathe on you."

His deep chuckle held little humor. "If I haven't gotten it by now, doubt I will. Half the damned department is out with it."

That explained why he'd turned up to answer her alarm call. She hadn't questioned it at the time, had merely welcomed his presence, his strength, the warm security of his arms around her. The father of her child, the man with whom she'd foolishly allowed herself to tumble into bed and into love, while she ignored the ramifications of getting involved with the local sheriff.

When those ramifications came home to roost, they'd bitten with very big, very sharp teeth. Lord, she'd been naïve to the point of stupidity, thinking they could separate their professional lives from the personal. Autry watched him, using the darkness and her lashes for cover. His strong hands with long, tapered fingers gripped the steering wheel, and his tall body, shoulders ridiculously broad, filled the car with his presence. His height, the raw strength of him, had always left her feeling breathless and feminine.

Heat flushed her face and she closed her eyes, a memory of him looming over her, pushing into her, making her come apart in his arms flashing through her mind.

Stop thinking about it. It's over. She took a deep breath and opened her eyes. Better to think about how she would stay safe. She couldn't shrug off the letters anymore. A different picture flickered in her head, someone lifting the window, creeping through her house, approaching her bedroom. She shuddered. What if he hadn't been scared away?

Stanton slowed, swinging the patrol car into Tick's long driveway. A vapor light cast a blue glow over the big white farmhouse. A lamp shining in the living room spilled a golden pool on the back porch. He braked behind Caitlin's Volvo and Autry reached for her small bag. Her wrist brushed his leg, the fabric of his slacks a little rough on her skin. Warmth traveled through her and something other than her baby flickered to life in her stomach. She straightened, clutching the bag like a shield. This was ridiculous. He didn't *want* her anymore, and even if he did, he wouldn't want her baby.

"Thanks for the ride," she said, her voice emerging as a tear-strangled rasp, and reached for the door handle.

"Autry, wait." His hand closed around her arm, sending heat tingling along her skin, even through the jacket and sweatshirt. The scent of him, male mixed with a crisp soap, enveloped her. "I wanted to—"

"I'm tired. I need to go." She had to get away from him before she gave into the terror-induced weakness and launched herself at him again. Without facing him, she inched toward the door; he didn't release her arm.

"Listen, please." He eased nearer and she dared to look at him. Under the security light, his hazel eyes glittered, the shadows highlighting the angles of his face. She tried to tug her arm free; he tightened his grip and pulled her closer. Autry stared up at him, the old passion flaring. His features hardened and he sighed. "Oh, hell."

He leaned toward her and Autry's breath stopped in her throat.

Chapter Two

Irrational jerk. That's what he was. Stanton ran a hand over his face, slight stubble pricking at his palm. He needed a shower, shave and a few hours sleep. Once Tick showed up, he'd settle for a fresh uniform shirt, his electric razor and some strong coffee.

What had he been thinking last night? He'd leaned forward to kiss Autry before his brain could overrule his habit. The level of anticipation had been scary. Only Caitlin's opening the back door and Autry's scrambling from the car had saved him from making a huge mistake. As far as he was concerned, Autry Holton was off limits, and no matter how her frightened eyes and the memories tugged at him, he wasn't going there again.

Even if he had to continue finding refuge in the most lame-ass excuse known to man. Yeah, he didn't like her defending Jeff Schaefer, but someone had to do it since the son of a bitch refused to plea out. Autry had defended obviously guilty clients before, always to the best of her ability. Stanton couldn't imagine her doing it any other way. That stubborn determination to stand by her duty had won his respect.

It was just that not only had Jeff Schaefer tried to kill Stanton's best friend, but Autry's refusal to have herself recused from the case gave him a hell of a reason to stay away from her. That wasn't an option anymore. He was going to have to interact with her, at least professionally, since that very same determination he admired seemed to be placing her in direct danger. His gaze dropped to the evidence bag on his desk, the notes she'd turned over to him lying face-up within the protective plastic. The threatening words in their big block letters glared up at him.

I'm coming for you, bitch.

Fury surged in his chest, strangling the air in his lungs. Someone threatening Autry. Someone attempting to get in her home.

Simply because she was doing her job?

He forced the anger down, locked it away in a tiny compartment. Right now, he needed to think more like an experienced cop and less like a protective lover—

Damn it, he wasn't Autry's lover anymore. They weren't even friends. More like professional acquaintances, what they should have remained in the first place.

With a deep breath, he stared at the note and twirled a silver pen between his fingers. None of the missives, penned on plain lined notepaper, the kind from pads found in any Dollar General in the Southeast, mentioned Schaefer. Stanton couldn't leap from A to Z, thinking the threats came only out of Autry's defense of the former cop.

One of *his* former cops.

He shook off the guilt that always accompanied the thought. What had they missed in Schaefer's background? What could they have seen to keep them from hiring him and turning him loose on an unsuspecting community?

"Think, Reed," he whispered into the quiet of the deserted station. What other options lay between A and Z? He grabbed a legal pad and leaned back in his chair. Flipping past three pages of budget figures, he headed a blank page with Autry's name. No, the simple act of writing her name didn't give him a thrill, set off a clenching sensation low in his gut. Hunger. Just his stomach reminding him he hadn't eaten since the night before.

A and Z. What came between?

He scratched a name and stared, a hoarse bark of a laugh escaping him. *Nate.* Now why the hell would he begin a list with Autry's reprobate brother? He formed a dark question mark next to the name and underlined it. Would Nathaniel Holton gain anything from frightening his sister?

Satisfaction, probably, of his weird resentment. Sibling rivalry gone really insane, maybe. But Stanton doubted even Nate Holton, screw-up extraordinaire, was stupid enough to send handwritten threats.

He moved the pen to the next line. Other cases. He wasn't privy to Autry's life anymore, so he didn't know everything she was working on, not like last spring, when he'd been so wrapped up in her that concentrating on anything else was difficult. But checking into her current and past cases was key. Maybe someone angry that she hadn't kept him out of prison? He scrawled another note. *Check on release/parole of former clients.*

An unknown stalker? Someone who'd formed an irrational attachment, a relationship only in his head? Those could be the most dangerous. Stanton's grip on the pen tightened, the silver ridges biting into his fingertips.

The next line received a single name.

Jeffrey Schaefer.

"Is there a reason you're strangling that pen?"

Stanton startled at Tick's deep drawl. Damn, the guy was quiet. With an easy movement, Tick settled a cup of coffee at the corner of Stanton's desk pad, covering a doodle of a six-pointed sheriff's badge.

"Thanks." Stanton tossed the pen aside and reached for the steaming cup. Tick dropped into the chair opposite, a mug cradled between his hands. Shaved and showered, dark hair combed, he appeared refreshed and relaxed, not like he'd spent the last four days pulling killer double shifts.

He waved a hand at the pad balanced on Stanton's knee. "Any ideas?"

Stanton passed it to him. With cautious sips of the hot brew, he eyed Tick's face while he read, gauging reactions.

Tick chuckled. "Nate's at the top of your list?"

Stanton shrugged, the caffeine seeping into him but doing little to soothe the tension twisting in him. "Came to mind first."

"Yeah. The little shit would love playing with Autry's head, sister or not. He's twisted that way." Tick returned the pad to Stanton's desk. "I'm with you on the Schaefer angle too. Her taking this case pissed off a lot of people. There's bound to be at least one weirdo out there who wants to see her punished for it."

With a harsh sigh, Stanton set his coffee aside. "You act like it doesn't bother you at all."

Tick made a face. "If I thought there was a snowball's chance he'd walk, I'd be screaming as loud as the rest of the yahoos. But there's no way, absolutely no way. She's good, but not that good. What am I going to do? Stop being her friend because she's doing her job?"

No accusation lingered in Tick's voice, but Stanton shifted in unease anyway. "Is that what you think I did?"

His dark gaze steady, Tick lifted his mug. "I think you used the whole thing as an excuse. You'd been getting antsy about being with her for weeks. Y'all were headed for serious things and your skin crawled."

Stanton glanced away. In the last ten years, he'd spent more time with Tick than with his own family and hiding anything was damn near impossible. The guy knew him too well after countless FBI stakeouts and operations, long hours spent trading tales in a BuCar. "I'd have ended up hurting her."

"You did hurt her." Steel and more than a hint of disapproval entered Tick's tone. "I guess it's just easier to tell yourself a little bit now is better than a lot later."

Wasn't it? If he'd let the involvement go further, they'd both have ended up in a world of hurt. Stanton straightened and met Tick's gaze again. "I need you to get those prints and casts over to Moultrie ASAP this morning. See if you can light a fire under the lab."

Seeming unimpressed with Stanton's shift to total professionalism again, Tick shook his head. "Always the Steelman, huh?" They stared at each other until a weary grin curved Tick's mouth. "Yeah, I'll get everything to Moultrie first thing. You going to check back in with Autry or you want me to do it?"

"You call her." Stanton reached for the topmost file in his inbox and lowered his gaze, sure Tick would pick up on the silent dismissal. As Tick left, Stanton flipped the folder open. He had a department to run, and checking up on victims and complainants was Tick's job, not his.

Cowardice and self-protection had nothing to do with it.

It was all about doing what was right for Autry. It always

had been.

Early morning sunlight glinted off windshields in the parking lot of the Haynes County Sheriff's Department. The jail complex sprawled across an open field, isolated from the nearby town. The low modern building with its shining fence topped with gleaming razor wire seemed worlds away from the rundown, outdated jail Stanton had inherited with the Chandler County department.

Stan would kill for this building.

Stop thinking about him. Autry removed her sunglasses and slid them into the case clipped to her visor. Gritty and dry from lack of sleep, her eyes burned. In Tick and Caitlin's guest room, she'd lain awake the rest of the night, reliving the terror of thinking the stalker had come for her, relishing the safety and security of having Stanton's arms around her once more.

She rested her forehead on the steering wheel, a muffled groan escaping her. Lord, she was weak where he was concerned. He walked in the room and she forgot he didn't want her. Instead, she wanted to burrow close, soak up his warmth, share their baby with him, look for joy in his eyes.

Yeah. Sure. As open as he'd been about not wanting another child, joy would be the last emotion he'd feel once he learned of her pregnancy. Angry, maybe. Trapped? Definitely. Resentful. No, please. She rested a hand on her stomach. Not resentful. She didn't want her baby to be anyone's burden.

That was the way Stanton would view it. Not a cause of celebration, but a duty, an obligation. She sighed. Could her life be a bigger mess right now? Hard not to think about how thrilled Tick would be if Caitlin told him she was pregnant and contrast that to what Stanton's reaction would surely be. Life possessed a weird, ironic sense of humor, sending her an unexpected, ultimately inconvenient pregnancy when that was what Tick and Caitlin wanted most in the world and seemingly couldn't have.

Autry lifted her head, smoothing her loose chignon. Sooner or later, she had to tell him, regardless of his reaction. With her stomach pooching out, she couldn't wait much longer, or Mr. FBI Eagle-Eyes would figure it out on his own. She shivered at that thought. Now that wouldn't be a fun conversation, filled with her stammering apologies and Stanton's cold fury. No. She had to tell him. Soon.

After Schaefer's trial was out of the way.

After they'd caught the psycho sending her notes and trying to break into her house.

When everything was normal again, and she was on equal footing with him, not a frightened, needy woman. That was the last thing she wanted, to appear weak and—

Oh, screw how he viewed her! This was her baby she was talking about here. Her baby. She had a responsibility to keep it safe, and if telling Stanton made him more determined to keep her safe, to keep the psycho away, then she should have told him last night. Or months ago, when the test stick first turned blue.

"This is getting you nowhere," she muttered. No closer to a decision, but late for her appointment. She pulled the keys from the ignition and grabbed her briefcase. Locking the door behind her, she strode across the deserted parking lot to the jail. Nervous nausea roiled in her stomach. God, she hated these meetings.

Heavy disinfectant hung in the stillness inside. Behind the bulletproof glass, the deputy manning the front desk looked up, a less-than-polite smile creasing her mahogany face. "Ms. Holton."

Autry made herself smile back. Why did all cops look at defense attorneys like oozing pond scum? "I have a meeting scheduled with Jeff Schaefer."

The heavy woman slid an attorney's pass beneath the window. A loud buzzing followed by a heavy click signaled the opening of the locked door. Autry pulled the massive metal door open and stepped into the hallway. The deputy met her, handheld metal detector in hand. Laying her briefcase on a nearby table, Autry extended both arms, allowing the deputy to pass the electronic wand over her body.

Her stomach fluttered and she frowned. The wand's rays couldn't be dangerous, could they?

The deputy deposited the detector on the table and ran her hands along Autry's body, performing a perfunctory search. Satisfied, she pointed at the briefcase. "Open that, please."

Autry flipped the latches and lifted the lid, the fine leather smooth and cool under her fingers. A gift from her parents, the case matched her father's, even down to the initials—VAH, for Virgil Autry Holton as well as Virginia Autry Holton.

The deputy glanced into the pockets, lifted the files within, and nodded. "All right."

Shaking her head, Autry closed the lid and clipped the pass to her jacket. The routine search niggled at her this morning. What did they think, that she'd try to help Schaefer escape? Turn him loose on the innocent again?

Wasn't she? Oh, she used the legal system to do it, but wasn't providing a quality defense for a man she believed guilty of heinous crimes the same as breaking him out? The oath she'd been so proud of, defended so stridently to Stanton, reached out, wrapping her in strangling tentacles. She'd defended clients she believed guilty before, had even taken a couple to acquittal, but none of them had been anything like the man waiting for her in the meeting room at the end of the long, narrow hallway.

None of them scared the life out of her like Jeff Schaefer.

The walls, painted an institutional beige, pressed in, trying to squeeze the air from Jeff's lungs. He hated being locked up like this, hated the loss of choices, freedoms, control. Didn't they get it? Didn't they know what a cop in jail faced, even under so-called maximum security? He shuddered, rubbing a thumb over the bruises at his wrists.

He didn't deserve this, any of it. They couldn't do this to him.

What he needed was to find a way out of this hellhole. A way to unlock that door.

A key.

Autry Holton would be the key to everything—freedom, vindication, salvation.

He smiled. Everything. Yeah. Autry could be everything he needed.

Schaefer waited for her in the small beige room, far

removed from the battered, green interrogation rooms seen on so many television cop shows. The walls might have been unimaginative, but were spotless, as was the brown carpet. The inexpensive furniture consisted of a table and two chairs with molded plastic seats. Sheriff Jason Harding ran a clean, no-waste department, and this room, like the others in the jail, reflected that philosophy.

"Hello, Jeff." Autry laid her briefcase on the table without a smile for the man sitting across the table. The orange jumpsuit he wore made his skin appear sallow, although it didn't diminish his clean-cut good looks. His dark hair, neatly trimmed, lay close to his head, and his earnest blue eyes remained steady on her. Watching her. She hated the way he studied everything she did.

He nodded. "Autry. How are you?"

"Good, thanks." She opened her briefcase. His gaze dropped from her face to her throat, then to the point where the table hid her stomach. Autry repressed a shudder and reached for the legal pad lying atop the files. He was already receiving letters in jail, women offering friendship and more. She couldn't fathom the idea.

"We need to talk about your trial date. Also, Tom McMillian called yesterday. He's willing to discuss a plea—"

"No." Schaefer shook his head, a short, adamant movement. "No pleas."

"Jeff, listen to me." Autry leaned forward, hands clasped before her. "You're facing a capital murder charge for Amy Gillabeaux's death. Tom's willing to take that off the table if you plead to all of the murders. He'll drop the two counts of aggravated battery from the incident with Tick and Caitlin—"

"No, you listen to me." Intensity deepened Schaefer's voice, and he bent toward her, stabbing a finger into the table. Autry tried to forget the knife wounds on Amy's body. Had his muscles tightened and flexed just that way as he swung the knife down? "I'm not pleading out. I didn't kill those girls and I won't say I did."

He believed it. Or at least, he wanted her to think he believed it. Maybe he'd convinced himself of his own innocence. But what about trying to kill Tick? Caitlin? He'd left witnesses. How could he deny that?

"Tom intends to put Tick and Cait both on the stand." She kept her voice soft and level. "That testimony alone will be damning and I'm not sure how we can counteract it."

Schaefer's gaze narrowed, the blue glittering between dark lashes. "I don't care who he puts on the stand. I'm not the dangerous one here. I can refute anything Calvert or Falconetti says."

He believed he could, anyway. Autry blinked and tried another tactic. "We're talking about a death-penalty case here, Jeff. Surely you don't want to die."

"I'd rather die than confess to something I didn't do." The words emerged between clenched teeth and vibrated with weight. He leaned closer, touched her hand, and she forced herself not to jerk away. Fear trickled through her. She straightened slowly, sliding her hand from beneath his. With her movement, his face relaxed and a slight smile touched his mouth. "You understand that, don't you, Autry? It's a matter of principle. You're defending me on one, even with everyone turning against you. We're in this together."

Together. The word shuddered through her. He was so smooth, so intense. Was this the Jeff Schaefer who'd smiled and charmed the girls, luring them to their deaths? In her diary, Amy had written of loving him. Had that smile and sincerity made her believe he loved her too?

She stiffened her spine, straightening further. "All right. If you don't want a plea, we won't take the deal. I feel bound to tell you, though, that I've never defended a capital case." Heck, she'd never defended a murder case. Lots of assaults, a couple of rapes and tons of petty crimes, but never a murderer. "Maybe you need a different attorney, someone with more experience. The Public Defenders Network has a capital specialist out of Atlanta. I could call him."

Schaefer shook his head again. "No, I don't want anyone else."

"But—"

"I want you." His voice throbbed with energy again. "I know you."

A frisson of fear moved down her spine. She didn't want the man before her knowing her in any way. If she were brutally honest, she wanted nothing at all to do with him, and maybe Stanton and the rest of the town were right—she should recuse herself from the case.

Only that was the easy way out and it went against everything she believed. The system worked, but sometimes that meant taking the good with the bad.

Sometimes it included walking hand-in-hand with evil, whether she wanted to or not.

She swallowed. Letting him see the fear and doubt wasn't an option. "Okay. We'll do it your way. I'll stay on the case and we'll go to trial."

His slow, satisfied smile only increased the constant nausea brewing in her stomach. "Thank you, Autry. You won't regret it."

"Well, I hope you don't." She dropped her pad in the briefcase. "I need to call Tom. I'll also begin putting together a list of possible defense witnesses. We'll have to turn that over to the DA's office, but we'll get theirs as well."

"I want you to let me know what you're doing along the way," Schaefer said, his voice sliding into smooth and polite again. A boyish grin, full of sheepishness, curved his mouth. If she'd been nineteen and mad about older guys as Amy had been, that expression might have blinded her too. "I want to be involved."

"Of course." Lifting her case, she pushed to her feet. She wanted away from him, as much distance as possible between them. "I'll be in touch."

She rapped at the door and the seconds crawled until two deputies appeared, one to unlock the door, the other to escort Schaefer to his cell. As they passed, Schaefer's scent, a blend of harsh soap and the permeating disinfectant, washed over her. Bile flooded her throat. Lord, that smell would be all over her.

She barely made it to the ladies room in the lobby, outside the lockdown doors. Retching, a hand pressed to her pounding heart, she emptied her stomach.

"Mrs. Milson, you remember me. Sheriff Reed." Stanton held his badge and ID aloft so the elderly woman could inspect them through the screen door. "You called the department to report someone missing."

Mrs. Milson peered at him, her thin brows drawn down, almost disappearing behind her huge, thick glasses. "I did no such thing."

Patience. Stanton smiled, hoping it looked like a smile and not like he was baring his teeth. "With all due respect, ma'am, you talked to Roger in dispatch not twenty minutes ago. Said you needed us to check out a missing person."

Still frowning, Mrs. Milson stared at him, tapping a finger against her lips. Traces of lipstick had crawled into the feathery lines around her mouth. "Did I say who it was?"

"No, ma'am." Why the hell hadn't he sent Tick on this call? Because Tick was still in Moultrie, dropping off the evidence from Autry's house. Damn it, he probably should have handled that himself. "That's why I'm here."

She shook her head. "Well, I just don't know...wait...maybe..."

He struggled for an encouraging expression. "Yes?"

"It could be Doreen Beall. Is she missing?"

The county commission owed him a raise for dealing with her. No way this was in his job description. Damn it, he didn't need to be here. He needed to be running down leads on Autry's case. He rubbed a hand over his neck. "Ma'am, I don't know."

"Well, you're the police, aren't you? You're supposed to know when someone's missing."

Teeth clenched until his jaw ached, Stanton nodded. "Yes, ma'am." He looked down at the petite elderly woman. She blinked at him. He pulled his notebook from his pocket. "Mrs. Milson, why do you think it might be Doreen Beall?"

She blinked again and narrowed her eyes. "Well, she's not here."

He lifted an eyebrow. "Is she supposed to be?"

Confusion twisting her wrinkled brow further, Mrs. Milson tapped a finger against her lips once more. "I'm not sure."

Shaking his head, Stanton stepped backward down the steps. "How about if I call Miss Doreen's daughter over at the grocery store and see if she knows where she is?"

Mrs. Milson's eyebrows snapped into a mistrustful frown.

"You do that."

Pulling his cell phone from its belt clip, he dialed the grocer. After a brief discussion with Doreen Beall's indignant daughter, he moved back up the steps. "Mrs. Milson? I've located Miss Doreen. She's safe and sound at home. So you don't have to worry about her anymore today."

Mrs. Milson nodded, still eyeing him with suspicion. She latched the hook. "Well, thank you. I guess."

He tapped the rim of his campaign hat. "Anytime."

The county's other unmarked unit pulled to a stop behind his in the driveway and Tick stepped out. "Having fun?"

Stanton tossed his notebook on the front seat of his unit, the movement short and irritable. "Working a missing person who's not really missing."

Arms crossed over his chest, Tick leaned a hip against the car's trunk. "Mrs. Milson lose Doreen Beall again?"

Stanton chuckled, the sad humor finally sinking in. "Yeah. Took her to her appointment at Dr. Shirah's and left her there. Miss Doreen's daughter is pitching a fit."

"Maybe she should start driving her mama around then."

"Well, she had to drive her home from the doctor's office. How did things go in Moultrie?"

"We're in the queue. Price said she'd see if she could get them to hustle our results since it's Autry we're talking about, but no promises. She's already running the fingerprints through the system." Tick hooked his thumbs in his pockets. "Came by Autry's place. Took another look around. Didn't find anything else. She's got Damon Watson over there, fixing her door."

Stanton frowned. "She's not staying at your place again?"

Tick shrugged. "Guess not. We offered, but she said she wanted to go home. Something about not running scared from some psycho."

"Son of a bitch." Stanton yanked his hat off and tossed it on the seat. What was with her? Didn't she realize how serious the situation was? She didn't need to stay alone in that house, not until they knew where the threat came from. "I've got to go talk to her."

Studying the evidence reports laid out on the dining room table, Autry rubbed at her aching temples. The rules of discovery required that Tom McMillian turn over copies of everything. The autopsy reports horrified her, but she owed Schaefer to go through everything, find a chink in whatever case Tom was building.

The idea of owing Schaefer anything made her sick. She ruffled her hair. If she was lucky, Tick had been his normal thorough ex-FBI agent self and the case would be airtight.

Lord, why didn't Schaefer just take the plea? And what was all that mess about her being the attorney he wanted, that he *knew* her? More of his mind games?

The next paper she touched turned out to be Caitlin Falconetti's profile of the killer, written before she'd uncovered what had seemed the final clue to Schaefer's duplicitous nature.

Narcissist...

Lack of empathy.

Absolute need for control.

What did being locked up do to someone with an overwhelming desire to control everything? What was going through Schaefer's head?

She shivered, chafing her arms.

A rap at her newly repaired back door echoed down the hallway and her heart thudded against her ribs. With a palm pressed to her chest, she edged into the hallway and to the kitchen. Who was out there? Was it *him*?

She hovered at the kitchen doorway, straining her ears, trying to catch a glimpse through the glass panes without being seen herself. This was ridiculous. She couldn't live her life forever afraid of every knock. With a deep breath, she stepped into the room and approached the door.

Another rap and her pulse ratcheted up a notch.

"Autry?" Stanton's deep voice filtered through the door and Autry's entire body sagged in relief. His baby moved, a tender, wavelike motion in her stomach.

"Coming." Her voice emerged tight and too small. She

stepped forward and stopped, glancing down at her jeans and T-shirt. Oh, Lord, would he see? She jerked the soft cotton shirt free of her jeans, covering the small bulge of his child.

His child.

Tell him, Autry. This is your chance. Tell him now before the lie goes any further.

Taking another deep breath, she opened the door and looked up into Stanton's angry face.

Chapter Three

Clutching the door so hard her fingers hurt, Autry stepped back and waved a hand toward the middle of the room. "Come on in."

Stanton stalked by her. The size of him made her small kitchen seem smaller. His presence sucked in all the extra air, leaving her breathless. Once upon a time, the sensation had exhilarated her. Now, it left her sad and filled with an aching loneliness.

She closed the door with a quiet click. "Any news?"

He shook his head, sliding her a look. His hazel eyes snapped with bad humor. "No. Just running the prints will take several days."

Then why was he here? She left the question unsaid. No matter his reason, she would take this opportunity to finally tell him the truth. She sucked in a deep breath, trying to draw in enough oxygen to quell the nerves flip-flopping below her heart.

"What are you doing here?" he asked, jaw clenched.

Autry lifted surprised brows at him. "I think that's my line, Stan."

"I'm serious, Autry. You think having the door fixed makes this place safe for you?"

She crossed her arms over her chest and dropped them almost instantly, not wanting to emphasize the slight roundness of her abdomen. "I won't be run out of my own home."

"Why do you have to be so damned stubborn? This guy tried to break in. No telling what he had in mind, although I have a pretty good clue from those notes. And you're back here as though nothing happened?"

She matched him glare for glare. "What do you want me to do? Move in with my parents? Put them at risk? Horn in at Tick and Cait's? They're newlyweds, Stanton, and hardly want a third wheel around all the time. What are you going to do, put me in protective custody?"

His eyes narrowed. "That's not a bad idea."

"Oh, no." Hands aloft, she backed away. "Don't start getting ideas. I didn't—"

"Not a bad idea at all." He folded his arms, the fine cotton of his polo shirt tightening over his biceps. "Wonder how long it would take me to get your dad to sign a protection order?"

"You wouldn't dare."

He leaned forward, gaze locked on hers. "Try me."

With a faked laugh, she looked away from those compelling eyes. She missed seeing them full of lazy desire and raw passion. The anger there hurt. "Be reasonable, would you? I'm *fine*. I have the security system, I'm sure you've already scheduled extra patrols by here, and believe me, I'm being more careful."

"I am reasonable." He blew out a frustrated breath. "I want you safe. I couldn't stand it if anything happened to you."

Her breath caught. Was he saying what she thought? "Stanton—"

"I'd feel responsible," he said, "if my department couldn't ensure your safety. We're understaffed right now and last night you were lucky Tick and I weren't both out on other calls."

Deflated, she looked away. Of course, he was only concerned with his professional responsibility. He didn't feel anything personal for her. When would she finally get that through her head? Her eyelids tingled with the stupid, too-easy tears. She covered her eyes. As much as she wanted this baby, she wouldn't miss all the weird pregnancy issues.

"Autry?" His voice taking on a note of odd gentleness, Stanton reached for her arm. His fingers warmed her skin, even through her T-shirt. He tugged her hand away from her face, his concerned gaze roaming her features. "What's wrong?"

So much for being on equal footing when she told him. Everything was so messed up now, it didn't matter anymore. She pulled free of his easy hold, lifting her gaze to his. "I'm pregnant."

The shock registered on his face first, sliding into stunned disbelief. He laughed, a short bark of sound completely lacking in humor. "What? Come on, Autry, enough games."

"It's not a game." She shook her head, hating herself for being letdown when his reaction was exactly what she'd expected. Damn it all, she'd let herself hope for more and she deserved whatever she got for that bit of stupidity. "I'm right at seventeen weeks. It-it had to have happened that last weekend, before...before we broke up."

His mouth opened, moving like a fish deprived of water, and he gave a quick jerk of his head, as though trying to clear his brain. "Autry, there's no way. It's impossible. I had a vasectomy, when John Logan was six—"

"Yeah, I know." Autry tilted her head to the side and pressed a finger to a non-existent dimple. "I mentioned that to my OB-GYN. She wasn't really impressed by how *impossible* it was that I was pregnant. Seems there's something like a two percent chance of vasectomy failure." She gave him a saccharine-sweet smile, full of the worry and sleepless nights she'd endured over this surprise pregnancy. "Guess you fall in that two percent, Stanton, honey."

He rubbed a hand over his eyes. "Oh, shit."

A red haze danced before her. "Is that all you can say?"

"I'm just—" He lifted his head, his staggered gaze meeting hers. "I'll marry you."

Fury dazzled through her, scalding her nerve endings, leaving her hot and raw. "Oh, no hell you won't. Get out."

She attempted to push him toward the door, but she might as well have tried moving Stone Mountain toward the Alabama state line.

"Hear me out." He caught her hands in his. "Autry, come on. Give me a minute to pull my head together, okay?"

After a futile attempt to free herself from his oddly gentle grip, she glared up at him. Damn him anyway for being so tall. "You can have all the time you need, as long as you're not here."

He flexed his arms and drew her closer, linked hands pressing to his chest. As he stared down, his face softened. "Autry, it's the best thing. The right thing."

"Yeah, the public defender hanging around with your illegitimate baby on her hip would probably make a re-election bid difficult for you."

Anger flared in his eyes. "That's not fair. This has nothing to do with my office or yours."

"Doesn't it?" She stopped struggling against his hold. "Wasn't that your excuse back in June? That our political careers didn't mesh? That you couldn't live with what I did, the whole defending Jeff Schaefer thing?"

His mouth firmed. "I think this changes that, don't you?"

The pain twisted through her. Autry closed her eyes. She *should* marry him, just for the sheer pleasure of hiring Suzanne Vansant to drag him through divorce court later. That couldn't hurt him nearly as much as he was hurting her now.

She didn't open her eyes. "I won't marry you."

He released her hands, warm palms cupping her face. "Autry, baby, we could make it work. We'd be good together and it's the right thing to do."

The right thing? Marrying him, when his only motive was duty? Anything but. She lifted her lashes, blinking away the blasted tears again. "I want you to leave now."

"Autry—"

"I'm not going to change my mind, Stan. Just...go."

Face set in tense lines, he dropped his hands. "Lock up behind me. I'll come by later to check on you."

She stepped back, away from the warm temptation of him. "I will. And thank you for checking."

He moved toward the door. "We'll talk later."

She didn't answer, merely went to close the door behind him. Sure, they could talk later, but it wouldn't change anything.

It wouldn't make him love her or want their baby.

Pregnant. How could she possibly be pregnant? Ah, damn

it. Another kid to screw up. He'd done such a great job with the first two, between his selfish ambition and single-minded devotion to the bureau. He had sons, about to be men, and he didn't know them, not really. Oh, he spent time with them now, as much as he could, aching to recapture something he'd let slip away, but it wasn't deep, wasn't real. He was the guy who visited with them, took them for pizza and ballgames.

A weekend father.

He shuddered and leaned back in his chair, scrubbed his hands over his face. Repeating the same mistakes...he couldn't. He hadn't wanted to face fatherhood again, but the reality stood before him. Autry carried his child.

His child, growing in Autry's womb.

The tiny spurt of primal joy, the first emotion to lift its head upon her revelation, flowed through him again. Another baby. Another chance at fatherhood. An opportunity to get it right.

Or to screw it up. His cynicism chuckled. *Do you have more time to give a kid now? How's running this place different from climbing the bureau ladder?*

He'd make time. He was building something here—a strong, honest department. Sure, it took up more of his hours than it should—since the breakup, he'd thrown himself into work—but he'd learned pretty quickly he could leave the department under Tick's more-than-capable leadership when he needed to. Last spring, Stanton had traveled to Tallahassee for four days when John Logan, his younger son, had his wisdom teeth removed. Tick had handled everything here, no problem.

He could pull this off.

With one big "if".

Convincing Autry to give him a chance.

In her parents' driveway, Autry parked behind her mother's sensible sedan. Her father's beloved pickup was gone, and as she swung from the driver's seat, Autry suppressed a relieved sigh. Her mother would be thrilled over being a grandmother again, once she got over her initial shock and worry. Her father? That was another story. As far as Virgil Holton was concerned, there was only one right way—his. Somehow, Autry didn't see an unplanned pregnancy as her father's right way, especially when she'd just refused to marry the father.

The old white farmhouse loomed in front of her, ferns swinging in lazy arcs on the wraparound porch. Her mother's ancient cat lolled on the top step, eyes closed, tail twitching. Ignoring the nerves holding her stomach hostage, Autry mounted the steps and walked around to the kitchen door on the side of the house.

The glass-paneled interior door was closed, and Autry tugged the screen door open to try the knob. Locked. She sighed. Obviously, her mother had taken off with her daddy to heaven knew where. She could let herself in and wait, or she could go home and try again another day. The latter appealed, but now that she'd finally told Stanton, she no longer had an excuse not to tell her parents of her pregnancy.

Lord, *why* did the idea of telling her father make her feel like a recalcitrant sixteen-year-old?

Leaning a shoulder against the doorjamb, she flipped through her keys and unlocked the door. The precious smell of home wrapped around her—rose potpourri, a fresh-baked cake, her mama's sweet tea. She pushed the door closed behind her, making sure the lock clicked back into place. Even here, she didn't feel secure enough to take any chances.

"Mama?" she called, just to make sure her mother wasn't somewhere in the huge old place, sewing, reading or taking a nap.

Silence answered her. She poured a glass of tea, added lemon, and wandered through the immaculate living room to stand in the doorway of her father's office. She'd loved this room as a child, the dusty smell of her father's law books mixing with his pipe tobacco. At her mother's insistence, he'd long ago given up the pipe, and black licorice drops had taken its place, but the warm, musty scent of the law books remained. Obviously, the law and her father's love for it had infected her at an early age.

She curved her free hand over her swollen stomach. Would her baby share that love? Or Stanton's devotion to law enforcement?

Marry him. She shook her head. He was insane and later he'd be glad she'd said no. Every conversation they'd ever had about marriage and babies had driven home one point—he'd lost one marriage, felt like he'd lost countless opportunities with his children, and he didn't want to try again. She'd simply been stupid enough to think he'd feel differently once he came to care for her as much as she loved him. So what had she done? Jumped into love and into bed with him.

And he'd dumped her.

The phone rang and she startled, tea sloshing over the side of her glass. Laughing at her state of nerves, she grabbed the cordless phone from her father's desk. "Holton residence."

"Autry?" The soft female voice brought a smile to her face. Her sister-in-law had left Autry's good-for-nothing brother months back and Autry missed her. Helen personified another reason why shotgun marriages were a bad deal—she didn't deserve Nate's resentment and bad temper.

"Helen! Hey, how are you? And the kids?" She walked back to the kitchen and grabbed a dishcloth for the spill, leaving her tea glass on the counter.

"I'm good. And the kids are fine, except Breanne has an ear infection." Helen faltered. "Actually, that's why I was calling. The doctor's office waived the fee, but I still have to fill her prescription and my insurance doesn't kick in for another month. I thought your mama might—"

"No worries." Autry swiped at the spill harder than necessary. Helen was too young, too smart and too darn sweet to be saddled with these kinds of worries. If Nate ever settled into a regular paying job, Autry would make sure he paid back child support. "I'll send you a check today. Just tell me how much you need."

"Autry, I can't take your money. I wouldn't have asked your mama except she told me that—"

"Helen, listen, I wouldn't offer unless—"

"Give me the damn phone." Nate growled the words and wrested the unit from her hand. Autry stumbled back, heart thudding against her ribs for a long, uncomfortable moment. Why hadn't she heard him come in? What if he'd been someone else?

She made a grab for the phone and he held her off. "Helen? Damn it, baby, talk to me. I want to know where you are...son of a bitch!" He punched the power button and threw the phone on their father's couch with a savage motion. "Where is she?"

Autry matched him glare for glare. "I don't know. We didn't get that far."

"Shit." He jerked a hand over his short hair, a shade darker than her own. A hint of stale alcohol clung to him and the constant drinking coupled with too little food gave his features a sallow, sunken look. "I have a right to know where my wife and kids are."

She didn't bother to point out Helen wasn't his wife anymore, hadn't been since the papers had gone through without his signature six months before. "What you have is a duty to support those children."

He snorted. "Who asked you?"

Folding the damp towel, she walked toward the kitchen, her injured foot aching. She wasn't here to argue with him. Trying to discuss anything with him was pointless, just like dealing with Mama when she got on a tear. "Nobody. Do what you want, Nate, you always do."

His heavy footsteps thudded on the polished hardwood floor. "Where are they?"

"I don't know." She tossed the dishcloth in the laundry room. "And even if I did, I probably wouldn't tell you."

"Uppity bitch."

Turning, she stepped right into the blow. The force knocked her against the doorframe and she staggered, holding the thick wood for support. A weird combination of light and dark exploded behind her eyes, pain radiating across her face. Cradling her aching cheek and jaw, she crouched and stared up at her brother's dazed expression.

He swallowed, throat moving, and shook his head, staring at his hand as though it belonged to someone else. He lifted stunned eyes, the same shade of dark blue as her own, to look at her. "Autry, I...I didn't mean to—"

"Get away from me." That cold voice couldn't be hers. She'd heard rapists, murderers, use that voice. She didn't move, using her curled position to protect her baby.

"Sister, I—"

"I mean it. Get away from me."

He backed up a step and turned, muttering a shaky curse. Eyeing him, Autry straightened and scrambled toward the side door. She fumbled for the lock, finally managing to free it. Letting the door flop against the wall, she hurried to the front steps and to the safety of her car.

Locked inside, she struggled to get the key in the ignition. Her chest heaved with uneven breaths and the nausea crowded her throat. God, he'd hit her. He'd *hit* her. Her own brother. She'd been disgusted by him before—he'd even stolen from her to support his drinking habit—but she'd never been afraid of him.

She was now.

What if he hadn't stopped with the one blow?

With tears blurring her vision, she finally got the car started. Gulping back a tearing sob, the entire left side of her face throbbing, she backed out of the drive. Could her intruder have been Nate? Had he planned to steal from her again?

Everything was too much—the notes, the break-in, Schaefer, Stanton and now Nate. She let the tears go, let them have their way, until she couldn't breathe. Finally, she pulled to the shoulder to get herself together. Forehead against the steering wheel, she sobbed out the fear and anger, let all the hurt come to the surface. She fumbled in her purse for a tissue, gave up, and scrubbed at her wet face with her fingers.

The hard tap on her window sent her heart into overdrive again and she jerked her head up, blood rushing through her ears, vision clouding for a moment. The tall figure standing outside her car kept her heart racing but for an entirely different reason. Sucking in a deep breath, she pushed the door open and stepped out.

Stanton towered over her, blocking the late evening sun. Chin tilted at a defiant angle, she looked up at him.

His first reaction was a harsh indrawn breath. "What the hell..." He curved gentle fingers along her jaw. "Autry, what happened?"

She closed her eyes. The warmth of his touch soothed the stinging somewhat and she didn't pull away. "Nate happened."

"He hit you?"

The disbelief in his words she completely understood. She

was still trying to convince herself he'd actually done it. Even with all the issues and the alcohol, he was her brother, her baby brother. Gulping back a fresh sob, she nodded.

"Son of a bitch." Stanton's features hardened, his lips fading to a nonexistent line. "Tell me from the beginning."

Fighting the weak tears, she did. While she stammered out the story, he smoothed her hair from her face, his gaze steady on her cheek and jaw. "We need to get some ice on that. I'll call Tick, have him pick Nate up—"

"I'm not pressing charges." She straightened, dislodging his gentle touch. Lord, she could just imagine her mother's reaction if she had Nate arrested.

"You don't have to, but I want him to answer some questions, like where he was last night when someone tried to break into your house."

"You don't think..." Her voice, sounding absurdly small, trailed away. Having those suspicions was one thing. Knowing Stanton shared them was something else entirely. "The notes too? Stan, he wouldn't. Would he? What would he gain from trying to scare me?"

He shrugged, a tight, uncomfortable roll of his broad shoulders. "I won't know until we question him."

She rubbed a hand over her eyes, unable to tell him how much worse the whole mess would be if it turned out to be Nate. Her mother's baby, locked away for making terroristic threats. Autry would be banned from home for life, or at least suffer a maternal cold shoulder for an extended period.

"Autry?" Stanton took her wrist in a gentle grasp and pulled her hand from her face. She sighed, and when she looked up into hazel eyes holding a tenderness she hadn't seen from him in months, she wanted to cry again. Lord, she'd turned into a crybaby lately, but maybe, just maybe she deserved it. He rubbed his thumb over her hand. "You need to ice that jaw and we need to talk."

"I know." She sucked in a shaky breath and fixed him with a stern look. "But you have to promise not to propose again."

His rare genuine chuckle rose between them. "Not tonight anyway." He leaned around her and opened the car door. "I'll follow you. Your place or mine?"

45

She didn't want to be in his home, where memories of them lurked everywhere, remembrances of what they'd never be again. The only reason he wanted anything to do with her now was the baby. Biting her lip to stop its trembling, she looked up at him. "Mine."

"Hey, Roger, I'm 10-7." Glad to finally be calling "out of service", Tick paused at the dispatch room's entrance. Holy hell, he was tired. Used to be a double shift was nothing. Maybe he was getting old. A grin tugged at his mouth. Or maybe the double shift wouldn't be a problem if he didn't spend half the night acting like the newlywed he was.

Roger thrust a pink message slip at him. "Sheriff wants you to call him."

Tick's grin died. Somehow, he knew whatever Stanton wanted would mean he was going 10-8, in service, again. "Thanks."

He tugged his cell phone from its clip on his way up the stairs. The message slip bore Autry Holton's home number instead of Stanton's cell. Now, that was interesting. Telling, maybe.

Settling into his squeaking desk chair, he punched in the digits. Autry picked up on the second ring. "Hello?"

Tears thickened her familiar voice and he frowned. "Autry, it's Tick. I had a message to call Stanton at your place. Everything okay?"

"Sure. Everything's fine. I just walked in the door, but Stanton's right behind me. Hang on."

She whispered, "It's for you."

In the background, Tick caught the clatter of a phone changing hands. He leaned back in his chair and closed his eyes, a slow smolder of anger coming to life in his chest. Crying easily had never been in Autry's nature, not even when she'd been a little kid, tagging after Tick and his brothers. Damn Stanton's hide for getting involved with her in the first place. Tick had tried to tell him at the beginning that Autry was a woman interested in long-term commitment—not the one for his gun-shy ex-partner-turned-boss.

He struggled to smother the sense of resentment toward

Stanton, the bitterness that rose way too easily these days, looking for any excuse.

"Tick?" The natural authority of Stanton's voice rumbled in his ear and Tick bristled.

"Yeah, it's me." He rubbed a hand over his eyes, now gritty and stinging with lack of sleep. "What do you need?"

"Go have a talk with Nate Holton."

Tick dropped his hand. "Why?"

"I want to know where he was last night." Stanton's voice hardened. "And if he had anything to do with those notes."

Delegating was one thing, but some things Tick figured Stanton could handle himself. "Then why aren't you talking to him?"

A pause hovered. "There are some things Autry and I need to talk about."

"Things?" Tick let the antagonism trickle into his own voice. "Is that why she's crying?"

"Nate hit her."

"What?" His anger blazed deeper, hotter. That little son of a bitch. He didn't have Helen for a target anymore, so he was turning on his sister?

"Seems Helen called the Holton place while Autry was there. Nate wanted Autry to tell him where Helen was, and when she wouldn't, he popped her in the jaw."

"Damn. Want me to arrest him or just put the fear of God in him?"

"Autry says she's not pressing charges, and we don't have enough to hold him on the attempted break-in yet. Have Williams over at the GBI lab pull his prints, see if they match up to that partial you took."

"Will do." The line went dead and Tick returned the cell to his belt. He grabbed the keys to his truck and jogged from the office. As bad as he hated to admit it, he was looking forward to this little conversation.

Nate Holton had had this one coming for a long time.

Desperate for something to occupy her hands and to

provide an excuse not to look at Stanton, Autry pulled open the pantry. "Are you hungry? I could fix us something—"

"I'm fine." He reached an arm around her and closed the cabinet door. With a gentle hand on her shoulder, he spun her to face him. "You need to put something on that bruise."

She laid a cautious finger against her cheek. Her lower cheekbone still felt as though it was going to explode. "I will. It's really not necessary for you to stay."

He cupped her chin and lifted her gaze to his. "Yeah, Autry, it is. We've got a lot to talk about. The baby. Us."

"There's not an us." Palms raised, she retreated, until her back met the unyielding cabinet door. "Stanton, you promised you wouldn't propose again. I'm serious about this. I will not marry you because you feel obligated."

"Finished?" He rested a hand on either side of her neck and smiled down at her.

"No, I'm not. I cannot believe you think I'd stoop to that kind of marriage, especially after...after..." She swallowed hard, her stomach lifting to a sweet flutter under that grin. "Stop smiling at me like that."

"Like what?" He leaned an inch closer, his smile widening.

She folded her arms over her chest, T-shirt pulling taut across the tiny bulge of their child. "Like I'm a suspect and you're holding the evidence to put me away."

His gaze dropped to her stomach and his smile slipped. He recovered quickly, lifting his eyes to hers again. The long muscles of his throat moved. "Autry, I think the best solution is for you to move in with me."

Chapter Four

"Are you insane?"

Stanton winced. "No. And you don't have to raise your voice. It makes perfect sense."

"To a crazy person. And believe me, buster, I'm not raising my voice, not yet anyway." Autry threw up her hands and rolled her eyes. "Move in with you? No. Absolutely not."

He was making a mess of this already. With a rough breath, he slid his hold from her chin to cradle her nape. "Autry, come on. I want you and the baby safe. Come stay with me until we get everything with the threats and the break-in sorted out. You can have the extra bedroom." He smiled, rubbing the velvet skin below the softness of her hair. Palpable tension resided in the muscles there, and he wanted to make it better, make the fear and the worries go away for her. "Completely platonic. No pressure."

Her lips parted and she shook her head, dislodging his easy touch. "You really have lost your mind. Us? Platonic? Do you really not remember what it was like between us?"

Considering he'd been trying to forget for four months? Hell, he'd dreamed about her. "I remember."

She tightened her arms, resting atop the swell of their child. His throat closed. That was his baby. His and Autry's—a mind-boggling, too-pleasant idea. She blew out a breath, a sarcastic puff. "And you think we can live together without going there again?"

He leaned closer and the sharp scent of her cotton-blossom lotion filled his senses. "Okay, so maybe not platonically."

"You're unbelievable." She placed her palms against his chest and pushed. Stanton planted his feet. His chest burned from the simple contact, made him want to pull her closer. "First you assume I'll agree to marry you just because I'm pregnant. Then you ask me to live with you, all blasé about the whole thing. Well, I have news for you, Sheriff Reed. I don't *need* you. I've made it just fine this far without you—"

"Were you fine last night?" At his words, her face paled and a flash of self-hatred streaked through him. But this was his child, his last chance, they were talking about here, and he'd do whatever necessary. "What if he comes back, out of nowhere? Will you be fine then?"

"You bastard." She closed her eyes, her skin whitening further. When she opened them, the blue depths blazed. "You don't play fair, Reed."

"Not when we're talking about my child." Not when they were talking about her. He'd spent the day dealing with flashes of what could have happened the night before, if he hadn't been in time. Damn it, he wanted her safe, and he could do that. Was that too much to ask? He cradled the sides of her stomach, her shaky sigh traveling up his arms. "Our child. I'm not putting it or you at risk with this guy out there."

She sagged, exhaustion constricting her mouth. "So it's all about safety, huh? A few days or weeks until you catch the guy. If I fall into bed with you, that's just a fringe benefit."

"That's not it at all. Listen to me." Resting his hands on either side of her again, he leaned in and held her gaze. He had to get this right. He had too much to lose. Something else had been flashing in his head all day—how damn lonely he'd been without her the last few weeks. "Yes, I want you and the baby safe. Absolutely. But I want a chance too. A chance to be the father this baby needs and deserves. To be..." He swallowed. "The man you deserve. Give me a couple of months. Move in with me. Or let me move in here, at least until we do catch this guy."

"Lord, you're crazy. I'm crazy for even considering it." She rubbed a hand over her eyes. "What is us living together supposed to prove, anyway?"

He slipped his hands up to frame her face, being careful of the darkening bruise on her cheek and jaw. Fury at Nate trembled in him again and he was vigilant to keep it out of his voice. "That we can make this work. We can, Autry. You know we'd be good together. Don't you think we should at least try? Our baby deserves that much."

She flexed her fingers against his chest, curling them into his shirt. "I don't know. I'm just...there's too much going on right now and you—"

"Can make some of it better." He muttered the words near her temple, inhaling her unique scent. He could make up for being stupid enough to let his fear convince him to let her go and too proud to crawl back to her. Arousal tingled to life low in him and he nuzzled her ear, aware of her quick intake of breath. "Let me, Autry. I'll take care of you, keep you safe."

She turned her head, lips whispering against his. "What about Schaefer?"

He kissed the corner of her mouth, slid his hands to her rounded waist. "Schaefer who?" He moved his lips over hers, tasting, teasing, tantalizing. "All I care about right now is you, me and the baby. We'll work everything else out later." He kissed her again and she flicked her tongue across his lips, into his mouth. He groaned. God, he'd missed her, missed the way she softened the edges of his life with her laughter and sauciness. "Say yes, Autry."

"A month," she murmured against his mouth and he resisted a smile. So like her to start adding clauses to an agreement. Always the lawyer. But he could work with a month. He'd solved major cases in less time. "That's all. If it doesn't work..."

"It will." He'd make sure of it. He'd be everything she needed, everything their child needed. "You'll see."

She tangled her hands in his hair, kissing him deeper, and he tasted something like desperation in her kiss. He lifted his head and nuzzled at her throat. "What'll it be, Counselor? Your place or mine?"

She pulled back and looked at him for a long moment. Her eyes shuttered and she smiled, a humorless expression. "Yours."

"Nate!" Tick banged on the metal door, careful to keep his

body low and to one side. He rested his free hand on his gun.

Inside, the trailer floor creaked. Blinds in the window rattled and Nate flung the door open. It bounced off the aluminum siding with a bang. He glared at Tick through bleary eyes and scratched his bare chest. "What d'ya want, Calvert? I was sleepin'."

More like drinking and half-passed out. Disgust curdled in Tick's empty stomach. How on earth Virgil and Miranda Holton had produced this good-for-nothing piece of crap was beyond him.

He narrowed his eyes, still letting his hand rest against the hefty weight of his Glock. "I need to ask you a few questions."

Unease flickered in Nate's murky gaze. "'Bout what?"

"Your sister."

"Which one?" Nate gave a disgusted snort and turned back into the trailer's dim interior. "I got two."

"Now why would I come asking you questions about Madeline?" Tick stepped in behind him, senses recoiling from the smells of stale alcohol, days-old garbage and a bathroom seriously in need of cleaning. Holy hell, how did the guy live like this? "We need to talk about Autry."

"Autry." Nate threw himself into the brown vinyl recliner and picked up a beer can abandoned on the side table. He laughed and swirled the liquid before lifting it to his mouth. "Daddy's little angel. Pure, perfect Autry." A hard smirk twisted his lips. "Wonder what Daddy would say if he knew she's been fucking your boss?"

Tick smothered a spurt of anger. How did a guy talk about his sister like that? And it wasn't like Nate should be throwing stones. Even before Helen had gone, he'd frequented the truck stop on 300 and its lot lizards.

He kept the anger off his face and lifted an eyebrow. "I don't know. Does he know you hit her?"

"Shit." Nate crushed the can under his foot. "So that's what this is about. Yeah, I lost my temper and I popped her one. She wouldn't tell me where Helen was."

Un-freakin'-believable. "So she deserved it, huh?"

"Yeah. What's the big deal?"

"The big deal is it's battery and you already have a record."

"Yeah, and if Autry was pressing charges, you'd have already had the cuffs on me. You can drop the bluff, Calvert, and get the hell out."

"Got a couple of questions for you first." He glanced around the dark, cramped living room. A ton of crushed beer cans littered the floor, a pile of clothes of indeterminate cleanliness took up half the couch and paper plates with food scraps covered the occasional tables. No writing pad in sight, not even by the phone. Course, no telling if the phone was even in service any more. "Where were you between two and four this morning?"

Nate tossed back his overly long hair, badly in need of a wash and a cut. "Here. Sleeping."

Tick nodded. "Can anybody verify that?"

"Yeah." Nate gave a satisfied sound, something between a chuckle and a belch. "Your wife."

Tick sighed. Like he'd never heard that one before. "So the answer is no."

Leaning back in his chair, Nate folded his arms behind his head, exposing tufts of underarm hair. "What's so important about last night?" He narrowed his eyes. "Let me guess. Somebody tried to invade Autry's ivory tower. Probably pissed off she's defending that son of a bitch Schaefer."

"Autry's receiving threats." Hands at his hips, Tick lowered his voice. "Let me find out they're from you and being Virgil Holton's son won't save you this time. Got me?"

Nothing flickered in the blank depths of Nate's blue eyes, but the insolent sneer remained. "Oh, yeah, I got you."

Tick held his gaze a moment longer and nodded. "Good. See you around, Nate."

He stepped out of the trailer and closed the door behind him. Keeping a close eye on the narrow mobile home, he walked to his truck. The scents of Nate's home lingered with him and Tick rubbed a hand down his jaw. Damn, he needed a shower.

She'd obviously lost her mind. Autry tossed a handful of panties into her suitcase. Not only had she agreed to Stanton's idea they should move in together, but she'd let him persuade her to begin tonight. In the privacy of her bedroom, she didn't have to lie to herself—she would feel safer with him. Maybe she'd actually sleep.

If she stayed out of his bed.

Heat flashed through her. They weren't talking about being merely roommates, her using his guest room. No, they were planning on a month of cohabitating, sharing everything from the morning paper to a bathroom to Stanton's big bed.

Autry sank to the edge of the bed, a hand over her stomach. Oh, this gamble was huge. She was betting on one more month, thirty days, to make Stanton fall in love with her. How did she think that was going to happen in a mere four weeks, when four months of dating hadn't done it?

Because the stakes were higher now. She rubbed at the slight swell of their baby. He had to feel trapped and that would lead to resentment if she couldn't make him love her. They could all end up hurting so badly.

Even knowing all that, she was going to try anyway.

"Insane," she muttered and pushed to her feet. So insane it might work.

She dumped jeans and T-shirts, pajamas and a couple of sweatshirts in her suitcase. She tugged her garment bag from the closet and loaded it with several of her suits. Matching shoes joined the montage in her suitcase. From her bedside-table drawer, she pulled the pregnancy book she'd been reading and tossed it in the case as well. She leaned over to latch it and moaned, the inevitable nausea climbing in her throat.

A hand clapped over her mouth, she scrambled for the bathroom. The horrible retching was over in minutes and she pushed to her feet, knees shaky. She brushed her teeth and tried not to look at her bruised face and red, damp eyes. Sure, Stanton would want that woman in his bed. She rested her forehead against the cool mirror.

She splashed cold water on her face and wrists, dried them, and walked out to the living room. "I think I'm ready..."

Her voice trailed away, a smile nudging at her mouth. Sprawled sideways, Stanton took up half her couch, his eyes closed, face relaxed in sleep. He probably hadn't eaten all day, or if he had, it had been greasy takeout grabbed with Tick and eaten on the run. That much hadn't changed in four months— he still let the job run his life.

He thought he was going to be taking care of her, but the truth was, as old-fashioned as it sounded, he needed someone to take care of him. She eased over to sit on the coffee table. She loved the planes and angles of his face, the fine lines radiating from his eyes, the jut of his chin, the slashes by his mouth. Her fingers tingled to stroke the strands of silver just beginning to highlight his temples.

He opened his eyes, the hazel depths sharp and clear. "Ready?"

Her face heated. He'd caught her staring at him like some lovesick teenager. "I thought you were sleeping."

"It wouldn't take much." He straightened with a groan and dragged his hands down his face. "It's been a long day. I was going to toss something on the grill, but how about if we stop at Winn Dixie and grab a rotisserie chicken instead?"

"Sounds great." The ordinariness of the situation overwhelmed her. What they were doing was far from ordinary. The sensation of her life spinning out of control spiraled through her again.

"I'll get your things." Stanton rose. "Autry?"

She didn't move from the table, but looked up at him and bit her lip. "Are we doing the right thing, Stan?"

His mouth curving, he dropped to a crouch before her. He cupped her thighs, thumbs caressing her knees, and her skin sizzled under his light touch, even through her jeans. "Yeah, baby, it's the right thing. We have to at least try."

"Then why does it feel..." She watched a frown pull his brows down and shook her head with a tiny dismissive laugh. "Never mind. Did I mention that pregnancy makes me a little weird and emotional?"

His face closed and his fingers tightened. "It does that to a lot of women. Hormones."

"Yeah." Foreboding settled in her chest, a sharp, pinching sensation. He didn't want this baby, not really, and did she think that would change in a month?

He patted her knee and straightened. "Bags in your

bedroom?"

She nodded, not looking at him. "Yes. But I can—"

"I've got them. Be right back."

His footsteps creaked on the old wood of her hallway. Autry closed her eyes. Right? Any of this?

Anything but.

Stanton dropped Autry's bags by the door and turned to take the grocery bags from her. They'd ended up with more than a chicken. "Let me get those."

She surrendered the bags, but rolled her eyes. "I'm not an invalid, Stan. I've been doing this on my own for months now, remember?"

"You didn't have to," he said, his voice quiet. "You know that, don't you, Autry? I'd have been with you from the beginning if I'd known."

"I know." She folded her arms across her chest, the self-defensive gesture he'd seen her use more than once the night before. "But I didn't want it to be because you had to. I still don't."

He unpacked the makings for their supper quickly and glanced over his shoulder at her. "Where do you want your bags?"

"This is so cold-blooded. Yesterday, we were nothing and tonight you're asking me if I want to sleep in your bed."

"You act like I'm just waiting to drag you off and ravish you. If you want to use the guest bedroom, that's fine."

"But that wasn't the agreement, was it?" She lifted her chin, a hint of defiance in the angle.

"Do you always have to be such a lawyer?" He leaned against the counter. "We agreed to live together for a month, to see if we could make a go of things, with marriage being the end goal. And yeah, I meant live together in every sense of the word, but hell, Autry. I know what the last twenty-four hours have been like for you. I wasn't planning on making any demands on you." He relaxed his death grip on the counter's edge. "Now, where do you want your things?"

"The guest room." She held his gaze, but her voice was soft, a little tremulous. "For tonight, anyway."

He nodded. "Fine. I'll be right back."

Hefting her suitcase and garment bag, he carried them through the living room to the guest room. An odd relief flowed through him. Autry was right on this point—a renewed sexual involvement too soon would muddy the waters even further. A little more space there was probably a good idea. Once he touched her, gave into the low hum of desire she always inspired, he wouldn't be able to keep a straight head where she was concerned.

He'd need that too, not only to keep her safe, but to muddle his way through the next month. He couldn't afford to screw this up.

She waited for him in the kitchen, placing salad greens and slices of fragrant roasted chicken on plates. Stanton paused in the doorway and watched. She moved with smooth grace, and the sweater she'd changed into before they left her house hugged the tiny bulge of her pregnancy. An urge to embrace her, fold his hands around the swell of their child, caught him by the throat. He didn't remember wanting that when Renee had been pregnant with their sons.

Autry glanced up, her expression tense, her eyes troubled. "Think it's warm enough to eat on the deck?"

"Probably. I can always light the fire bowl."

Once they were settled at the deck's glass-topped table, a fire flickering in the copper and iron bowl in the corner behind them, he watched her play with her food, pushing the lettuce around her plate and only nibbling at the chicken.

He cleared his throat. "How has it been? Physically, I mean."

Surprise flickered in her blue eyes. "I'm still fighting morning sickness that lasts all day, if that's what you're asking."

"I'm sorry." What else could he say? Hell, it was basically his fault. He was the one who'd told her it was safe to make love. He was the one with a faulty vasectomy. "What did your doctor say?"

With her fork, she danced a slice of tomato around the edge of her plate. "Just that it wasn't anything to worry about. It'll go away." She rested her chin on her hand, expression glum. "With my luck? The day I have the kid."

The conversation only made it more real, even though, sitting across from her with the table hiding her stomach, he couldn't see a lot of changes in her body. Her breasts might be a little fuller, but if anything, her face was thinner, the line of her clavicle sharper.

He frowned. "You're gaining weight, right?"

She pinned him with a look and reached for a roll. "You know, sometimes I can see why Renee divorced you. You don't ask a pregnant woman that, Stan."

"You do when she's carrying your child. Are you gaining what you should?"

"Yes. I am. Right now, everything is fine. Anything else you'd like to know?"

He cleared his throat again, looked away then back to hold her gaze. "Do you know the sex?"

Her eyes softened. "Not yet. I'm scheduled for a sonogram on my next visit, a couple of days from now, and we might find out then. It's one of those new four-dimensional sonograms." She paused, head bent for a moment, and pushed the tomato around her plate again. Finally, she lifted uncharacteristically shy eyes to his. "Would you like to come with me?"

An opportunity to see his baby growing within her? To make sure she actually was okay? More than he wanted to admit. "I'd like that. Thanks."

Yawning, she stretched and rolled her shoulders in a small circle. "Lord, I'm exhausted. And I've got a ton of prep work to do."

Stanton pulled his gaze from her breasts. Yep, definitely fuller, a little rounder. She'd filled his hands nicely before and he itched to find out what that fit would be like now. He swallowed, hard. "Why don't you grab a shower while I clean up? You can relax and do what you need to do, make an early night of it."

"That sounds wonderful. I think I will." She folded an arm over her head and tugged on the elbow with her other hand, a move he remembered seeing Tick's ex-girlfriend the yoga instructor do. The movement lifted her breasts higher beneath the thin cotton sweater. "What will you do?"

Probably suffer unrequited lust even after a cold shower. He laid his fork across his plate. "Go to bed early, try to get some sleep. Pulled doubles the last three days, and I'm beat."

He rose, stacking her plate on top of his and grabbing the serving platter with the remains of the chicken. She reached for their glasses and the breadbasket. "Are you sure you don't want help cleaning up?"

With his hands full, he couldn't tuck that errant wisp of chestnut hair behind her ear or stroke a comforting finger down her bruised face, as badly as he wanted to. "I've got it. Enjoy your shower."

She pushed the patio door open with her elbow. After setting the glasses and basket down, she glanced at him. "Um, do you mind if I use yours?"

He shot a quick look at her. She'd always loved the openness of his semi-outdoor shower, one of the main reasons he'd bought the big cedar contemporary overlooking the Flint River. He'd loved the things they'd done in that glass cube, open to the stars and night air. "Sure. Go ahead."

"Thanks." With an impish smile, she disappeared down the hall.

Stanton rubbed a hand over his face. He needed to call Tick, find out what Nate had had to say. Maybe, just maybe, that would take his mind off the woman getting naked in his bathroom.

Tick took the back steps two at a time. His stomach gnawed at his backbone and he still felt grimy and soiled after his little conversation with Nate. He flipped through his key ring and unlocked the back door, well aware Caitlin never left a door or window unlocked in the house. He felt like crap. But home? Coming home felt pretty darn good.

The mail sat in a neat pile on the kitchen island and scents of spicy tomato sauce and melted cheese lingered in the air. Lasagna. Or Caitlin's incredible spaghetti Bolognese. His stomach gnawed harder and his mouth watered.

Caitlin's laptop stood open on the dining room table, glossy crime scene photos lying amid scattered reports and a legal pad full of her neat handwriting. He tossed his keys on the island and picked up a photo, grimacing a little at the dead girl's face. She was just a baby, not more than fourteen or fifteen.

He dropped the photo. "Cait?"

"I was wondering when you'd straggle in." She emerged from their bedroom clad in a faded Quantico trainee shirt and brief gray gym shorts. A pair of his boot socks covered her feet and he grinned. Beautiful runner's legs, but the coldest feet known to man. Married little more than a month and he was still getting used to those feet hitting his calves in the middle of the night. Still getting used to being a husband after years as a bachelor.

Smiling, she went into his arms and he wrapped her close, kissing her. Tugging his mouth free, he buried his face against the sleek mass of her black hair.

"Lord, I missed you." He exhaled hard, the tension already draining out of his body. "It's been a long day. Sorry I'm late."

"It's okay. I held supper for you. It's in the microwave." She arched into him, arms twined around his neck. He trailed his mouth down to the hollow of her shoulder and she sighed. "You need to eat something. I'd lay money you skipped lunch."

"You'd be right." He pulled the neckline of her T-shirt to one side, giving him greater access to her soft skin.

"Tick?"

He made a noncommittal sound in his throat.

"You're not the only one who's late."

"Yeah?" He scraped his teeth lightly against her shoulder, the gnawing in his gut turning to a different type of hunger.

"Mm-hmm." She ran her hands beneath the hem of his shirt, caressing his spine. "Three days."

The words and her thinly veiled excitement penetrated the desire. Her period was late, but that wasn't a big deal. It wasn't like he could set his watch by her irregular cycle, caused in part by a missing ovary and Fallopian tube.

He lifted his head. "Cait, precious, come on. Don't get your hopes up. Dr. Astin's not even starting you on the Clomid until next month—"

"I took one of those home tests, just to make sure."

He closed his eyes, steeling himself. This whole trying-to-have-a-baby thing was going to be one wicked rollercoaster ride and somehow he knew the first dip was about to hit. "Cait, we agreed we weren't going to do this to ourselves."

"It was positive." She was biting her lip, obviously trying to hide a grin.

Hopeful joy spiked in him and he squashed it. "Those things aren't always reliable. Deanne got two false negatives when she was pregnant with Charlie—"

"Yeah, that's what I thought too. A false positive." She leaned back in his arms, her dark green gaze glowing. "So I did it again, three different times, with three different brands."

That was his Caitlin, covering all the angles. A burn of excitement started in his chest. "And?"

"And I got three more positives." The grin spread across her face. "So I dropped in on Layla at the clinic. We did another urine test and a blood test."

"Both positive."

She nodded.

An answering grin tugged at his mouth. "For real?"

"Would I kid about this?"

"Good Lord." He ran a hand through his hair. She was pregnant, without all the fertility drugs and artificial insemination, the in-vitro process and everything else they'd researched in the last few months, getting a head start before they'd even exchanged vows. He laughed, hugging her close and rocking from side to side. "Holy hell. You're pregnant."

She wrapped her arms snugger around his neck, her husky laugh bubbling between them. "I know."

"A baby." The rocking wasn't enough, and he lifted her, swinging around with a wild whoop. Laughing, he set her on her feet, still bound in his embrace. He slid his hands to her stomach. "Our baby."

"Yes." She bit her lip again and a sheen of tears glimmered in her eyes. "Our baby."

The joy was unbearable and he wanted to yell again, to shout it for everyone to hear. Instead, he leaned down to kiss her. His mouth whispered over hers, lowered again, clung. "I love you, Falconetti."

She pulled him close, her kiss fierce and possessive. "I love you too, Calvert."

At that moment, he had to be the happiest man in Chandler County, Georgia, and absolutely nothing could change that.

Chapter Five

Autry woke to the rich smell of fresh coffee. Half-asleep, she inhaled the well-loved scent. Her stomach rebelled, nausea wrapping rough fingers around her throat. With a groan, she rolled from the bed and dashed for the small bath off Stanton's guest room.

"Baby," she mumbled around her toothbrush after retching her lungs out again, "you'd better make up for this when it's time for the terrible twos. I expect you to be quite well behaved."

"Autry?" A quick rap at the closed bedroom door accompanied Stanton's voice. "You up? Breakfast's on."

Ignoring the way his deep tones sent a rush of warmth through her, she rinsed her mouth and spit. "Be right there."

She didn't bother with her hair, but threw a robe on over her pajamas and padded to the kitchen. Cereal and bowls of fresh fruit waited on the small table, along with glasses of juice. She cast a longing look at the coffeemaker and covered her mouth and nose.

Stanton pulled the milk from the refrigerator and turned. His brows descended in a concerned frown. "What's wrong?"

Breathing through her mouth, she shook her head. He followed her line of sight and groaned. Setting the milk on the table, he reached for the carafe. "The coffee. I'm sorry. The smell made Renee sick too, but I didn't think..."

His voice trailed away as he walked outside and Autry envisioned him pouring the rich liquid off the side of the deck. Lord, what a waste. He stepped inside, the glass-paned door closing behind him with a muted snick. A small apologetic grimace twisted his brows. "I'm sorry, Autry. I just didn't think."

"It's okay, Stan." She glanced down at the table. Oh, heaven help her, he'd remembered exactly how she liked her cereal—a banana and strawberries sliced on top, a few blueberries tossed in for good measure. She frowned. There'd been no fruit in his refrigerator last night and they hadn't picked any up at Winn Dixie, either.

She tucked her tousled hair behind her ears. "Did you go shopping?"

A crooked smile curled his mouth. He set the milk in the middle of the table. "Yeah. I remembered you liked fruit in the morning and I was out, so I skipped my run and went to the store instead."

This was what had started her slow tumble into love with him in the first place—these small kindnesses, the little ways he paid attention to her likes and dislikes. She hadn't intended to love him at all. She'd been exploring an unexpected attraction, had told herself she could handle a short fling with the handsome new sheriff, no worries.

She really had to stop listening to herself like that.

He pulled out a chair for her. "Did you sleep well?"

How was she supposed to answer that? Exhaustion had pulled her under pretty quickly, but she'd woken often during the night, disturbed by nightmares as well as the knowledge he was mere feet away. "Better than I thought I would, thanks."

He poured milk over his cereal. "Feel okay this morning?"

Was this how it was going to be? This awful stilted conversation, them tiptoeing around each other? She picked up a banana slice from her cereal and popped it in her mouth. "Same as yesterday morning. Stanton, we're not doing this."

Nervousness flickered in his eyes. "Doing what?"

She reached for the milk. "Having too-polite conversations. Acting like strangers turned roommates. I'm a big girl. Like I told you, I've made it through four months of this pregnancy without you watching my every move. I'm not a fragile flower who can't take a little stress."

He laid his spoon down and leaned back, frustration darkening his face. "This is out of my league. I don't know what I'm supposed to do."

"That's my line, Sheriff. You have two children already,

remember?"

The short bark of his laugh dripped self-deprecation. "Yeah, but I was finishing my last year in the army when Renee was pregnant with Hadden. I was in Germany and she stayed in Houston. When she was carrying John Logan, I was at Quantico and doing my compulsory training with the bureau. It's not like I was around then either."

She sipped her juice. "Well, the first thing you're not supposed to do is drive me up the nearest wall with those overprotective instincts of yours."

"I think I can handle that."

"Last night...why did you ask me if I knew the sex?" She fiddled with her spoon, watching him beneath her lashes. "Would you like another son?"

He looked up at her, his expression guarded. "I haven't really thought about it. Curiosity, I guess."

Mere curiosity. Silly of her to be hurt by that, when he'd never wanted to be in this situation with her. She pushed the cereal away, any appetite gone. "I'm going to get dressed. Thank you for the fruit. You really didn't have to go to all that trouble."

"No trouble." His body still and tense, he fixed her with his steady, watchful gaze. "What's wrong?"

"Nothing." With a scornful laugh, she blinked back more of the stupid, weak tears and walked out of the kitchen.

His chair scraped on the floor and he caught up to her in the hallway, taking her shoulders in a gentle hold and turning her to face him. "Wait."

Maybe he couldn't see how close her emotions were to the surface. She smiled, her face aching. "I need to get dressed. I have a meeting at nine—"

"It's barely seven. You have plenty of time." His thumbs caressed her shoulders and he leaned closer. "What did I do?"

"Nothing." She shrugged and his hands fell away.

"Nothing didn't put that look on your face." Frustration roughened his voice. "I said or did something wrong and—"

"You didn't do anything. I told you, I'm silly and emotional right now and it just doesn't take much to get me going."

He lifted an eyebrow, his eyes still confused and

unconvinced. "You're sure?"

No. She wanted to press closer, bawl against his chest, and have him promise he'd come to want their baby, to want her. "I'm positive. Now, I really have to get dressed."

He stepped back. "Okay."

She walked away, aware he didn't move, feeling the weight of his gaze until she closed the bedroom door behind her.

Would you like another son?

Autry's question dogged Stanton all morning. Most of his deputies had returned to duty, having recovered from the flu, and he was back behind his desk, swamped in paperwork. With every report reviewed, every timecard signed, every irate county commissioner soothed, the idea of having another son beat in his head.

Or a daughter. A little girl, who'd probably end up with his dark brown hair, but who might, just might, get her mother's blue eyes and sassy attitude.

His mother would love having a granddaughter. He scratched a note in the margin of Tick's report on Autry's break-in, a reminder to have the GBI's crime lab run a handwriting analysis on the notes. What kind of things did a guy do with a daughter? Hell, like he even knew what kind of things to do with a son.

A hushed hum of activity drifted in from the squad room—a couple of deputies clocking out after a split shift, the rumble of his other investigator Mark Cook's deep voice, Tick's good-natured cursing because the coffee can was empty. Something was up with Tick—all morning he'd been whistling and bouncing around the station like a hyperactive kid who'd missed a dose of Ritalin.

And the weird tension that seemed to cloak him lately whenever he was around Stanton felt diminished. Stanton tapped his pen on his blotter. For months now, since Caitlin Falconetti had walked back into Tick's life, Stanton had the odd sensation Tick was pissed off at him and hiding it. In the ten years they'd worked together, there'd never been this much strain between them and hell, Stanton was glad whatever it was seemed to have vanished for the moment.

Tick appeared in the doorway, soda in one hand, computer printout in the other. "Got the list of recent parolees that Autry represented. Couple of possibilities, guys who've returned to the area." He glanced down at the list. "Martin Kinney, armed robbery, did the minimum sentence at Lee State. He's living at his mama's over on 112. And Hunter McLeod, just released from the CI over in Valdosta. He's moved in with a girlfriend at the Miller Place apartments."

Stanton leaned back. "What'd he do time for?"

"Sexual assault."

"Great." The last thing he needed was images of a convicted rapist trying to get into Autry's house. He shuddered.

"After lunch, I'm going to run them down and—"

"Come get me when you're ready. I'll go with you."

"Two days in a squad car and being behind a desk is killing you." Tick stepped inside, closing the door. "Listen, I thought you'd want to know the office scuttle has Autry's car outside your place last night."

Stanton ran a hand over his hair. "She's moving in for a while."

"Putting a new spin on 'to serve and protect'?"

"She's pregnant, Tick."

"Holy hell." Surprise flared in Tick's dark gaze. "Must be something in the water. Damn it, Stan, that wasn't supposed to happen."

"You're telling me."

Tick's laugh emerged rusty and a little rough. "You got snipped for nothing."

"Go ahead. Have a good laugh." Eyes narrowed, Stanton glared at him. "What did you mean, something in the water?"

The tension Stanton had thought diminished rose between them again. Tick rolled up the printout and stuck it in his pocket. "Cait's pregnant."

And he was absolutely overjoyed—the emotion was all over him, the reason for all that vibrating energy he had this morning. So why the waves of ill-temper suddenly rolling off him?

Stanton shook his head. "That's...great."

"Don't lie, Stan."

The abrupt hostility took Stanton back for a half-second. "Tick—"

"But yeah, it's pretty damn great that we didn't have to go through all the freakin' fertility treatments." The flare of antagonism banked again, Tick rocked back on his heels. "So what are you and Autry going to do?"

No way Stanton could explain the convoluted mess they'd talked themselves into. "We're going to take it one day at a time, see what happens."

Irritation fired in Tick's eyes. "A little casual about the whole thing, aren't you? This is a kid we're talking about. *Your* kid."

"Don't you think I know that? Why do you think I'm—" Stanton bit off the words.

"You're going to break her heart." Weariness dragging at his features, Tick dropped into one of the chairs before Stanton's desk. "I knew it. I told you she wasn't your type."

"Yeah." Stanton reached for a pen and slashed his signature at the bottom of the daily jail headcount. "About like I told you about Falconetti."

"Well, you were wrong, weren't you?" A hard edge entered Tick's voice, the enmity flickering to life again.

"Guess I was." He wasn't going to point out that one month and a pregnancy didn't a successful marriage make. His pen stilled over the second report. But wasn't that the agreement he and Autry had? One month to prove to her they could make it work.

He seriously needed to renegotiate for more time.

After a sharp rap at the door, Cookie stuck his head in. "Yo, boss. You've got a visitor at the front desk."

What now? Stanton tossed his pen down. "Who is it?"

Cookie grinned. "Your ex-wife."

Renee, here? Stanton exchanged a look with Tick and pushed up from his chair. A pharmaceutical rep, Renee traveled the area frequently, but didn't usually come by. Lord, he hoped nothing had happened to one of the boys.

She waited for him at the front desk. A red suit set off her dark hair, caught up in a sleek knot. A bright smile lit her face.

"Stan! Hello, Tick." She leaned up to kiss Tick's cheek. "You look wonderful. Marriage agrees with you."

"You look great too." Tick tagged Stanton's arm. "I'm going to grab a bite, but I'll catch up with you and we'll do those interviews. Good to see you, Renee."

Once he disappeared through the front door, Renee fixed Stanton with a look. "Now you...I've seen you looking better."

"Thanks a lot." He gazed down at her. Amazing that as much as he'd felt for her once upon a time, everything from love to hate and all the cold places in between, her presence held only warm friendship now. "Not that I'm not glad to see you, but what are you doing here? Boys okay?"

"They're fine." The dimple in her left cheek flashed. "I thought I'd save you a stamp and pick up the child-support check."

"Funny, but I mailed it yesterday."

She rolled her big green eyes. "Oh, the check's in the mail. Where have I heard that before?"

"Not from me. Really, why are you here?"

"I had sales calls in the area and I decided to take you to lunch."

"That sounds great." He grinned. "Diner across the street okay?"

They walked to the little storefront diner and she filled him in on their sons' latest accomplishments and elicited a promise that he'd attend Hadden's next basketball game.

Once they'd settled into a booth and ordered, Renee folded her hands atop the table and narrowed her eyes. "Now, what's going on?"

He opened his mouth, closed it, gave up the idea of lying and sighed. "Autry's pregnant."

Lips parted, Renee stared. "Stan, you had a vasectomy."

"You know, that topic's been covered several times in the last day or so."

Her expression troubled, she ran a finger around the rim of her tea glass. "I thought the two of you were kaput."

He cleared his throat. "We were, but we're going to give it another try."

Renee's frown deepened. "For the baby's sake, of course."

The disapproval in her voice bothered him. "It's the right thing to do, Renee. I want us to try. This baby deserves that much, doesn't it?"

"What about what Autry deserves?"

"I'm going to try to be what she needs." The frustration crowded his chest again. He had no clue what that was. Even this morning, in the hallway, he'd known she needed something from him, but damn if he could figure it out. "I won't...I won't be the way I was with you."

Renee lifted her arched brows, her eyes cool. "You mean an emotionally unavailable ass?"

Even if he wasn't in love with her anymore, the words still hurt, despite the truth in them. He hadn't been an involved husband. "Yeah. Exactly."

Her gaze softened with concern. "Stanton, you're my friend and I love you. On some level, I always will, but for a smart man, sometimes you are the most clueless individual. Do you know when I knew our marriage was over?"

"About the time you packed my bags for me?" He tried to keep the lingering bitterness from his voice.

She fixed him with a look. "When I realized I knew more about Tick's goals than yours. Your partner had more genuine conversations with me than you did." A sad smile lifted the corners of her mouth. "It's very hard to be in love with a man who's never really there, even when he's sleeping beside you."

He glanced away. "Renee, I—"

"Stan, I'm glad you found Autry, really I am. I like her. I want you to be happy." She covered his hand, fingers cool on his wrist. "But if you want this to work with her, it's got to be about more than the baby. You've got to find out who the guy inside is—the one you've been hiding from for years—and let her see him."

The waitress brought their plates. Stanton stared at his turkey club, his appetite gone. All he wanted to do was make things right with Autry—to keep her and their baby safe, to be there for them.

And it wasn't enough.

"Well, at least I have you thinking." Renee crunched into a carrot stick.

If she only knew. Hell, he didn't know where to start. He picked up his sandwich and forced himself to bite into it.

Renee leaned forward. "What do you want, Stan? I mean, when you think about making a life with Autry, what do you really, *really* want?"

A memory flashed, June, that weekend before they'd arrested Schaefer. Waking in the middle of the night in Autry's bed, the warmth of her pressed along him, her hand over his heart. Sleepy and sated, he'd pulled her closer, suffused with an emotion so strong and pure he never wanted to let her go.

That was in the dark. In the light of morning, that connection, the level of feeling had scared him. He knew from experience he wasn't capable of sustaining that kind of emotion. With Renee, he'd felt it in snatches, but it had always subsided once he returned to duty with the bureau, in the chase again, his mind and energy focused on some pocket of organized crime.

He wanted to be the guy who felt that for Autry all the time, who inspired the same sentiment in her.

That guy just plain wasn't him. He didn't have it in him. Hadn't he already proved that?

"Stan?"

He glanced up and met Renee's concerned gaze. "I don't know."

"Then don't you think you'd better figure it out?"

He smiled, shrugged again, and made a desperate attempt to change the subject. "What about you and Don? You two set a date yet?"

The remainder of their lunch passed with light conversation about Renee's engagement and John Logan's misadventures as a learning driver. When Stanton returned to the department, Renee's question—what he really, *really* wanted—continued rolling over in his mind.

Inside, he stopped at the front desk and picked up his messages. While he flipped through them, the door swung open,

of fall breeze. The pink message slips he'd laid tered away and he made a grab for them.

The trembling nervousness in Autry's voice sent s skin.

rc open, he messages forgotten. Autry's pale face, her big eyes, the same expression he'd seen the night of the break in— all of it kicked his heart into overdrive.

With a step forward, he took her hands. "What happened? Are you okay? The—"

She clutched at him and shook her head, her chest moving with her uneven breathing. "I'm fine. I just...I got another one."

"Another note."

She nodded. "It was under my windshield wiper when I walked out of the courthouse."

"Okay." He smoothed a stray lock of hair behind her ear, not caring that all activity around the front desk and in the hall had stopped, that the front desk secretary and two deputies watched every move he made. "Come on in the office."

He ushered her through, his hand at the small of her back. Inside, he grabbed an evidence bag and a pair of gloves. "Got it with you?"

"Yes." She dug into her purse and pulled out a folded piece of lined notepaper. Her expression as she passed it to him was apologetic. "I know I probably shouldn't have touched it, should have called you to meet me, but I just wanted out of there."

"It's okay." Flashing her a reassuring smile, he took the note with a gloved hand. She was beginning to calm down, some of the tension relaxing from her posture. "I want to have Tick go by and dust your car for prints, canvas the area to see if anyone saw anything. You can take the Explorer."

"Thanks." A half-hearted smile played around her lips, and she placed a hand over her stomach.

He unfolded the paper and slid it inside the clear evidence bag. The same blocky handwriting. Four simple words.

He can't stop me.

Fury flared in him, but he kept his face devoid of expression when he met her eyes. "I need to know everything. Where you've been today, what time you arrived at the courthouse, who you spoke to, what time you found this."

She fidgeted with her jacket hem. "I had a nine o'clock meeting with a client at the Thomas County jail. I left there a little after ten. Dropped by the office, picked up my briefs. I arrived at the courthouse around eleven-thirty. The hearing was over at twelve-fifteen and I went straight to my car. Once I found the note, I came here."

He pulled his gaze from the note and slanted her an inquiring look. "You walked?"

Her small laugh was self-deprecating as she sank into the chair before his desk. "It was only a block and I was afraid to get in the car. Lord, I'm getting paranoid."

"No, you're not. You did the right thing. Only next time, *call me.*"

"Please don't say next time, Stan. I don't want there to be a next time." She lifted her eyes to his, the blue dark with fear. "You have to find him and make it go away. If you don't, I swear I'll go crazy."

"We'll find him." He dropped the plastic-encased note on his desk and crossed to kneel before her. She blinked rapidly and he gripped the chair arms, the clean scent of cotton blossoms wrapping around him. "We'll get him, Autry, I promise. Tick's already running down leads, and I'm going out with him later. I'll make this go away, baby. I swear."

"I believe you." She curved a hand along his jaw, and every nerve in his body tingled.

What did he really, *really* want? For this moment to never end. For them to remain locked in this bubble of isolation, for his failures and the stalker and Jeff Schaefer to just not exist. For it to be simply him and Autry, going on and on and on.

Everything he thought he couldn't have. If only he could figure out how to be what she needed...

With a rough breath, he took her wrist, turned his head and pressed a kiss to her palm. Her fingers flexed against his face, a brief caress. He didn't want to break the connection, but he pushed to his feet and moved to put the expanse of his desk between them. "I need to call Tick."

Hand pressed to her thudding heart, Autry watched him pick up the phone and dial. His deep voice washed over her and her heartbeat calmed. In his steady presence, the fear faded. If she could only trust him with her heart as easily as she could her physical safety.

"Thanks. I'll be here." He replaced the receiver and looked at her. "He's going to dust the car. I'd like to have it towed over to Lawson Automotive, have them check it out, just in case."

She nodded. "Okay."

"Do you have any other appointments today?" He detached his keys from his belt.

"No, only going back to the office for the rest of the day."

"If we picked up your laptop and files, could you work from here?"

She shrugged. "I guess. Why?"

He leaned against his desk, playing with the keys. "Your office is isolated. The backstairs offer a concealed way in and out. I'd rather not have you alone over there right now. I'd just feel better if you were here."

It made sense, but frustration slammed through her. "God, I hate this. He's taking over my life."

"I know this is hard," he said, voice soft, his gaze steady on hers. "But I don't want to take any chances."

His very real worry raised her fear again. "You think he really wants to hurt me, don't you?"

"I don't know. Very few stalkers actually escalate to violence, but one is too many. We'll go get your stuff. I'm going to take off with Tick and you can have the office to yourself." A crooked grin curved his mouth. "How much safer can you be than right here?"

Safer maybe, but a prisoner all the same. Everything seemed to be spiraling out of her control. Her eyes burned. "Why is this happening? Damn it, Stan, what did I do to deserve this?"

"Nothing." He pulled her up and into his arms, hands stroking her back in soothing sweeps. "You didn't do anything, baby. I mean it, Autry. This is not your fault."

"I just want it to go away." She turned her face into his throat, his warm scent filling her senses. A hint of returning stubble rasped against her skin and he kissed her cheek.

The door opened. "Hey, you ready to go..." Tick's voice trailed off, and he cleared his throat. "Sorry. Should have knocked."

Stanton released her. "Why start now?"

Autry wiped at her eyes and turned to face Tick. She shaped her trembling lips into a smile. "Hey, Tick."

"Hey." He smiled, but it didn't quite reach his eyes, a cold anger glinting in them as he glanced at Stanton. "Stan tells me congratulations are in order."

Beneath her lashes, she studied Stanton. He remained expressionless. Lord, he was so guarded. She sighed. "Thanks, but can you keep that quiet? I haven't told my parents yet."

"No problem." He shrugged. "I've got prints off the car, but ten to one says they turn out to all be elimination prints. Keith Lawson picked it up and he'll call you once they've checked it out."

Stanton nodded. "Good deal. Autry's going to work from here this afternoon. Let me take her over to get her things and we'll run out on those interviews."

"Can you give me an hour first?" The line of Tick's shoulders was tight. "I never made it to lunch. Had to go back up Troy Lee on a traffic stop."

"Yeah." Stanton's mouth went taut.

Autry watched the tense nonverbal interplay between the two. Something was up there, something big enough to strain their easygoing friendship.

Tick held Stanton's gaze a moment longer then shrugged. "I'll call you when I get back."

"Sure." Stanton turned, dismissal in the movement. "Autry, let's go get your stuff."

Frowning, she looked after Tick as he stalked through the squad room. "He's tense."

"Pissed off at me." With a gentle nudge, Stanton ushered her from the office.

"May I ask why?"

"Hell if I know." He held the side door for her, the brisk autumn breeze flirting with her hair. "He's been that way since—"

He snapped his mouth shut on the words. She sighed, sure he'd been about to invoke Caitlin's name. Wanting to lighten his suddenly dark demeanor, she tucked her hand through his elbow and tilted her head toward the side street.

"Come on and stop worrying. He'll get over it."

"Yeah. Maybe."

They walked to her office, in one of the historic, slightly dilapidated buildings facing the courthouse. He stepped back to let her precede him, his gaze tracking over the street and the sparse traffic.

"Sheriff Reed!" The local newspaper editor's voice boomed from the corner.

Behind her at the foot of the steep, too-dark stairwell leading to her office, Stanton groaned. Two steps above him, Autry turned as Ray Lewis puffed up to them. "Glad I caught you, Sheriff. I was wondering if I could ask you a couple of questions about that string of burglaries in the north end of the county."

"Tick could probably answer those better than I could—"

"It's your department and you don't know enough to answer a couple of simple questions?"

Stanton stiffened at the sly insinuation and Autry rolled her eyes and leaned forward to tap his arm. "Talk to him. I'll go up and grab what I need."

He frowned at her over his shoulder. "I don't think—"

"You'll be right here," she said, aware Ray listened with avid curiosity. "I'll leave the door open and I won't be but a second."

His mouth thinned, but he nodded. "I'll be straight up."

With the male voices rumbling behind her, she hurried up the stairs and down the short hallway to her office. She flipped through the files on her desk, picking up everything concerned with the Schaefer trial. She stacked them in her briefcase and laid her notebook computer atop them.

The voices below stopped. She glanced around. What had she done with her planner?

Footsteps creaked in the hallway. Pulling her leather agenda from under a law encyclopedia, she dropped it in her briefcase. "Stan? I think I'm ready."

The footsteps stopped at her open doorway and she glanced up.

The person standing in her door wasn't Stanton and she froze. "What do you want?"

Chapter Six

"What do I want?" Beau Ingler stepped into the office. His eyes darkened with anger and loathing. "I'll tell you what I want, Autry. I want to know how the hell you can defend the son of a bitch who murdered my sister!"

Her heart stuttered. She'd known Beau Ingler all her life—they'd gone to school together since kindergarten, his family attended the same church as hers, and five months ago, she'd cried as his sister was laid to rest.

"Beau, I—"

"How can you?" His face reddened, hands clenching and unclenching at his sides. Fear uncurled in Autry's stomach. Was he the one? Oh Lord, where was Stanton? "Your mama and daddy raised you right. I know it. And you're helping that...that piece of murdering trash. Why? For the money?"

That was laughable, but far from funny right now. The money? She was a public defender and most of her clients were indigent. She shook her head, wanting him calmed down and out of her office. "No, Beau. I'm doing it—"

"Because it's her job," Stanton said as he appeared behind Beau. His steady gaze caught hers for a moment and gratitude and warmth flashed through her. "Her duty."

Beau looked between them, his features twisted with disgust. "You can't agree with this. Oh hell, maybe you can. He was in your damn department—"

"Mr. Ingler, I understand you're upset." Firm authority laced Stanton's tone. "But the system has to be allowed to work and Ms. Holton is only doing her job. Your harassing her about that is not going to help."

"Harassing her." Beau's laugh was an ugly thing and Autry cringed. "She's helping him get away with murder and you're worried I'm harassing her."

"Mr. Ingler, I'm asking you to leave." Stanton didn't move, but his posture remained alert. "Jeff Schaefer will pay for what he did. Let the system work."

"Yeah, sure. Wish I could say it was good to see you again, Autry." With one last disgusted look, Beau brushed by Stanton. His footsteps thudded on the backstairs.

Stanton moved into the office. "Are you all right?"

She nodded and clenched her hands to stop their shaking. "Yes, I'm just..."

To her absolute horror, she burst into tears. Sudden sobs tore at her throat and she buried her face in her hands. Residual fear trembled in her.

Strong arms came around her, pulled her close to an equally strong chest.

"Go ahead," he whispered, stroking her back. "Let it out."

She folded her hands into the soft cotton of his shirt. Her face against his throat, she cried harder. How was she supposed to function, never knowing who was threatening her, where he might be, what he might do next?

Stanton held her tighter. "It's all right, baby," he murmured into her hair. "I'm here. I won't let anything happen. I promise."

"L-look how easily he...he got up here." She lifted her head, rubbing at her hot, wet cheeks. "Stanton, wh-what if he was the one? Anything could have happened and—"

"But it didn't." He cupped her head in his hands, brushing tears from her face with his thumbs. His eyes intense, he held her gaze with his. "And it's not going to, because I won't let it. I mean it, honey, I won't let anyone hurt you. I swear."

She pulled away, immediately feeling the loss of him, and pushed her hair back from her face. "You can't be with me twenty-four-seven."

He hooked his thumbs in his belt and studied her. "Why don't we make the working out of my office thing permanent, at least until we make an arrest. You can forward your calls—"

"I don't know. I can't make that decision right now, okay?"

She took a deep breath. If she gave him an inch, anything more than this one decision about where she was to work this afternoon, he'd take over completely. The scary part was right now she wanted to let him. "I have to get through today first."

"All right." He nodded toward her desk. "Ready to go?"

She rounded the desk to close her briefcase. "I'm ready."

He took the case from her and escorted her downstairs, across the street and into the sheriff's department. The whole way, Autry's skin prickled as unwanted thoughts about unseen watchers followed her.

Stanton parked the unmarked unit behind Tick's dusty pickup. As he walked up the brick path to the back porch, a breeze tossed a few stray pine needles down from the swaying trees. With Autry firmly ensconced in his office, he felt better, although the incident with Beau Ingler left a lingering tension at his nape. He passed a hand over the stiff muscles there. Letting her go up to that office alone, even for a minute, had been the height of stupidity.

He skirted a stack of two-by-fours, a sign of Tick's constant renovating, to knock at the kitchen door. When he'd returned to the department, Lydia, with her usual unflappable aplomb, had handed him yet another pink message slip—this one from Tick, directing Stanton to pick him up at home.

No reason as to *why* he'd gone home in the middle of the day. Stanton cast a glance at the driveway. Falconetti's vehicle was nowhere in sight. He rapped at the doorjamb again.

"It's open."

Inside, the house was neat as always. A few of Falconetti's things had joined Tick's, but the home still bore more of his personality than hers. The ironing board stood open in the kitchen, the iron atop it and plugged in.

"Hey." A towel knotted at his waist, Tick strode from the bedroom, uniform shirt in hand. "I'll be ready in a sec. I just need to run an iron over this."

Stanton eyed Tick's damp hair. "You come home for a nooner or what?"

"I wish." Tick spread the shirt out and attacked it with the iron. "Ran up to El Vaquero's to meet Cait for lunch. She ordered the gazpacho, and somebody's rugrat ran into the server. I ended up wearing it—my shirt, my hair—man, it was even in my holster. I had to clean my gun, and my truck will smell like freakin' pico de gallo for a month."

A chuckle rumbled in Stanton's throat, a welcome relief from the constant tension of the past few days. "You're lucky she didn't order fajitas."

Tick set the iron aside, unplugging it. "Yeah. Be right back." He took the shirt and disappeared into the bedroom. In a couple of minutes, he returned, tucking his shirt into a pair of crisp khakis. "So how's Autry?"

Stanton darted a glance at him. There was that edge in Tick's voice again. "A little shaken up. First that note, then Beau Ingler jumped on her case about the defense—"

"I meant physically." Tick sat on the ottoman to pull on his socks and shoes. "The whole pregnancy thing. How is she?"

"She's having a lot of nausea, I think." Stanton ran a hand over his nape. "She has a doctor's appointment this week. They're doing a sonogram." Tick nodded, staring at the tips of his polished duty shoes, and Stanton's gaze sharpened on his face. "Tick? You okay?"

Tick dragged a hand along his jaw. "Yeah. All I could think about last night and this morning was what a flippin' miracle this baby is. It wasn't supposed to happen this way, you know. And then Cait saw Dr. Astin this morning and at lunch we got into all the things that could go wrong, if her uterus can't take the strain and ruptures... You don't want to hear this, do you, what with Autry and all."

His ex-partner was right—Stanton didn't want to think about all the things that could go wrong. But he knew Tick well enough to understand he wouldn't have brought it up if he didn't need to talk about it. "Are you borrowing trouble? What are the odds something could go wrong, according to the doctor?"

Tick ran a smoothing hand over his still-damp hair. "For the uterine rupture? About two percent. The normal risk is less than a half percent."

"The normal risk?" He was missing something here, probably because he went out of his way to not discuss

Falconetti with Tick. Not like Tick ever listened to him about her anyway.

"Hers is higher because of the attack."

Attack? He was really missing something. "Tick, partner, I'm lost."

"Don't worry about it." The sharp note was back. Tick blew out an audible breath and rubbed his face.

Annoyed, Stanton rested his hands at his hips. "If there's something you need to say, out with it, Calvert."

"Let it alone, Stan."

Tick had obviously decided he was going to clam up. Stanton restrained himself from rolling his eyes. From long experience, he knew Tick wouldn't talk until he was good and ready.

"You said two percent, right? That means you have a ninety-eight percent chance everything will go right. Focus on that."

"Yeah." Tick's gaze dropped to his shoes again. "I know you're right. It's just that two percent, you know? A woman can bleed out from a uterine rupture. She could die if that happens under the wrong conditions."

A shudder traveled down Stanton's spine. He'd have a list of questions ready for Autry's doctor's appointment. "Yeah, and we could get hit by a chicken truck at the Stagecoach Crossroads. Greater odds that would happen. She'll be fine."

"She has to be." Tick looked up, the dark depths of his eyes completely serious. "Because I can live without being a father, Stan, but I can't live without her."

Tick's words stayed with Stanton during the drive out to Mildred Kinney's neat brick ranch on Highway 112.

I can't live without her.

Stanton's first instinct was to laugh off the statement, to point out Tick had managed the first thirty-five years of his life just fine without Caitlin Falconetti. Except that in the last five months, since Falconetti had come back to him, Tick had become someone different—still the intent law enforcement officer he'd always been, but somehow the constant simmering energy he'd always carried seemed more focused now.

Marrying Renee had not done that for Stanton. Neither had fourteen years of marriage.

Those few short months with Autry had, and it scared the hell out of him. He was starting to get an inkling of what Tick had meant—*I can't live without her.* Tick could survive without Falconetti in his life, but it wasn't really living. Stanton's stomach squeezed. Is that what he'd been doing? Merely surviving without Autry?

He rubbed a hand over his face as Tick stopped the unmarked unit behind a run-down pickup. The rusted robin's-egg blue Chevy leaned forlornly to one side, a sharp contrast to Mrs. Kinney's manicured lawn and late-model Ford sedan.

"I think I went to high school with this guy." Tick pushed the door open. "He'd have been a few years behind me, though."

Unfolding from the car, Stanton glanced at the printout. "He was one of Autry's first cases."

"*The* first." Tick fell into step beside him on the concrete walkway lined by neatly squared-off boxwoods. The corner of his mouth quirked up in a wry smile. "Mrs. Kinney is in Mama's Sunday School class. She had Mrs. Kinney on her prayer list for months and I got a complete rundown of everything. He robbed the Tank and Tummy at gunpoint. The gun wasn't even loaded."

Stanton chuckled. "He's lucky Jeanette didn't take it and beat him to death with it."

The pathway rounded the house's corner. A neat backyard stretched to the pecan grove butting the property. A slight man, random streaks of silver glinting in his black hair, knelt at the patio edge and tinkered with a weed trimmer.

Stanton and Tick stopped at the path's end. Stanton cleared his throat. "Mr. Kinney?"

"Yeah?" Kinney glanced up, his eyes a dull blue in the bright sunlight. Surprised, Stanton realized he was far younger than he first appeared—late twenties, maybe thirty—but his face, even his body, seemed prematurely aged. Five years in prison would do that.

"I'm Sheriff Reed, this is Investigator Calvert—"

"I know who you are." Kinney wiped his hands on a greasy

rag and pushed to his feet. "What do you want?"

"We need to ask you a few questions."

Kinney's chin lifted to a defiant angle. "About?"

"Where were you the night before last?"

"Here." Anger flashed in his eyes. "And yeah, my mother can verify that."

"Talk to us about Autry Holton," Tick said.

Kinney frowned. "What about her?"

"She was your defense attorney, right? You went to prison for five years. A lot of guys would be pissed."

"Because I paid the price for what I did?" Kinney straightened, thin shoulders tight under his shirt. "I made the decision to rob that store and I deserved what punishment I got. Probably deserved more, but Ms. Holton got me the minimum. She did right by me and I don't hold any grudge against her."

"That was successful." A cynical grin twisted Tick's mouth. He swung the patrol car into a left on Old Lonesome Road. "Did you believe his whole 'I don't hold any grudge against her' bit?"

"Hard to say." Stanton turned his attention to the scenery outside—peanut fields, tall pines, chicken houses. "He sounded sincere enough, but he fits the whole stalker-stereotype profile—unassuming, lives with his mother."

Tick cleared his throat. "Speaking of profiles...I've been meaning to bring this up. I think we should get—"

"No." Not no, but hell no.

"Stanton, it can't hurt to have someone look at those notes and see if they can give us an offender profile."

"Fine. Call the GBI."

"I did. The backlog at the profiling unit is as bad as the one at the crime lab. They told me they could get to us in six to nine months. I'll have a kid by then. So will you."

"Damn it." He would have to take back that "no". Even if Caitlin Falconetti grated on his absolute last nerve, she remained one of the best profilers he'd ever seen. If her insight could help them locate whoever was threatening Autry, he'd get over it. "Let her have a look, see what her take is."

"Will do."

The radio crackled. "Chandler, C-2."

Tick reached for the handset. "Go ahead, Chandler."

"Are you available?"

"10-4."

"Be advised, reported 10-15 at 3850 Long Lonely Road."

Tick's eyebrows went skyward and he glanced at Stanton. "10-9, Chandler."

"Reported 10-15 at 3850 Long Lonely Road. Are you available?"

"10-4, Chandler. ETA, five minutes." He returned the mike to the clip and pressed harder on the gas. "I heard that right, didn't I? A burglary call. At Ash's."

"Yeah." Scenery flickered by, trees blurring as Tick took the curves on the back road with the ease of a hometown boy. Stanton pinched the bridge of his nose. Another burglary—the fourth in the last two months. Five, if they counted Autry's attempted break-in. He frowned. Once she'd shown him those notes, he'd jumped to the conclusion the prowler had to be the writer.

What if the two were unrelated?

"Tick, did we get prints from the other burglaries? Or footprints?"

"A partial thumb from the Smithwick place." Tick braked for Ash's driveway. The metal roofs of the chicken houses gleamed under the midafternoon sun. "Couldn't get a cast from the footprints. And, yeah, I told Williams to run the prints from Autry's against the one we had."

The patrol car bounced over a couple of ruts in the red-clay drive. Next to the plain farmhouse, Ash's pea-green Ford sat dejectedly. Tick drew to a stop behind it. As they climbed out, Ash stepped onto the porch, his expression tense and harried.

"What's going on?" Stanton pulled his sunglasses from his pocket and slid them on.

Ash settled a battered cap on his hair, the sandy tone made brighter by long hours in the sun. "Somebody busted the lock on the shed while I was in town. Came home to find the door wide open and everything cleaned out."

Tick clipped his keys on his belt. "What all did they take?"

"My toolbox, all the lawn stuff, even the leftover bags of fertilizer I had stored."

Stanton slanted a glance at the shed, halfway between the house and the chicken houses and standing beneath a spreading oak tree. The door remained open. "You touch anything?"

With a terse chuckle, Ash lifted his eyebrows. "I've been hanging out with you two forever. What do you think?"

Tick laughed and walked to the car. He pulled the evidence kit from the trunk. "Let's take a look. What time did you leave home?"

Ash shrugged, a tight, tense roll of his shoulders. "Around eleven. Had to wait at Lawson's because Keith hadn't gotten back from Thomasville with my tractor part. Made it home about ten, fifteen minutes ago."

The grassy area around the shed yielded no footprints and Tick wasn't able to lift any usable prints from the door or building.

Stanton shot Ash an apologetic glance. "We'll do what we can, but I can't make you any promises."

"Yeah, thanks." Ash grimaced and tilted back his cap. "My insurance company will be glad to hear it."

"You know, it would be one thing if there was some pattern to what they took." Frowning, Tick flipped through his notebook. "Television and a laptop at the Faircloth place, jewelry and household items from the Smithwicks'. Why garden stuff here?"

Ash gave a frustrated laugh. "Probably knew I didn't have anything worth taking in the house. What are they going to do, steal my first edition copy of *The Great Gatsby*? They can pawn the lawnmower or run the weed trimmer at the flea market."

"Dougherty County PD will check the pawnshops in Albany for us, but I gotta tell you, Ash, you probably won't see any of it again." Stanton ran a hand over the tense muscles at his nape. "That kind of stuff moves fast."

"Great."

"Listen, we have to go. We've got another interview to do this afternoon, but I'll run you over a report once I've written it up." Tick snapped his notebook closed. "I'm sorry about this, Ash. Hey, if you need to borrow anything—weed whacker, lawnmower—just drop by the house."

"Thanks." Traces of disgust lingered in the single syllable.

Stanton and Tick strode to the unmarked unit. Stanton caught his eye across the roof and sighed. "Guess now Ray will have something else to print in the paper."

Tick laughed, a harsh, humorless sound. "Wait until he finds out about Autry's attempted break-in. She'll get the front page for sure."

"Ah, hell. That's all she needs right now." Stanton jerked the passenger door open. "Come on and let's go have a talk with Mr. McLeod."

Head rested on her hand, Autry stared at Tick's report on Amy Gillabeaux's death. The words swam together and she straightened, rubbing her eyes. An ache gripped her lower back, so she twisted, stretching her spine. In her stomach, a slow flutter greeted her and she curved a hand over the movement and smiled. Her own personal bright spot.

The autopsy report lay below Tick's and she picked it up. Time of death estimated to within twenty-four hours of Amy's disappearance. Sometime in the hours before her death, she'd had sexual intercourse. She'd been twelve weeks pregnant when she died.

Autry tunneled a hand through her hair. Tom McMillian would try to use that pregnancy as part of Schaefer's motive for killing Amy. The DA would argue Schaefer had killed her because her pregnancy threatened his persona as the perfect cop. He'd back that up with Amy's possession of another victim's credit card, claim that Schaefer had used her to help cover up that murder.

And Schaefer expected her to find a way to make a jury doubt that.

Even better, doubt the testimony of the local investigator and hometown golden boy, along with that of a veteran FBI profiler.

Why didn't he just take the deal?

Her cell phone buzzed and she dug it out of her briefcase, glad for the distraction. Frowning at the unfamiliar number on the display, she flipped the phone open. "Autry Holton."

"Ms. Holton, this is Jason Harding." The Haynes County sheriff, calling her? Her sense of misgiving deepened. Harding cleared his throat. "I hope I didn't catch you at a bad time."

"No, it's fine. What can I do for you, Sheriff?"

"I'm at Chandler County General Hospital. There's been an incident involving Jeffrey Schaefer."

"An incident?"

What sounded like a sigh traveled over the connection. "Our jailers stopped an attack. Schaefer suffered some injuries, including a blow to the head. Protocol requires he be checked out in the ER. He's asking for you."

She closed her eyes. When would she extricate her life from this guy? "Tell him I'll be there as soon as I can."

Ending the call, she closed the phone and rubbed her temples. She had to find a way to get to the hospital. It was only a few blocks away and before she wouldn't have thought twice about walking. But now...the memory of that note under her windshield, flapping in the slight breeze, squeezed her throat. Now everything had changed.

Walking was out of the question.

She couldn't very well call Stanton and ask him to stop what he was doing to chauffeur her around. However, he'd left her the keys to his Explorer. She gathered her phone and dug his extra keys from the depths of her purse.

Nerves contracted her stomach. She could understand why some people lived in fear of going outside. Too many unseen threats lurking around every corner. Hers were unseen, but all too real.

She scribbled a note to Stanton and left it with Lydia at the front desk. The skin at her nape prickled as she crossed the narrow parking lot and climbed into his SUV. The daily bustle of the small county seat carried on around her—people trickling in and out of the courthouse adjacent to the sheriff's department, two women laughing together outside the bank across the street. Normal, everyday activities, but her life felt anything but normal right now.

And the last thing she wanted to do was spend more one-on-one time with Jeffrey Schaefer.

A breeze holding a hint of fall chill tickled Stanton's ears and nose as he climbed from the unmarked patrol car. Their quest to interview Hunter McLeod had proved unsuccessful—he wasn't home and his girlfriend had been less than forthcoming. She claimed he was somewhere on the Flint River, fishing on his day off.

Stanton rolled stiff shoulders, rotated his lower back to relieve the tension sitting there and stopped, staring at his designated parking space. His Explorer was gone.

Foreboding trickled over him, followed by a wave of anger. She wouldn't. Not after that note, not after Beau Ingler had scared her so badly.

"Where's your truck?" Tick paused at the unit's hood.

Stanton clenched his teeth so hard his jaw ached, then forced himself to relax the muscles. She was an adult. One of the most intelligent, capable women he'd ever known. If she'd taken his truck and gone, she'd had a damn good reason and used every precaution.

"I'm assuming Autry took it. The question is where." He tugged his phone from his belt and punched the speed dial for her cell. After four rings, her voice mail picked up. The fear wrapped icy tentacles around the base of his spine. "Autry, it's Stanton. Call me when you get this please."

Smothering a curse, he slapped the phone closed and returned it to his belt. Tick's amused expression irritated him, and he glared. "What?"

"You've got it bad. Can't stand to have her out of sight, can you?"

His scowl deepened, his jaw tightening once more. "She's carrying my baby, and some nut's threatening her. Yeah, I like knowing where she is. That doesn't mean I've 'got it bad'."

Arms folded over his chest and his expression terse, Tick leaned against the hood. "This is me, Stan, remember? Why don't you just admit you love her and that it scares you shitless?"

"I'm not—" Stanton snapped his mouth closed. He didn't love her. Hell, he wasn't capable of loving anyone, not the way a man was supposed to love a woman—deep, abiding, above all else. He wanted her, he cared about her, yeah. But love? He didn't know what that was, not really. He pointed at Tick. "This isn't open for discussion."

"Damn, you're defensive."

"I'm not defensive. We have a job to do, or have you forgotten? Get those notes over to your wife so she can do whatever it is she does and help us get a handle on this guy."

"Sure thing." The cold set of Tick's features eased, a cheerful grin curving his mouth. Stanton sighed. God, surely he didn't get that kind of look when he talked about Autry. Of course he didn't.

A silver Mercedes whipped into the parking lot, gleaming under the weak afternoon sun. Tick straightened, his gaze sharp and alert. "That's McMillian."

The district attorney stepped from the luxury car, a well-cut navy suit highlighting his tall, fit frame. His grim appearance made Stanton's gut go taut.

"We have a problem," McMillian said.

"Nice to see you too, Tom." Tick's wry tone belied his tense expression. "What's up?"

McMillian ran a hand over his receding hairline, his blue eyes intelligent and glacial. "The Moultrie crime lab called a little while ago. They finally have the results back on Schaefer's DNA test."

"And?" Stanton leaned a hand against the roof of the car. He didn't have a good feeling about this, at all.

"Schaefer didn't father Amy Gillabeaux's baby."

"Oh, holy hell." Tick rubbed a hand over his mouth. He glanced at Stanton.

Stanton narrowed his gaze at McMillian. "How badly does that affect your case? I mean, it just means Amy was sleeping with more than one guy and that's not going to come as a surprise to anyone. It doesn't mean Schaefer didn't kill her."

McMillian rested his hands on his hips. "It screws my motive argument all to hell—that he killed her because she was pressuring him about the pregnancy, threatening to expose him. I can still argue she was doing that, but it weakens the theory."

Tick dragged a hand through his hair. "That baby was the only thing we had that really put them together sexually. She never named him in her diary and the clerk at the hotel in Tallahassee, where we thought they'd been together, never could pick Schaefer out of a photo array."

Disdain constricted McMillian's features. "Oh, you can bet Autry Holton's going to take this and run with it when she finds out."

"Then we need to find another way to link them," Stanton said. "Somebody's bound to know something and we just missed it the first time around."

"Find it and do it quick." McMillian shook his head. "This case has always been too circumstantial for my liking. Juries want to see physical evidence—DNA, fibers, fingerprints. And we just don't have it. We've got Schaefer's print on Sharon Ingler's car, but Autry can raise doubt there. Hell, she got his journals and the victim souvenirs excluded because that dumbass deputy of yours opened the front door before the warrant was signed. She's too damn good sometimes. I need more and I need it fast."

"I'm on it." Tick straightened. "We're not letting this son of a bitch get off."

"Good deal." McMillian shook Stanton's hand, slapped Tick on the shoulder. "Keep me informed. And time really is of the essence here. The hearing to set a trial date is tomorrow morning. I can try to put it off a few days, but Autry may ask for speedy trial, especially if she thinks we're looking for further evidence. I have to disclose these DNA results, but I'm going to hold out as long as possible."

McMillian strode back to his car and the sleek Mercedes purred onto the side street.

Tick sighed. "Shit."

"Yeah." Stanton rubbed at his jaw. "Throw everything on your desk Cookie's way. I want you focused on this."

"Everything on my desk includes Autry's case."

"I can take it. Just get Falconetti to go over those notes."

"I'll run them over now. Then I'm going to Tallahassee, pass a photo array by that desk clerk one more time." Tick shook his head. "We can't let him walk on this, Stan. If he does, he'll go somewhere else, do it all over again. Only he'll know what mistakes not to make."

"Don't throw in the towel just yet. It'll be hard for him to wiggle out of the aggravated assault charges with both you and Falconetti testifying against him."

"Yeah, and if that's all he's convicted of, he'll be out of prison in a couple of years. He's a control nut. Think about what prison would do to a guy like that, what he'd be when he walked out."

Stanton suppressed a shudder. He didn't want to think about it. "Then find the evidence to make sure that doesn't happen."

"Will do." Tick pulled his keys from his pocket, jingling them. "What are you going to do about Autry?"

"Find her."

"No, I mean about the DNA results. Are you going to tell her?"

"I can't."

"Oh, man, you're screwed when she does find out."

"Just go find someone who can put Schaefer with Amy Gillabeaux, Tick." His silence might mean he was screwed with Autry, but if Schaefer walked...

They all were. Including his next victim.

Chapter Seven

Hamburger.

Parts of Schaefer's face actually resembled raw meat, fresh from the grinder. Autry had heard the old cliché, but she'd never seen it until now. A huge purple bruise encircled one eye, the lid completely swollen shut. The skin over his cheekbone had burst in more than one place. His lip was split and bloodied. He winced as Layla Jackson, the physician's assistant on duty, cleaned the lacerations.

Sympathy flashed through Autry and she buried it. What was she thinking? The man had killed people and she felt sorry for him because he'd had the living hell beat out of him? No. She refused to.

Removing her gaze from Schaefer's face, she looked up at Sheriff Harding. "Now what happened, exactly?"

Arms folded over his chest, Harding shrugged. "A fight broke out in the exercise yard. While the jailers were breaking it up, another prisoner jumped him."

Autry brushed a loose hank of hair behind her ear. "Mr. Schaefer was remanded to your jail because there were fears about his safety in the Chandler County facility. You knew that, didn't you, Sheriff?"

Harding barely blinked. "Jail is a tough place, Ms. Holton. Your client is an ex-cop, charged with some pretty heinous crimes. A lot of people don't like him. We can go twenty-four-hour solitary for his own protection, if you like."

"No." Schaefer struggled to a more upright position, the handcuffs at his right wrist rattling against the bedrail. His fingers compressed on the mattress's edge. "I'll be fine."

Harding flicked a glance at him. "My decision. Not yours."

Schaefer's expression tightened, but he remained silent. Layla tilted his chin up and inspected the largest cut on his cheekbone. "No stitches. We'll put a butterfly bandage on that and finish cleaning, and you're out of here."

Her stomach rolling, Autry looked away. "Will the other prisoner be charged?"

Harding nodded. "Paperwork's already been filed."

"Good." She glanced at Schaefer, not meeting his eyes. "All right then, I'm going to—"

"Can you stay?" Schaefer's voice rose slightly. Harding tensed. "I wanted to talk to you. Alone."

She clenched her hands behind her back. "Of course. Is that all right with you, Sheriff?"

"Sure thing."

"All finished." Layla stepped back, cleared her debris of gauze and cotton swabs and tugged off her gloves. "I'll get the discharge instructions."

She disappeared outside the cubicle. Harding tilted his head toward the door. "Five minutes, Ms. Holton. I'll be right outside."

Once Autry was alone with Schaefer, the room seemed suddenly smaller. Or maybe he just seemed larger, without the table between them. She refused to look at the metal bracelet at his wrist, to let him see the fear trembling beneath her skin.

She swallowed. "Why did you need to talk to me?"

With his good eye, he held her gaze. "You promised to keep me informed. I haven't heard from you."

Autry smothered a sigh. "I'm still working. Putting together a defense takes time. Tomorrow is the hearing to set your trial date. I'm going to ask for a continuance—"

"No." He shook his head, a sharp, emphatic movement. "I want it over soon. No delays."

"I don't think you—"

"I said no." Anger crackled in his words and Autry jumped.

He leaned forward. A muscle flickered in his jaw. "You don't understand what it's like, being locked up. Having no say in anything—when you sleep, when you eat, when you relieve yourself. Never being alone. There's always someone around you and you don't know what anyone will do next."

"But rushing to trial isn't the answer." She pitched her voice to a quiet, gentle tone and tried to keep in mind that Jason Harding waited just outside. One scream and he'd come running.

If she got the chance to scream. Had Amy? Or any of the other girls? A shudder ran over her spine and she hoped the fear didn't show. She'd read Caitlin Falconetti's profile—the FBI agent believed Schaefer fed off his victim's fear. Autry refused to give him a taste of her own.

"*I want out.*" The words emerged terse and intense, as though Schaefer gritted his teeth. "Do you get that? I want out as soon as possible. No continuance."

She straightened. "Fine. I'll ask for the next available date."

Schaefer relaxed. "And you'll keep me informed."

"Of course." She loosened her hands, blood rushing back into her aching knuckles. "Are we finished?"

He nodded, a crooked smile curving his damaged mouth. "Thanks, Autry."

The glimpse of intensity beneath the handsome exterior was scary. Was that what his victims had seen, only when it was too late to get away?

Head held high, she slipped out of the room and leaned against the wall. Her breathing came in shallow bursts as residual adrenaline flowed along her veins. Vertigo attacked her, feet and the floor seeming to tilt.

"Ms. Holton? Are you all right?" Concern softened Harding's voice.

Autry opened her eyes on a slight smile. "I'm fine. Just a little dizzy."

"You're sure?"

She nodded, making her smile brighter. "Absolutely."

He didn't drop his gaze from her face. "I'll make sure you get a copy of the incident report."

"I appreciate that." Breathing through her mouth, fighting off the dizziness and nausea, she tugged Stanton's keys from her purse and walked away. Even though it made her feel paranoid, she asked the ER's security guard to escort her to the parking lot. Locked securely in the Explorer, she rested her head on the seat and closed her eyes.

She could smell Stanton, the essence of his scent lingering in the SUV's upholstery. The sensory memory triggered a mix of emotions—safety, desire, loss. She released a long, shaky breath. What was she going to do about him? Letting him continue making decisions for her, acting the protector, couldn't go on. He was the one man she needed to be on equal footing with, and life kept shoving obstacle after obstacle at her—Schaefer, the threats, even her baby.

Pressing her eyelids closer together, Autry buried her fingers in her hair, nails biting into her scalp. The whole Schaefer issue would eventually go away, his case would end one way or the other, and he'd be out of her life. In five months, she'd give birth and she and Stanton would just have to deal with sharing parenthood, separate or apart. She could handle all of that.

But the threats...the stalker...

That could go on indefinitely. What if it didn't have anything to do with Schaefer? What if the person never went away? Her whole life would change. Had already changed. How was she supposed to deal with that?

No answers swam to the surface of her mind, her thoughts still swirling in an endless, sucking whirlpool. With a sigh, she reached for the ignition and opened her eyes.

She yelped, a high, startled sound, heart hitting a racing tempo in a nanosecond. The next instant, recognition of the strong silhouette at the SUV's hood sank in and she released her deathgrip on the steering wheel.

She lowered the window. "Lord, Daddy, you scared me to death. What are you doing here?"

"I had a check-up with Dr. Shiver." Her father smiled, although the affectionate expression didn't wipe out the concern darkening his blue eyes. "And I have a couple of questions for you, Buckshot. Want to tell your old man why you're leaving the hospital in the middle of the afternoon and driving Stanton Reed's truck? Or better yet, why Tick was dusting your car for fingerprints in front of the courthouse earlier today?"

She supposed she was lucky he wasn't asking her why she'd spent the night before at Stanton's. It wasn't like keeping a secret in this town was possible, even if she had managed to keep a whopper of one far too long. Her secrecy weighed on her and she took a deep breath. For once, in her father's steady presence, the hated tears were far away.

Pushing the door open, she tumbled from the truck and into his embrace, inhaling deeply of his licorice and Old Spice scent. "Oh, Daddy. I've got so much to tell you."

"Well." Autry's father passed a hand over his forehead. "A baby."

Her chest squeezed. Was that disappointment deep in his eyes? Around them, the diner bustled—spoons clinked against china cups, conversation buzzed between patrons. But they seemed surrounded by a bubble of isolation, a result of the two secrets she'd disclosed over sweet tea and slices of pecan pie.

She fidgeted, twining her fingers together in her lap. "I know what you're probably thinking...that I should have been more careful, especially after everything that happened with Helen and Nate—"

"You just let me do my own thinking, Buckshot." Affectionate exasperation laced his voice. "Maybe I was thinking about having another grandson or granddaughter to take fishing."

Autry buried her head in her hands and groaned. "Mama won't take it that way." Stupid, to be thirty years old and still afraid of her mother's reaction to perceived mistakes. At the thought, a spurt of irritation shot through her. Her baby might be unexpected, but a mistake? Even Stanton hadn't approached it that way and obviously he hadn't wanted to become a father again. Damned if she'd let her mother use the word.

"Don't worry about your mama right now." At her father's gentle sternness, Autry lifted her head. He watched her, his blue eyes intense and worried. "I want to hear about these notes and why you didn't come to me." He frowned, the wrinkles in his forehead deepening. "Or take them to Stanton sooner."

"Asinine of me, wasn't it? I don't know why I..." She fingered the lemon slice perched on the side of her glass. A condensation droplet meandered down to splash on the faded Formica tabletop. She did know why—Stanton'd hurt her when he'd dumped her back in June and she hadn't wanted him to think she was using the notes, or the baby, as a way to get close to him once more. A tense smile tugged at her mouth. "I didn't tell you because I realize you've always expected me to take care of things on my own. At first I thought it was a one-time thing that would go away, and then, well, I didn't want to look like a weak, scared female."

He lifted his tea and sipped. "You're a smarter woman than that, Autry."

She shrugged. "But Stanton's involved now, and Tick, and if anyone can find this person, they can."

A troubled expression crossed his lined face. "And if they don't?"

The frisson of hopelessness traveled along her spine again, and she squashed it. "They will. I'm sure of it."

Because if they didn't, she'd have to live her life always wondering when the next note would come, if the next time there wouldn't be a note, just an attack from nowhere. She'd seen stalker cases before, had even defended a woman accused of stalking an ex-husband. Too often, they escalated to violence.

"And how long will you be staying at Stan's?"

She didn't miss the pointed question lying behind the innocent inquiry. More water drops trailed down her glass and she traced them with her finger before meeting his gaze. "Awhile. We've agreed we're going to try to make things work, because of the baby."

Her throat narrowed, aching. Because of the baby. Not because he wanted *her*. Because she was pregnant and he felt he had to do the right thing. Lord, duty sucked sometimes. She was trapped into defending Schaefer and Stanton had to feel trapped into this mess with her.

She'd been crazy to go along with him, to think maybe he'd come to love her. Her eyes blurred, and she blinked. She would not cry in front of her father. Doing so would embarrass her beyond belief and could only impact his professional relationship with Stanton negatively. Why hadn't she considered all the ramifications before getting involved with Stanton in the first place?

You did. You just didn't care at the time.

A heavy scowl brought her father's thick gray brows down. "I don't like the sound of that. You don't have to settle, Autry. You're intelligent, beautiful and—"

"And you're my father and completely biased."

He ignored her. "And if Stanton Reed doesn't want you for those reasons, then he doesn't deserve you. Draw up custody and support papers and find a man who'll see what a treasure you are."

She reached for his hand. His fingers, strong and dotted with age spots, curved around hers. "Daddy, I have to try. My baby, your grandchild, deserves that much."

She wanted him to agree with her, to tell her she was doing the right thing, but he remained silent, his thumb moving across her knuckles in a soothing sweep. His frown didn't lighten. She laughed, trying to alleviate the doubt on his face, although the sound was strained even to her ears. "Daddy, I'll be fine. I know what I'm doing."

He lifted his gaze to hers, his eyes troubled. "Do you, Buckshot? Do you really?"

"Stanton?" At Autry's soft voice, he looked up from one of the endless reports that always seemed to grace his desk. Her absence had trapped him in the office, so he'd spent the rest of the afternoon trying to catch up on the paperwork. Worrying about her had kept him from getting half what he normally would done.

He cleared his throat. "Hey."

Autry's lips curved into a tight bow. "Did you get my note?"

Tossing his pen down, he leaned back. "I got it." It hadn't lessened his worry any. His eyes narrowed. "Jason Harding called to tell me what happened with Schaefer."

She nodded and stepped inside, pulling the door closed. Her hair rippled across her shoulders and his fingers itched with the desire to bury themselves in the thick chestnut strands. "I ran into my father when I left the hospital. We went for tea. I...I told him about the baby."

Her hesitation clenched Stanton's stomach. She worshipped her father, and if he'd denounced her out of his traditional values, she'd be devastated. "What did he say?"

Arms folded over her midriff, she leaned against the door. "I think he's looking forward to having another grandbaby. He says he is, anyway."

"Did you tell him about us?" Stanton flipped the folder closed and pushed away from the desk. His movements tense and short, he walked to the file cabinet and shoved the manila file into place. His back to her, he rifled through the second drawer. God help him, he was afraid to look at her.

Tick was right. He was a damn coward. Scared to death that now her father knew about the pregnancy, she'd leave, seek protection at her family home, and his chance to win her back would be gone.

Her footsteps whispered on the tile. "I did. He's worried I'm making a mistake."

He clutched the edge of the file drawer until his fingers hurt. She'd walk away for sure now. He spun to face her. "I want more time."

She blinked. "Excuse me?"

"Our agreement. A month's not long enough." He pushed the drawer shut. Under his skin, he felt like his pulse pounded at every nerve. "We need more time."

She stared at him before shaking her head. "What are we doing?"

He frowned. "What do you mean?"

"This whole agreement. This isn't the way it's supposed to be between people who are having a baby together." She motioned between them. Her voice sounded tight and weak, but he didn't see a trace of tears. "What we're doing is beyond insane."

She was scared too. Did she feel like he did, like he was teetering on the edge of an abyss, no clue what would push him off? He skirted the desk to lean against it. Reaching out, he gripped her arms above her elbows, his hands gentle. "Come here."

She tried to tug free. "Stanton, don't—"

"Hush and listen." He drew her between his thighs, the warmth of her curling around him. His thumbs rubbed the soft skin of her arms, and his body hummed at their proximity. "I want this to work for us, Autry, but you can't build a lasting relationship in a month. We need more time."

She bit her lip, blue eyes clouded with doubt. He needed some other way to show her what he felt, what he couldn't articulate yet. He pulled her closer, until her lower abdomen bumped against his groin, until her breasts, swollen and probably sensitive, pressed into his chest, until her mouth met his. He held his breath. God, she felt like home.

"Autry," he murmured against her lips, desire racing along his nerves. This he was sure of, the way she made him feel, the way she could make him sigh and groan once he was in her arms. She pressed closer and wrapped her arms around his waist, fingers tiptoeing over his spine.

Opening her mouth, she flicked her tongue against his. He stiffened and pulled her tighter. The taste of her, kissing her, was like touching a bare electrical wire, consuming him alive. Exhilaration exploded in him, a wild companion to the desire tingling to life low in his gut. Flexing her fingers, she raked her nails along his back in a light pattern. His kiss deepened, hands slipping to her hips to fit their lower bodies more closely together.

She hummed a sigh into his mouth and rubbed against him. He'd always loved being with her like this. The need to forget everything but her, to ignore the problems, seized him.

Autry caught her breath and pulled her mouth from his. "Wait."

He stared at her, caught in a haze of desire. "What?"

He tightened his hold at her hips, but she reached for his hand and splayed his palm over her abdomen. "Feel."

His brow furrowed in intense concentration. Autry watched him, her bottom lip damp and a little swollen from their kiss. Her pulse beat under his palm, but whatever she wanted him to feel simply wasn't there.

He shook his head. "I don't feel anything."

She pressed her hand harder over his. "Nothing?"

He lifted his gaze to hers, disappointment a cold knot in his chest. "No."

She released his hand, leaving him curiously letdown. The sense of connection drained away as their desire had moments before and he was left empty, bereft.

This is what it would be like when the whole mess fell apart. He'd never be free, not really, and it wasn't because of the baby. It was her, the way she consumed him with a look, a touch.

She straightened and stepped away, a hand over their baby.

He frowned, watching her. "Autry?"

She shook her head, but didn't quite manage a smile. "It's nothing. Just someone walking over my grave."

Frustration gripped his throat. Damn it, he wasn't any good at this. "You look—"

The phone buzzed behind him. "Sheriff Reed?" Lydia's voice filled the small room. "Tick's on line three."

"Thanks." Stanton gazed at her a moment before twisting to pick up the receiver. "Tick? What's up?"

"Just left the motel in Tallahassee. The clerk couldn't pick Schaefer out of a new photo array."

"Great." Stanton ran a hand over his nape and blew out a breath. She'd turned away to gather her things, to give him a semblance of privacy, he guessed. The line of her shoulders looked tired, dejected.

Exactly the way he felt.

"Cait and I are going to dinner at Wutherby's. She's been looking at Autry's notes. Thought you two might want to join us. About seven?"

Dinner out would probably be great for Autry, might even give him a chance to get his feelings together where she was concerned. For that, he'd even tolerate Caitlin Falconetti.

"Sounds good. See you there." He dropped the receiver back in the cradle. "How do you feel about meeting Tick and Falconetti for dinner?"

Autry eyed him over her shoulder. "You *want* to go to

dinner with them? You, spending an entire evening in Cait's presence?"

He grimaced. "I'm not that bad where she's concerned and you know it."

"You were pretty verbal when she arrived last June. Not exactly a happy camper, you know?"

His mouth quirked. "You did a damned good job of taking my mind off it."

Her cheeks flushed and she darted a glance at his desk chair. Late one night during that weekend before Schaefer had been arrested, they'd dropped by the department for him to pick up some papers. He'd already been bitching about Falconetti's presence. His belly clenched as Autry bit her lip. She had to be remembering too. Telling him to shut up about it, she'd pushed him into that leather chair and straddled him. She'd kissed him, one caress leading to another touch, until they'd been partially naked and straining together, and he'd whispered a laughing "shhh" against her lips.

She shook back her hair. "Dinner out sounds good."

A warm breeze, rare for late October, blew across the deck at Wutherby's. Lights, strung between the pecan trees nestling the restaurant, cast globes of colored lights on the tables and seventies-retro disco music pulsed from speakers placed at strategic spots. A handful of couples occupied the tiny dance floor at one end of the deck.

Stanton laid his fork down on his half-full plate. Lingering desire, coupled with an odd sense of loss, smothered his appetite. Next to him, Autry pushed a piece of grilled chicken around her own plate. Throughout dinner, the mood at their table had been subdued, a direct contrast to the happy laughter and chatter surrounding them.

The early notes of a Gloria Gaynor hit filtered through the speakers. Tick glanced toward the door and brightened. "Hey, Buckshot, there's Casey and Irene Roberts."

Autry lifted her head, a smile flirting around her mouth. "Wow, she looks great." She met Stanton's gaze. "Irene is my third cousin, once removed. She and Casey just got married last month."

"He and I are somehow distantly related on Mama's side." Tick eased back his chair and stood, extending a hand. "Come on. Let's go speak to them."

Autry laughed and let him lead her away. A smile tilted the corners of Falconetti's mouth. "I think that's his subtle way of leaving us alone so we can talk about those notes."

"Probably." Stanton lifted his iced water and sipped. "So what did you come up with?"

Falconetti eyed him. "Well, for starters, you're a perfect suspect."

"Be serious."

"I am." She gave him a look of pure innocence, but Stanton refused to be taken in. He crossed his arms over his chest and waited. She lifted a shoulder in an elegant shrug. "The most common type of stalker is the simple obsessional. Usually known to the victim, many times a former intimate acquaintance. Often the desire to reconcile serves as the motive."

"Cut it out, Falconetti."

She waved a hand at the other side of the deck, where Autry laughed and tossed her hair over her shoulder, leaning down to admire the pretty little blonde's diamond ring. "You two are reconciled, right?"

"Cut the shit and tell me what you have, all right?" God, how did Tick live with her?

"Or you have a vengeful-resentful stalker. In his head, she's done something wrong, and he wants revenge."

"Something wrong." Stanton passed a hand over his jaw. "Like defending Schaefer."

"Maybe. Or it could be something as small as he smiled at her in the post office and she didn't respond."

He watched Autry bestow a hug on the new groom. "Think she knows him?"

"At this point, I couldn't say. There's nothing to indicate that in the notes, and often vengeful-resentful stalkers aren't known to their victims. But it could just as easily be someone she has daily contact with." Falconetti's smile appeared again.

"Like you."

Stanton regarded her coolly. "Tell me again what Tick sees in you?"

"My winning personality and really hot sex." Sobering, Falconetti reached for her glass. Ice tinkled against the sides. "There is another possibility."

He glanced heavenwards. "I can't wait."

"About two percent of all stalking cases involve false victims."

Anger licked at his gut. "Don't go there, Falconetti."

"You have to consider the possibility, Reed. She might not be the victim here." Falconetti brushed a strand of black hair behind her ear. "It might be you."

Chapter Eight

"Go to hell, Falconetti." Stanton leaned forward, stabbing a finger into the table. "She wouldn't do that."

"You broke things off with her and now she's living in your house. Tick says she was working out of your office today. Looks like your life has been wrapped around her since the night of the break-in at her place. If her goal was to get to you, I'd say she succeeded."

He wasn't even going to let the insidious idea into his head. Bending closer, he held Falconetti's icy gaze. "Listen to me and listen good. It's not her."

She didn't flinch. "How can you be so sure?"

"Because she's pregnant with my child. That's why she's in my house, in my office. Because I'm trying to keep her safe."

"Tick didn't tell me about that. Well, that could change things." A cool smile lifted one corner of Falconetti's mouth. "If she really is pregnant."

The memory of Autry's body pressed against his, the hard little bulge of her belly, the swollen softness of her breasts, filtered through his brain. No way she could fake the changes in her body. And no way he was actually considering Falconetti's crazy theory. "She is."

Falconetti leaned back, fiddling with the ends of her hair. "Your offender is probably a white male, twenties, high school educated, average intelligence, maybe below average."

Stanton frowned, as much at the description as the sudden turn in the conversation. He should have known she was only pushing his buttons. "Below average?"

She arched an eyebrow. "Smart stalkers don't send notes and provide you with handwriting samples."

"Describes half the guys in the county, though."

"He won't be able to stay away from her. He'll want to see the reaction to the notes—he feeds off of it. And be forewarned—having you around her, a barrier, could piss him off. If you're not with her, she needs to be especially careful."

Stanton nodded. Fear unfurled in him. He knew Autry well enough to realize she wasn't going to let him babysit forever. Sooner or later, she'd want her life back.

He can't stop me.

The words from the last note flashed in his head. He swallowed hard. She could have her life back but it would involve a twenty-four-hour guard if he had anything to say about it.

Gloria Gaynor trailed away, replaced with a slower Bee Gees number. Tick escorted Autry back to the table, but instead of sliding into his chair, he leaned over Falconetti, an arm around her neck, mouth close to her ear. "Dance with me, precious."

With a sultry smile, Falconetti pulled him to the dance floor and went into his arms, his hands linked at the small of her back, hers on his biceps. Autry watched them, her expression wistful. "He's crazy about her."

"Crazy would be the word," he said and could have bitten his tongue off when she turned cold blue eyes in his direction. He held up his hands. "All right, I know. Lay off."

Lips pursed in a narrow line, she shook her head. "He's your best friend and he's in love with her. You could try harder to accept her."

"In love or in lust?"

With an exasperated sigh, she gripped his chin and turned his attention to Tick and Falconetti on the dance floor. "Look at them. Really look. What do you see?"

His skin tingled beneath her touch, but he obeyed and surveyed them. They swayed with the unique, unmistakable rhythm of an intimate couple. Falconetti's lips moved, and Tick grinned and lowered his head.

"What do you see?"

Stanton shrugged. "He wants her. Big surprise, he always has. They'll go home and go to bed—"

"Absolutely clueless. That's what you are. He adores her, and to her, he's everything. She focuses him and he softens her."

He laughed, although frustration filtered through him. Why didn't he see what she did? "Whatever, hon. Looks like good old sexual attraction to me."

"Maybe because you only see what you want to." She grabbed her purse and pushed away from the table. Stanton stared after her as she threaded through the crowded tables.

Oh, shit. He'd screwed that all to hell. Snatching up their bill, he followed. She had the keys to his truck and he wouldn't put it past her to leave his ass here, stalker or no. At the hostess station, he handed off his bill and cash then headed for the door at a near jog.

"Autry!" She stood in the anteroom before the door, her shoulders hunched. "Autry, I—"

"He's changed everything." She stared at the door, a forlorn expression making her seem lost and vulnerable. "Before I wouldn't have thought twice about walking out there. Now...I can't go out alone. God, he's changed *me*."

Her voice quavered and the constriction in his chest loosened. Ignoring the curious glances of a couple entering the restaurant, he pulled her close, enfolding her against him. He rubbed a hand over her hair. "Oh, baby, I'm sorry. It's going to be all right—"

"Don't say that." She tugged away and he glimpsed a glitter of tears along her lashes. "It's not all right, and even if you catch him, I'm not sure it ever will be. Look what he's done to me. I'm afraid all the time, I'm letting you make decisions for me, I question everything and everybody...I'm not me anymore."

"Yes, you are." He cupped her face, wanting to soothe the fear and the anguish away.

Her lashes fell and she turned into his hand. "I want to go home," she whispered. "I just want to go to bed and forget all of this."

After that kiss earlier, he wanted to take her there so bad

he could taste it, but that wasn't what she needed from him right now. He brushed his mouth over her cheek. "Let's go then."

This had to stop.

Autry put her lotion away and wrapped a towel around her body. Irritation and unfulfilled desire had her nerves jumping and the worst part was she had herself to blame even more than Stanton. Sure, he was clueless about other people's emotions, let alone his own. She'd known that going in. Now suddenly, she wanted him to change into Mr. Perfectly-in-touch-with-his-feelings? So being pregnant had made her emotional and now completely irrational. Instead of sitting around whining about how blind he was, maybe she needed to show him where to go.

He'd asked for more time. That had to mean something.

They were having a baby together. She wanted to forge a relationship with him. He said the same thing.

What was she accomplishing by holding him away?

Sleeping in the spare room wasn't getting her any closer to him, wasn't in any way binding him to her.

So what are you going to do?

Taking a deep breath, she knotted the towel at her breasts. Before her spurt of courage and resolution could desert her, she marched into the bedroom and gathered her things. Her hands full, she slipped down the hall to Stanton's bedroom. The door stood slightly ajar and the fresh smell of his soap hung in the air.

Her stomach turning slow rolls, she nudged the door open with her knee. The bedside lamp shed soft light in the room. Stanton lay on the bed, arms under his head, clad only in his khaki slacks. At her entrance, he glanced her way, his eyes dark and shuttered.

Her simmering level of irritation, with him and herself, flashed into anger. She tossed her overnight bag on the floor. "Just tell me one thing. What the hell is your problem?"

Surprise flared on his face and he levered up to lean on his elbows. "Which problem are we talking about?"

"What do you really want? Is this all about the baby and your so-called duty? Or do you want me at all?"

He moved to a sitting position, throwing his legs over the side of the bed. He kept his gaze trained on hers. "Of course I want you."

She clutched the knot between her breasts. "If there were no baby, would we be together?"

He opened his mouth, closed it, swallowed hard enough his Adam's apple bobbed. "I don't know."

Irrationally hurt, she laughed. "What am I saying? The only reason we're together now is because I got pregnant."

"Autry..."

"It doesn't really matter how much time I give you." How could this hurt so much? "Nothing changes the fact that you didn't really want *me.*"

His head jerked up. "That's not true."

"You dumped me. If that doesn't say 'I don't want you', I don't know what does." Why was she doing this? Hell, why was she even here? What she should do was march back to her room, get dressed and demand he take her to her parents' house.

Shaking her head, she spun and stalked to the door.

"I was afraid, all right?" The words emerged in a near-hiss, as though he pushed them out between clenched teeth. "What I felt for you scared the hell out of me, and I got as far away as fast as I could. Happy now?"

"Afraid." She couldn't quite catch her breath, couldn't quite believe what he was saying. Holding her breath, she turned.

"Yeah." He ran both hands through his hair, leaving the short brown strands disheveled.

"Why?" she whispered, still clutching at her towel.

He shook his head. "I'd already failed with Renee, hell, to the point she had an affair. I was scared of screwing everything up with you too, and it just seemed easier to get out, let you find somebody who could be what you needed."

Renee had cheated on him? He'd never revealed that before, and as badly as she wanted to explore that, see how it related to their relationship, she needed more to make him understand what was most important.

She took a step forward. "I needed you."

"Oh, yeah, I'm a real prize. An emotionally unavailable ass, as Renee says."

Unavailable? She wouldn't say that. Reserved, yes, until she'd managed to get under the layers of professionalism and seriousness. Then she'd glimpsed the real man underneath—honest, compassionate, intuitive, blessed with a wry sense of humor.

She took another step toward him. "I think I'd say more confused than unavailable. Whenever I've needed you, you've always been there."

"Autry, you don't get it." The words were rough, torn from him. "If I failed again and lost you..."

She closed her eyes, his words thrumming through her. He did care; there was hope. She simply had to reach out and take it, show him the way. They could have so much more than she'd dared dream. If only one of them took the first step.

Opening her eyes, she caught his ravenous gaze. Those eyes whispered of starvation, of a wanting that went far beyond the physical.

She reached for the knot and let the towel fall to the floor.

Cool air rushed over her bare skin. She stood before Stanton's hungry eyes, nervous, exposed, titillated. He gripped his knees, staring at her.

Resisting the urge to cover herself, she stepped closer. "You can't lose me, Stanton. I'm yours." She reached for his hand, splaying his fingers across her naked abdomen. "We both are."

With a muffled groan, he wrapped his arms around her waist and buried his face against her. "God help me, Autry, I've been lost without you."

His mouth caressed the skin above her navel. Strong fingers stroked her back. The titillation slid into full-blown desire, painful pleasure pricking low in her belly. The ache spread lower, unfurling between her thighs.

He pressed open-mouthed kisses down her stomach and she buried her hands in his hair. The contrast of his skin against hers, the strength of his arms about her, weakened her knees. She could fall, though, and be assured he'd catch her. With his size—tall and broad and just big all over—he made her feel dainty, feminine, ultimately desirable.

"Our baby," he murmured against her belly, sliding his hands lower to cup her buttocks. "My baby."

"Take me to bed, Stan." She ran her fingers over his nape and shoulders, loving the warmth and texture of his skin. Loving him. "I want you."

"Oh, I'll take you." His chuckle vibrated on her skin. He nipped at the jut of her hipbone and a shiver raced over her. Strong fingers dipped between her thighs, a tantalizing sweep of sensation. The muscles in her legs quivered.

He eased to the floor, kneeling before her, his mouth dancing along her thigh. The intimate ache intensified, her body feeling loose and open. He swept his hands up her sides, palms warm and a little rough. He cupped her breasts, thumbs rubbing over her hardened nipples.

"Like that?" he murmured, nuzzling the curls at her mons.

"Oh, yes." She arched into his touch, breasts tingling and aching.

He nudged her legs apart, kissing the inside of her thigh. Anticipation sizzled through her.

The first touch of his tongue almost sent her over the edge. She moaned, fingers tangling in his hair, as he laved and caressed, tortured and soothed. While his mouth pushed her higher, his hands kneaded and teased her sensitized breasts. He was everywhere, his lips on her, fingers pressing into her flesh, male scent invading her senses. Pressure and pleasure radiated within, building between her legs, flowing into her belly, surging through her whole body. Her legs trembled and she tugged at his hair, seeking to assuage the unbearable tension.

"Stanton...please..."

The orgasm burst within, a strangled cry escaping her lips. She tightened her hold on his hair and waited for him to pull away. Instead, he increased his ministrations, pushing her higher until the intensity peaked again, until she was gasping his name over and over.

She collapsed into his arms and he folded her close, his

mouth meeting hers. The sharp taste of her own desire blended with the hot silk of his mouth and she moaned again, fumbling at his button and fly. He was hard, ready, and she wrapped a hand around him, wringing a groan from his throat. Steadying herself against his shoulder with her other hand, she lifted and poised over him. She caught his gaze, dark and smoky with desire, and slowly slid down, until all of him was inside her, with her body still trembling around him. She gasped, pausing to catch her breath, as her body stretched to accommodate his.

Pleasure contracted his face, eyes sliding closed. He gripped her hips harder. "God, Autry."

Pressing into his shoulders, she lifted and squeezed her muscles around him. The exquisite feel of him hard within her took her breath. She dropped again and cupped his jaw. He lifted his lashes, gaze burning into hers.

"Yours, Stan," she whispered, easing up and down on him, their bodies sliding wetly together. "We're yours."

His mouth found hers, hands at her hips helping her move on him, until the pleasure built in her once more, washing over her moments before he stiffened and groaned, thrusting higher.

With aftershocks trembling in her body, she sighed and buried her face against his throat. Against her lips, his skin was hot, salty.

He rubbed his hands over her back and kissed her jaw then her temple. He pressed his cheek to hers, a gentle contact. "God, I've missed you."

She turned her head, capturing his lips. "Show me."

Gathering her close, he lifted her to the bed. He stripped away his slacks and made love to her again. The slow, thorough exploration left her drowsy and sated in his arms, whispering more reassurances that she was his and he'd never lose her. Only as sleep closed in did she realize he hadn't said he was hers.

Tick dropped the banker's box on the dining room table. Tension and dread sat in a knot at the base of his neck. He didn't want to delve into the darkness hiding in this box, into what his own failure had cost his hometown.

"What are you doing?" Caitlin opened the refrigerator and pulled out the milk. Once they'd arrived home, she'd swapped her dark suit for a tank top, pajama pants and the ever-present boot socks.

He lifted the first file from the stack. "Going through the Schaefer case again."

She grimaced over the edge of her glass. "Why?"

"Because." Copies of Amy's diary entries hit the table with a thud. "Schaefer didn't father Amy Gillabeaux's baby. I need to find another way to connect them."

She drained the milk and set the glass in the dishwasher. "Need any help?"

He glanced up from the initial report on Sharon Ingler's disappearance. Memories of that night, walking through the dark pine woods, yelling for Sharon while Schaefer waited yards away, flashed in his head. The fury pressed in on him again.

Smothering the rage, he laid the report aside. "No, precious, I've got it. Go on to bed."

"Tick, it's eight o'clock. Bed? You've got to be kidding me."

The threat of that two percent risk and what it could mean to her health hovered in his head. "You should get some rest."

"Did you not hear me at lunch today? Dr. Astin said everything looks good, I'm in great physical condition and—"

"Cait." Their gazes clashed across the island. He blew out a long breath. "I'm going to worry, all right? I just am."

She skirted the island to link her arms around his neck. "Your overprotective male tendencies are damn cute at times, Lamar Eugene, and I love that you want to take care of us. But you're not going to drive me or yourself insane for the next eight months. Are we clear on that?"

"Crystal." He kissed her, letting the anger and worry slide into the sheer pleasure of her presence. Arms draped about her waist, he tugged her closer and inhaled her unique scent, warmth and spice and pure Caitlin. "So is that offer to help still open?"

"Mmm." She brushed her mouth against his cheek and tugged away. "Of course."

The house quiet around them, they settled in at the table

with legal pads and the reams of copies, scratching out notes. He laid out the department's patrol schedules from the previous spring and picked up Amy's diary entries. She'd never mentioned Schaefer by name, but if he could link the nights she described her sexual encounters with what appeared to be a cop to nights Schaefer had been on duty...well, maybe that would go a long way toward convincing a jury the two had been intimately involved. Transcripts. He'd need the radio transcripts to show any blocks of time in Schaefer's shifts when he'd have had time for a little backseat tryst.

Just because Schaefer had turned out not to be the father of that baby didn't mean Amy hadn't tried to convince him he was.

He just needed something, one little thing, that would definitely tie Schaefer to each victim, beyond the similarity of the killings, beyond the randomness of the victims.

They had been random. Victims of opportunity. The old nicotine urge tugged at him and he reached for one of the peppermints scattered across the table. The cool spiciness of the candy exploded in his mouth. Opportunity. He reached for the shift schedules again. A link had to exist, somewhere.

"Damn it." He pinched the bridge of his nose. If the link was here, he sure didn't see it.

"I know." Caitlin leaned back with a wince, covering her lower abdomen with one hand. "I don't see anything either."

Unease tingled to life in him. He laid a hand on her thigh, rubbing in a light circle. "All right?"

"Yes. It's just a twinge." She shrugged and straightened. "Something about the uterus stretching. I had them last time, early on."

Her gaze lifted to his, the loss of that first baby, the one taken from them by the brutal attack she'd suffered, hanging between them. He swallowed. "You're sure."

"Tick, it's a twinge, not a cramp. There's a difference, believe me. Dr. Astin and I covered this as well. When it's a cramp or there's blood, then we worry."

Holy hell, he needed a cigarette. He rubbed a hand down his face and crunched down on his mint, shattering it into tiny shards.

"We should be able to work this backward." Caitlin's husky voice pulled him back to the task at hand. She shifted and tucked her ankle beneath her. "All right. She mentions him, at least we think it's him, on May sixteenth and again on the twenty-second. Was he on duty or not?"

He flipped back through the schedules. "Not."

Paper rustled. Caitlin twisted in her chair to rest against him. "There's no activity on his credit card those nights. Or Amy's."

He rubbed his hand down her arm, reading over her shoulder. A heavy knot of frustration settled in him. "Nothing."

She flinched. He felt the small movement all the way through him. "Cait, I don't like this."

"Tick, I really don't think it's anything to worry about." She touched his hand, her fingers light on his skin. "I'm serious, I had the same twinges with that first pregnancy."

Maybe, but it didn't make him feel better. "You cannot expect me to go through this without smoking."

"Yes, I can." She handed him a peppermint, a familiar mischievous glow in her green eyes.

Almost two hours later, he pushed away from the table. Cellophane candy wrappers littered the pine surface, along with crumpled sheets of yellow paper, filled with his and Caitlin's crossed-out notes. They couldn't find a discernible pattern between Schaefer's shifts and Amy's diaries, or even between Schaefer's shifts and the victims' disappearances.

Holy hell, at this rate, Autry might actually be able to get the guy off. If she did...

Schaefer would come after Caitlin. A shudder traveled down Tick's body. He knew it, as surely as he knew he'd die loving her. In Schaefer's journals, the ones Autry had managed to get excluded, he'd detailed fantasies of killing Caitlin, who he saw as more of a challenge than his previous victims. Just reading those entries had turned Tick's stomach.

If Schaefer got out, walked away...

Tick would kill him before the bastard touched her. It was that simple.

He rubbed a hand over his eyes. Lord, he was tired. Those

doubles and the stress were catching up to him.

Caitlin slipped from her chair. "I'm going to get—"

The words ended on a hiss of pain and she cringed. The hair lifted on his nape, his heart thudding, adrenaline pouring into his system.

She looked at him and pain darkened her eyes almost to black in her pale face.

"What's wrong?"

"That was a cramp." She bent slightly, hand covering her abdomen. "And I think I'm bleeding."

He reached for her, faltering at the ugly red stain suddenly blooming at the apex of her thighs. His stomach dropped. "Oh, Lord."

"This isn't good, Tick." Her husky voice broke and she bit her lip.

"Come on." He lifted her easily and carried her through to their bed. Keeping one hand on her hip, he grabbed the phone and fumbled through the bedside table for the OB/GYN's card, although he knew in his heart what that blood and her pain meant.

Punching numbers with one hand, he stroked the dark silk of her hair with the other. Eyes closed, she winced and curled her knees toward her belly. Tears trickled from between her lashes, a sob making her breathing harsh.

He leaned down, brushing his mouth against her cheek. "Hush, precious. It's all right. Everything's going to be all right."

The insistence of a ringing phone penetrated Stanton's exhausted slumber. Cursing, he slipped his arm from beneath Autry and rolled over to grab the offending receiver. "Reed."

"It's Tick." He sounded drained. "I need to take a couple days off."

Stanton squinted at the clock. "It's four in the morning, Tick. Couldn't this wait? And why the hell are you wanting to take time off when you know what McMillian needs?"

"Cait miscarried."

Oh, shit. Stanton sat up, pinching the bridge of his nose. Autry shifted beside him, murmuring. Stanton sighed. "I'm sorry."

"Yeah, so am I." Desolation lingered in Tick's voice. "Listen, I'll take care of the Schaefer stuff from home, but it'll be a couple days before she can go back to work. I want to be with her right now."

"Yeah, sure." Stanton cleared his throat. "So how is she?"

"Groggy from the sedative. They had to do a D&C, but she can go home in a few hours."

Stanton chafed a hand over his disheveled hair. "Take what time you need. And Tick? I really am sorry."

"Thanks. Later."

The line went dead. Stanton replaced the receiver and slipped back into bed. Rolling to his side, he gathered Autry close. She rubbed her cheek on his arm and sighed. He spread his hand over the hard bulge of her belly. Even if he couldn't feel it, their baby lay under his palm. Growing. Moving. Waiting to be born.

He closed his eyes, moving his fingers in a small circle. Falconetti had been fine at dinner and now her baby was gone. The speed and lack of warning was scary.

Autry had said it herself earlier—she was only with him because she was pregnant. If they lost this baby, he'd lose her for sure. His chest went tight and cold. He could keep her safe from the stalker, but how could he protect their child from the capriciousness of nature?

Damn sure he'd have a list of questions for Autry's doctor in the morning.

Chapter Nine

On the monitor screen, orange lights flickered, slowly evolving into recognizable images. Autry stared, excitement trembling under her skin. An arm. The bend of a knee. A tummy, umbilical cord attached.

She flicked a glance up at Stanton, wanting to see his reaction as badly as she wanted to see the reality of their baby. He stared at the screen, his jaw slack, eyes amazed. She smiled and squeezed his fingers, wrapped around hers. He looked at her, grinning, and warmth swirled through her.

The technician moved the transducer over Autry's stomach, increasing the pressure. The picture flickered, shifted, morphed into a new angle. "Would you like to know the sex?"

Autry met Stanton's gaze, and at the fascinated awe on his face, her heart constricted with happiness. She nibbled at her lip. "Do you want to know?"

"Yeah." His attention slid back to the display. "I do."

Autry turned to the waiting medic and nodded. "Please."

A smile tipped the corners of the tech's full mouth. "Then say hello to your daughter."

A girl. A thrill rushed through Autry, similar to the first primal one she'd felt when the pregnancy test stick had turned a shocking shade of blue.

"And there..." the sonogram wand trailed up the side of Autry's abdomen, "...is her face."

"Oh my God," Autry breathed, staring. A tiny mouth pursed, and minuscule fingers curled along a rounded cheek. The baby's thumb flexed. "Stanton, do you...?"

"I see." His voice emerged strained, a little choked, and she looked up at him. He stared at the screen with a rapt expression. A wide grin lit his face. "I don't believe it. Look at her."

"She's real." She couldn't decide which she wanted to watch more—the awesome sight of her baby or the fascination on Stanton's face.

"She's beautiful." Ignoring the sticky gel on her stomach, he cupped a hand along her side.

The technician's soft chuckle burst the bubble of isolation around them. "All right, a few more measurements and we're done."

Stanton pulled his hand away, but kept his gaze trained on the monitor during the remainder of the procedure. When they met with Dr. Hampton in her office after the sonogram was finished, he was full of questions—was the baby's development okay, what were the risks of miscarriage at this point, were there any precautions Autry needed to take?

A tiny frown tugged at her eyebrows. Hands between his knees, he leaned forward, the force of his attention focused on the doctor. His concern centered on the baby. She wanted to laugh at herself, but the damned tears gripped her throat again. She had what she wanted—he'd become an interested father—but was left wanting more. Was it too much to ask that some of his concern extend to her?

Dr. Hampton smiled, an indulgent expression Autry figured she reserved for nervous fathers-to-be. "Everything is going just fine. The baby's development is normal, no problems with mom or baby." She glanced at Autry's chart. "Autry, you're gaining weight nicely—not too fast or too slow. I'd say at this point we're looking at a textbook perfect pregnancy. Any other questions? Concerns?"

Stanton clasped his hands. "You're sure?"

"I'm positive." She scribbled a renewal prescription for Autry's prenatal vitamins and slid it across the desk. "Here you go. We'll see you next month."

At the front desk, Autry stopped to schedule her appointment. Stanton held the door for her and she slid her sunglasses on as they stepped into the bright morning sunshine. A light breeze played with the leaves on a crape myrtle by the walkway and stirred Autry's hair.

Stanton pointed his remote at the Explorer and pressed the unlock button. "So you really are feeling all right? I mean, you've been under a lot of stress—"

"What is with you?" She put a hand on his arm and glanced up into his face. He shrugged, muscles flexing under her fingers, and a sensory memory played over her, of the same movement against her palms last night, as she rode him. Her face flushed and her body warmed, a low, tingly sensation in her belly. "Stanton?"

He glanced away, then swung his gaze back to hers. The hazel depths were haunted. "Falconetti had a miscarriage last night."

Surprise and sadness slid through her. Caitlin pregnant? "Oh no, that's awful." She shook her head. "When did she find out she was pregnant?"

"Tick just told me a couple days ago. He sounded pretty cut up about losing it."

"I'm sure," Autry said, her voice soft. She dropped her hand from his arm and turned toward the truck. "Do you mind if we stop by my place? There's some of that gel on my blouse, and I want to change before the hearing."

"No problem."

In the passenger seat, she fastened her seatbelt and adjusted it to lie low over her abdomen. With him beside her, the warm male scent of him filling the air, she had to fight off memories of the night before. In his arms, forgetting everything but him had been too easy. This morning reality was everywhere she looked and she didn't want to face it yet.

What she wanted was his touch, more of him, anything but having to admit she could reach him more easily on a sexual level than any other. But maybe she could use one as a step to the other. Keep one connection open until it built to something else. She shifted in the seat, half-turning toward him.

"Stanton?" She ran the back of her knuckle over the side of his neck. Muscles jumped under her light touch.

He braked for a stoplight. "Hmm?"

"Last night was fantastic." She eased her fingertip into the collar of his shirt.

A smile quirked at his mouth. "Yeah, it was." The light turned green, and he accelerated. A hand covered her knee, palm a little rough against her bare leg. "Seeing her this morning...that was the most amazing thing I've ever seen."

Autry stared at the contrast of his tanned fingers against her paler skin and renewed desire tingled through her. She stroked his wrist. "Me too."

"Have you thought about names?"

In abstract terms, she had, when she hadn't been worried about crazed stalkers and helping a murderer go free. "I know I don't want her to have anything Tick or my dad can shorten into a weird nickname."

"Or something too different." He grimaced. "Hadden says every new teacher he's had since kindergarten has called him Hayden at first."

She frowned. She hadn't considered that. "If you'd known, would you have called him something different?"

"I didn't name him." His mouth formed a thin line. "Renee and I had agreed on Thomas. She changed her mind when he was born. Guess she figured it was her due since I was an ocean away." He squeezed her knee. "Tell you what...on the way home, we'll pick up one of those baby name books and start going through it. How does that sound?"

Sensation tingled out from the point of contact between his hand and her leg. She cleared her throat, not wanting her voice to come out husky and full of need. "I'd like that."

He swung the Explorer onto her street and a moment later into her driveway. Loss washed over her as she stared at her little house. It didn't look like a safe haven anymore. She fumbled through her purse for her keys as Stanton came around to open her door.

His hand under her elbow, he escorted her to the back door, the fresh wood of the repaired doorframe not yet painted. When she stepped into her kitchen, the house smelled different, as though fear had tainted the rooms. She shivered.

"Autry?" He stared down, his eyes concerned, and she made herself smile for his benefit.

"I'm going to change. I'll just be a minute." She hurried

down the hall to her bedroom, not giving in to the urge to check every shadow for an intruder. She changed blouses quickly, half-listening to the sounds of Stanton rustling through her refrigerator. If she knew him, throwing out milk and other items with past-due dates.

Sure enough, when she returned to the kitchen, he was holding a can of whipped cream aloft to check the "use by" date. The muscles in his forearm rippled with the movement. He shot her a wry glance. "Why do you have three cans of whipped cream in here?"

Her cheeks warmed. "It's my craving food."

He raised an eyebrow at her. "Straight out of the can?"

"Yes." She crossed to take the bright can from him. "Is that a problem?"

His mouth curved. "Not at all. If you'd told me, I'd have gotten you some for my place. We'll pick some up on the way home."

"Thanks." She shook the can and popped the top free to squirt a small amount on her finger. With a sublime sigh, she sucked the sweet cream off her fingertip. At Stanton's harsh intake of breath, she met his gaze. He stared at her, hazel eyes dark and hot.

Impish desire seized her. On this level at least, she could keep a connection open and she wanted to be connected to him again in that elemental, man-to-woman way that always thrilled her to the core. She nudged the refrigerator door closed before spraying another puff on her finger. Eyes locked on his, she lifted her hand and spread the white fluff on his mouth. On tiptoe, she brushed her tongue over his lips, licking away the sweetness, blended with his taste.

He gasped once and tangled his hand in her hair, taking her mouth in a hard, deep kiss. She sucked his tongue between her lips and he groaned, backing her into the refrigerator, hips pressed into hers. Her fingers flexed on the can with a compulsive grip and whipped cream exploded between them.

Surprised, she squealed and Stanton pulled away, the white stuff in his hair, on his jaw, smeared down his shirt. He swiped a hand down his chest, glanced at the mess and grinned. Autry laughed.

Linda Winfree

"Think it's funny, do you?" He ran his sticky finger down the side of her neck, and still laughing, she tried to squirm away.

"Stanton, stop..." The words died in her throat as his mouth followed the trail of cream, sucking, licking, nipping. She moaned, the sensation shooting straight to her belly and lower, to pool between her legs. Yes, definitely connected. He slid his hands along her thighs, pushing her skirt up to cup her hips and pull her into him.

He lifted her, draping her thighs over his, so his legs supported her body. The upward movement dislodged one of her refrigerator magnets, which tumbled to the floor with a soft clatter. Autry slipped an arm around his neck, playing with the hair at his nape while his mouth continued doing magical things.

"Beautiful," he murmured against the hollow of her throat and she felt his mouth move in a smile. "Sweet too."

She shifted her hips, rubbing against the hardening bulge behind his fly. He sucked in a breath, hands tightening on her, and she laughed. "My court appointment isn't for another hour. What time do you have to be in at the department?"

"I'm just the sheriff. A political figurehead." He licked a dollop of whipped cream from her collarbone, his tongue slick and a little rough. "Cookie's there and the place can run without me for an hour."

"Political figurehead, my ass." She nipped at his earlobe. However, his job, the political aspects between them, were the last things she wanted to focus on right now. Instead, she wanted him, hard inside her, making her forget the real world for a while.

His fingers busied themselves, unbuttoning her blouse. He fumbled, tugged a little hard on one tiny pearl button, and it pinged to the floor. A thrill of desire tingled down her spine. She liked him eager. "We can do a lot in thirty or forty minutes. Take a shower—"

"Have dessert." With a deft movement, he released the front clasp on her bra.

"We haven't had lunch yet." Her voice emerged breathless and shaky.

"That's the problem with you lawyers," he murmured near her ear. He plucked the can of whipped cream from her hand. "Always getting hung up on technicalities."

He flipped the can upside down, and with a gurgling hiss, it released rosettes of cream on her sensitive nipples. She gasped, at the sudden coolness, then the heat of his mouth closing over them in turn.

She laughed again, arching into him, hands tangling in his hair. "Lunch is vastly overrated anyway."

Damn, he couldn't concentrate.

He couldn't get rid of the huge grin, either.

Stanton stretched, tuning out the speaker addressing the local civic club. His entire body ached, as if he'd gone through a major run followed by a strenuous workout, but damn if he cared. Being with Autry again was worth any lingering discomfort.

Once hadn't been enough—he'd taken her in the kitchen and afterward she'd seduced him in her shower as they washed away the sticky remnants of whipped cream and enthusiastic lovemaking. He'd ended up late for Rotary and she'd almost been late for her hearing. His tardy entrance had garnered a couple of dark looks from two of the county commissioners, but their disapproval didn't come close to touching the warm glow of contentment in his chest.

He sipped at his tea. Content. Yeah, that's what he was. Having Autry in his life again offered a sense of balance, an escape from the everyday loneliness. And nestled in her womb was the most beautiful, amazing thing he'd ever seen—his unborn daughter. The level of excitement engendered by seeing her surprised him. He found himself impatient, ready for her to be born so he could hold her, look for Autry's features or his own personality in her. He'd been so busy, consumed by his career, when his sons had been born that he'd missed that.

He wanted to nurture, foster that relationship with his daughter. Along the way, he'd learn how to repair the one with his boys, too. He could start by taking them for pizza after Hadden's game, telling them about their sister.

A new life seemed to open before him, another chance, new beginnings.

All because of Autry. Stanton smiled. He'd make this work with her. He had to. Tick had said he could live without anything but Falconetti and Stanton was finally understanding the most important thing.

Autry was the "anything but" woman of his life.

His smile died. She'd told him she was his, that he'd never lose her. Too bad he couldn't make himself believe it. Yeah, he had a new chance.

What he didn't have was a clue how not to screw it up.

He was still pondering that as he dodged county commissioners and the newspaper editor on the way to his truck. God, sometimes he hated the political side of the job. He wanted to run a decent department to the best of his ability, not make nice with politicians. Hell, now he knew why Tick had wanted the investigator's position rather than the appointment to sheriff.

"Sheriff, one more question!" Ray Lewis puffed up to the Explorer's hood. "Any truth to the rumor that Autry Holton is receiving death threats?"

A chill slithered down Stanton's spine and pooled in his gut. "Where did you hear that?"

Ray smiled, looking satisfied. "So it is true?"

"I'm not going to comment on—"

"Is that why she's staying at your house?"

Anger flashed through Stanton, dissipating the cold knot in his belly. He straightened. "Let's get one thing straight. What I do in my personal life is not fodder for that rag you call a newspaper. My relationship with Ms. Holton is not open for discussion. Got that?"

"Some citizens would consider the sheriff seeing the public defender a conflict of interest."

"Some citizens should mind their own business. My seeing her is not an issue." He jerked the truck door open. "Excuse me."

Settled in the driver's seat, he pulled the door closed and jammed the key in the ignition. He reached for his sunglasses and flipped the visor down.

Photographs rained into his lap.

He stopped breathing, staring at the glossy prints of Autry...outside the courthouse, with her father in the hospital parking lot, with Stanton entering the Winn Dixie, on the front porch of Stanton's house.

"God," he whispered. Nerves kicked off in his gut, followed by a wave of pure rage. The son of a bitch was warning *him*. Telling him he could get to her, get to Stanton, any time he wanted.

Like hell. Stanton would see him dead before he'd let anything happen to Autry, to their daughter.

He gazed at the photos, anger still cramping his stomach. He couldn't touch them, risk destroying any fingerprint evidence. No telling what he'd disturbed by getting in the truck.

His locked truck. Someone had managed to get inside, tuck the photos under the visor and leave it locked again.

Were the photos all they'd left? His gaze shot to the ignition. What had he set off by putting the key there? Or maybe there was a pressure-sensitive device under the seat, triggered by his weight, set to go off when he left the vehicle.

Jesus.

He eased his cell phone from its clip and punched in half of Tick's number before he remembered. He couldn't call Tick in, not now, even if he couldn't think of anyone else he'd rather have watching his back. Frustration stung his chest. He didn't want this call going through dispatch, with every scanner in the county able to hear what was going on.

Mouth taut, he punched in a second number and waited.

"First available date?" Tom McMillian asked. He lounged in one of the chairs before Autry's father's desk, an ankle crossed over his knee. "You must be awful damn confident."

Autry smiled, ignoring her flickering nerves. Confident, about this case? More like scared to death she'd actually win. "My client wants a speedy trial. He has that right."

Her father reached for the calendar at the desk's edge. "Well then, let's see what we have." He flipped. "November first."

"That's only ten days away." Tom straightened and Autry looked his way, searching his face. His blue eyes narrowed, and his jaw clenched. Interest flared in her—he *wasn't* confident about his case.

Autry caught her father's glance and nodded. "November first is perfect."

"All right." He scribbled on the calendar. "I'll notify the clerk of court. Now, any other business?"

Tom shifted in his chair and pulled a folded document from his inner coat pocket. He separated two sheets and handed one to Virgil and one to Autry. "New evidence disclosure."

Her stomach pitching, Autry glanced at the paper. DNA test results. Her attention sharpened. DNA results proving Jeffrey Schaefer had not fathered Amy Gillabeaux's unborn child. She looked up to find Tom watching her, his expression guarded. She suppressed a smile. Well, no wonder he didn't want a quick trial date. Part of his motive argument had just unraveled with those strands of DNA.

Clearing his throat, her father shuffled the report into the file on his desk. "Well, if that's all, I have another hearing in ten minutes."

Gathering her things, she smiled a goodbye at her father and stepped into the hall. In the quiet courthouse, her low heels clicked on the polished white marble.

Tom joined her, his loafers making only a hushed whisper against the floor. "Voluntary manslaughter with sentencing recommendations. My last offer."

Autry glanced at him as they walked toward the stairs. "I'll approach him, but he won't take it. He wants a trial, Tom, vindication in the form of a jury acquittal."

At the top of the stairs, he caught her arm in a gentle grasp. "You know he did this."

She looked at his hand and shrugged away. Her paranoia was turning everyone into a possible suspect, making every gesture questionable. "What I think about him is irrelevant. I have to provide him an adequate defense. You know that. And if he doesn't want to plead out, I can't make him."

"Advise him. Strongly. This is the best offer he'll get."

Irritated, she waved the disclosure document at him. "Do

you really think he'll consider it once he finds out about this? My God, Tom. He's not stupid. He'll know what this means. Hell, he's probably known all along what these results would be."

Tom's mouth drew into a line. "Don't tell him."

She stared at him, not believing what she'd heard. "I can't do that. It's unethical. I could be disbarred."

"No one ever has to know. We can make it disappear."

She shook her head, backing down to the next step. "I don't believe you. Make it disappear? It's been entered into the court record! It exists. The GBI has a record, the sheriff's department would have a record..."

Her voice trailed away, realization sinking in. The sheriff's department. She glanced at the date on the report again. Yesterday. Stanton had known and never said a word. Her throat closed, aching. He'd been with her, made love to her, all the time knowing something that could make or break her case. Probably already had Tick looking for more evidence, something to counteract the damage this could do to the state's argument.

And she couldn't blame him for keeping quiet. His job demanded it. Hers would too. She sighed. Another secret. One more way in which they couldn't be totally connected. If they forged a real relationship, but stayed in their current professions, there would always be this secrecy between them.

With a shaky breath, she straightened and fixed Tom with a look. "I won't hide this from Schaefer. He's entitled to a decent defense and he'll get it."

He straightened his already perfect tie. "If he walks, it'll be because you helped him."

She narrowed her eyes at him. "No. If he walks, it'll be because you charged him before you were sure of your case."

Turning her back on him, she walked away.

"It's clear."

Stanton flinched as Cookie, his second investigator, slammed the hood closed. During the examination of the truck, his nerves had jangled with each noise. With the infinite methods available of wiring an explosive to a vehicle, he hadn't known which of Cookie's movements might set something off. Regardless, he hadn't been willing to wait two hours for the bomb squad from Ft. Benning to show up.

Cookie appeared at the open driver's door, evidence bag and a second set of gloves in his gloved hands. "I called Lawson Automotive. Thought you'd want them to go over everything before you drove it again."

"Thanks." Stanton reached for the gloves and snapped them on. He lifted the photographs from his lap and slid them into the plastic bag. Letting Cookie take the bag and seal it, he eased from the seat, part of him still expecting to be blown away by a huge fireball.

Nothing happened and he stiffened shaky knees. Damn, this was what Autry was dealing with on a daily basis. He'd known it, but hadn't really gotten it, not until now. The rage flowed through him again. When they found this guy, when Stanton managed to get his hands on him...

The son of a bitch would pay for terrorizing Autry, for putting her and Stanton's daughter at risk. Everything was as simple as that.

"You all right, boss?" Cookie folded the chain-of-custody seal over the top of the bag, watching him. "You're a little pale."

"I'm fine." He gestured toward the Explorer. "Let's get this dusted for prints before Lawson gets here."

The painstaking process of lifting fingerprints from the vehicle took forever, even with both of them working. When Lawson's tow truck rumbled into the dusty lot, they'd dusted maybe two-thirds of the vehicle. Another, more familiar, engine followed the tow truck's big diesel and Stanton lifted his head, frowning. Tick's pickup slid to a stop behind Lawson's big yellow rig.

Stanton straightened and watched Tick emerge from the driver's seat. He was dressed farmboy casual—jeans so worn they were almost white, faded Jimmy Buffet T-shirt, a John Deere gimme cap pulled low over his eyes. A dark shadow of stubble covered his jaw.

Stanton lifted a hand in a wave. "What are you doing here?"

Tick shrugged, his face tense under the cap bill. "Had to pick up a prescription for Cait. Saw Lawson pulling in, wondered why the hell you were dusting your truck for prints."

Cookie grinned and dropped yet another evidence bag holding print tape into the banker's box. "Does Falconetti know you're out in public dressed like that? I thought she had rules."

"She's asleep." Tick glanced at Stanton's truck. "SOB come after you this time?"

"Photos of Autry." Stanton clenched and unclenched his fists. "Wants me to know he's everywhere she is."

"And that he can get to you too," Cookie said.

Tick nodded at Lawson's tow truck. "Having it checked out, huh?"

"Autry drives it as well. I'm not taking any chances." Stanton rubbed his nape, trying to relieve some of the awful strain sitting there. It didn't go away.

"Good deal." Tick jammed his hands in his pockets. "I'll give you a ride back to the station."

Stanton frowned. "I thought you wanted a couple days off."

Tick's gaze followed Cookie, ambling back to the Explorer. "Cait's pissed as hell at me. Figure I'll let her sleep it off."

Stanton lifted his brows. So that explained the tension emanating from him. "Want to talk about it?"

"Nothing to talk about." Tick's shoulders rolled in a tight movement that matched his expression. "Doctor told her we could try for another pregnancy in a month or so. She wants to, and I said no way." He glanced sideways, and Stanton caught the flash of agony in his dark gaze. "Damn it, Stan, I'm not risking her again. All that blood and as much pain as she was in...not to mention the emotional toll she doesn't want to admit to. It's not worth it. We can adopt. Or live without having kids. But I won't let her risk herself with another pregnancy."

Somehow, Stanton didn't see Falconetti giving in and accepting Tick's dictate, and he was well acquainted with Tick's own stubbornness. He shrugged off the epic battle of wills brewing on the horizon. "You know where I am if you ever do want to talk."

Mike Lawson wandered over, his middle-aged pooch straining the buttons on his grease-stained work shirt. His teenaged son Keith followed, longish hair poking out from under a cap bearing the garage's logo.

Mike nodded. "Afternoon, Sheriff, Tick. Want me to run it into the shop for you?"

Stanton nodded, anger trembling under his skin once more. "I need you to go over everything for me, Mike."

"Will do." Mike passed a hand over his shiny brow. "Got in it while it was locked, huh?"

"Yeah." Stanton glanced at the Explorer, where Cookie was wrapping up the print work. "They didn't jimmy the lock, though."

"Not real difficult to get in one of those." Mike hooked his thumbs on either side of his brass belt buckle. "All they need is your VIN number and thirty bucks to buy a remote for the locks. Maybe not even that. Beau Ingler's wife has an Expedition and he was telling me the other day her remote unlocked an Explorer and an F-150 in the Wal-Mart parking lot."

Stanton stiffened and exchanged a look with Tick. Interest flared in Tick's gaze and a grin played about his mouth. Stanton knew that look—it was like the baying of a bloodhound once he was on the scent. Grief and marital strife aside, Tick was in the game. Stanton was glad of it too.

Because his next step included a little talk with Beau Ingler.

And if there was even an inkling Beau was the one terrorizing Autry...Stanton might need Tick to keep him from killing the guy.

Chapter Ten

Autry stood still under the metal detector wand. The Haynes County deputy waved her toward the interview room, and she drew a deep breath. On the other side of the steel door was the one man she never wanted to have anything to do with again.

She was about to make him very, very happy.

The thought made her ill, a nausea that had nothing to do with her pregnancy.

Aware of the deputy's narrowed stare, she knocked once and pushed the door inward. "Hello, Jeff."

"Hey." His voice was hushed, a little weary, and still held traces of pain. He sat at the table, hands clasped on the top. No handcuffs.

She stepped forward. Light from the window fell on his face, highlighting the bruises and stitches. "We have a trial date. Ten days, November first."

He nodded, but his eyes remained dull, lifeless. When he didn't say anything, she pulled out the second chair and sat across from him. "There's also been a new evidentiary disclosure. The test results are in on Amy's baby's DNA."

He didn't move and his expression didn't change. "I'm not the father."

She held his dead gaze and shook her head. "No, you're not."

One corner of his mouth quirked. "There goes McMillian's motive."

Linda Winfree

"He can still argue she told you the baby was yours. That she threatened to expose your affair, force you to marry her."

His smile grew and the icy malevolence made her heart stutter. "He can say whatever he likes. He can't prove any of it, and that's what counts."

Nausea rose in her, a chilly sweat breaking on her upper lip. He'd done it. He'd killed the five girls, murdered two witnesses to cover up his crimes. If there'd been any doubt in her mind before, that smile and his easy, joyful satisfaction at possible acquittal convinced her otherwise.

The sudden urge to flee, to get as far away from the man as possible, seized her. She glanced at her watch. "I only asked for a few minutes. You probably won't hear from me again until early next week. I have a case to present before then, but I'll make arrangements to meet with you a day or so before jury selection begins."

"Thank you." He leaned forward, the frightening intensity appearing in his blue gaze again. "I appreciate you keeping me informed. I appreciate everything you've done to help me, Autry."

To help him. She repressed a shudder. Help him do what? Walk away so he could murder again? Sweet heaven, she had to get out of here.

Metal clattered on metal and Beau Ingler's muttered cursing filled the still afternoon air. Edgy anger smoldered in Stanton's chest, making him jittery. He hated the simmering fury, the way it worked its way through him like some mind-altering drug. He hated being angry, period, but the last time he'd felt like this had been that night when he'd been packing for Quantico and Renee had told him about the affair, the possibility the baby she carried wasn't his.

He'd wanted to hit her, hit the guy who was supposed to have been his friend. Instead, he'd carried his bags to the car, and on the way back inside, punched the doorframe. Split his knuckles wide open and he'd gone to Quantico with a hairline fracture of his hand.

Sizzling in him now was the same desire to strike out, but not because he'd been betrayed. Because Autry had been

134

threatened, frightened.

Because those damn photos scared the shit out of him.

Stanton nodded at Tick as they approached the red Massey Ferguson tractor outside the Inglers' massive barn. Beyond the building, the family's fields stretched, a patchwork of green and beige. To their left lay the produce fields and store, large pumpkins glowing orange in the green vines. The scent of freshly turned dirt hovered over the farm, rich and warm, mingling with the heavier aroma of diesel fuel close to the barn.

Tick cleared his throat. "Beau? Can we talk to you a minute?"

Beau Ingler straightened to regard them over the tractor, his features set in rigid lines. "I guess I got time."

"You been here all afternoon?" Tick glanced across the fields. Stanton watched Beau's expression, glad they'd agreed Tick would do the talking. He was afraid of what might tumble from his lips if he opened his mouth.

Beau shrugged. "Other than running into town to pick up a part, yeah. Why?"

"What route did you take?"

"Highway 3." Irritation darkened Beau's face beneath his cap, sporting a fertilizer logo. "What's this about anyway?"

Stanton folded his arms over his chest, holding in the anger. "Your wife drives an Expedition, doesn't she?"

Beau shot him a glare. "I asked you a question. Tell me what this is about."

"We're just checking something out," Tick said, his voice even. "Mike Lawson said you told him your wife's entry remote unlocked other vehicles."

"That's why you're here?" Beau's scowl deepened. "If this is the best y'all can do, no wonder Jeff Schaefer got away with what he did for so long. No wonder my sister's dead."

Tick grimaced, his eyes flickering with guilt. "Beau, I'm sorry about Sharon—"

"Yeah, I bet you are." Beau shook his head. "Whatever you're checking out, I didn't have anything to do with it. Now, unlike the two of you, I have things to do."

He snatched up his toolbox and stalked into the barn. Tick

sighed, a long-suffering puff of breath. "That went well."

Stanton gazed after Beau. He was too closely involved to be able to read the other man—his emotions tangling together and overriding his objectivity. Everywhere he looked, he saw another threat to Autry's safety and he wasn't sure which ones were real and which were the result of an overactive protective drive.

He nudged Tick's shoulder. "You've known him a long time. You think he's the one?"

Eyes narrowed, Tick stared at the barn. "Hard to say. His daddy and Virgil go way back. We all grew up in each other's houses, went to school and church together, so it's hard to imagine him wanting to hurt Autry. But he adored Sharon. His baby sister murdered? Well, I can see where something like that can change a guy."

"Williams at the crime lab in Moultrie said she might be able to tell us which photo center developed the prints, once she has time to look at them."

Tick's disgusted snort stretched Stanton's already tense nerves. "When will that be? Six months from now? Cookie and I can check out the local places, but anybody with half a brain who watches television cop shows would know to drive a distance out to get the film developed. I'll verify Beau's alibi."

"Don't you think you should be at home—"

"No. My wife made it awful damn clear she doesn't want me around right now." Turning away, Tick trudged to his truck. "You coming?"

Stanton followed him. Behind the wheel, Tick stared across the fields, his hand motionless on the ignition. "She's freezing me out, Stan, sucking all the pain down inside. Thinks if she ignores it, it'll all go away."

"Maybe it's the only way she can cope right now." Stanton shifted on the bench seat, uncomfortable with the conversation. Not because of his dislike for Falconetti, but because he recognized himself in Tick's description. He'd done that with his emotions all his life, from the pain of his father's untimely death to his anger over Renee's betrayal. Even with his feelings for Autry. Those emotions in particular had scared the hell out of him. In turn, he'd shoved them down, locked them away securely and run as fast as he could.

Tick fired the engine. "This isn't the way it's supposed to be. I'm her husband. It's my place to help her shoulder this, but damn if she's going to let me."

Stanton ran a hand over his nape. "Wish I knew what to tell you, other than maybe to give her some time."

As he glanced over his shoulder to turn the truck around, Tick shot him a sardonic look. "Hell, you probably understand her better than I do. Y'all are just alike."

"You could have gone all day without saying that, Tick."

Once they were back on the highway, Tick lapsed into silence, the quiet of the truck cab broken only by the whir of tires on Highway 19 and the low crooning of Tim McGraw from the radio. Stanton tapped his fingers against his knee. He couldn't really see Beau Ingler as a threat. The man had made no secret of his anger, had blasted Autry to her face. If he'd wanted to hurt her, he'd had an opportunity that afternoon in her office.

Stanton shuddered at the memory, at the what-could-have-happened scenarios running through his head. He'd been careless and stupid, putting his professional duty and the need to address Ray's questions before Autry's safety, just for a few seconds.

Damn if he'd do it again. If need be, he'd take some time off until the trial was over. Except he didn't see how he could. Tick had just lost a very wanted child and wouldn't be a hundred percent for a while. Stanton tapped his knee harder. Cookie. The investigator could probably handle the office for the duration and Stanton could work from home or the courthouse or wherever.

Yeah, the county commission would love that.

Shit, man, just decide what's more important to you—Autry or your damn job.

Autry and his baby, definitely. But his duty, the promises he'd made to the people of Chandler County...those were important too. He knew Autry well enough to know she wouldn't want him to shirk his obligation. From what he'd heard, Virgil Holton had preached duty and responsibility to Autry since before she could walk.

At the first stoplight in town, Tick took a right, heading the back way to the courthouse square and the sheriff's department. He swung the pickup into his designated parking spot and killed the engine.

Stanton eyed the parking lot between his office and the courthouse. Only a few cars dotted the asphalt, but he could only imagine how crowded the courthouse would be for Schaefer's trial. He frowned. "We need to up our security level for the trial. Keep that in mind when you're working up the staff schedule for that time, would you?"

"Sure thing." Tick rubbed a hand over the steering wheel. "I'm not going to hang around. I want to go check on Cait, see if I can get her to talk to me. But I'll make some calls later, verify Beau's alibi and start trying to run down where those photos came from."

"Thanks." Stanton slid from the truck and stood, propping the door open with one hand. He looked away, cleared his throat, glanced back to hold Tick's dark gaze. "I'm sorry, Tick."

"Yeah. Me too." He gunned the engine. "Later, Stan."

Stanton stepped back and slammed the door. Tick backed out and the truck roared away. Late afternoon stillness descended on the square, a handful of courthouse employees straggling to their cars, patrons stopping at the produce stand next to the sheriff's department. All the trappings of a small, peaceful town.

An icy sensation trickled down Stanton's spine. The hair lifted at his nape. He glanced around. His imagination, or someone watching him? The images from the photos flitted through his mind. He hoped to God the notes, the photos were simply someone playing head games with them, but if not, he'd be ready.

He'd protect Autry and their baby with everything in him.

Autry's little car pulled into the lot behind the courthouse. Warmth rushed through him at the sight of her and a smile tugged at his mouth. Damn, if just seeing her made him happy, he was in trouble.

Briefcase in hand, she swung out of her car. He met her at the sidewalk edge and reached to take the case. "How was your hearing?"

She shrugged and an urge to hug her bubbled within him.

He wanted to fold her close and hold her, but the memory of those damned photographs lingered.

Autry smiled, but the expression didn't reach her serious gaze. "We have a court date. November first. And Tom turned over his new evidentiary disclosure. DNA results on Amy's baby."

Stanton grimaced. "Are you pissed because I knew about that?"

"No, I wouldn't expect you to tell me." She looked up at him, the sun creating a shining halo on her chestnut hair. "Does it bother you? That we'll always have those kinds of secrets between us?"

"Become a prosecutor and we won't."

"Funny." She frowned at his empty parking spot. "Where's your truck?"

"It's a long story." He glanced around and took her arm, urging her toward the sheriff's office. His skin prickled with awareness of a possible unseen watcher again. "Let's not have this conversation out here. Come inside."

"You're making me nervous."

"Well, that makes two of us."

"Oh Lord, that *really* makes me nervous."

"Autry, please. I don't want to be out here right now."

She relented and let him draw her inside. The department was quiet, the squad room empty. He ushered her into his office and closed the door. Watching him lay her briefcase aside and retreat behind his desk, she crossed her arms over her chest.

"Okay, what's going on?"

He picked up the photos in their plastic evidence bag and came around to lean against his desk. He held out the bag, his stomach clenching at what he was about to do. "These turned up in my truck today."

She stared at the photos. Turning her gaze away, she thrust them back at him. "Take them. I've seen enough." She closed her eyes, but not before he glimpsed the glitter of tears that probably had nothing to do with pregnancy hormones. "It's never going away, is it? Not really."

His hand closed around her wrist and he tugged her

against his chest, wrapping her in a close embrace.

"I'll make it go away," he whispered near her ear. He tightened his arms, wanting to absorb all of her pain and fear. "I will."

She slid her arms around his waist and hung on. "I believe you."

"Good." He laid his cheek against her hair and inhaled the sharp, clean scent of her. Hands moving over her back in soothing circles, he drew her as close as the bulge of their baby would allow. "Because I mean it. You're safe with me, Autry. Both of you."

***

Autry laid her legal pad aside and stretched. The notes for her opening statement insisted on swimming before her eyes and she didn't need them anyway. The words were branded into her brain, along with the ramifications of winning this court case.

She uncurled from the armchair in front of Stanton's fireplace and wandered into the kitchen. Her cotton pajama pants swished against her legs, and in her belly, the baby rolled, the movement harder, more prominent than in previous days. She patted the little bulge and opened the refrigerator.

A thud echoed down the hall and she jumped, heart kicking to double-time. Stanton's muttered curse followed and she pressed a hand to her throat, pulse slowing. Since the photos had turned up in his truck, there had been no more notes, no more evidence of her stalker.

It seemed he'd gone away.

But the fear sure as hell hadn't.

Grabbing a bottled orange juice, she ambled down the hall to the third bedroom, which served as his home office. In the past two weeks, she hadn't returned to the bedroom his boys used, but had spent her nights in Stanton's bed. They'd settled into an easy routine—early dinners, followed by Stanton reading or watching a movie while she worked on her case notes, going to bed together, sometimes to make love, other nights falling asleep wrapped close. He was gentle, affectionate, attentive.

She couldn't for the life of her figure out why he was afraid of messing up with her. A couple of times, she'd started to broach the subject, but she hadn't wanted to disturb the precious warmth of their evenings.

She paused in the doorway, one hand curved over their baby. Soon. She would ask soon, maybe even tell him how she felt, find out if maybe he was beginning to love her too.

Stanton stood at the window, measuring the distance to the corner. Autry sipped her juice. "What are you doing?"

He jumped, the tape measure retracting with a metallic clatter. With a sheepish grin curving his mouth, he shrugged. "Figuring out where to put the crib."

An irresistible smile tugged at her lips. "Isn't it a little early for that?"

"Probably." He ran a hand through his already tousled hair. Oh, he was cute, with his feet bare under faded jeans and a T-shirt. The simmering attraction flared in her belly and she sipped at her juice again, trying to drown it. Lord, maybe that whole thing about pregnancy increasing a woman's libido was true. Hers sure seemed to be in overdrive lately.

Or maybe it was just Stanton.

He glanced around the office, with its plain masculine furniture and metal desk. "I thought maybe I'd get one of those office armoires to hold my stuff. I didn't want to put Hadden and John Logan out of the extra bedroom, make them feel like they were being displaced or anything, you know?"

Her smile widened. Another change she'd noticed over the past two weeks—he'd been reaching out more to his sons and they'd responded with cautious enthusiasm. "Sounds like a plan."

He gestured at the white walls. "I guess you'd want to paint."

Her breath caught. "It's your house."

His gaze met hers and she saw uncertainty flash in the hazel depths. "Yeah, but I'd started thinking about it as our house." He laughed, a short, self-deprecating sound. "Insane, huh? We haven't settled anything between us."

At his words, her stomach clenched as her heart lifted simultaneously. Warmth tingled through her. She stepped farther into the room, eyes locked on his. "Is that what you want? To make this our house?"

He swallowed, his Adam's apple bobbing hard, and glanced away. She held her breath during his long pause, but didn't release it even after he looked at her again. "I want a future with you," he said, his voice rusty, as though he forced the words from deep inside. "Both of you."

She released the trembling breath. Setting her juice on the desk, she crossed to stand before him, her knees quivering to match the muscles in her abdomen. Head tilted back, she stared up at him. "I want that too, Stan, but I have to know it's about more than the baby." She paused and dampened suddenly dry lips with her tongue. His eyes darkened. "I need to know how you feel about me."

He blinked, his expression closing, the glow in his eyes dimming. "Autry…"

She reached for him, grasping his arms with light hands. "Stanton, this is important. I need to know I matter."

Frowning, he stared at her.

And didn't say anything.

Her heart folded in on itself, becoming a small, cold knot of nothing in her chest. She turned away. Lord, she should have known, shouldn't have let the fantasy get to her, make her hope for more. Fighting back a wave of tears, she escaped into the hallway. She dashed away a couple of stray drops that dared fall.

Strong hands closed on her shoulders, tugged her back against a solid chest. His spicy scent surrounded her and a hint of stubble scratched her ear.

"You've always mattered," he whispered. "Don't you know that?"

She struggled in his easy hold, pulling loose to face him. "How would I? You're not exactly free and easy with your emotions. You let me go easily enough."

"I told you, I was scared." He backed her into the wall, a hand on either side of her neck. In the dim light, his eyes glittered. He leaned closer. "It's not that you don't matter,

Autry. You matter too much."

"I don't understand you," she whispered. She closed her eyes to block out his too-persuasive gaze. "If I mean that much, why did you leave me?"

"Because I wanted you to have the best." He murmured the words, nuzzling her temple. His deep sigh stirred her bangs and he pulled away. Cool air washed over her in the absence of his warm body. "And that's not me."

The dejection in his voice pierced her heart and she opened her eyes. He looked down at her with an expression she'd caught glimpses of the first time they'd been together—a longing, that sense he starved for something more than just the moment.

She tucked her hair behind her ear. "Why not?"

"Pick a reason. I'm too old for you, I screwed up one marriage already—"

"Have you ever screwed up a case?" She pinned him with a stern look.

Surprise flickered in his eyes. "Yeah. Everybody does."

"Did you give up being a cop?"

Muscles moved in his throat. "That's different."

"No, it's not." She held his gaze, desperation curling through her. This seemed a make-or-break opportunity and damn if she intended to break. Or let him do it either. "You didn't run from the job. And you can't keep running from this."

"I don't know what to do." The rough words seemed torn from him. "I don't want to hurt you and I'm not sure how to keep from doing that."

Love me. She couldn't say it. A huge gulf lay between "you matter" and "I love you". He cared. He wanted her. Couldn't that be enough for now?

The baby rolled in her womb and she reached for his hands, curving them over the small mound. The movements, growing stronger within her over the last few days, had proved elusive for him. She watched his face. "There she goes again."

He frowned, concentration furrowing his brow. A slow smile broke over his face and he lifted his gaze to hers.

"I feel her." He laughed, tension evaporating from his

features. "God, that's amazing."

She stroked his wrists, gaze trained on his awe-filled face. Yes. For now, this would be enough. She just needed to keep this emotional connection open between them. Surely, the rest would come.

It had to.

Stanton drifted through layers of sleep to awareness. Early fingers of dawn filtered through his thin curtains. Autry lay sprawled across his chest, her breath warm and humid on his skin. Her stomach was a hard bump against his hip and memories of feeling their daughter move within her rose in him. Transfixed by an emotion so strong and pure it stole his ability to breathe, he tightened his arm around her.

He wanted to hold on to them, to never let them go. He wanted their baby, but even more, he wanted forever with Autry. The fear tried to lift its head, but the sheer contentment of having her with him crowded it out. Maybe that was the key...focus on the positives, fight against the fear. Maybe holding on to the way he felt about her, the way she made him feel, would lead him in the right direction.

She stirred, murmuring, and he rubbed his palm over her hip. Her lips moved against his chest in a small kiss. "What time is it?"

"Early," he murmured and whispered his mouth over her temple. Her rumpled hair brushed his cheek.

She lifted her head and smiled at him, a sleepy expression that stunned him with its simple beauty. "Morning."

He chuckled, happier than he had a right to be. "Something like that."

She tapped his chest and subsided, her cheek over his heart. Her sigh vibrated through him. "Today's the day."

He didn't have to ask what she meant. After four days of jury selection, she and Tom McMillian had finally agreed on the twelve people—nine men, three women—who would decide Schaefer's conviction or acquittal. Today, the trial opened in earnest.

"Nervous?" He rubbed a small circle low on her back, where he knew it ached as her pregnancy advanced.

"Afraid I might actually win." With another sigh, she rolled away to stare at the ceiling.

Stanton levered up on an elbow to look down. He curled a strand of her soft hair around his finger and studied her troubled face. His chest squeezed. He wanted to make it better for her.

And he knew her well enough to realize she wouldn't want him to. He released her hair and stroked the back of his finger down her cheek. A surge of emotion, strong and pure, coursed through him. "Autry, I..."

I love you. The words trembled on his tongue, but wouldn't move beyond his lips. Was that what he felt? Would it be enough?

Better to wait until he was sure.

He rubbed his thumb along her chin. "I know doing the right thing here hasn't been easy, but you've done it. No matter what happens, I'm proud of you for doing it."

A tiny smile curved her mouth and she laid her hand along his jaw. "Thank you." Her eyes dimmed and she pulled away to sit up. "I need to shower and get moving. No sense dragging this out."

She slid from the bed and disappeared into the bathroom. Stanton subsided onto his pillow, hands folded behind his head. Maybe he should have said the words. And maybe he'd done the right thing. Maybe neither of them was ready for that yet.

What he really ought to do, though, was stop thinking about himself and focus on what Autry needed.

He rolled from the bed. Juice, breakfast, support, whatever she needed from him. Maybe he couldn't give her the words yet, but he could give her the actions.

Autry stepped into the courthouse from the side door and her stomach rolled. For a moment, she was afraid she'd throw up, then and there, and the nausea didn't have anything to do with her pregnancy. She couldn't remember ever being this sick with nerves over facing a jury. Townspeople crowded the lobby and hallway, waiting to venture through the stand-up metal detectors and head upstairs for the trial. A few looked in her direction and she caught a handful of disparaging and disdainful glances before she turned away.

As the deputy manning the side entrance waved a handheld detector over her body, she shuddered and found herself grateful for Stanton's steady presence. He was quiet, but solid, everything she needed right now. His hand on her arm, he escorted her to the attorney's meeting room just off the stairway.

"Are you going to be okay?" His gaze traveled over the people moving up the stairs.

She smiled, although it was the last thing she felt like doing, and clenched her fists, nails biting into her palms. "I'm fine."

He shifted so his body shielded her from the townspeople's view. "Listen, I won't be far away. Schaefer will be in shackles the entire time, up until he enters the courtroom. One of us will be outside this door until you're ready to go and he'll be under guard the whole way too. No one's getting near you. I promise."

She swallowed, the nasty metallic taste of fear coating her mouth. "You think he'll try something today, don't you? The stalker, I mean."

"I don't know." He reached out a finger as if to touch her face and let his hand fall. She ached for that brief touch. "But I don't want to take any chances." A quick smile quirked at his mouth. "I have to take care of my girls."

She rolled her eyes, struggling for normalcy among the fear and nerves. "You're going to be insufferable about her, aren't you?"

"Only when she starts dating." His radio squawked, dispelling the sense of intimacy around them. He replied and she let the garbled conversation with its ten codes and terse male voices wash over her. Instead, she closed her eyes and focused on calming her nerves.

"That was Harding." Stanton's voice pulled her too soon from the fantasy she'd been building—a hospital room, their daughter in her arms and Stanton bending over them with love in his eyes. Reluctantly, she lifted her lids and looked up at his serious face. His gaze was dark and shuttered. "Transport's here. I'm going to meet Cookie around back and bring Schaefer in. Sure you're okay?"

"I'm *fine*." If her voice trembled a little, it was simply nerves. Pretrial jitters. Never mind she'd outgrown those jitters during her first year of trial work.

"All right." He leaned in and opened the door, the unique blend of his spicy soap and fresh deodorant enveloping her. He nodded toward the deputy manning the metal detector and another standing between the twin staircases. "Monroe and Troy Lee are right here if you need anything before I get back. Tick and Chris are around too."

With a tight smile and a nod, she stepped into the small room. She'd been in it dozens of times before, but as he closed the door behind her, her stomach jumped again. Black iron bars covered the two tall windows. The door offered only one way in and out.

Sighing, she laid her briefcase on the table and straightened her back. She rubbed at the tiny ache there and wandered to the window. Below her, in the parking lot between the courthouse and the sheriff's department, Stanton and Mark Cook stood by as Jason Harding helped Schaefer climb from the white transport van. Even at this distance, Autry could make out the tension bunching Stanton's shoulders. Schaefer wore the dark blue suit she'd provided, the shackles a stark silver against the fabric. The line of his body was tense, his movements jerky.

Trapped. He looked trapped.

Autry could understand that, even with disgust roiling through her.

Because she was trapped with him.

Eight-fifty-five.

As they walked up the stairs to the courtroom, Autry glanced at her watch. Her stomach still jumped and twisted periodically. Schaefer walked beside her, his face expressionless, the shackles gone. She ran the high points of her opening statement through her head and tried to ignore him. Tried to ignore what she was doing.

Behind her, the authoritative and distinctive sound of Stanton's footsteps was a welcome reassurance. Mark Cook murmured something and Stanton chuckled. Harding replied, his voice an indistinct echo in the massive marble hall, now empty of spectators.

They stopped before the large mahogany double doors. Troy Lee Farr, Stanton's youngest deputy, snapped to attention, his gaze skittering over Schaefer's face, resting uncomfortably on Autry for a second before focusing on Stanton. His leather belt creaking, he stepped to the side and opened the door. "Morning, Sheriff."

Stanton nodded and held the door. "Troy Lee."

He motioned for Autry and Schaefer to precede him. Autry caught his gaze and he smiled, a quick reassuring tilt of his mouth before the professional mask descended. The baby chose that moment to turn over within her womb and she resisted the urge to lay a hand over her, to protect her from being tainted by the mere presence of Jeff Schaefer.

Amy Gillabeaux hadn't had a chance to protect her unborn child from Schaefer.

Who deserved more from the justice system? Amy? Or Schaefer?

The urge to flee gripped Autry and she lifted her head, facing down the people she'd known all her life, now turning to look at her with anger and disdain. Or not deigning to look her way at all. She focused instead on the bench where her father would be seated and concentrated on taking slow, deep breaths to still the nerves jumping in her belly.

A ripple of whispers moved through the room as they approached the defense table. The jurors eyed Schaefer. Autry watched them, trying to read their expressions, seeing nothing but stoicism at this point.

She stepped back to allow Schaefer to take the inside chair. A bailiff stood against the far wall, next to the door to the judge's chambers. The court recorder was already in place.

Harding and Cook sat behind them. Autry glanced at Stanton, saw him looking down at his cell phone. He grimaced, caught her gaze and shook his head. Turning away, he strode back to the doors and disappeared into the hallway.

The doors closed behind him with a soft thud.

Through the next few minutes, her senses seemed

heightened as the bailiff called the court to order and her father took the stand. For a second, she fancied she could hear his black robe rustling. The scent of dusty law books and licorice curled around her, settling the nerves somewhat.

She pulled herself together as Tom McMillian addressed the jury. While he outlined the state's theory of the crime, she scratched notes on her legal pad.

Finally, it was her turn.

She stood, resisted the urge to straighten the edge of her suit jacket. Smiling, she stepped forward and faced the jury.

Chapter Eleven

Heart thudding an uncomfortable rhythm against his ribs, Stanton thrust open the courthouse doors and jogged down the wide steps. Hadden calling him at nine o'clock in the morning couldn't be good.

He flipped his cell open. "Hadden?"

"Dad, I got it!" Exuberance bubbled in Hadden's voice, only deepened into manhood in the last year or so. "Mrs. Roberts just handed me the letter. I got it!"

It. What was it? Stanton raced through all the conversations he'd had with his eldest son in the last month— they'd been more frequent the last couple of weeks. It. Finally, something clicked into place. The "Character in Athletics" scholarship he'd applied for. "The scholarship?"

"Yeah. A full ride for my first year at FSU. And it's renewable. I can't believe it."

"That's great, Had." Pride created a warm glow in Stanton's chest. The boy was a good kid; Renee had done an excellent job raising him. It wasn't like Stanton could take much of the credit for how he'd turned out. But with his daughter...he had a second chance. He wouldn't screw that up.

"I'm proud of you, son." He cleared his throat and glanced at his watch. Just after nine. "Listen, I have to get into court, but how about I drive down tonight? We'll go get a pizza and celebrate. You can tell me all about it."

"That's fine." Hadden lowered his voice. "I need to go before I'm late for second period. See you tonight."

"I'll be there around seven." Stanton hesitated to break the connection. "I meant what I said, Had. I'm proud of you." He swallowed. "And I love you, son."

Silence stretched between them. Stanton wasn't sure he'd ever said the words to either of his sons. Hadden coughed. "You too, Dad. See you tonight."

Stanton folded his cell and returned it to his belt. Saying it felt like a release, leaving him lighter and warmer. What would giving Autry the words feel like?

He glanced toward the second floor windows. The early morning sunlight washed the glass and white marble in a golden glow. Once he returned from Tallahassee, he'd tell her tonight. He frowned. Would the words be enough?

His gaze traveled to the stores across the street, to the gilt script on the window at Hodges Jewelers. He needed to do this the right way, to offer her a sign of his devotion as well as the words.

What if she said no again?

Then he'd deal with it. He'd back off, be patient, give her the time she needed. And he'd love her all the while.

Because he did. Admitting it merely to himself lifted some of the tension he'd been carrying around since June when he'd let her go.

He rotated his shoulders, as if he could feel the weight sloughing off them. Smiling, he turned to reenter the courthouse.

A deafening noise rolled over him.

The concussion knocked him off his feet.

Blinking, he stared at the concrete sidewalk, inches from his nose. His body ached, heart racing, ears dull and ringing as if stuffed with cotton. His hands formed an instinctive cradle over his head.

Debris—glass and concrete and marble—rained around him.

The dust invaded his nostrils and throat and he choked on the thick acrid smoke.

God, what was happening?

He pushed up to his knees, entire body trembling.

Paper fluttered to the ground. Dust fell like snowflakes. Larger chunks of concrete thumped down, clipping his shoulders and back, his hands where they covered his head.

He shook his head and stared at the courthouse. The western side doors hung from their hinges at a weird angle. The windows were gaping holes, the glass and frames gone. Gray smoke poured from the openings, joining the black cloud billowing skyward.

A creaking, grinding sound came from deep in the earth and the western walls toppled inward with a raucous roll of sound.

His stomach clenched and rolled, bile pushing into his throat.

God. Oh, no. Please.

Sounds filtered in—the high-pitched squeal of the bank's alarm, car horns and alarms, the roar of a hungry fire, glass tinkling to the concrete, chunks of debris hitting metal and sidewalk with muffled thuds.

Screams.

People poured from the businesses surrounding the courthouse.

He pushed to his feet, the training taking over. *Call it in.* His radio. He jerked the square from his belt and keyed the mike, called his dispatcher. Silence, broken only by static, answered him.

Hell, the department. He eyed the smoke billowing behind the courthouse. What had happened to his department? What the fuck was going on?

He ran for the corner, fumbling with the radio to pick up the city PD's frequency. "C1 to Coney. 10-20, county courthouse. 10-70, 10-33, 10-18. Repeat, 10-70, 10-33, 10-18!"

Stumbling over a chunk of marble, he skidded to a stop at the edge of the courthouse square and stared. The back wall of his department building was gone. Thick black smoke rolled from the parking lot, flames shooting from vehicles.

The eastern half of the courthouse had disappeared, smoke and dust fluffing out of what had been the basement.

The courtroom was in the east wing.

An image flashed in his mind, Autry standing at the defense table, uncertainty darkening her blue eyes as he walked away to take Hadden's call. His mouth dried.

Autry. Oh, Jesus. Where was she?

She couldn't be in that rubble. She couldn't be. Something had to have pulled her out of the courtroom, out of the courthouse, and she was somewhere safe.

Because he simply couldn't make his mind wrap around the idea that somewhere in that pile of smoldering concrete and marble lay the woman carrying his child. The woman he loved.

Sirens wailed to life from the city's emergency center, a block away, and blended with the bank and car alarms still shrieking.

A small car, next to the ones already burning, exploded with a roar, a fireball shooting skyward. Metal flew and Stanton ducked. Staying close to the broken building, away from the fire and vehicles in the lot, he scrambled toward the east wing. In that mass would be survivors, injured, needing help. If they were lucky, there would be no bodies to recover.

Autry would be just fine, waiting for him on the sidewalk when he got to the end of the building. She had to be.

He climbed over a pile of marble blocks, where the back of the courthouse had simply sheered off. A flash of hot pink caught his eye. Fabric, stained with red, still clothing a human torso. A silver pin shaped like a lighthouse lay attached to one shoulder.

An arm and the head were nowhere to be seen. The legs had disappeared. His stomach pitched again. Let Autry be all right. Let him find her before it was too late.

His men. He'd left Cookie and Troy Lee in there. Chris and Monroe, too.

Tick. Dear God, his *partner*. They'd worked Oklahoma City together, when Tick had been a rookie agent. They weren't FBI anymore, but Tick was still his partner. Still like his right hand. Stanton stared at the destruction, with paper fluttering to earth like dusty angels' wings. His stomach pitched. How much of that paper debris had he watched Tick meticulously tag in evidence bags in Oklahoma? He couldn't do this without Tick.

He sucked in a breath and immediately wished he hadn't. The stench of burning fuel and rubber swamped him, combining with the sights and sounds and fear to turn his stomach one last time. He spun, vomiting in violent, helpless waves.

The sirens wailed closer, followed by the *whup-whup* of the city's police cars. Voices boomed over loudspeakers, asking people to vacate the streets, to begin walking west, to clear the area so they could help the victims.

The heaving over, Stanton straightened and once again moved toward the east wing. A foul taste lingered in his mouth and throat, not helped by the sooty air he breathed. His movements were shaky and uncoordinated, entire body weak and trembling. Shit, he had to get himself together or he'd be no good to anybody.

Running feet pounded on pavement, voices yelling instructions. Water exploded from fire hoses and the fire hissed, angry and tortured.

He slid on a hunk of concrete, his ankle twisting, the rough surface scraping skin from his arm. The pain registered, but was so far removed from the reality around him that he brushed it off. The agony in his chest, the fear and worry, the absolute devastating truth that Autry wouldn't be waiting for him, superseded any physical hurt.

City officers in their dark blue uniforms ushered bank employees to the end of the block, herding them east. Officers and civilians alike glanced over their shoulders, shock and horror, the same dazed awe Stanton had faced at first, on their faces.

Things like this didn't happen here. It happened other places, to other people, but not here.

"Reed!" Dix Singleton, the city's police chief, sprinted down the sidewalk and stumbled over rubble to meet him. "What the hell happened?"

"Explosion," Stanton muttered, his chest tight, throat burning. No telling what the fumes he'd inhaled had been. "Between the courthouse and the sheriff's office."

His office. His employees. His gaze darted toward the building again and he took a step toward it. He needed to be there. Only he needed to be here for Autry too.

A fireball erupted from yet another parked car. Singleton jerked and ducked, his eyes wide. "Goddamn. The gas main?"

Stanton glanced at the blazing vehicles, the spray from a fire hose doing little against the flames. "No." He shook his head, trying to pull his thoughts together to do his job when all he wanted was to rush into the rubble and find Autry. "The gas main would still be burning. Probably came from a parked vehicle."

Oklahoma City flashed through his head again. A truck parked in front of a building, one hundred sixty-eight lives lost, countless more destroyed. Jesus, had he let that happen here, to the people who depended on him? To Autry, who everything in him screamed was his to protect?

"A bomb?" Singleton tugged a hand through his hair. "I'm gonna call for help. We're going to need the GBI, probably their bomb squad. County inmates for digging, the county equipment."

Ambulances screamed to a stop in front of the post office, behind the fire trucks. EMTs in blue and white streamed into the street.

Police officers were already in the rubble, yelling, moving chunks with their bare hands.

There were no tan county uniforms among them.

Stanton jerked his gaze from the courthouse to what was left of the sheriff's office. "...get GEMA on the way here. Call in LifeFlight." Singleton's voice seemed to follow a stream of consciousness and it took Stanton a second to realize he was calling directions into his radio. "And maybe the FBI from the local office in Albany..."

FBI. Stanton closed his eyes. Someone would have to find Falconetti, in federal court in Albany, and tell her what had happened. That Tick might be among the missing. Even worse, among the dead. God, he wanted to wake up from this nightmare.

Because it couldn't be real.

Or maybe it was. Maybe it was real.

And he was in Hell.

Caitlin jogged lightly up the steps to the Albany regional FBI offices. The defendant in the case she'd been set to testify in had pled out at the last possible moment, and she should be happy that was off her plate.

Instead, lingering irritation simmered under her skin. Tick Calvert had to be the most stubborn man alive, and when he got an idea in his head, there was no changing his mind.

Or so he thought. She wouldn't let him win this one. Since her miscarriage, he'd been withdrawn and absolutely adamant they wouldn't attempt another pregnancy. She passed a hand over her flat stomach, the nagging little pain tugging at her heart. She wouldn't deny that losing this baby hurt, almost as much as losing the first much later in her pregnancy had, but she refused to let fear of another loss hold them back. They'd argued over it again that morning, until Tick had stormed out to his truck without his customary "love you, precious" or even kissing her goodbye.

She was mad as hell, not hurt. That squeezing around her heart was anger. Not the ache of separation from the man she loved.

"Hey, Falconetti, we're not running a race. Slow down, would you?" Agent Demetrius Taylor caught up with her at the top of the steps.

She shot him a cool look. "You know, if you quit smoking, keeping up with me wouldn't be a problem."

"You know, if you were less bitchy, we'd get along better." He swiped his ID through the electronic lock at the back entrance. "We're supposed to be partners. Bond and be best friends and all that bullshit."

"Bullshit is right," she muttered and swept into the building. Partners. Taylor was the guy she worked with, not her partner. She'd buried her partner more than four months ago, thanks to the son of a bitch standing trial in Chandler County. The shame of it was they couldn't prove he'd killed her. Schaefer wasn't facing charges of murdering Special Agent Gina Bocaccio.

The more Caitlin watched Tick bury himself in the evidence, the more she worried Autry Holton might work some miracle of defense and get him off. A shudder worked its way over Caitlin's body. Schaefer, on the loose. He'd planned to kill her, to make her beg before strangling her, all in front of Tick.

She'd danced in the darkness of enough killers to know

that if Schaefer walked out of that courthouse, he wouldn't be able to resist the challenge she represented for him. Before he disappeared to begin killing again, he'd come after her. But like him, she learned from her mistakes.

This time, if need be, she'd be ready for him.

"So I guess you're going down to Chandler County, huh?" Taylor glanced sideways at her, his face more unguarded and readable than any FBI agent's should be. "Schaefer's trial starts today, doesn't it?"

"Yes." She tugged open the office door.

"Yes, you're going, or yes, it starts today?"

"Both." She shrugged at the exasperated noise he made in his throat. Changing her personality for him wasn't an option. If he wanted to be her *partner*, he might as well get used to her now.

The level of activity in the office stopped her dead at the doorway, adrenaline kicking to life in her stomach. The small office's four other agents pulled on duty jackets, checked holsters, pocketed cell phones, all while glued to the small television next to the coffee station.

"What's going on?" Obviously something more than the background checks they'd been swamped with the last week. Excitement joined the adrenaline.

All eyes jerked to her before the four men exchanged shuttered glances. Bruce Milton, agent in charge of the office, cleared his throat. "Falconetti, there's no easy way to say this."

Oh, God. Those had to be the worst words in the English language and every cop knew what lay behind them.

Tick. Had something happened to Tick? No. Please. She clenched her hands, nails biting her palms, and waited.

Milton gestured at the television. "There's been an explosion at the Chandler County courthouse. We've been called in to assist."

An explosion. She stared at the television, where a pretty blonde reporter stood on the main street in Coney and addressed the camera. Behind her, fire trucks blocked the street, ambulances raced by and officers swarmed.

Blue uniforms. City cops.

Not a tan sheriff's uniform in sight.

No tall figure with black hair always in need of a cut and the charcoal suit she loved on his lean form.

He'd walked away from her in anger that morning, wearing that suit, and she'd let him.

"...local authorities won't confirm any fatalities," the anchor said, her expression earnest. She turned and pointed to the courthouse, barely visible in the distance. Smoke rolled behind the decimated structure. "But it's apparent the courthouse has experienced extensive damage. The GBI is on scene now, George, and we have seen the LifeFlight helicopter from Worth County Hospital arriving and leaving. Obviously, there are life-threatening injuries involved here..."

Caitlin shook her head. She shouldn't have let him go like that. Dazed, she turned to Milton. "I'm going with you. I...I need to change." Her slim suit skirt and heels, perfect for court, would only be a hindrance now. "Give me five minutes."

It only took her three. With jeans, a T-shirt and sturdy boots paired with her FBI-emblazoned duty jacket, she scrambled into the bureau-assigned vehicle she shared with Taylor. For once, there was no argument about who would drive. Her hands shook too badly to steer and her attention was too focused on prayer and recriminations to watch the road.

She closed her eyes and conjured Tick's face in her memory, the sound of his voice, his touch on her skin. He would be fine. He always was. He had to be.

She'd waited too long to find him and she had no intention of letting go now.

Getting into Coney proved to be a nightmare. All traffic had to be rerouted, producing one mother of a traffic jam. Caitlin wanted to scream as they presented IDs, had them verified and finally proceeded to the courthouse square. Yellow tape cordoned off the vicinity and a rough triage area had been set up in the parking lot next to the bank, opposite the courthouse. Firemen trained hoses on the cars smoldering in the lot between the courthouse and the sheriff's office.

Caitlin's breath caught in her throat. The back wall of the sheriff's department was gone. In the park north of the building, two refrigerated semi trailers waited. Temporary morgues, she realized, as firefighters lifted a sheet-draped body into the closer of the two.

Following her colleagues toward the makeshift command center, she scanned the parking lot. Tick's truck, the windows shattered, the white paint obscured by dust and ash, sat in its customary spot. Her chest tightened. He'd been here. There'd been no miraculous occurrence to keep him from that courtroom.

In the rubble, officers and inmates worked side by side, clearing debris, yelling for survivors. The smell of scorching rubber and concrete dust lingered, the air so thick Caitlin could taste it. Taylor thrust a filter mask at her. "Put that on."

She obeyed, boots crunching over glass and pebble-sized chunks of marble. Dusty papers, the edges charred, whispered under her feet. She glanced at them—file folders, legal briefs, tax records.

A sheriff's department report, filled with a distinctive, slashing handwriting that took her breath again.

She stopped, snatched it up, smoothed it against her chest. The top corner was singed away, but Tick's signature remained at the bottom. She traced her fingers over the letters—*L. E. Calvert, Jr.* With shaky hands, she folded the paper and tucked it into her jacket pocket. She looked up to find Taylor stopped in front of her, his face lined with sympathy as he watched.

"We'll find him, Falconetti. I've known him for years; he wouldn't go down easily. He's here and we'll find him."

She swallowed, the acrid dust invading her throat again, mingling with the lump of tears. "I know."

The command center, set up at the corner of the courthouse lawn under a funeral-home tent, was a den of bustling activity and a cacophony of voices. A local police officer sprinted by them, rolled papers in hand. "I got them!"

Gasping, he spread them over a table and the men under the tent moved to set whatever was handy at each corner, holding the paper flat. At the edge of the crowd, Caitlin glimpsed blue paper and white lines—blueprints of the courthouse.

Milton introduced himself to Dix Singleton and Caitlin watched him shake hands with Will Botine, head of the local

GBI offices. She turned away, wanting to throw herself into the search, to find her husband.

A tall, familiar figure detached himself from a group of rescuers and her heart lightened. Reed. If Reed were here, Tick wouldn't be far behind. Maybe she'd gotten her miraculous delay after all.

She hurried from the tent. "Reed!"

He spun, his face grimy with soot and dust above an equally gritty mask. Blood oozed from a long scrape on his arm. He tugged the mask down and graced her with a curt nod. "Falconetti."

Stopping in front of him, she reached for his uninjured arm. Urgency flooded through her, and over his shoulder, she scanned the area.

"Where's Tick? He's with you, right?" He opened his mouth, closed it, and panic curdled in her belly. "Where is he?"

He shook his head, pain glittering in his hazel eyes. "I don't know."

"You have to," she whispered. Her gaze jerked to the mound of rubble, what had to be tons of marble and concrete and rebar. "*You have to.*" She covered her mouth, stifling the sob clawing to get out of her throat. "Oh, God."

"Don't fall apart on me, Falconetti." His face was grim. "We're going to need every available pair of hands. We'll find him. I swear."

She nodded, forcing the FBI training to the forefront. He was right. She didn't have time for the luxury of tears and panic. Straightening, she sucked in a deep, calming breath. "What happened?"

He chafed a hand over his hair. "Looks like a car bomb. Went off a little after nine. We...we've had fatalities. I don't know how many. Even more injured. God knows how many still missing." He swallowed, muscles in his throat moving in spasms. "That courtroom was packed. It seats close to two hundred people. And that's not including the staff in the offices. So far, our survivors have come from the west wing, the part still partially standing."

She wouldn't think about the implication in his statement. Instead, she stared at the sheriff's office, looking injured and forlorn. Her eyes burned. "The department?"

"We were lucky. Only one dispatcher and two jailers on duty. Roger ended up with a busted arm because of falling debris. One prisoner with minor injuries. Everyone else was okay. All off-duty personnel are en route."

Blinking back tears, she glanced at him. "What about Autry?"

His eyes darkened. "Not yet."

Taylor jogged up to them. He held out a pair of work gloves. "Come on, Falconetti. Let's go find your guy."

Tugging on the gloves, Caitlin nodded and met Reed's tortured eyes. She put on a smile, her face aching. "And Autry too."

Chapter Twelve

The dark hung all around him and he couldn't move. Tick wasn't sure which was worse. The blackness held noises though—distant moans, muffled yells, machinery roars. Beyond that was a shaky creaking that scared the hell out of him, as if whatever lay above could come crashing down any second.

He fought the panic crawling over him, forced his breathing to a slow, even pace. God only knew how big the pocket around him was—he'd tried to map it with his left hand, but a hunk of concrete pressed against his shoulder, prohibiting movement of that arm. Jolie Williams, whom he knew from the GBI crime lab, lay pressed at an awkward angle on top of his right arm. The particular perfume she fancied filled his nose, mingling with the choking dust. He could wriggle the fingers on both hands, his toes too, so he didn't think he faced any permanent damage there. He simply lacked room to move.

And he couldn't see a damn thing. He stared into darkness blacker than any night—an absolute absence of any possible light.

With the disorientation, he couldn't even be sure how much time had passed, how long he and Williams had been trapped here. How much air they might have left. A shudder ran through him, the panic trying to fool his lungs into working overtime. He squeezed his eyes shut and prayed, all the while making sure he breathed with an even rhythm.

What had happened?

One second, he'd been at the door of the witness sequestration room, convincing Monroe he really needed a cigarette. The next...

He didn't remember the next second, his memories a jumble of noise and disorientation, debilitating fear and a slow return to awareness.

An explosion of some sort. Maybe the gas main on Scott Street had blown.

And maybe it hadn't been an accident.

The whys and hows weren't going to matter, though, if no one found them. He opened his eyes, squinting into the dark. It had to have been only hours. It couldn't be days yet, could it? His stomach growled and thirst dried his mouth, but it was normal hunger. Not days-without-food hunger. He'd skipped breakfast because of that fight with Caitlin, so maybe it wasn't even lunchtime...

Caitlin. His chest went tight. *Lord, thank You she wasn't here.* This was the last place he wanted her. What he wanted was her safe, free from danger—

He hadn't told her goodbye. Pain coursed through him. She'd pissed him off, with her insistence they try for another pregnancy despite the risks to her health, and he'd walked out. *Father God, please. Don't let her last memory of me be that one. Not me stalking out on her in anger and self-righteousness.*

His eyes watered and he closed them again. If that was the memory he left her with, it would be his own fault, letting his stubbornness get in the way of their talking. He hadn't wanted to listen, had wanted her to merely agree with him. Now, he faced the very real fact he might die without having a chance to make it right.

With a smothered moan, Williams shifted her head. The stiff spikes of her short hairstyle brushed his throat and dust settled on them.

Tick wiggled his fingers, the tingling of lost circulation moving up his arm. "Williams?"

She groaned, a strained laugh puffing against his shoulder. Against skin. He rotated the joint and his arm scraped along concrete. His shirt was torn. Frustration curled through him. He'd tucked his cell phone in the inside pocket of his suit jacket, which he'd tossed over a chair upon entering the sequestration room. God only knew where it was now.

Probably with his unopened pack of cigarettes.

"Calvert," Williams breathed, with that sound like a laugh again. "S'that you?"

"Yeah." He tried to sweep his left hand along the debris, managed six inches or so, felt nothing but rebar and dust and rubble. "You okay?"

"Not...sure." She shifted against him, pressing a hand against his midsection for leverage. "Stuck. Can't move. Shit, it's dark."

"Hurt anywhere?"

"Don't know. I can't...Calvert, I can't feel anything below my waist." Panic flooded her choked voice. Her nails dug into his abdomen. "Why can't I feel anything?"

"I don't know. But, don't move, okay? If you're injured, we don't want to make it worse." He flattened his hands, feeling along the surface beneath them. Marble, covered with dust. A fallen wall? The floor maybe. "Just be still until they come for us."

She subsided, breath coming in panicked bursts against his shoulder. He stretched his left hand, the muscles along the top of his shoulder protesting. His fingers brushed human flesh—a hand, long slender fingers, a ring. Wet and not moving. Gritting his teeth, he slid his hand farther.

And touched protruding bone. Nothing beyond that.

He squashed the scream that pushed up in his throat.

An engine kicked over above them, at a distance to his right. The noise filtered through the rubble, vibrating into him. Not a jackhammer. A generator maybe? A crane?

Voices, dim and far away.

Hope surged in his chest. If he could hear them, maybe they could hear him. "Hey! We're down here! We need help!"

Williams moaned, a weak mewl.

"Sorry, Joles," he whispered and gathered oxygen for another shout. "Hey, help!"

The concrete next to his shoulder shifted. The creaking grew stronger. Tick tensed. Above them, a roar and Williams screamed.

Oh, holy hell.

It was crashing in on them again.

Stanton grasped the chunk of stone and tugged. His feet slid on the uneven pile and his elbow smashed into a gap in the debris. Pain shot up his arm and he levered to his feet. His gaze trailed over the huge layers of wreckage.

They weren't getting anywhere. In nine hours, they'd pulled survivors from the mess, but most had come from the western sections of the courthouse.

Most of the dead were lifted from the courtroom wing.

Eyes closed, he rested his forehead on his wrist. Nine hours. Nine hours since he'd looked into Autry's eyes. Nine hours that she'd lain God knew where, and he couldn't find her. Couldn't help her.

He hadn't kept her safe, not after he'd promised to do exactly that. Images of the injured flashed in his head and his stomach cramped when he thought of Autry—hurt, bleeding, in pain. What about the baby? What would happen to her? They needed him.

There wasn't one damn thing he could do but move fucking chunks of rock.

"Reed?" Falconetti's husky voice was subdued and weary. He lifted his head and she extended a bottle of water. Dust smudged her face and tiny scratches marred her arms.

"Thanks." He pushed his mask down and lifted the bottle, drinking even as guilt lashed at him.

Falconetti fiddled with her own bottle, her gaze dull and distracted as she peered out over the rescue site. "Was he in the courtroom? Do you remember seeing him there?"

"I..." He shook his head. His thoughts had been only of Autry, what she was feeling as she prepared to face the jury. "I'm not sure. I didn't look for him."

She nodded, the muscles in her throat flexing. "I just wondered."

A yell came from yards away, where a crane lifted large slabs from the wreckage. Stanton spun, only to see more of the building slide away, crashing to the rubble below.

"Oh, God," Caitlin whispered, blanching. "What if there's someone under there—"

"Don't think about it. We're going to find them." Stanton turned away to tug at the chunk of white marble again. "We will."

As hours passed and daylight faded, he found it hard to believe his own reassurances. The painstaking process dragged on, and with each lifeless victim removed, his heart ached.

"Hey!" One of the Coney firefighters waved wildly from a small pit near what had been the courthouse's southern wall. "I've got two. Alive!"

Autry? Please. Let it be her.

Stanton scrabbled over jagged chunks and lethal spikes of rebar. He joined the firefighter in tossing aside the loose debris. Excited hope jumped under his skin and made him dizzy. As they worked, green fabric came into view. Familiar hunter green fabric, with a golden patch of embroidery bearing a six-pointed star. Stanton dropped to his stomach, peering into the small space.

"Cookie?" He reached in, pressing his fingers against the other man's pulse points. The beat was strong and relief flowed through Stanton.

Cookie's eyelids flickered and a weak smile curved his mouth. "Hey, boss. Been waitin' for y'all."

"How do you feel?"

"Wrist hurts and I really need to take a leak. Other than that? I'm good."

The firefighter was already helping the second survivor from the pit—a woman wearing a multicolored pantsuit, blood oozing from a cut above her eyebrow. She cradled her arm, the elbow twisted at a weird angle.

Stanton met Cookie's pain-blurred gaze. "Think you can slip out?"

Cookie shook his head. "One of my legs is pinned. I don't think it's broken or anything, but I can't move it."

"All right, let's see if we can get you out of there."

He stayed with Cookie while the rescue team cut and lifted the building materials free. After checking him over, a medic tagged his wrist with a green plastic band—injured, but not serious or life threatening.

Once Cookie was off to have the wrist evaluated and the gash on his leg stitched, Stanton attacked the rubble in the area with renewed hope and conviction. When he'd walked out of the courtroom, Cookie had been standing right behind Autry. He didn't remember the blast, but if they'd been that close, she had to be near.

She had to be.

He was struggling with yet another slab of marble when another yell, this one more subdued, came.

"I've got a body."

As Will Botine picked his way through to the location, Stanton turned away. He'd find her before it was too late. He would.

Botine and the officer who'd found the body conferred for a moment, voices rising and falling in the evening air. One word stood out to Stanton, sent his heart to a screeching halt.

Holton. He'd heard Botine say Holton, and suddenly, Stanton's lungs refused to work.

Pushing up from the area where he'd been working, he headed for Botine as fast as he possibly could.

Caitlin splashed lukewarm water on her cheeks and pushed her dusty hair away from her face. Tears scalded her eyelids and she sucked in the urge to cry. She covered her eyes and blew out a long breath.

My God, she just wanted him back.

She bit her lip, until metallic blood flowed against her tongue. She wanted to keep hoping, but clinging to positive thoughts grew more difficult with each lifeless form discovered. The survivors numbered fewer and fewer as the hours wore on, and even though she tried to tell herself that in other situations—earthquakes, other explosions—rescuers had located victims alive days later, her heart froze in agony each time someone called for a body bag.

"Falconetti?"

At Taylor's tentative tone, she turned, schooling her features into her bureau facade. He tugged his mask down to lie about his neck, and when she glimpsed the sympathy in his ebony gaze, her chest contracted. "What?"

"They want you to come take a look at a...they want you at the morgue."

She closed her eyes, all oxygen whooshing from her body in a soft moan. She nodded.

"I'll go with you," he said, his voice quiet and firm.

Making the two-block walk to the makeshift morgue took sheer will, forcing one foot in front of the other. With each step, memories beat in her head—the cocky young lawman she'd first met at Quantico a decade ago, the confident man who'd slowly won her trust and convinced her to take a chance on loving him, the cherished husband she lived for.

It wasn't long enough. She'd only loved him a few months— not nearly the seventy years or so he'd promised her.

She sighed, a shuddery sound bordering on a sob. Taylor glanced at her. "I'm sorry, Falconetti."

"Not now, Taylor." If she thought about what she was about to do, she'd lose it completely. One foot after the other. One more memory to catalog. Maybe the last memory.

The backdoor slamming shut behind him so hard the glass rattled, his truck firing to life. She'd glared at the door, anger and pique twisting through her.

Oh, that couldn't be it. That couldn't be the last moment between them.

At the two refrigerated trailers, GBI personnel worked at tagging bodies, rezipping bags and transferring them to the shelves inside. A line of bags waited, gaping open. Caitlin's stomach rolled. Was he inside one of them?

No. She shook her head. Those dark, compelling eyes, closed forever? She wouldn't believe it.

A slim woman stepped forward, concrete dust marring the smooth pecan tone of her skin. Her eyes darkened with sympathy. "Falconetti, I'm sorry to ask you to do this."

Caitlin glanced at her. She knew her; Tick had introduced them a few weekends ago at some political fundraiser. Agent Price, GBI. "Where...?"

Price gestured toward a body bag at the far end of the row. Caitlin frowned. The ends lay flat, only a small bulge in the middle. Horror filtered through the numbness.

"The...the remains aren't complete, but there are some personal effects..."

Oh, God help her. Not complete? Nausea roiled in her belly.

Dimly aware of Taylor at her side, she followed Price down the long line of black vinyl bags. At the last, Price leaned down, lifted a tattered, scorched piece of charcoal fabric. Black dots danced at the edges of Caitlin's vision, her breath growing short. Another memory flitted through her mind, that gray suit flattering the lean line of his body, moving with his loose, easy stride.

Price slid a small silver square from the remaining pocket. His cell phone. Caitlin closed her eyes and turned away, teeth tearing into her lip. Behind her lids, she could still see the bright yellow SpongeBob sticker his niece had stuck on the phone during Sunday's church service. He'd fussed later because he couldn't get it off.

Dipping her hand into the pocket again, Price withdrew a pack of cigarettes. The unopened cellophane crinkled under her touch, and Caitlin covered her mouth, holding back a horrified laugh. How many times had she nagged him about those things, told him one day they'd kill him?

"There's a wedding ring and a watch. We haven't removed them but if you want to wait until—"

"No." In order to believe, she had to see.

Price leaned down and widened the bag's opening. Caitlin held her breath and leaned over.

Charred flesh—layers of black, white and ash gray. An exposed rib where the muscle had burned away. Her stomach pitched. Against the curled fingers, a dull glint of gold. A wide wedding band, with a distinctive coin edge.

She clutched her stomach and bent double, gasping. Taylor grabbed her arm. "Breathe, Falconetti. It's okay. Just breathe—"

"It's not him," she said, her voice a torn whisper. "That's not his ring. It's not him."

"Are you sure?" Price sounded relieved.

Caitlin nodded and straightened. She wiped her damp eyes.

"I'm sure. It's not him."

Joy bubbled through her. She tugged away from Taylor's easy hold and glanced at the rubble. Renewed energy surged through her.

For her, at least, there was still hope.

"Botine!" Stanton stumbled over a tangle of rebar; he caught himself from landing on his face. The skin peeled from his arm above his wrist, but he ignored the stinging and scrambled to his feet.

Wiping his brow, Botine straightened. Above his filter mask, his eyes were dull, his face drawn. "Reed."

Stanton slid down the slight incline to the depression where Botine stood. The sheet-draped figure lying in the rubble inexorably drew his gaze. His throat closed and he cleared it with a rough sound.

"Who is it? I heard you say Holton—"

"It is." Botine pinched the bridge of his nose and wiped his eyes. "Do you believe this—"

"Which Holton?" Stanton scrambled across the jagged hunk of marble and reached for the sheet. "Is it Autry?"

He flipped back the white fabric and looked into blue eyes, fixed, vacant, staring. His body sagged.

"It's Virgil." Botine spoke over his head.

It wasn't her. He had a reprieve; he could still hope. Stanton dropped his head. Tremors raced over his body, the shakiness of extreme relief. But her father...when Stanton did find her, she'd be devastated. If he found her before time ran out. He ran a hand over his nape and leaned against the wall of debris behind him, knees weak.

What if it was already too late?

He shut his eyes, throat closed and hurting with a rush of tears. He couldn't do this. The strength to handle the waiting and the not knowing, the constant barrage of images in his head, didn't lay within him. He could take dealing with pain and death when it involved strangers.

But not Autry. Not his daughter.

God, help me. Please. The prayer whispered through his

head, surprising him. He hadn't prayed since before his father had died and he'd been twelve then. *I can't do this alone.*

"Reed?" Falconetti's husky voice, soft and weary, washed over him. He shook his head, fighting off the sob that wanted to claw its way out of him. Her fingers drifted over his shoulder, the contact tentative. "You need to take a break."

He lifted his head, staring at her. "What?"

The tired lines of her face softened, sympathy glowing in the worry-darkened green of her eyes. "You've been at it almost twelve hours. You need a break, some water, something to eat, maybe some sleep."

Sleep, with Autry still under there? Falconetti had lost her mind. He shook off her hand. "I'm fine."

"No, you're not." She straightened. "Neither of us will be until we find them. But you can't keep going like this. Take a break. Ten minutes."

He looked away, his gaze traveling over the yards of destroyed building and lives. Bleak despair tried to horn into his heart and he pushed to his feet. "I can't."

"Reed—"

"I can't. I have to keep looking."

Caitlin shoved her dusty gloves in one back pocket and tugged two bottles of water free from one of the large coolers. Reed wasn't going to stop but at least she could keep him from getting dehydrated.

"You're not listening to me!" The distraught voice carried from the barriers blocking the street and Caitlin glanced over her shoulder at the tall brunette accosting Cookie there. "I can help—"

"And you're not listening to me." His voice calm and authoritative, Cookie folded his arms over his chest, one wrist bound in a fresh, hot-pink sling. "Only authorized personnel beyond this point."

"People could be dying while you're standing here arguing with me." The brunette faced him down with something close to hatred twisting her face. She was casting looks over his shoulder, her gaze then darting to his arm. Caitlin set the water bottles aside. The woman had the edgy look of someone who'd been pushed too far emotionally, and as capable as Cookie was, she might be more than he could handle alone right now.

"Lady, people *are* dying." He sighed, his face softening for a second. "I understand you want to help, but you're not authorized to be here—"

"Who is she, Cookie?" Caitlin stopped beside him.

Cookie slanted an inquiring glance in the woman's direction. She straightened. "Madeline Holton, Jacksonville PD."

"Jacksonville?" Caitlin raised one eyebrow. "You're a long way from home."

Madeline shrugged. "My family lives here."

"Holton." With his uninjured arm, Cookie rubbed his chin. "Related to Autry Holton?"

"She's my sister." Madeline's voice steadied. "Virgil Holton is my father."

Oh no. Caitlin sighed. Cookie half-turned, a look passing between them. Great. She hated family notifications. She jerked her chin at Madeline. "Do you have your creds?"

Nodding, Madeline dug them from her jacket pocket and handed them over. Caitlin took the black wallet and examined the badge and identification. Finally, she nodded at the barrier. "Let her in."

Cookie raised his eyebrows. "You sure? Botine—"

"I'll answer to him." The GBI head wasn't fond of her anyway, so one more transgression couldn't matter much. Besides, the guy had his hands too full right now to worry about Caitlin overriding his authority. "Let her in."

He stepped back and pulled the barrier to the side. Madeline slanted a glare at him and skirted the bright orange wood. She glanced at Caitlin's own identification, dangling about her neck. "Thanks, Agent Falconetti."

"Sure." Caitlin brushed a few loose strands of hair away from her face. "Ms. Holton, there's something you should know."

Madeline stilled, her gaze locked on what was left of the courthouse. Caitlin turned, trying to survey the chaos through the other woman's eyes. Bright floodlights cast huge pools of white on the piles of wreckage. Men and women moved about, their freakishly huge shadows flickering and dancing on the courthouse square. Tramping feet and large machinery had destroyed the thick green lawn.

Arms arrow-straight at her sides, Madeline directed her attention on Caitlin.

"What do I need to know?"

Caitlin sucked in a deep breath. She simply didn't have Tick's or Cookie's finesse for doing this. "I'm sorry, Ms. Holton, but your father's body was recovered a little over a half hour ago."

Madeline's expression turned icy. "What?"

"I am sorry." Caitlin gestured over her shoulder. "Let me take you to the morgue area. You can see him."

"No." Madeline shook her head. "You're wrong. He can't be dead."

"Ms. Holton—"

"He's not dead," Madeline snapped. "He's not." She strode toward the ruined courthouse.

Caitlin followed. With a gentle hand she caught Madeline's arm in a firm grasp and pulled her to a stop. She held the woman's deep hazel gaze. "Believe me, I wouldn't say it if we weren't sure. We have a positive ID. I'm sorry."

The line of Madeline Holton's shoulders moved up and back to a near-impossible straight angle. "Take me to him."

Thirty minutes later, Caitlin slumped onto the curb and rested her forehead on her knees. She was so tired, her muscles trembling with weariness. Her stomach grumbled and twisted, but she'd been unable to choke down any of the sandwich a volunteer had handed her earlier. Milton and Taylor had gone to catch a nap under one of the tents dotting the courthouse lawn and had tried to convince her to do the same. The same way she'd attempted to persuade Reed to take a break before he dropped.

She understood his refusal. Because she couldn't leave Tick. He was here, somewhere, and she wasn't leaving him.

She rubbed her eyes. Earlier, she'd expected Madeline Holton to fall apart once she saw her father's body. The other woman surprised her—she'd stared down at him, blinked once or twice, and then turned away, ready to help search. She'd never uttered a word.

It didn't mean she wasn't grieving. Caitlin shuddered. After the recent miscarriage, she hadn't cried over her lost baby. The searing hurt at this second loss had been too great and the tears wouldn't come.

Tick had cried for both of them.

And she'd pushed him away.

If anything happened to him...she wouldn't have enough tears.

Caitlin rubbed her gritty eyes. She had to get up. Keep looking. He needed her. She pushed to her feet, the world spinning around her. Breathing slowly, she closed her eyes, waiting for the dizziness to pass. A deep breath, another, until everything steadied once more. She lifted heavy lids and pushed her hair from her face.

She turned, making her way back to the rescue operation. Reed worked tirelessly in the rubble, with a determination she recognized because she lived it as well. He paused, wiping his brow, shoulders slumping with dejection. He'd been quiet, not talking to those around him, and that she understood too. The right words to describe the agony of not knowing didn't exist.

One thing was obvious—big, bad, show-no-emotion Stanton Reed was deeply, crazily in love with Autry Holton.

Picking her steps carefully, she joined him and the two GBI agents working with him. The piles of debris didn't seem to be getting any smaller, although truckloads of the stuff were steadily being carted away. She glanced over her shoulder at the parking lot, where the GBI bomb squad and evidence response team worked together, trying to piece together the tragedy.

For once, she didn't want to be in on working the puzzle.

What she wanted was nowhere to be found.

The closer of the two agents shifted a slab of marble and swore. "I've got a hand."

Another one. Caitlin pressed the heel of her palm into her eye. When would this stop?

The agent dropped to his stomach, shining his flashlight into the space beneath the slab. "Hey, there's two intact bodies here." He squirmed closer, trying to get his arm inside the passage. "Can't get close enough to check for a pulse. My arm's too thick."

Reed slid down to crouch next to the agent. "Then they're survivors until we know otherwise. Bag the hand." He tagged the second agent's arm. "Go get a medic."

Caitlin eyed the dark crack between the slab and the rubble below. If they could tilt the slab, she might be able to slip at least her arm and shoulder in. "Reed, think it's stable enough for me to get in there?"

"Are you insane, Falconetti? If it shifted, then we'd be looking for you too." He ran a hand along the edge of the marble. "But the four of us might be able to move this without the crane."

With cautious movements, she edged down beside him. "At least let me see if I can get close enough to check for a pulse."

His mouth a thin line, he nodded. "Fine. But be careful."

She eased by him, a few pebbles of concrete sliding down the slope, tapping away. On her stomach, she stretched an arm inside the space. Her fingers encountered only more rubble and thin air. Levering up, she shook her head. "I can't reach them. Hand me your flashlight, Reed."

He complied and she scooted closer to the opening. The space was tiny and any hope the two were alive dwindled. She played the light over the area. The back of a woman's head, her hand against her ear. No signs of life.

"One's female."

Beneath her, the rubble creaked, an eerie shifting deep in what had been the basement. Her stomach clenched.

"That doesn't sound good, Falconetti," Reed said. "Come on. We'll let the crane lift it off."

"Wait a sec." She wiggled closer, shining the light into the hole again. "I want to see if I can..."

The words strangled in her throat.

The flashlight beam highlighted Tick's face. His eyes were closed.

He didn't move.

Chapter Thirteen

Voices, from a distance, shook Tick from his fitful slumber. A beam of brightness bounced off his eyes, and he shielded them with a hand. "Get that damn light out of my face."

"Tick." Caitlin's reverent whisper, delivered in a choked voice, washed over him. "Oh, thank God. Are you all right? Are you hurt? We're going to get you out, but this slab...we might need the crane for that..."

He closed his eyes again, a wave of thankful tears singeing his lids. Hands clenched, he gulped against the lump in his throat. Lord, he'd always loved her voice, but now it was truly the most beautiful thing he'd ever heard. He opened his eyes again, the weak tears sliding free. He blinked and squinted, trying to peer through the gloom, wanting, *needing,* to see her.

"Cait?" he asked, his own voice emerging as a raspy croak.

A metal flashlight clanged against rock, the beam bouncing around the space once more. "Yes?"

He slid his hand along the floor, seeking the opening, craving her touch. Concrete scraped his palm. "I love you, precious."

"I love you too." Her voice cracked on the words, and he closed his eyes once more, listening to her yell for someone to get him the hell out *now.* A smile curved his mouth, even as a harsh sob shook his chest. He wanted to wipe his eyes, but didn't have enough room to move his left arm to do so and his right remained trapped by debris and Williams.

"Cait?"

"I'm right here."

"Jolie Williams is here with me. She...I don't think she's in such good shape." She hadn't awakened after the second crash, but he'd been able to keep a check on her pulse by twisting his left hand up to encircle her wrist. Each time, he'd found it thready and growing weaker.

"Okay, I'll..." Her words trailed away and male tones filtered down to him. The light disappeared. "Tick? They want me to move. Botine thinks they can cut through the slab quicker than they can maneuver the crane. I won't be far away."

"Okay." He let his head rest against the hard marble once more. A few more minutes. A little longer and he could touch her, hold her. Minutes. That was all.

The sudden whine of a massive saw cut through the silence and he startled. Williams moaned, but he felt rather than heard it. The noise deafened him and the vibrations ran through his body like a shock. His heart accelerated to a painful speed, his lungs constricting. With fear thick in his mouth, he stared up into the darkness, wondering what would happen if they miscalculated. Would the stone fall in on them? What if they cut too deeply and hit them with the saw? Squirming to move his aching arm, he pressed a protective hand over Williams' vulnerable head and prayed.

Once the saw stopped, he listened to rescuers scrambling over the debris, moving chunks aside. He didn't hear Caitlin's voice again, although he strained his ears for it. The concrete shifted, pressing painfully into his shoulder, and he sucked in a yelp. Lord, they needed to be careful. Just his luck to have one of them send a piece of marble crashing into his head moments before he would have been rescued.

The material shifted, a thin line of light appearing above him. Artificial light, the too-bright glow of spotlights. The voices grew closer and more debris disappeared, the crack widening to a hole, then a larger opening. He closed his eyes on a whispered prayer of thanks. They'd been found; he was moments from safety.

The largest piece of the slab moved. Small chunks of concrete rained on him and he turned his face away.

"Damn, son, didn't think I'd find you lying down on the job," Botine's voice boomed above him.

Tick opened his eyes and managed a weak grin. "Took y'all

so long I needed a nap."

Botine hollered for medics and within moments an EMT slipped into the new clearing. She ignored Tick for the moment, her attention concentrated on Williams. That was fine with him—other than being sore as hell, he was reasonably sure he hadn't suffered any major injuries.

"Looks like a spinal cord injury." Urgency filled the EMT's voice. "Possible internal bleeding. Tell LifeFlight to stand by."

Tick's gut twisted. It was worse than he'd feared. Damn it, her body had shielded his from the brunt of the second crash— he knew that. *Lord, please, let her be all right.*

Over the next twenty minutes, he lay as still as possible, while the EMTs prepared to lift Williams from the hole. Finally, they were rushing her toward the helicopter and Botine tugged Tick to his feet. His head spun and he stumbled, life returning with stinging force to his legs and arms.

Once the fuzziness stopped dancing at his peripheral vision, he glanced around, seeking Caitlin. "Where's Cait?"

"Agent Taylor pulled her over to the triage tent to wait for you." Botine cleared his throat. "We...we weren't real sure what we'd find when we got through all that debris. What shape you'd be in and all." His eyes crinkled with a smile hidden behind his filter mask. "She bitched at him the whole time too."

Joy bubbled in Tick's chest. Yeah, that was his Cait. He stepped up onto the next layer of debris and faltered as his legs trembled, the muscles feeling like overcooked spaghetti.

"Whoa." Botine grabbed his arm, steadying him. "Let's go get you checked out."

Picking their way over the piles of rubble took forever, but Tick rarely moved his eyes off the woman waiting for him on the sidewalk, just beyond the orange barriers. He ached all over, every single muscle in his body protesting something, and blood trickled from the wound at his shoulder. But that was all right...he was alive and Caitlin was here, waiting.

Mere feet from her, he pulled his arm from around Botine's shoulders, shaking off the other man's support. Lord, all he wanted was to hold her close, to soak her in, convince himself this was real and not some desperate hallucination.

Two EMTs intercepted him, steering him under a funeral-home tent for inspection. He tried to shrug away, his arms weak. "Guys, come on. I want to see my wife—"

"She'll wait." The first paramedic flashed a penlight in his eyes while the second placed a blood pressure cuff around his arm.

"She will," Caitlin said, hovering at the edge of the tent. Tick caught her gaze, hunger to be near to her beating in his chest.

They cut his shirt away and the first EMT whistled. "Shoulder's gonna need stitches."

Tick never looked away from Caitlin's dark green eyes. "Slap a bandage on it. I'll be fine."

"Check out those bruises," the second EMT said. He prodded Tick's chest with gentle hands. "Any trouble breathing?"

Searing pain shot across his chest and he gasped, but didn't drop his gaze from Caitlin's. "Not until you did that."

"Bruised ribs."

"Guys, I'm fine." Tick shrugged irritably away. "I just need a shower and some food—"

"Let them take care of you." Caitlin tugged at the end of her lank, messy ponytail. "I'm going to see if I can dig up some clean clothes for you."

She slipped away and Tick stared after her, incredible frustration burning through him. Damn it.

The EMT brushed disinfectant over the shoulder wound and the stinging took his breath. He closed his eyes, and when he opened them, Caitlin was nowhere in sight.

Tick stuck his head under the lukewarm spray, trying to wash away the dust and the memories. The emergency showers, in a trailer partitioned into four small bathrooms and usually utilized during trips to hurricane areas, were on loan from a local church, and although the water pressure wasn't the greatest, at least he was beginning to feel human again. Like he'd gone twenty rounds with a superior boxer, but human.

The water stung the open cut on his shoulder. The EMTs

had wanted him to head over to the hospital for stitches and observation, but he wasn't having any of it. Not when Autry and God knew who else was trapped in there. Not when he was on his feet, able to help.

Alive. He closed his eyes, welcoming even the harsh bite of shampoo and soap hitting the gash. Every sensation, painful or pleasant, proved he'd survived.

Rinsing away the last of the soap, he shut off the water and reached for one of the thin towels. Water continued to run in the adjacent shower unit.

He wrapped the towel about his waist and glanced in the mirror. Tiny cuts marred his face and neck and he had a hell of a bruise forming on his jaw. At his ribs, large contusions were red and angry. He ran a hand over his chest. That was gonna hurt tomorrow.

The door opened and Caitlin eased inside, a bundle of clothing in her arms. She met his gaze in the mirror, her eyes wet. "You wouldn't believe what I had to do to get—"

Spinning, he jerked her into his embrace, mouth covering hers. She moaned and wound her arms around his neck, the clothes dropping about his feet. Pressing closer, she opened beneath him and he plunged his tongue between her lips, ravenous for the taste of her. They clung, her palms sliding over his back and waist in desperate caresses. Assuring herself he was real. He knew it because he was doing the same thing, roaming from the small of her back to her hips, along the curve of her waist to her ribcage.

Hungry, he explored the familiar depths of her mouth, drinking in her dark taste. Her hands moved lower and the thin towel joined the clothes at his feet. She clutched his hips, fingers digging into his flesh when she surged tighter against him. He squeezed his eyes closed, fighting the tears that lay too near the surface.

His lungs ached and he slid his mouth from hers, trailing kisses over her jaw while he caught his breath. With the sweet, salty smell of her filling his senses, emotion squeezed his throat. "Cait, precious, I was afraid I'd never see you again."

Arms about his waist, she turned her head and sought his mouth. "I love you." Her hoarse whisper feathered across his lips. "I thought I'd lost you..." She brought her arms up, hands tangling in his wet hair. A husky laugh puffed against his throat and she pulled his head back so she could meet his gaze. "Don't you ever scare me like that again."

He stared at her and slipped his hands beneath her T-shirt, rubbing his thumbs over her spine. Even coated with a layer of dust and dried sweat, her skin remained the softest thing under his touch. With his tongue, he moistened lips dry and chapped, still able to taste her.

"I'm sorry," he said, his throat so constricted that even the torn whisper hurt. Having her close wasn't soothing the need in him. He wanted her closer, wanted everything. He needed *her.* "About this morning. About the baby and—"

"Don't." She wound her hands tighter in his hair. "You don't have to. I should have listened to you, talked to you. All I could think about while...while you were down there..."

Her voice broke and he lowered his head, kissing away the pained words.

"Shh. Hush," he murmured against her lips and nuzzled her temple. She urged him nearer and found his mouth, her kiss full of the same wild need he couldn't shake.

"Touch me." She whispered the words into his mouth, hands tugging at his hair. "I need to feel you, Tick. Make me believe it's real."

The need arrowed into his gut and he ran his palms under her shirt and up her sides, cupping the firm curve of her breasts. Her deep moan of relief rewarded him and he let the craving take over.

Breaking their kiss, he fisted the edge of her T-shirt and yanked it over her head. Gaze locked on hers, he tossed it aside. Want and desire settled in him heavily, but this went beyond passion or even making love. This had more to do with claiming and being claimed, assuring themselves he was alive and they were together once more.

Still watching her, he didn't bother with the clasp on her bra, but jerked it over her head as well. He pulled her into his arms, chest to chest, skin against skin. His shoulder protested the movement, but he ignored the discomfort. All he wanted was her.

She buried her face against his throat, mouth and tongue

moving over his skin, sending tingles racing over his nerves. When she touched him, hands skimming over his ribs, down his hips and finally around his erection, he groaned. His knees wobbled and a rough laugh escaped him.

She stroked him, sensation shooting through him, and he reached for her wrists. "It's too much." He kissed the sensitive skin below her ear and released her hands to fumble with the button on her jeans. "I need you."

With a soft laugh, she pushed his fingers away. "You've got me. You always have."

The rasp of her zipper filled the sudden silence left by the shower next door stopping and sent urgency zinging through him. He shoved the denim out of the way, taking the delicate silk of her panties with the jeans. Smothering her mouth with his again, he lifted her to sit on the edge of the cheap vanity. His heart thudded and sensations skittered through him with each touch, each kiss, each sigh.

He ran his hands along her thighs, long, lean muscles quivering under his caresses. His mouth left hers to nip kisses along her jaw, down her throat, and he slipped a finger between her legs to find her ready for him. His turn to moan, the overriding urge to be inside her, to prove to both of them he remained, wringing the sound from him.

"Holy hell, I love you." Speaking hurt, his ribs aching, but the only things that mattered were her, in his arms, and being alive.

"I want you," she murmured, teeth scraping his throat. "I *need* you, to know this is real, that you're here."

Her words jolted through him and he spread her thighs wider. She pulled him closer and he plunged inside with one swift, even stroke. She gasped, the tiny noise loud in the small room.

"Shh." He chuckled against her mouth and pushed into her, reveling in the snug grasp of her body. He supported her with one hand, pulling her into his thrusts, and cupped her face with the other, kissing her.

The plastic basket holding toiletries tumbled to the floor. Caitlin leaned back and wound her legs about his hips. Her nails bit into his scalp, and the slight pain joined the unbearable pleasure swirling in his body, pushing him closer to the edge.

"Harder." She urged him closer. Sweat trickled down the side of his neck, his hair tumbling onto his forehead. She pressed into him, her eyes sliding closed, breath coming in small pants. "All of you."

"Open your eyes. Look at me."

She obeyed, the green irises black with wanting, and he felt the first of the tiny contractions within her. Her lids lowered and she bit her lip. "Tick, I—"

"Look at me." He rasped the command, fighting back his own climax.

Her lashes lifted and he pushed higher, harder, staring into her eyes. Her body pulsed around him, back arching. "Tick—"

He caught her harsh cry with his mouth, plundering hers in rough strokes. His stomach contracted, lungs threatening to burst, ribs on fire. The tension exploded and he thrust deeper, spilling within her.

Gasping, he rested his forehead against hers and waited for his heart to slow down. She kissed his jaw, running her fingers over his back in slow, easy caresses. "I don't want to stop touching you. The whole time, all I could think of was how I didn't want it to end with this morning between us—"

"I know." He brushed his mouth over hers. "I know."

She scored her nails lightly down his spine. "We've got to get back out there."

"Yeah." He closed his eyes, inhaling their mingled scents. Reality could wait one more moment for them, though. He'd waited a lifetime today for her.

A hard, swift knock at the door stiffened his body and he jerked, gaze flying to the doorknob to make sure it was locked.

"Tick?" Cookie's voice held genuine concern. "You all right? You've been in there a while."

Caitlin buried her face against his throat, her silent, strangled laughter vibrating through him. Tick swatted her butt and cleared his throat. "Yeah. Cait brought me some clothes. I'm getting dressed."

"Oh. Wondered where she'd disappeared to." Even the door

didn't diffuse Cookie's wicked glee. "So she's with you?"

"She is." Tick sighed. "We'll be right out."

Cookie laughed. "Take your time."

His footsteps faded down the hall, the trailer vibrating slightly as he slammed the exterior door.

Tick glanced in the mirror over Caitlin's shoulder and grimaced. His hair stuck out in fifteen different angles. A slight film of sweat had dried on his skin, leaving him sticky. "Damn, I need another shower."

Caitlin's husky laugh wrapped around him. She kissed his collarbone. "I thought you might. That's why I brought my clothes along, too."

He chuckled, the rumble in his chest a warm relief after the day's fear. "Oh hell, Cait, I love you."

Under the funeral-home tent making up the makeshift command center, Stanton slumped in a folding chair and tried to pay attention to Botine's rundown of where they were. The constant noise of the rescue and his own exhaustion made his ears buzz, and his lids felt weighted, slipping down over his gritty eyes whenever he relaxed his guard.

"The current number is forty-three confirmed dead. Seventeen injured. Luckily, only half of those injuries have been critical." Botine cleared his throat. "We're estimating over a hundred still missing. I don't have to tell you how imperative it is that we find any survivors as soon as possible."

Then hush and let them get back to searching. Stanton leaned forward, pinching the bridge of his nose. Autry remained among the missing. *Why* hadn't he told her he loved her? Why had it been so hard to say? Damn it, if he could only find her...he'd make sure she had the words. He'd shout them for everyone to hear and never flinch. Nothing else mattered.

He'd had everything—Autry, their baby—and he'd allowed his fear to get in the way of showing her that.

No more. If—*when*—he found her, he'd make sure she knew just how damn important she was in his life.

"Stanton?" Botine clapped a firm hand on his shoulder. "It's time you got some rest."

Stanton shook his head. "I'm fine—"

"That wasn't a suggestion, Sheriff. It was an order. Take a break, get some food and some sleep. Two hours minimum before—"

"Agent Botine!" A young city police officer skidded to a stop under the tent. "We've found a major pocket in the east wing. Numerous bodies, but looks like several survivors too."

The east wing. The courtroom.

Stanton shook off Botine's hand and sprinted for the destroyed building. Excitement and fear warred within him, sending his pulse skyrocketing. He scrambled down the miniature mountain of rubble. Voices carried to him.

"God, what a mess. I've never seen anything like it." A firefighter rubbed a hand across his forehead. "They're all jumbled together."

Stanton shuddered. It was true—in the pit newly uncovered, both complete and partial remains lay tangled. They were going to find survivors in this?

They had to.

He had to.

Tugging his gloves from his back pocket, he pulled them on. He'd forgotten his filter mask, but he plunged into the fray regardless. Across the depression, he spotted Tick, moving with the slow caution of someone with sore muscles but also with his customary dedication. Falconetti worked near him.

Over the next half hour, Stanton helped extricate four bodies. A nearby team lifted one of the Ingler boys, critically wounded, from the rubble, and he was rushed to the LifeFlight helicopter to be airlifted to a regional hospital.

"Hey, Reed." Botine picked his way over the chunks of marble and concrete. He extended a plastic evidence bag. "Found it under one of the bodies we just bagged."

Stanton ran his wrist over sweaty forehead and took the bag. A Haynes County Jail identification card bore Schaefer's name and photo. He lifted his gaze to Botine's. "He's dead?"

Botine grimaced. "Had three bodies twisted together, all of them beyond recognition, but sure looks that way. We'll be doing DNA tests and looking at dental records to be sure."

Stanton returned the bag to Botine's hand. He couldn't be sorry Schaefer was dead—the man had brought too much grief to too many people—but all he felt was a gaping emptiness. They'd found Schaefer, Cookie...all had been near Autry. Where was she?

"Stan!" Tick's hoarse shout sent a chill racing down his spine. "Get over here!"

His stomach knotting, he fumbled his way across yards of debris. Tick lay on his stomach, peering into a break in the concrete. Stanton dropped to his knees beside him, his shins aching with the pressure. "What?"

Tick trained his flashlight into the small hole. "I think it's Autry."

The quiet resignation in Tick's voice scared the shit out of him. He reached for the flashlight. "What do you mean, you *think*?"

Tick held on to his end of the light. "She...her face is partially turned away. And there's a lot of blood."

Blood. Stanton closed his eyes and swore. Flattening, he wriggled closer to the opening and shone the beam inside. The first thing he saw was a hand, palm up, slender fingers curled inward. A silver bracelet glinted at the wrist.

His heart stuttered. He'd watched Autry fuss with the clasp on that bracelet in his truck this morning. They'd found her. He focused the light up her arm, to her chest, seeking signs of life. Her torso moved with shallow breaths and he lowered his head for a moment, tears burning his eyes, his hands shaking. She was alive. Thank God.

He lifted his head. "Autry? Baby, can you hear me?"

She didn't respond. Twisting, he met Tick's sympathetic gaze. "Get a medic, now."

Tick pushed to his feet, hollering for an EMT, and Falconetti climbed to the top of the rubble. "I'm going to get help."

Stanton used the light to peer farther into the gloom, fear squeezing his chest. Wood lay across her abdomen, what looked like one of the attorney tables. A chill invaded his body. The baby. Oh Lord, what about her?

He moved the light upward and the sight of blood covering

her face punched him in the gut. He shifted closer, trying to reach through to her. The opening wouldn't allow more than his forearm to enter; her fingers lay just out of reach.

"Autry, sweetheart, it's Stanton. Honey, I'm right here. Everything's going to be okay..." He cleared his throat and brushed at his wet cheeks with the back of his hand. "You're going to be fine."

Within seconds, volunteers appeared from all over and began shifting debris under a firefighter's direction. A medical team joined them, emergency kits ready. As the layers of concrete and marble were removed and her face and upper body came into view, Stanton sagged. The blood trickled from a gash at her hairline, and although it was several inches long, it appeared superficial. The medics moved into place, one checking her vitals while the other began a quick physical exam as the volunteers shifted the wooden table away.

"She's pregnant." He directed the statement at the first EMT. Stanton knelt by her head, staying out of their way, but needing to be near her, to touch her. He stroked his thumb over her wrist, her skin cool to the touch.

The EMTs exchanged a glance. The second EMT ran a hand over her abdomen, testing, probing. The woman glanced up at Stanton. "Do you know how many weeks?"

Stanton nodded, lacing his fingers with hers. "Twenty. Almost twenty-one."

The EMT looked at her partner and reached for a pair of scissors, and as she talked, began cutting away Autry's skirt and stockings. "Start oxygen and get an IV line in. Possible pelvic fracture, appears the membranes have ruptured and contractions have started. We want to move her to the local ER as soon as...oh my God."

Stanton's stomach dropped. "What? Damn it, what's wrong?"

The EMT ignored him, her attention on her partner. "Get a stretcher. Now."

The male paramedic ran and Stanton leaned forward as the remaining medic scrambled into action, getting the IV started, removing materials from her kit. "What's going on?"

The woman lifted her gaze to his and he flinched from the

sympathy there. "Her injuries have obviously triggered preterm labor—"

"They can stop that, right?" Stanton shook his head. She couldn't deliver now. It was way too soon. Even he knew that. "Right?"

"No, I'm sorry. Not this time."

"How do you know?" He refused to give up. Not when he'd finally found her.

"Because when I examined her, I could see the baby's head."

Chapter Fourteen

Stanton rested his forehead against the wall of glass overlooking the emergency center's parking lot. Empty gurneys waited on the sidewalk, proof the hospital expected an influx of injured from the explosion.

They weren't coming.

He closed his eyes. Autry, Tick, Cookie...they'd been among the lucky ones. Most of the people pulled from the wreckage hadn't been. The death toll had risen to almost sixty—a massive number of families affected in the small community. He'd have rather seen every one of those gurneys filled, rather than the endless supply of body bags waiting at the courthouse square.

Autry was alive, somewhere in the maze of the emergency room's cubicles, and he should be relieved, joyful. Instead, fear overwhelmed him, choking every breath. Yes, she'd been one of the lucky ones, but he'd glimpsed the rubber band the EMTs placed on her wrist. Not the green Cookie and Tick had gotten, indicating they were among the walking wounded. They'd snapped a red band on Autry's wrist. Red. Immediate, life-threatening injuries. The fear wrapped tentacles around him again. Both she and the baby could die.

Tick's words pounded in his head.

I can live without being a father. I can't live without her.

Losing the baby would devastate him.

But losing Autry?

If he lost Autry, he'd have nothing.

"Are you Reed?" The female voice held an odd familiarity, something about the rise and fall of the words, although it possessed more of a clipped coastal accent than the slow Southern drawl he'd grown accustomed to.

"That's me." Straightening, he turned. Surprise skittered through him, and he stared. Looking at her was like looking at Autry—the same fall of chestnut hair, the stubborn pointed chin. God, he was hallucinating. He shook off the sensation of drowning in déjà vu. At second glance, the differences were plain—her mouth was a thin, tight line, her hair a shade or so darker, and her hazel eyes were dead, void of emotion.

She looked him over. "I'm Madeline Holton."

"Autry's sister." The sister he'd heard Autry mention once, in some offhand manner, and then she'd refused to speak of her again. He swallowed. "I'm sorry about your father."

"We all are." She folded her arms over her chest and regarded him, her expression cold.

Stanton ran a hand over his nape. "How's your mother?"

"How do you think? She's devastated. She had to be sedated." She lifted her eyebrows. "What happened here, anyway? Wasn't your department in charge of security for the courthouse?"

He blinked at the thinly veiled accusation. For the last fourteen hours or so, he'd been asking the same thing, castigating himself. "I'm sorry, but I can't discuss the particulars with you, Ms. Holton. All information has to go through the GBI—"

"That is such bullshit, and you know it. My father is *dead*, Reed. My sister could be dying and you're handing me the chain-of-command line? Nate said you used to be a Fed and damn if the training doesn't still show."

He smothered a rush of anger. For all he knew, she was attacking him out of grief, out of fear for Autry. Hell, he could empathize. The agony of waiting had him wanting to jump down somebody's throat too. "I'm not heading up the investigation. You should direct your questions to Agent Botine with the GBI."

She narrowed her eyes to dull hazel slits. "Why are you here?"

"Because Autry is."

"And she's so important to you, is that right?" She stepped closer. "Is that why you dumped her when she came up pregnant?"

He definitely heard Nate Holton's slant in her words. His stomach muscles quivered with anger, but damned if he'd get into this here with Autry's sister. Or anywhere for that matter.

"Nothing to say?" An ugly mocking tone made her voice coarse. "You don't deserve to be here. All of this is your fault. If you'd done your job, my father would be alive and my sister wouldn't be here, would she?"

Damn, she was right. He knew it, had known it from the moment he figured out that explosion had nothing to do with a gas main. He didn't deserve to be here. He should be the one in *there*, fighting for his life. Not Autry. Not the baby.

"Stanton?"

At Jay Mackey's harried voice, he spun. Clad in scrubs, the physician hurried across the waiting room. Stanton flinched from his grim expression.

Oh, God.

Madeline stepped up beside him. "How is she?"

Jay slid a glance in her direction, before his gaze met Stanton's. "She's stabilized for now and on her way up to the surgical unit—"

"Surgery?" Madeline's voice emerged an ugly squeak and Stanton repressed an urge to shake her, tell her to shut up and let Jay speak.

"There's some internal bleeding we need to stop." Jay's face tightened further. "She was close to bleeding out from that. If y'all had found her an hour later, might have been too late."

Stanton didn't need to hear that, didn't need to know how close he'd come to losing her forever. "But she'll be okay? What about her head? She was bleeding."

"A fairly superficial cut, but head wounds bleed a lot. We stitched it up and her CAT scans came back clear. That's reassuring. She has some major bruising to her pelvic area, but thank God, her pelvis is intact. Pelvic fractures can be nasty things."

Stanton cleared his throat. Jay wasn't mentioning the baby. Stanton opened his mouth, closed it, sucked in a deep breath.

Jay fiddled with the ring on his right hand. "About the pregnancy..."

The pregnancy. Not the baby. The pregnancy. The air whooshed from Stanton's lungs, like he'd taken a kick to the solar plexus.

"The amniotic membranes ruptured and Autry was in preterm labor when she was found."

"The EMT said she could see the baby's head."

Jay nodded. "She was crowning already. There was nothing we could do to stop the premature birth at that point. We had to deliver. There wasn't even time to get up to the obstetrics floor."

Stanton's eyes burned. Too early. He didn't need to be told how too damn early it was. But he needed something. "And?"

Jay's jaw clenched, his sharp blue eyes sympathetic. "The neonatal team took her upstairs. She's on a ventilator, but her lungs are underdeveloped, and even at its lowest setting, there's the risk of blowing out one or both of them."

"So the prognosis is what exactly?" Madeline's brittle voice cut through him like shards of glass and dislike bristled in him. They were talking about his daughter and she was throwing around words like *prognosis*.

Jay glanced at the floor. "The reality is we're saving smaller and smaller babies every day, but she's a preemie below the threshold of viability." He looked up, meeting Stanton's gaze. "I'm sorry, Stan, but even with the ventilator, it's just a matter of time. The neonatologist is going to tell you the same and he's going to need you to make some decisions—"

"I'm Autry's next of kin," Madeline said and once more Stanton resisted the urge to tell her to shut the fuck up and get away from him. "He has no legal right to make those decisions."

"Actually, he does." Jay shifted his gaze to her and Stanton got the idea he was enjoying this single part of the conversation. The doctor slanted a slight smile at Stanton. "Autry has a medical power of attorney, for her and the baby, on file at Dr. Hampton's office. She changed it last week, giving it to you."

Ignoring Madeline's irritated huff of breath, Stanton closed his eyes and thanked God for once that Autry was such a lawyer about things. He opened his eyes and met Jay's gaze.

"I need to see my daughter."

He'd never seen a baby so small.

Staring down into the incubator, Stanton held his breath. Eyes closed, she lay sprawled froglike. He'd expected her to be curled into the fetal position, like his boys had slept as young infants, but other than her elbows and knees being bent, she lay straight and still. Her chest, ribs visible under her skin, rose and fell with the pulse of a machine. Tiny wires and tubes invaded her body and his stomach turned over.

How much of that could she feel? He didn't want her to hurt. Instead he wanted to touch her, hold her close, protect her.

Love her.

His throat closed.

"What are our options?" He had to force out the words.

"She's too premature to survive. Dr. Mackey has told you that?" The neonatologist stepped forward.

Stanton nodded.

"We can keep her on the ventilator, risk bursting her lungs, and she might live a few days at most. Or remove the ventilator and give her pain medication to make her comfortable for the next few hours."

Stanton closed his eyes. So there were his choices.

Prolong the inevitable. Keep her here and cause her pain.

Or let her go.

Oh Autry, baby, I need you to help me through this. I need you to tell me what I should do.

Opening his eyes, he stared at his baby's face. He stroked a fingertip across a tiny palm and her fingers flexed. She was so perfectly formed—ten minuscule fingers, ten matching toes. She was skinny, not much longer than his hand and fine hair covered her body. Wrinkled and a little red, she looked like a wizened old lady. On her head were dark swirls the same color as his own hair. This was the baby he'd first felt fluttering within Autry's womb only a day ago.

His daughter.

She was his baby and daddies were supposed to do the best thing, the right thing. He swallowed against the massive lump in his throat. His only choice was to do the best thing for her.

"Take her off."

Over the next few minutes, there were forms to sign, matters to tend to, while a nurse removed the ventilator tube and the other wires, leaving only a single IV line in place.

Finally, it was done and he stood over her again, watching the ragged rise and fall of her breathing. He cupped her head, the swirls of hair incredibly soft under his tentative touch.

The nurse approached. "Mr. Reed? There's a pastor here, if you'd like one. He's been with some of the victims' families in the chapel."

Did he want one? From deep in his memory, his father's voice rose, murmuring prayers with him at bedtime. Stanton stroked the baby's head and nodded. "Please."

The man appeared in moments, his face haggard yet serene. "Sheriff? My name is Ed Thurley and I am truly sorry."

Stanton nodded again, unable to speak. He recognized the man—Tick's pastor.

Thurley clasped Stanton's shoulder. "Does she have a name, son?"

Memories flashed in Stanton's head—Autry poring over the baby name book he'd purchased, throwing out wild suggestions and laughing. Finally, they'd tentatively decided without the book, choosing one of each of their grandmother's names.

He trailed a finger down a tiny cheek. "Claire. Jane Claire."

"A beautiful name for a precious little girl." Thurley bowed his head and Stanton followed suit, letting the soft prayer wash over him. His heart hurt. His whole body ached with this loss.

Thurley prayed and read briefly from the Bible. Stanton thanked him before he left and was once more alone with Claire, watching her struggle for breath.

He glanced up at the nurse, across the room tending to another small infant. "Can I hold her?"

Her face softened. "Of course."

She wrapped a blanket about Claire's small body and settled them into a Kennedy rocker, draping the IV line out of the way, before leaving them alone again.

Stanton cradled Claire in his arm, stroking her cheek. Her tiny body jerked, fingers flailing before curling into small fists.

"Shh, Claire," he whispered, brushing his lips over her forehead. "Daddy's got you. Daddy's right here."

He watched her, memorizing her features, the unique baby scent mingling with the harsh scent of Betadine. With one foot, he set the chair rocking and rubbed her back with feather-light touches. He would miss out on so much by not being allowed to be her father, to watch her grow up—guiding first steps, teaching her to ride a bike, letting her cry on his shoulder over her first heartbreak, walking her down the aisle at her wedding.

A tear dripped from his chin and splashed on her foot, but he didn't brush at his wet face. She deserved his tears, his grief, the overwhelming love in his heart.

He lifted her higher, kissed her cheek. "Claire," he murmured close to her ear, "Daddy loves you."

More than he could ever say. More than she'd ever know.

The scent of hospital disinfectant invaded every pore of Stanton's body, until he swore he'd never get rid of the smell. Outside the NICU, down the hall from the waiting area, he slumped against the wall, heels of his hands pressed into his eyes.

He hadn't known it was possible to hurt this much. He should have known, should have realized with the birth of his sons, that this kind of loss hung out there, waiting.

Hell, when it came to being a father, he'd been a loser, a failure. A royal fuck-up. He didn't deserve the boys, didn't deserve the tiny little girl who'd drawn her last breath in his arms.

His Claire.

Oh God, how was he going to tell Autry?

What if Autry died too? What if he lost her?

Suddenly, his legs refused to hold him anymore and he slid

to the floor, a harsh sob raking its way out of his throat.

"Stan." Tick's voice and strong hands lifting him to his feet. "Come on. Let's get out of the hallway."

His legs weak and trembling, Stanton let Tick half-lead, half-carry him to the deserted waiting area.

"I came over to check on Autry and Jay told me I might find you up here." Tick's tone was reserved.

"I had a daughter, Tick." Stanton dragged a hand down his face. "She was *real*. I held her and watched her move. And she's just...gone."

"I'm sorry."

"She's just...gone." He buried his face in his hands, tears dampening his palms. Another sob tore at his chest, shuddering through him. Tick clamped a warm hand on his shoulder and they sat in a silence broken only by Stanton's rough weeping.

Long minutes later, Stanton scrubbed at his gritty face. A sigh heaved through him. "I can't do this, Tick. I don't have it in me."

"Yes, you can. You have to. It'll hurt like hell, but you'll do it for Autry."

Something about the grim, raw proclamation penetrated the mind-numbing grief. Stanton dropped his palms and blinked the blurry film of tears away. Tick leaned forward, elbows on his thighs, hands between his knees, turning his wide platinum wedding band in a slow circle.

"You don't forget and it never quite goes away, but you get through it because she needs you, because as hard as it is for you, somehow it's even worse for her."

They weren't only talking about Claire and him and Autry and they weren't only talking about Falconetti's recent miscarriage either. He'd known Tick too long not to pick up on that.

Tick continued rotating his ring about his finger. "When Cait called you while I was undercover in Mississippi, you remember that?"

"Yeah." That had only been a little over a year ago; Stanton could still feel how pissed off he'd been that Falconetti seemed ready and willing to jeopardize Tick's safety by trying to contact him. But what did this have to do with anything and why was Tick bringing it up now?

"She was pregnant, nearly five months along, and she wanted me to know." Tick cleared his throat, a harsh jagged sound. "A few days after that, this obsessive bastard who worked for her grandfather tried to kill her. He did kill our baby and the fertility issues we're having come from that attack."

Stanton closed his eyes, sure now what that edge he'd been picking up on in Tick's voice really was.

"If I'd known," Tick continued, in a rough near-whisper, "I realize I wouldn't have been there to stop it happening, the attack or her losing the baby. I mean, I couldn't have just hopped the next plane, but afterward...afterward, I'd have known and she wouldn't have been able to keep it from me as long as she did. I'd have been there when she needed me most, wouldn't have let her push me away like I did."

Stanton rested his forehead on his clenched fists, elbows digging into his knees.

"I don't know how Autry will react to this," Tick said. "I never would have thought Cait would shut me out like she did this time around and I guess that means we still have some growing together to do. But I know one thing. Losing a baby like this can make or break a relationship. And as bad as it hurts, you have to get up, dust yourself off and get back in the game. Autry's going to need that from you."

Autry woke to a blanket of numbness. She blinked, trying to clear her fuzzy vision and bring the room into focus.

Hospital. She was in a hospital room. Her gaze traced up the IV tubing leading from her right hand to the half-full bag hanging over the bed. She looked further.

Stanton slept in the chair by the bed, his head tilted at an unnatural angle, arms folded over his chest. His face was ravaged. Why did he look so sad?

Something had happened, something was wrong, but she couldn't remember what it was.

Thinking was too hard, with her brain drugged and fuzzy. Darkness rose at the edges of her mind, and she let it suck her under.

The next time she opened her eyes, daylight filtered in at the window. Stanton still dozed in the chair and she experimented with movement. Her limbs worked, but beneath the painkillers, she still hurt. She frowned. What had happened?

She cast about in her memory for the last thing she remembered...

Standing in front of the jury.

Beau Ingler jumping to his feet to scream at her, at Schaefer.

Jason Harding moving back to escort him from the courtroom.

Her father, his gavel pounding, ringing in the room.

And nothing.

She moaned, frustrated, and Stanton jerked awake. He leapt from the chair.

"Autry? Sweetheart?" He leaned over her, his face haggard, eyes dull.

She moistened her dry lips. "What happened?"

He touched her cheek, his fingers gentle. His Adam's apple bobbed with a swallow. "There was an explosion at the courthouse."

An explosion? She shook her head, scalp stinging with the movement. What was he talking about?

His lashes fell and his mouth tightened. "You were trapped for several hours. When we found you...you'd gone into labor."

The words hit her like stones. Her baby. She moved, explored her abdomen, found it oddly flat and soft. Pain screamed across her skin with the contact.

She looked at Stanton, remembering as if from a dream the infinite sadness of his face, even in sleep, and she knew.

"No." The word slipped from her lips on a moan and she shook her head, closing her eyes to the pain on his face. If she didn't see it, then it couldn't be true. "Oh, no."

A sob broke free on a keening wail that hurt her ears.

"Baby, I'm so sorry." Stanton cupped her face, his voice

near.

Sobbing, she opened her eyes, staring at the ceiling. "Lord, please, no. No, no, no..."

A nurse appeared. "Sheriff Reed, you have to leave now."

"Wait, let me stay with her—"

A burning coursed through Autry's veins and then...

Blessed darkness.

Autry stared at the seascape hanging on the wall. If she didn't think about it, if she just avoided the truth, the pain stayed at bay for longer periods of time. Until her hand brushed her stomach or her mind wandered from the painting and she remembered.

Her baby was dead.

The knowledge cut through her and she drew in a shaky breath, focusing on the painting once more.

Stanton was gone. She wasn't sure how much time had passed since the nurse had shuffled him out before sedating her, but from the angle of sunlight brightening the room, it had to have been hours. Anger boiled in her. How dare the sun come out like that? Didn't it know her daughter had died?

She fisted the covers, her body aching. She welcomed that pain, as it drew her attention from the agony that left her heart shrunken and icy.

On the television, images flickered without sound. The local news, with almost constant footage of the courthouse disaster. A ticker ran headlines and informed her the death toll neared eighty.

Did they include her baby in that number?

The door whispered open and one of the nurses bustled in to check her IV and vitals. The gray-haired woman smiled down at her. "Your mother is outside to see you. And your sister too."

Surprise shivered through Autry. Madeline? Here?

The nurse smiled again. "I'll send them in now."

The first glimpse of her mother shocked her. Her normally neat silver bun skewed, her mama pleated the wrinkled hem of her blouse between her fingers. She stared at Autry, her mouth working, and the tears spilled over. "Oh, Autry. Oh, my baby."

She enveloped Autry in a smothering hug, the IV line tugging slightly, and over her mama's shoulder, Autry met Madeline's cold gaze. Her sister glanced away, her movements tense and edgy, arms crossed over her chest in her "I really need a smoke" stance. Autry swallowed a sigh. Same old Maddie.

Her mama pulled back, wiping her face. "All my babies together again. I just wish..." Her voice broke, but she smiled, the expression forced. "Madeline, come hug your sister's neck."

Madeline rolled her eyes, but moved forward obediently. She leaned down to wrap a cursory hug around Autry's shoulders. "Hey, Autry."

"Hey, Maddie." Autry made herself smile as Madeline tugged free. "I'm glad you're here, but you didn't have to come all this way."

Madeline glanced over her shoulder at their mother, whose eyes welled with tears again. "I felt like I was needed." Her gaze tracked Autry's IV line. "Dr. Mackey says you'll be here a week at least. You're lucky it wasn't worse."

Worse? Than losing her baby? "Where's the baby? I want to see her."

Her mother laid a hand on hers. "Now, Autry, I don't think that's such a good idea."

Autry squeezed her eyes closed. "I need to."

"That's not going to help you forget—"

"Forget? Mama, I'm not ever going to forget." Autry struggled to sit up, pain shooting up her leg, cramping across her abdomen. Stitches, from surgery to repair her bleeding spleen. "Please. Find out where she is. I need to hold her, just once."

Madeline shook her hair away from her face. "Calm down. I'll see what I can do."

Her heart pounding as if she'd run miles, Autry subsided against the pillows. Lord, she wished Daddy were here. He'd smoothed over her mother's prickliness when Miranda had first learned of the pregnancy, when she'd worried about what all her friends would say about her pregnant, unmarried daughter, and surely he'd understand her need to see her baby.

The memory flitted through her mind again, her father's voice booming for order, his gavel banging on polished wood. She stilled and lifted her gaze to her mother's. "Where's Daddy?"

A spasm twisted her mother's face. "Oh, Autry."

"Mama?" To her horror, her voice cracked. "Have they found him? Is he all right? Tell me he's not still in the rubble."

"No, baby, he's not." Her mama patted her hand, tears streaming down her wrinkled cheeks again. "Honey, your daddy's dead."

"He can't be." The words spilled from Autry's lips and she shrank from her mother. "It's a mistake. He can't be dead."

"He is, darling. He is." Her mother leaned forward and embraced her, nails scratching against the too-sensitive skin of her back, even through the hospital gown. Autry stared at the wall over her shoulder. This couldn't be. God wouldn't be so cruel, taking both her baby and her father. No. It wasn't happening. If it was happening, she'd be shaking with the same sobs as her mother. But inside, she simply felt cold, numb.

So it couldn't be true.

The door opened and Madeline entered, accompanied by a nurse pushing a small plastic bassinette containing a tiny bundle of blankets. With a muffled sob, her mother pulled away and wiped her cheeks.

Autry watched as Madeline lifted the bundle and carried it to the bed. Like watching a movie. She shook her head. Her emotions had fled her body and she stood on the outside of everything, a mere observer. She welcomed the sensation, the lack of pain.

"Here she is," Madeline murmured and placed the tiny body in her arms.

Eyes closed, the baby resembled a miniature wax doll. There was no warmth, almost no weight to her, and holding her seemed like just another part of the movie. Autry brushed the corner of the blanket away. Ten fingers. She touched them and found them cold.

"She has Stanton's hair." Her voice sounded cold, matter-of-fact to her own ears, and she looked up in time to catch concern flicker in Madeline's lifeless eyes. "We were going to call her Claire, after Grandma Holton."

Madeline watched her. "Daddy would have liked that."

Autry shrugged and dropped her own gaze back to the minuscule narrow face nestled in the blanket. "He said he was looking forward to having another grandchild."

"He was always a dreamer," her mother said, patting her knee. "An idealist. I always used to think that's where you got it from."

Her father's idealism had driven her mama crazy. Look what her own idealism had done. She sighed, wondering why even the self-recriminations didn't hurt. "Have you seen Stanton?"

"Reed?" Madeline's voice sharpened. "He's over at the courthouse."

Autry nodded, not looking up, fingers stroking the dark hair atop her daughter's head. Of course. Now there was no baby, he didn't need to be here. She could understand that.

Her mama squeezed her knee. "Sometimes these things work out for the best, Autry. You'll see. There'll be other babies, at the right time, after you're married."

Married? Other babies? After this, Autry didn't think so.

"Mama?" Madeline stepped forward, lifted the baby from Autry's slack hold and handed her to the nurse. "You didn't eat anything this morning. Why don't you go down to the cafeteria? I'll be right there."

"All right." Her mother leaned forward to hug Autry again. Autry raised her arms to return the embrace, her heart a cold, dead thing in her chest. "I love you, baby."

"You too, Mama."

Madeline waited until the door closed, leaving them alone, to speak. "Mackey says you'll need some time to recuperate. You should come back to Jacksonville with me. This place is poison, Autry, believe me."

Having Madeline of all people offer to take care of her should have shocked the hell out of her, but the whole world was upside down. "I'll be fine. Like Mama said, sometimes these things happen for the best...but I'd appreciate it if you'd ask

Stanton for my things from his house."

"I'll do that." Madeline waved toward the door. "I'd better go check on Mama. For what it's worth, Autry? Reed looked like someone had kicked him in the balls when they told him about the baby. Having that ventilator removed was probably one of the hardest decisions the guy ever had to make."

The sun was setting when Stanton finally made it to the hospital again. The state bigwigs from the GBI, not to mention a handful of his former colleagues from the FBI, had corralled him in an interview, wanting his initial impressions of the explosion. The nurse who'd kicked him out of Autry's room when she became hysterical had assured him she'd sleep for most of the day.

Having to leave her after witnessing her grief had broken his heart.

All day, he'd ached to be with her, to hold her, to share her grief, and maybe find relief for his own.

He'd begun to think he was never going to escape from the duties that kept rising all around him, never going to make it back to her.

Carefully holding the single white rose he'd cut from Mrs. Lydia's yard with her permission, he eased open the door to Autry's room. The room's only illumination came from the fluorescent light above the bed, but that was enough for him to see Autry lay awake, staring at the ceiling. Warmth gathered in his chest, driving out for a moment the chill of loss and horrors that had surrounded him the last two days.

He let the door close behind him. "Autry? Sweetheart?"

She looked at him and his heart stuttered. Her eyes were as lifeless as her sister's. She dropped her gaze to the rose in his hand. "Is that supposed to make up for her being gone?"

Unease gripped his chest. "Autry—"

"How could you let them take her off the ventilator?" Her shaky voice hit him like a body blow. "How could you let her die?"

He shook his head. Surely she didn't think that. She had to understand he'd done what he had to do, what was best for their baby. "Is that what you...Autry, baby, no. It wasn't like

204

that—"

"Why are you here?" She narrowed her eyes, blue glittering slits of pain. "Guilt?"

Stanton swallowed. His worst fear was coming true. He'd lost Claire and now he was losing Autry, too. Only this was far worse than he'd imagined. "Because I love you."

She laughed, a harsh, ugly sound. "Oh, now you love me."

"Autry, please don't do this."

"Don't do this? Don't *do* this?" Her voice rose, cracking on a brittle note. "My father is dead. My baby is dead. Because some maniac got around your security. You let this happen. You told me everything would be all right and I believed you. I believed you and you let this happen."

Thinking it himself was one thing. Hearing Autry say it was worse. "Autry, please—"

"I want you to leave."

"You don't mean that."

"I do. I can't handle you right now." She turned her face away. "I want you to go."

Chapter Fifteen

Juggling two canned Cokes and a pair of wrapped breakfast sandwiches from Midway, Tick nodded at the GBI agent manning the roadblock barriers and headed for the courthouse square. The thudding repetition of diesel motors and air compressors cut through the early morning. Although the eastern sky lightened, the sun wasn't quite up and spotlights cast artificial brightness on the ruined building. During the night, the temperature had dropped with the arrival of a cold front and frost dappled what grass remained.

Rescuers swarmed over the wreckage still, although they'd not had any new survivors since shortly after two in the morning. The bodies were still coming, nevertheless, and every call for a body bag turned his stomach with another stab of guilt.

They'd been snowed by Schaefer, turned the murdering bastard loose on the county.

And it didn't take a rocket scientist to figure out this disaster was linked to his trial.

He ducked under one of the funeral-home tents that lined the street. Most of the cots beneath the tent were empty. On one, Demetrius Taylor, Caitlin's partner, lay with an arm over his ear, snoring. A couple of city officers dozed as well, faces and clothing streaked with dust and dirt.

On the cot in the far corner, Caitlin slept on her side, duty jacket pulled tight around her, head pillowed on what was left of his charcoal suit coat. He'd had a hell of a time getting her to take this break and catch a couple of hours of rest. Careful of his hurting ribs, he eased to sit beside her. He set the cans on the asphalt, balanced the sandwiches atop them and shifted so he could see her sleeping face.

Her chin was bruised around an angry scrape. He smoothed back disheveled hair and bent down to brush a kiss over her cheek. "Cait?"

Her eyes flickered open and a sleepy smile curved her full mouth. "What time is it?"

"A little after seven." He continued to stroke her hair, sifting his fingers through the thick strands. "Botine wants to debrief at seven-thirty."

She nodded, lashes fluttering down for a second before she blew out a long breath and shifted to sit cross-legged facing him. With gentle fingers, she touched his bruised jaw. "How do you feel?"

"Like I got hit by a Mack truck. Brought you breakfast." He reached down and snagged one can and its waxed-paper-wrapped cargo. Once his hands were free, he dug in his jacket pocket for the red-foil-wrapped squares there. "And dark chocolate."

"Thank you." She angled in to kiss him then pulled back, wrinkling her nose. "You've been smoking."

He popped the top on his own can. "Do you blame me?"

"No."

He smiled at that and they ate in silence broken only by the sounds of machinery, the low hum of the searchers' voices and Taylor's occasional rasping snore. After he'd eaten his sandwich and half of hers, he rolled the wrappers into thin cylinders and dropped them into his empty drink can. He reached for her hand, rubbing his thumb over her wedding rings.

"I love you," he said in a fierce whisper.

"I know. I love you too."

Still holding her hand, he looked away. Stanton was in the rubble once more, working with tireless dedication despite the grief and exhaustion ravaging his face. Tick didn't think he'd said two words to anyone since he'd come back from the hospital that last time.

Swinging his gaze back to Caitlin's green eyes, he leaned forward. "I can be a stubborn ass when I want to be."

207

"No." Her fingers tightened around his. "I never noticed that."

"I'm serious." He tugged on her hand, pulled her toward him. "The idea of losing you scares me. I want a baby with you, but not if it means endangering you."

"I want to have your baby. Our baby." She held his gaze, her murmur as ardent as his had been. She rested a finger against his lips. "One more try. Just one."

"One." He cradled her chin, careful of the contusion there. "And then we consider adopting."

She closed the distance between them, taking his mouth in a sweet kiss to seal their bargain.

"Falconetti, if you get pregnant again," he muttered against the corner of her lips, "be prepared to have me all over you for the duration. I don't plan on letting you out of my sight."

She turned her head to kiss him again. "Oh, Calvert, I like the sound of that."

"Our official death toll stands at eighty-seven." Botine glanced over his shoulder at the decimated courthouse and cleared his throat, an abrasive sound that grated on Stanton's already strained nerves. "We expect it to go higher. The reconstruction team says we've got melted plastic, a red polymer. Initial tests indicate diesel fuel residue."

"Diesel and fertilizer?" A hand over his ribs, Tick shifted on the chair next to Stanton's.

Botine nodded. "Could be. No timing device has been recovered as of yet."

Stanton caught the look Tick slanted his way. He had no doubt what was tumbling through Tick's mind—the whys and wherefores of what had happened.

"We're figuring the timing of this was no coincidence."

Tick dropped his head. "You think, Sherlock?"

Falconetti, leaning against the table beside them, nudged his shoulder. "Behave."

Botine rubbed a hand over his jaw. "Stanton? Those notes you sent over to the lab, the ones Autry Holton had received. Think those are tied to this?"

Stanton frowned. His gut said no. There'd been something personal about those notes, the fear they inspired. This explosion...why kill dozens if Autry had been the target? He shook his head. "I don't think so. We're still following up on that case. If there's a connection, we'll find it, but—"

"We won't make it the focus of our investigation," Botine finished for him. He tilted his chin toward Falconetti. "Agent? Any thoughts on the mind behind something like this?"

"Reed's right. It's probably not the same guy sending Ms. Holton threatening notes." She brushed a loose strand of hair behind her ear. Her gaze strayed to the courthouse, rescuers thronging over the rubble in the early morning light. "The letter writer was angry, but his anger was focused on one person. This perpetrator wanted to make a larger statement."

"By killing eighty-seven people?" Agent Taylor, Falconetti's partner, swigged from a bottled water. "That's a huge motherfucking statement."

She fixed him with a look. "The people, the number killed, are incidental to him. He's felt ignored, like an issue of some sort, something important to him, had been brushed aside."

Botine's face hardened. "Well, he has our attention. More than he's gonna want before it's over."

The meeting broke up, officers and agents heading back into the fray. Stanton rested his hands on his knees, gathering his strength for one more go. His head wanted to spin a little, the ground tilting crazily if he stood or moved too fast. Food would probably be a good idea, if he thought he could choke something down without it coming right back up.

Beside him, Tick hadn't risen either, a frown pulling his brows together as he stared at the pile of rubble.

"Tick?" Falconetti paused at the edge of the tent, pulling on her gloves. Taylor loomed behind her.

Leaning forward, Tick shook his head, his gaze trained on the destruction. "You said a statement."

"Well, yes." She gestured behind her, an absent wave of one hand, her eyes locked on Tick. "Terrorist acts usually are. They're meant to provoke a response or to strike out at someone, maybe a group, for some perceived wrong."

Tick shifted, turning his attention to Falconetti. "This

wasn't about Schaefer."

"No." An infinite sadness shifted over her face. "It wasn't."

With a muttered oath, Tick looked away. Irritation crawled along Stanton's skin. He hated when the two of them did this, talked in the damned shorthand that seemed particular to their relationship.

Scowling, he caught Falconetti's shuttered green gaze. "What?"

"Don't you get it, Stan?" Weariness and defeat dragged at Tick's voice. "This wasn't about getting to Schaefer. Someone could have accomplished that with a good hunting rifle. This...this was about us."

The words slammed into him.

About us.

Because of them, because of *him*. Echoes of Autry's accusations, pounding into him. Claire gone, Autry hating him now. All of these people dead, their families devastated.

Because of him, because he'd screwed up.

"Reed?" For once, Falconetti's voice was soft as she addressed him. He ignored her.

He closed his eyes and pushed up to his feet. Time to get back out there.

Tick's sure hands steadied him when he rocked where he stood. "Whoa, Stanny-boy. Man, you have to get some sleep."

Stanton shook him off. "I'm fine."

Tick's reply was a frustrated grunt. His gaze tangled with Falconetti's and she shook her head slightly at her husband. Anger flickered in him. There they went again, the connection pissing him off more than it normally did.

"Come on." He tagged Tick's chest, a little harder than necessary, and Tick sucked a pained breath between clenched teeth. "We've got work to do."

Autry stared out the window. The problem with hospitals was they gave a person too much time to think. She didn't like what kept running through her head, but the more she pushed the intrusive thoughts away, the stronger they nudged.

Who was she now?

Yesterday morning, she'd been Virgil Holton's daughter. She'd been a card-carrying member of the public defenders' network.

A soon-to-be mother, filled with joyful anticipation.

Stanton Reed's lover, falling deeper into that relationship every single second.

She closed her eyes, clenching the sheets. She'd been, if not *sure*, at least hopeful, optimistic, that once this trial was over, she could move forward.

Now...

Now she didn't know anything anymore, except she'd lost both the man who'd shaped who she was and the child she'd wanted. Would they still be here if she'd recused herself from taking Schaefer's defense, if she'd given in to her own unease? She pressed her lips together against an anguished moan and a wash of overwhelming guilt.

What kind of daughter, what kind of mother, was she?

"Hey." A light tap at the door followed Stanton's quiet greeting and her eyes snapped open. Lord, please don't let what she felt show on her face.

She eyed him, standing just inside the open door, his stance uncomfortable. Under a dark layer of stubble, his face was worn, his eyes dull and shuttered. Her stomach clenched. He seemed a stranger to her, even after everything they'd shared.

She swallowed. "Hey."

He hefted the overnight bag in his left hand. "Some of your things from the house. I thought you might need them."

"Thanks." She didn't know what to say to him. Surely she should know what to say? She pleated the sheet between her fingers, wishing he'd go so she wouldn't have to struggle for words.

He moved forward and set the bag on the vinyl chair in the corner. He darted a quick glance at her. "How do you feel?"

Talk about a question open to millions of interpretations. She brushed a hand through her hair, lank despite her mother washing it to get rid of the blood, dust and debris, and went for the easy one. "A little sore."

He shifted from one foot to the other, looking as awkward as she felt. His gaze trailed over her face. "You look good."

Before, she'd have laughed and called him a liar. Before, she'd have relished his presence. Now, she wanted him gone, wanted to be alone. She laid a hand over her abdomen, the stitches burning. "I'm tired."

His gaze dropped to her midsection, and pain flickered in the hazel depths of his eyes. "Autry, I—"

"I'm sorry about before." She rushed into the apology, desperate to keep him from mentioning the baby. His pain she couldn't handle right now. "I was unforgivably rude."

"Rude." He laughed, although it held no humor, and rubbed a hand over his mouth. "Is that what you call it?"

This was too hard. Couldn't he see that? "Stanton..."

He fixed her with a look. "I didn't have a choice about the ventilator. She was too small." His lashes dropped, his jaw clenching. His voice roughened. "I did what I had to."

A scream pushed up in her throat and she smothered it, forcing herself to use an even tone. "I know, and I'm sorry for what I said to you. I shouldn't have—"

"No." His eyes opened, no glimmer of emotion in them. Nothing. Just...dead. Autry shuddered. She knew how that felt. "You have a right to your feelings, but I need to know where I stand with you."

She didn't miss the question in the quiet words. With a deep breath, she looked away. "Do we have to talk about this now? I really am tired."

"You're right." His expressionless voice fell flat between them. "I should go. But Jarrod O'Shea may come by to see you."

Jarrod? Why would Jarrod come to see her? She frowned at Stanton before it sank in. O'Shea and Willis Funeral Home. Of course. She brushed at her hair again, her throat tight. "Oh. Okay."

Stanton jammed his hands in his pockets. Her gaze followed the long angry scrape on his arm. A huge purple bruise spread over his elbow. His throat moved in a swallow. "Whatever you want to do, I'll go along."

Tears hurt her eyes and she blinked. "I don't know what I want."

He cleared his throat. "If you'd rather, I can handle the arrangements."

She sucked in a shaky breath. "I think I'd like that. I'm just not...I don't think I can do it."

"Then you don't have to." His voice lowered to a gentle, caressing tone. "I'll do it."

"Thank you." She darted a look at him and glanced out the window once more. "Lord, I'm tired."

"I'll go." His footsteps whispered on the tile floor. "Goodbye, Autry."

The door clicked closed.

He'd lost her. Resting his head against the file cabinet, Stanton rubbed at his eyes. Ever since leaving Autry, he'd tried to shift gears, to focus on getting the sheriff's department set up in temporary housing. He'd hoped the physical exertion of moving furniture would help. Instead, his mind wanted to dwell on that conversation with Autry, with her withdrawal.

He'd never seen her without the life and spark that had drawn him to her. Like inside, she'd died too. He ached with the need to hold her, to take away the pain she was holding at bay.

He was the last thing she wanted. She'd barely been able to tolerate having him in her hospital room earlier. He'd felt it, seen it—in her eyes, her face, her nervous demeanor.

"So what are you going to do?" Tick dropped a banker's box of files next to the door.

Stanton dusted his hands, stepped back from the cabinet. "About what?"

"About Autry."

He shot a glance in Tick's direction. The other man leaned against the door, arms folded over his chest, an intent expression on his bruised face. "What can I do, Tick? She's..." Stanton shook his head. "It's over between us. I can see it in her eyes."

Tick's mouth thinned. "She's been through a lot."

"Don't you think I know that?" Anger simmered along

213

Stanton's nerve endings. "I don't want to make it any harder for her."

"So that's it. You're giving up."

Stanton blew out a frustrated breath. "I have to think about what she wants. Right now, that's not me."

Tick gave him a disbelieving look. "What about what she *needs*?"

"Same difference."

"Like hell it is. Damn, Stan, how can you be so stupid where women are concerned?"

"And you're an expert, right?"

"Smart enough to know there's a difference between needs and wants. Maybe if you'd gotten what Renee needed, she wouldn't have wanted to sleep with someone else."

The anger boiled into fury and Stanton took a step forward, hands clenched. "You son of a bitch."

Tick rolled his gaze heavenward. "Yeah, whatever. So tell me this. What do *you* need right now?"

Stanton froze. The anger drained away as the words pounded in his head. What did he need? Autry, plain and simple. He needed to hold her, to let her nearness soothe the awful gaping emptiness of having a child...and then not. He needed to share his grief with the one person who could understand it best.

Autry wanted him gone.

Maybe she needed him near more.

He tugged off his gloves. "Listen, think you can handle this? I'm going back over to the hospital for a while."

A grin quirked at Tick's mouth. "All this furniture? Sure, Stan, no problem. It was only half a building that fell on me."

"Get Troy Lee to help you. He'll be here later."

Tick grimaced at the mention of the young deputy. "I'd rather do it myself. He'll find some way to screw it up."

"I'll call Ash, send him over here. He's been itching for some way to help and Botine won't let anybody but LE or rescue on site."

"Just get out of here and go get your life in order."

"Autry?"

At Madeline's soft voice, Autry lifted heavy lids. They'd given her a pain medication earlier and she'd finally given in to the drowsiness. She'd welcomed the darkness, the opportunity to forget.

She brushed her hair away from her face and levered up on the pillow. "What time is it?"

"A little after five." Madeline shifted the overnight bag to the floor and settled into the vinyl chair. "You look better."

Better than what? Death? Autry rubbed her eyes. "Where's Mama?"

Madeline's expression contracted. "Home. I finally convinced her to take one of the sleep aids Mackey prescribed for her. She was sleeping when I left."

Autry darted a glance at her sister. "Alone?"

"Lenora Calvert's with her." Madeline looked away, staring at something outside the window for a moment. "What's going on with Nate?"

Autry closed her eyes. She couldn't handle Nate's issues right now too. "What do you mean?"

"He disappeared yesterday evening and hasn't shown back up. Did you know his phone's disconnected?"

No, but she wasn't surprised. Autry sighed. No point in hiding. "He probably tied one on and passed out at home. He'll show up at Mama's when he's hungry or needs his laundry done."

"Where's Helen? And the kids?"

Irritation spiked under Autry's skin. If Madeline was so concerned about the state of their family, why not stay in touch? Couldn't she realize Autry really didn't feel like a game of twenty questions right now? "She left. The divorce was final months ago."

Madeline grimaced. "We've got to do something about Nate. Get him into AA. Help him land a decent job, clean up his act."

"Damn it, Maddie, stop pretending you care. If you'd cared, you'd have been here before now."

Madeline jumped from the chair, pacing to the window with

215

jerky movements. "The only reason I'm here now is because Daddy...you know why I'm here."

The flat words held no trace of remorse. Autry gripped the edge of the sheet. Didn't Madeline care at all that she'd broken their daddy's heart all those years ago? Broken it every day after that by staying away? Didn't she get that Autry hadn't been able to make up for Madeline's defection, even by being all their father asked?

Her stomach turned over. She'd tried, damn it. She'd tried so hard to take that look out of his eyes.

It had never disappeared.

The door opened and a hospital worker bustled in with a cheerful smile and a dinner tray. "Dinner time. Hope you're hungry."

She settled the tray on the table and wheeled it to the bed, adjusting the top over Autry's legs. "I'll be back to pick that up in a little while."

With listless hands, Autry lifted the lid. Chicken, broccoli, mashed potatoes. She popped the top off the plastic beverage cup. In a lazy swirl, steam drifted upward from dark coffee.

Madeline tucked her hands in the back pockets of her jeans. "Doesn't look too bad."

The aroma of coffee hit Autry's senses...and didn't make nausea rise in her throat. Oh Lord. She could handle the smell of coffee again. The reality crashed in and her throat closed, tears rushing to her eyes. She shoved the table away, coffee sloshing over the side of the cup.

"Get it out of here."

"Autry, I know it's hospital food, but you need to eat."

"Get it out of here!"

Madeline pulled the table away. "Autry—"

"Now!" The tears spilled, tearing sobs shaking her chest. "And you go too. Back to Jacksonville or to hell...just go. You wanted out and you didn't care what it did to Daddy or Mama or any of us..." The sobs stole her ability to breathe and she pressed a hand to her chest, over her pounding heart, the stitches in her abdomen pulling with sharp tugs of agony. She welcomed the physical pain, nothing compared to the anguish pouring through her.

She pulled up her knees, muscles aching, and curled against the tearing hurt.

"Autry." Unease hovered in Madeline's voice.

She cried harder, unable to stop now that she'd begun. "Go *away.*"

"What the hell's going on?" Stanton's authoritative tone cut through the room. On a shuddering breath, Autry lifted her head, a blur of tears casting a shimmering veil over her vision. She wiped at her wet cheeks, the uncontrollable sobs still ripping at her. He glared at Madeline and crossed to the bed, arms closing around Autry's shaking body. His scent, warm, spicy, a little sweaty, enveloped her, and she buried her face against his chest.

He stroked her hair. "Autry, baby, it's all right."

"No." She shook her head, the cotton of his polo shirt abrading her cheeks. "It's not. It's real, Stanton. She's *gone.* And Daddy too. *It's real.*"

"I know, sweetheart, I know." He murmured the words against her cheek, the bed dipping with his weight. "I'm so sorry."

She cried in his arms, until the tears were spent, until the sobs were nothing but small, shuddery gasps. He stayed, holding her, whispering endearments and reassurances, infusing her with a strength she didn't have within, until the exhaustion claimed her once more.

Hours later, the murmur of Stanton's voice pulled Autry from her doze. She opened her eyes, the room lit only by the fluorescent light over the bed. Beyond the window, night hovered. Stanton sat in the chair, phone to his ear, scribbling on an envelope.

"Thanks. Bye." He replaced the receiver and stuffed the envelope in his pocket before glancing up. His smile didn't quite reach his sad eyes. "Feel better?"

She passed a hand over her eyes, gritty and sore. "I feel drained. A little fuzzy still."

"Pain meds." He leaned forward, hands between his knees. "Autry, we have to talk. You know that, don't you? About us."

She looked away, nerves jumping in her stomach. "I know." She laced her fingers together, needing something to hold on to. "I know I'm all over the place, Stan—"

"I think you have a right to be," he said, his voice quiet, and she slanted a shaky smile in his direction. "I can deal with it."

"I'm glad you can." She rubbed a hand over her cheeks. "I'm so confused."

"Then talk to me, baby."

Tell him what had been bouncing around in her mind? Face what he'd surely think of her? She sucked in a shaky breath. "You'll hate me."

"Hell, Autry, don't you know I could never do that?" He closed his eyes, opened them, fixed her with a fiery stare. "I'm in love with you."

Panic poured through her and she clenched her hands to stop their trembling. "Don't say that."

He leaned closer, his expression intent. "I am. I should have told you sooner, as soon as I figured it out, but I was scared."

He was scared? He had no clue.

"So why are you saying it now?" she whispered.

"Because I learned there are worse things I should be afraid of." His jaw tightened. "Like losing you."

"You can't say this. Not now. I can't handle it."

"Then I won't say it again until you're ready to hear it." He reached for her hand, rubbing his thumb over knuckles. "But it doesn't make it less true."

She stared down at their linked fingers. "Do you ever think about your decisions? Where you'd be if you'd made different ones?"

"Every damn day." He squeezed her hand. "Honey, you've been through hell in the last thirty-six hours. I'd be worried about you if you *weren't* questioning everything."

She closed her eyes on a wave of tears. "I'm an awful person."

"Ah baby, you're not." Cloth rustled, and the edge of the bed dipped, warm arms enfolding her. "Don't say that."

Lord, she was weak. All she wanted was to stay in his arms, let him shoulder her problems. Just like all her life she'd let her father direct her decisions? She tugged away.

"My father's dead, and I'm thinking about myself, how it affects me. Like whether or not everything I've ever done, I did for someone else. After Madeline dropped out and left, Daddy wanted me to go to law school, so I went. He suggested criminal defense as a specialty instead of family law. He believed in giving back, so I went for the public defender's office instead of private practice."

"If you don't want to continue in defense, don't. You don't have anything to feel guilty for. People's needs, what they want out of life...all of that changes. But you also don't have to make those decisions now. You need to rest, to get well."

She bit her lip. "I'm not sure about you either."

Beside her, he stiffened. "Explain."

Hugging her midriff, she looked away from his shuttered hazel gaze. "I don't know if I wanted you back because I wanted you, or if it was because—"

"Of the baby," he finished for her, his voice reserved. She didn't miss the hint of pain there, though. He rubbed a hand over his knee. "And now there is no baby."

A rough sigh shuddered through him and her chest tightened. "I'm just not sure. I'm such a mess..."

"Listen." He smoothed her hair behind her ear, his touch tender. "You've been through a lot. You're hurting and you're confused. I'll back off; you can have whatever time you need. But don't give up on us, Autry. Not yet."

She looked away. "When Jay releases me, I'm going back to my house."

He cupped the back of her head, tilting her face up so their gazes met. "Are you sure? We haven't found the person sending those notes—"

"Do you think he can hurt me worse than he already has? Blowing up the courthouse, killing my father, our baby?"

"It may not be the same guy. Falconetti seems to think it's not. I'd feel better if you came home with me. You can use the extra bedroom."

A shiver ran over her and she glanced at the darkness beyond the window. What was she more afraid of—the unknown threat or living with Stanton again? "I'll think—"

"Sorry for interrupting." At Madeline's flat voice, Autry jerked. She glanced at her sister, standing just inside the door, two vases of flowers in hand. "I left my purse earlier." She stepped forward. "These were downstairs."

Autry shifted, uncomfortable with her. "Thank you for bringing them up."

Madeline set them on the bedside table and gathered her purse from the window ledge. She slung it over her shoulder. "I'll see you later."

"You don't have to go." Autry made herself smile for Madeline's benefit, cringing a little at the memory of her emotional outburst.

Madeline cast a pointed look at Stanton, who'd risen to his feet, arms folded over his chest. "Oh, I think I should. I'll come by tomorrow."

Autry sighed. "Madeline..."

"You want the cards from these?" Madeline tugged the tiny white envelopes free and held them out. "I'm going to go look for Nate."

"Thanks." As her sister slipped from the room, Autry slid the first card from its covering. A smile tugged at her lips and she held the vellum square up to Stanton. "From the sheriff's department. Tick's handwriting."

He chuckled and took the card. "Which means the others are probably from him and Falconetti."

She checked the envelope while she pulled the card free. "Different florist."

The black block letters jumped out at her and she dropped the square, fear pushing into her throat. She swallowed. No. Lord, not now.

"Autry?" Concern shook Stanton's voice. He lifted the card from her lap. "Oh, shit."

Autry closed her eyes, but it didn't make the words go away. They remained, imprinted on her mind.

I'm still here.

Chapter Sixteen

His department was a disaster.

Stanton frowned at the dispatch report. The radio room was up and running in their temporary quarters, and they were working full rotations again, despite four injured officers and the loss of two patrol cars.

Somehow, they'd missed two calls in as many days. The first, an abandoned vehicle call, a local state trooper had picked up.

The second, a prowler call, from Mrs. Milson, early that morning. Nobody had yet picked up that one. Stanton dropped the report on his desk and rubbed a hand over his nape. Obviously, he needed to tighten the reins. Between attending countless funerals, he'd spent the last few days closeted with Tick and Will Botine's agents, sifting through evidence and scenarios while Cookie oversaw the department's involvement in the ongoing rescue mission. He'd been too wrapped up in other things to fully watch over the day-to-day operations.

He really needed a chief deputy. Tick had taken those duties as they crafted a new department, but Stanton needed him able to focus on the investigative division. He scribbled a note for Lydia to call the newspaper, run an employment ad. After everything he'd had to say to Ray Lewis when he'd phoned to place Claire's obituary, it wouldn't do for him to call. Lewis was after his head, running a series of editorials blaming the sheriff's department for "security lapses" at the courthouse the day of the bombing. In the last he'd outright called for Stanton's resignation.

Linda Winfree

There were times when Stanton wondered whether he should. Quit and go back to the bureau. He rubbed a thumb over the framed photo on the corner of his desk. Hadden and John Logan grinned at him from the candid shot and he'd tucked a small printout of Claire's sonogram in the corner. Were these the same doubts Autry was facing?

She wasn't talking to him. They were having conversations, but those interactions were mere surface talk. Nothing real. Just hi-how-are-you-what's-new kind of stuff.

It was driving him absolutely-fucking-nuts. He wanted to force his way beneath the layers of self-protection she was building, make her see him, push her to really talk to him, confide in him.

And that was the quickest way to lose her he could envision. His daddy hadn't raised a fool and he knew when not to push. What scared him was the insistent little voice that whispered he'd already lost her.

No. Not yet. It wasn't over yet. She'd agreed to keep the relationship on a casual level. Granted, she'd sounded like her old lawyer self at the time and he'd half-expected her to draw up a contract, but that was something. She hadn't told him to get the hell out of her life.

His gaze fell on the phone. The need to connect with her, to hear her voice, was like a physical urge. Even if it was a hi-how-are-you-what's-new conversation.

God, he was a sap.

A sap with no willpower.

The scary thing was he didn't care.

He reached for the phone, punched in the direct number for her hospital room and listened to the rings.

"Hello?" Her voice was breathless, a little husky, and he closed his eyes. His body insisted on equating that tone with making love to her and he shook off the shiver sliding over his nerves. He was in sad shape.

"Hey, it's Stanton. Thought I'd check in, see how you felt today." He rested his head against the back of the chair. Yeah, he was smooth. Like a fourteen-year-old calling the girl he liked for the first time.

"Um, pretty good, actually." Cloth rustled over the line.

222

"Jay said I could go home today."

"That's great. Want me to drive you? I could take off—"

"No, that's okay." She spoke too quickly, the words tripping over themselves. "Madeline's here. She's going to run me home, probably hang out for the afternoon before she heads back to Mama's."

"All right." He suppressed the pinpricks of hurt. Casual. She'd agreed to casual. Not her fault his feelings went a lot deeper than that. The image of those words blocked on that florist card pulsed in his head. He'd tried tracking down who'd sent them, but had run into a brick wall with the harried and overloaded business owner. "And Autry? Be careful."

"I will." Her voice softened slightly.

He cleared his throat. "Mind if I run by this evening?"

"That's fine."

"I could pick up some takeout."

"Um, sure."

Frustration curled through him and he resisted an urge to grit his teeth. Patience. He would be patient if it killed him, but it sure felt like it would. "Great. I'll see you tonight."

"Bye." The line went dead.

He replaced the receiver and pinched the bridge of his nose. This was like beating his head against a wall. He lifted the dispatch report again. Maybe rather than send out a deputy, he'd pick up the slack and go himself.

Because he really needed to get out of the damn office before the walls closed in on him.

Autry let her fingers linger on the receiver, fighting the impulse to call Stanton back and tell him, yes, she'd like him to drive her home.

But letting him come over for dinner was probably muddying the waters enough. She needed some time to stand on her own, take charge of her life, before she allowed him any closer. The last few weeks, with them together—she'd looked upon him as a protector, the father of her baby. She needed to back off, look at him as a man, figure out what she needed from him before they moved forward.

"Ready to go?" Madeline breezed in, her dark hair swept up in a chic, messy knot. An orderly waited at the door, wheelchair ready.

Autry grimaced. "Can't I walk?"

"It's the rule." Madeline smiled, perfectly plucked eyebrows lifting. "You're always the one following the rules, remember?"

"Yeah." Autry rose, the healing incision pulling a little, and walked to the chair. Following the rules, making the safe choices. Where had it gotten her?

Madeline shouldered the overnight bag. "Let's rock and roll."

At the pun, Autry rolled her eyes and glowered at her sister. "You're in an awful good mood."

As they maneuvered down the hall, Madeline chuckled. "Called the department, told them to expect me back Wednesday of next week. The idea of leaving this place always makes me happy."

Autry fingered the stitched seam along the front of the wheelchair seat. "So the funeral arrangements are final?"

Madeline darted a look at her. "Yes. Monday, eleven o'clock."

Autry nodded, looking away as the orderly punched the down button at the elevator. Monday morning. And Monday afternoon, she and Stanton would bury their daughter. She laid her hands over her abdomen. They'd talked about those arrangements last night, in a tense, uncomfortable exchange before he left. A private burial, just the two of them, a few close friends and family.

At least she'd have two days to prepare herself to face the emotional hell that day would be.

Madeline's car waited under the portico downstairs and Autry folded herself into the passenger seat and closed her eyes. The engine revved and Madeline shifted into gear. "I'm surprised Reed wasn't here this morning."

On a sigh, Autry opened her eyes. The restored historic district, with its quirky, trendy shops set in old houses, flashed by. "He offered to drive me. I said no. He's bringing dinner over tonight."

Madeline made a sound in her throat, suspiciously like a snort. "He's a sucker for punishment, isn't he?"

Autry rolled her head on the seat and glared. "What is that supposed to mean?"

"You've told him it's over and he's still hanging around."

"It's not over." Autry shifted, uncomfortable with the conversation. "It's...I need some time to make up my mind about what I want from him."

"Bullshit." Braking for the stoplight at Highway 19, Madeline looked at her from the corner of her eye. "You either know or you don't. You're scared."

She was not. Autry swallowed the denial. "Can we talk about something else, please?"

Madeline waved a hand in the air and swung into a left hand turn. "Whatever you want. Pick a subject. Anything to foster sisterly bonding."

"Like you've ever wanted to bond with me."

"Nice to know you can be something other than perfectly mannered at all times."

Her head ached. Maybe she should have let Stanton pick her up. "There's no talking to you."

"You sound just like Daddy." Madeline's fingers clenched on the steering wheel and she pressed down harder on the accelerator. The little car jumped forward and the chicken plant flashed by, followed by the Coney city limits sign.

"Don't start." Autry tightened her seat belt. "He's dead, Madeline. You won't have to listen to him anymore. Not like you ever did."

"You did enough listening for both of us. And Daddy didn't talk. He handed down dictates."

"That is not true." Autry pushed her hair away from her face, the strands limp against her fingers. "You never quit, do you? He's *dead*, Madeline. Your stubbornness outlasted his. You won. What more do you want?"

"You think I won?" Madeline's laugh was short, disbelieving.

"You're the one who said you'd come home over his dead body."

Madeline paled. "You've conveniently forgotten what he said. You think I have? Him standing at the bottom of those stairs, yelling at me?"

Autry blinked. He had shouted. She'd been fourteen, accustomed to her sister and father's battles, but her reserved father raising his voice had been new, frightening. "I don't remember what he said. I remember the two of you yelling, your door slamming, Mama crying. But I don't remember what he said."

Madeline laughed again, an ugly, cynical sound. "Well, I do."

Autry frowned, trying to focus on the memory beneath the emotions.

If you walk out that door, Madeline, don't bother coming back.

Her daddy's voice, rough with pain, hoarse from yelling, rose in her mind. Autry shot a quick glance at her sister. Madeline drove, fingers flexing on the wheel. "He said, if you walk out that door..."

"Don't bother coming back." A harsh smile touched Madeline's mouth.

"And you didn't."

"What was the point?" Madeline shrugged. "He'd said what he had to say and I wasn't crawling back to be his mindless robot."

Autry turned to watch the pine trees as Madeline slowed to turn left onto River Road. "That's what you think I am."

"Don't put words in my mouth. I *think* you loved him and wanted to please him and maybe you got in the habit of putting aside your own wants and needs to make him happy. And maybe, just maybe, you're afraid the same thing will happen with Reed."

A chill wrapped around Autry's heart. Was that it? Was she afraid of losing her identity to Stanton's?

Madeline threw on the brakes and stopped short of the stop sign at the Flint crossroads. "Fuck."

Autry looked up. "What?"

"We're supposed to be going to your house and we're

halfway to Mama's. Why didn't you say anything?"

Because she hadn't been thinking. Someone else had been in the driver's seat and she'd been along for the ride. Looked like that was turning out to be the story of her life.

Autry sighed. "We're this close, we might as well go see her. It'll make her happy."

Madeline chuckled and pressed the accelerator. "There you go again, thinking of everyone but you. You'd better wise up, little sister, and start looking out for number one."

Stanton knocked at Mrs. Milson's front door and waited. A chilly breeze ruffled through her azaleas and hydrangeas, planted close to the house and seriously overgrown. He frowned. That near her windows, they offered too much cover to a would-be burglar.

Footsteps creaked in the hallway and the door eased open. Mrs. Milson glared up at him, her eyes hazy behind her large lenses. "Yes? What do you want?"

He'd so been here, done this before. He produced a professional smile and lifted his badge with identification showing. "Good afternoon, Mrs. Milson. You called the sheriff's department? About a prowler?"

She folded her arms over her chest. "Took you long enough to get here."

He nodded. "Yes, ma'am, and I apologize for that—"

"He's done gone anyway."

"Ma'am?"

She waved a hand toward the ramshackle shed taking up one corner of her yard. "He ran off this morning. Saw him headed into the woods."

Stanton studied the shed. The door hung open at an angle, the interior dark. Overgrown yellow-tip shrubs surrounded the building. Beyond the shed was a rusted wire fence, the posts listing at a drunken angle. "What did he look like?"

Mrs. Milson huffed a sigh. "Only saw him for a moment. Tall, skinny, dark hair. He was walking funny."

Stanton nodded. "All right. I'm going to check out the building. Stay here, please."

He pulled his flashlight from its ring and unsnapped his holster. Approaching the outbuilding with caution, he glanced through the dusty windows. Weak sunlight broke up the shadows, but nothing moved within. He edged to the door, but saw only an ancient lawnmower and assorted junk. A pile of tarps and drop cloths lay in one corner, near a stack of rusted paint cans. Stepping inside, he shone the flashlight over and behind the accumulated junk.

Nothing.

Backing out of the shed, he eyed the ground. The grass seemed undisturbed. He studied the woods, his nape prickling. Something just didn't feel right, but he didn't see anything out of place.

He returned his flashlight to his belt and walked back to the porch where Mrs. Milson waited. At the bottom of the steps, he stopped and rested his foot on the second riser. "I don't see anything, Mrs. Milson. If he was there, he's gone now. I'll file a report and have a deputy run by here as often as possible over the next couple of days. If you see anything, don't hesitate to call and we'll get someone out here."

She harrumphed at him and stalked into the house. Stanton sighed. "Nice day to you too, ma'am."

Keys jingling at his belt, he jogged to the patrol car and called in to dispatch before turning around in the yard. The radio crackled, drowning out the whir of tires on the blacktop. Frowning, Stanton zeroed in on the conversation, Tick verifying his arrival at another burglary.

Bubba Bostick's hunting cabin. Stanton braked, slowing to a near stop. Bubba's cabin was...less than a mile away. He'd just passed the turnoff for it. On impulse, he swung into a three-point turn and headed that way. He took the right into the long, narrow path that led toward the river, underbrush scraping along the sides of the Crown Victoria. When it opened up at the rustic one-bedroom lodge, he stopped behind the marked unit Tick was driving. Bubba's cherry red Ford stood to one side, and the men talked on the front porch, Tick nodding and frowning while Bubba gestured.

Stanton's boots crunched on fallen acorns as he strode toward the steps. He nodded a greeting. "Bubba. Tick."

Bubba grimaced. "Sheriff."

"What's going on?" Stanton jerked his chin at the front door, slightly ajar, the screen ripped from the outer frame.

Tick scribbled in his notebook. "Somebody busted the lock. Can't find any footprints out here, pine straw's too thick. Couple spots of blood in the kitchen, like maybe he cut himself getting in."

"What did they take?" Stanton shifted his attention to Bubba, the one county commissioner who seemed to like what they'd done with the sheriff's department in the last nine months.

"Cleaned me out of saltines and Vienna sausages. Took my case of Coke from the back porch. Probably hauled it all in the blanket off the couch. Hell if that ain't gone too."

After a few more minutes of conversation, Stanton walked with Tick back to the patrol cars. Hands at his hips, he gazed over the unit into the thick woods. "This is strange."

Tick quirked an eyebrow at him, jotted one last note and tucked his notebook away. "What is?"

"I just came from Mrs. Milson's. She claims a man was in her yard, hanging around her shed a couple of days ago."

Tick squinted, looking north, toward the Milson place. "Probably a squatter. A transient off the highway."

"Off the *highway*?"

"It happens." Tick shrugged. "It's only ten miles and you get guys who come through the area once or twice a year. They know the river's back here, that there's good fishing. Easy meals, plentiful firewood."

Stanton scratched his jaw. "Wonder if that explains our other burglaries."

"No. Money items taken during those, stuff somebody could sell or pawn for a quick buck. This is somebody hungry. I'm telling you, it's a squatter. Lord only knows when he actually broke in. You heard Bubba say he hadn't been out here in two weeks. The guy's probably halfway to Atlanta by now."

It sounded logical enough, but something continued to niggle at him. "What about Mrs. Milson's story?"

Tick pinned him with a look. "This is the same woman who called us and reported a UFO sighting because she could see the new lights on the water tower, remember?"

"Yeah. I guess."

With a sigh, Tick rolled his eyes. "Tell you what, tomorrow after church, I'll get Chris and the dog and we'll go through the woods, see what we turn up."

"Tomorrow?"

"Yeah, tomorrow." Tick shook his head. "He's gone to Valdosta for training, remember? Besides, my chest hurts like hell, and Cait and I haven't had dinner at home together all week. It's been a sandwich at the courthouse or while we're meeting with the GBI. I need a break. And from the looks of it, so do you. Go get something to eat, see Autry. You'll feel better."

Her house didn't feel right.

Autry transferred the last of her toiletries from the overnight bag to the bathroom and paused in the doorway, staring into the bedroom. She rubbed at her arms. The air of the place felt off—not only dusty and unused, but just plain wrong.

Or maybe it was her.

Tired and out of sorts, she wandered into the living room. Madeline had gone shortly after dropping her off, back to their mother's. Autry had been grateful for the solitude, but now the silent emptiness wrapped around her, almost smothering in its intensity.

She curled up on the couch and reached for the remote. The television flickered to life, the bright prattle of the local news anchors dulling the silence. Days later, the courthouse bombing continued to be the top story, with tales of rescues and updated death tolls mixed with eyewitness accounts.

Each day, there were fewer rescues, a higher number of dead.

Autry closed her eyes. So many lives gone, so many chances unfulfilled. She had the opportunity to make a new start, to begin her life from this point and make it whatever she wished it to be. What did she want? Look out for number one, Madeline had said.

She'd already started. She was here, in her home, despite the supposed reappearance of the stalker. So he'd sent her flowers. Big deal. There was nothing he could do that would rival the horror of the explosion, her loss, and she would not let him send her running scared again. She wasn't going to run to Stanton for protection. That part of their relationship was over, but it left her facing the same question.

What did she want?

Her fingers slid over her lower abdomen and she bit her lip at the emptiness, remembering the tiny flutters. Pain sheared through her. Another baby. Did she want that, at some point in the future? Would Stanton? She'd watched him grow accustomed to the idea of their daughter, watched him become attached, but accepting an accidental pregnancy was a far cry from planning one.

She pulled the throw to her shoulders. What did she need? A man who would let her make her own decisions, who wouldn't be intimidated by that, who would respect the choices she made.

I'll back off; you can have whatever time you need.

He was trying. She yawned. He was right. She'd been given a second chance and she had plenty of time.

They had plenty of time.

No sense in rushing things.

Exhaustion pulled at her and she gave in to a light doze, still aware of the television droning.

Her doorbell rang and she jerked to awareness, feeling like her thudding heart had taken up residence in her throat. Only the bell at the front door worked and no one she knew ever used it. She sat up, clutching the throw, and eyed the door. The bell rang again.

No way was she answering that.

Two more short rings.

This is ridiculous. You're a grown woman. You can look through the damn peephole.

Casting the throw aside, she rose and crept to the door, making sure her feet made no sound on the wood floor. Hands braced on the door, she peered through the peephole. The tension drained from her body. It was only Keith Lawson, holding a clipboard and her car keys. His daddy's wrecker waited in the driveway, her car on the rollback. A shaky laugh left her lips on a breath and she reached for the chain. Lord, her mother had taught him in Sunday School when he'd been little and she'd been afraid to answer the door.

She threw the deadbolt and opened the door.

Keith smiled. "Hey, Ms. Holton. I was beginning to think you wasn't home."

"I'm sorry, Keith. I was taking a nap."

He nodded and jerked a thumb over his shoulder. "Brought your car. The sheriff asked me to drop it off." He held out the clipboard. "Just need you to sign here."

She took his proffered pen and scribbled her signature on the form. "Thank you."

Tapping the clipboard against his palm, he glanced down at his feet. "Real sorry about your daddy. It's a terrible thing. He was a good man, my daddy says."

Her throat closed, and she swallowed hard. "Yes, he was. Thank you."

Keith rubbed a grease-stained thumbnail across the edge of his clipboard. "Can't say I'm sorry about Jeff Schaefer being dead, though. Not after what he did to Amy. Or those other girls."

What could she say to that? Legally, not to mention ethically, she couldn't discuss this with him. "I'm sure there are many who would agree with you."

He ducked his head and glanced away. "Well, I'd better be going. All right if I just leave her in the drive?"

"That's fine." She accepted the keys.

With a wave, he bounded down the steps to the truck and began unloading her car. A familiar Explorer turned into the street and eased to a stop at the curb. Stanton unfolded from the driver's seat and she crossed her arms over her middle, trying to suppress the way her pulse accelerated at the sight of him. Heaven help her, she loved the way he moved, his long stride and the tentative smile on his face.

He jogged up the steps and held aloft a white bag. "I

stopped by Ming Yong's. I hope Chinese is okay."

"Chinese is fine." She stepped back to let him enter. Keith's wrecker lumbered away. The warm scent of fresh fried rice wafted over her and her mouth watered. Lord, she was hungry. She hadn't wanted to eat for days, but suddenly she was ravenous. "What did you get?"

He handed her the sack. The heavenly smells of shrimp and broccoli and hot crab rangoons rose to tantalize her. In the kitchen, she set the bag on the table and inhaled, her eyes sliding closed on a pleased sigh.

A warm hand cupped the back of her head and her eyes flew open. She barely registered his nearness before his mouth covered hers in a fast, hard kiss. Then he was gone, the table between them, his hands tucked in his pockets and a frustrated expression on his face.

She touched her mouth and his eyes darkened, fixed on the gesture. "Go ahead, bitch me out. It was worth it."

"I'm not..." She shook her head, still able to taste him. Turning away, she fumbled in the drawer for forks. "Are you hungry?"

He laughed, a brief puff of sound behind her. "Yeah, something like that." A rough exhale filled the air. "I'm sorry, I probably shouldn't have done that, but it's been a hell of a day and I was glad to see you."

"It's okay." Her hands stilled, and she pulled in a deep breath before facing him. "I'm glad to see you too."

With a grimace, he tugged a hand over his hair. "This is hard, Autry, going from where we were to here."

She clutched the forks to her chest. "I know. I'm sorry."

Pain flickered in his eyes. "It doesn't have to be this way. Come home with me."

"I thought you said you were going to back off?"

He glanced away, a muscle flicking in his jaw. "You're right. Come on. Let's eat."

Her appetite nonexistent now, she lifted the cardboard containers from the bag. She watched the tense line of his shoulders as he pulled glasses from her cabinet and crossed to the refrigerator. Ice clinked. She popped the top open on the first box. Steam rose and fat shrimp glistened against a bed of bright green broccoli. Her stomach roiled.

The refrigerator door opened with a small sucking noise, but no sound of his rummaging for beverages followed. Autry glanced up to find him staring into the depths of her refrigerator. Over his shoulder, she glimpsed the bright red of a whipped-cream can. Memories rolled over her, laughter and lovemaking here in this room. Her heart clenched.

"I can't do this." Stanton stepped back and closed the refrigerator. He spun to face her, his expression pained.

She wrapped her hands around the counter's edge. "What do you mean?"

His Adam's apple took a sharp bob. "I can back off and wait for you, but I can't come around and act like we're just friends. I want too much."

"I'm sorry," she whispered.

"Don't be. I want you to be sure." He tapped a fist against his thigh. "I'm going to take off. When you make up your mind, you know where to find me. I'll be waiting, Autry, as long as it takes."

Chapter Seventeen

Ringing. Tick frowned and threw an arm over his ear. The sound didn't stop and he groaned. He wasn't dreaming.

Caitlin nudged his side, sending a shock over his still-healing ribs.

"Tick," she murmured, "phone."

He reached for the cordless. "Maybe it's for you."

"Yes. An emergency background check, I'm sure."

Lifting the phone to his ear, he pushed up on the pillow. Caitlin shifted, pressing her face into the hollow of his shoulder, her leg over his thigh. He cleared his throat. "Hello?"

"Tick, man, I'm sorry to wake you." Cookie's subdued voice raised the hair at Tick's nape. "I'm over at Mrs. Milson's. I think you ought to come out here."

Tick disentangled himself from Caitlin's easy hold and rolled to sit on the edge of the bed. The green numerals on the clock glowed three-thirteen a.m. "What's wrong?"

"The newspaper guy noticed her lights were off. Seems she always leaves the porch light and the living room lamp on. He decided to check on her. The front door was open." A harsh sigh traveled over the line. "Tick, she's dead, and it ain't natural causes."

Already on his feet, Tick grabbed khakis and a department polo from the closet. "I'm on my way."

He dropped the phone in the charger. Sheets rustled, and with a soft click, light flooded the room. Blinking, Caitlin eyed him, midnight hair tumbling about her shoulders. "What is it?"

He threaded his belt through his holster and belt loops. "Possible homicide."

"Who?"

"Nance Milson." He sat on the bed and tugged on socks and his shoes, adrenaline already pumping into his system.

"Oh my God."

"Yeah." Reaching over, he opened the nightstand drawer and pulled out his cuffs, wallet and badge. His department cap dangled from the bedstead and he grabbed it, tugged it on. He leaned in to brush his mouth over Caitlin's. "I'll lock up and set the alarm. Go back to sleep. I probably won't see you for breakfast. You know how long this'll take."

She tangled her fingers in his collar and pulled him in for another brief kiss. "Be careful."

"You know it. See you later."

Outside, frogs croaked in the damp night air. He jogged down the steps to Caitlin's Volvo. Damn, he'd be glad when Lawson finished fixing his truck. Her car made him feel like he was driving a tin can.

Nance Milson's home was a mere four miles from his. When his old frame house had belonged to his grandmother before her death, the two women had been good neighbors, often visiting to swap recipes and help can vegetables. He'd spent countless days as a teenager cutting her grass, weeding her garden and dodging her wrath. He frowned. Mrs. Milson was nosy and absentminded, a total pain in the ass as far as the sheriff's department went, but why would anyone want to hurt her?

When he arrived, Cookie's unmarked unit shared the long, rutted driveway with a regular patrol car, blue lights spinning a lazy whir in the dark and casting an eerie glow about the yard. The headlights and spotlights on both cars were trained on the house. The paper carrier's rattletrap Buick sat to the side. Yellow crime scene tape cordoned off the drive and Chris Parker leaned against the patrol unit's trunk, interviewing Wayne Andrews.

Tick ducked under the tape. "Hey, Chris."

"Morning." Chris muffled a yawn. "Cookie's inside."

"Thanks." He stopped at Cookie's unit, the trunk open to display the evidence recovery kits, and grabbed a pair of gloves, snapping them on. He surveyed the house's exterior. The screens were intact, if a little rusty. No trampled bushes. No signs the door had been forced.

Flashlight in hand, he eased around the side, careful where he placed his feet. The jalousie window in the storage room, near the back door, was open, the glass tiles extended enough to allow a man to wedge his arm in. Maybe far enough to throw the lock open. He shone the light around the concrete steps. A couple of footprints in the damp clay stood out.

Backtracking, he entered through the unlocked front door. Lights blazed in the living and dining rooms. "Cookie?"

"In here." The deep drawl flowed down the narrow hall and Tick followed it to the tiny bedroom at the rear of the house. The musty smell of a closed-up dwelling grew stronger, competing with the sharp odors of body fluids.

Cookie stood just inside the door, sketching the layout of the crime scene in his notebook. He didn't look up. "That was fast."

"I live four miles away." Not touching the doorway, Tick peered into the room. "Damn."

Cookie glanced up then, his sharp eyes a stormy gray. "Yeah. She didn't make it easy for him."

"You dust yet?" Tick studied the destruction in the room, signs of a major struggle apparent, from the overturned lamp to the twisted bedcovers and mattress hanging halfway off the bed. Long gouges at the side of the bed marred the dull hardwood floor. Mrs. Milson's thick glasses, twisted and cracked, lay nearby, amid the shards of a broken glass.

"Nope. Secured the scene. Called the coroner. Talked to Mr. Andrews, the paper carrier. Chris is taking his statement." Cookie gestured at the room. "Want to call the crime lab or are we doing it?"

Tick shook his head. The crime lab in Moultrie was straining under the evidence from the explosion. No need to call them out to process a scene he and Cookie were capable of handling. "We'll do it."

Cookie nodded. "Body's on the floor, other side of the bed. Rigor's setting in. Probably been dead a few hours."

Moving with care not to disturb anything, Tick stepped

around him, far enough in so he could see. Mrs. Milson's body lay awry, arms bent at an awkward angle, her old-fashioned nightgown twisted about her form. Her head was tilted back, mouth agape, clouded eyes staring.

"Check out her neck." Cookie snapped his notebook closed. Over his shoulder, Tick tossed an inquisitive look at him. "Just look."

With a shrug, Tick eased closer. Dark bruises mottled the crepey skin of the elderly woman's neck. "She was strangled—" The words died in his throat and he closed his mouth with a snap. Surely he wasn't seeing what he thought he was. "Holy hell."

"Yeah. That's why I called you."

Tick leaned over, inspecting the darker bruise, a small, flawless semicircle pressed into her throat. The impression of a button left when the murderer pressed his arm across the woman's throat, crushing the windpipe, cutting off all oxygen. "Cookie, there's no way. It's impossible."

"I just wanted you to see it."

Tick frowned. Obviously, Cookie recognized the similarity in that mark too. Not exactly the same but close enough that unease was pouring over his spine like icy rain. "It has to be a coincidence."

"Yeah."

"Because there's no way." Except stranger things had happened.

"Yeah."

"Cookie, Schaefer died in that explosion." He waved a hand at the body. "This is a coincidence. Just a fluke that the mark looks like the ones on his victims. Besides, those came from his watch. This looks like...a button, maybe?"

"Yeah." Cookie fixed him with a long-suffering look. "You calling the sheriff, or am I?"

"Shit." Tick looked down at that damning bruise again. Sometimes close enough was still too close to ignore. "I'll do it."

With Will Botine on his heels, Stanton met Tick on the porch. "What the hell is going on?"

"What's this about Schaefer?" Botine asked, irritation lacing his voice. He hadn't been real happy when Stanton had called him just after four and asked him to ride along out to the Milson place.

Tick held out a couple of Polaroid photos. Stanton took them, squinting at the glossy paper under the dim porch light. "What am I looking for?"

"Here." Tick tapped his index finger against the image. "See that bruise on her neck?"

Botine leaned in to look as Stanton peered closer. Stanton glanced up. "Looks kinda like the mark on Amy Gillabeaux's neck."

Tick nodded. "Our Jane Doe, Sharon Ingler and Vontressa King, too. When Williams did the autopsies, she said it probably came from a watch. Schaefer's Timex matched up perfectly."

"This isn't from a watch. Too small," Botine said, scratching his stomach. "Besides, Schaefer's dead. We found his identification and a body."

"A body so damaged it couldn't be visually confirmed as being him." Tick rested his hands at his hips. "I'm just saying…it looks like his MO and we don't have confirmation of his death yet. What if he managed to walk away from that?"

Stanton frowned. "Walk away? Come on, Tick. We found Autry under twenty feet of rubble and you think Schaefer walked away?"

"They were in different parts of the courtroom, remember?" Tick's face took on an intent expression, dark eyes glittering in the dim light. "She was in front of the jury box. We did find those people under several layers of debris. But Schaefer? He was across the room. Ray Lewis was sitting behind him."

"And Ray was near the top," Botine said. "Only reason he didn't free himself was a chunk hit him in the head, knocked him out."

Still frowning, Stanton dropped his gaze to the photos. "Explain the ID card, then."

Tick shrugged. "Maybe it wasn't on him. Maybe he'd laid it on the table."

"Okay, so if it's him, why Mrs. Milson? The smart thing for him to do would be to run, get as far away as possible."

239

"Maybe this was as far as he could go. If he's injured, he might have trouble moving." Tick waved a hand at the looming darkness of the woods behind the house. "He's familiar with the area, he knows Mrs. Milson is a little off, that we might not take her seriously."

Stanton nodded. As much as he hated to admit it, the idea had some merit. And Tick's instincts as an investigator were normally dead-on. Schaefer loose in his county again? Stanton repressed a shudder. The prowler call, the break-in at Bubba Bostick's cabin trailed through his mind. "We need to search the woods."

"Chris and Monroe are already out there with a couple of the day-shift guys."

Stanton shot him a look. "What did you do, call out the whole damn department?"

Tick blinked. "Well, yeah."

Stanton rolled his eyes, visions of being called on the carpet about budget excesses tumbling in his head. Oh, hell, let 'em bitch. "If he's trying to keep a low profile, why kill her?"

"Desperation, maybe?" Tick shrugged again, a negligent roll of his shoulders. "Hunger, pain, thirst. Found half a sandwich in the kitchen. Purse contents are scattered in the bedroom. Her keys are in the ignition of her car. Bet it wouldn't start. It's ancient as hell and the battery connections are corroded."

"So he's on foot." Botine glanced toward the woods. "Why the woods, though? I mean, all that's on the other side is the river. Makes more sense he'd go east, through Hardison's fields. He'd come out at the highway."

"That's almost ten miles, though, and what's he going to do when he gets there?" Stanton studied the photos again, unease shivering through him. "He needs a vehicle if he's going to get anywhere. Mrs. Milson's didn't work out for him. But he's smart, he wants the cover the woods offer while he moves. Where's the next closest home?"

Botine pointed south. "The Gurleys' place. Five miles down the road."

"Down the road. Seven through the woods." Tick frowned, his head whipping north toward the woods. He paled. "Oh, shit."

The chill of disquiet trickled down Stanton's spine again. "What?"

With jerky movements, Tick pulled his cell phone from his belt. "The next closest house as the crow flies? Mine. Four miles north through the woods."

Botine chuckled. "He'd have to be nuts to show up at your place."

"He's not crazy, but he's also not scared of me. Thinks I'm inferior. Stan, you saw those journals. You know what he'd planned for Cait." Eyes closed, he slapped the phone closed on an oath. "No freakin' signal, as usual."

A garbled radio transmission carried to them from the patrol cars, Troy Lee's voice murmuring in response. His car door shot open and he jumped to his feet. "Hey, Tick!"

Stanton froze, aware of Tick stiffening beside him. Foreboding crashed over him, no longer a mere trickle. Troy Lee ran for the porch. He stopped at the bottom of the steps, his expression earnest and strained as he looked up at them. "Roger says your alarm company just called. Your backup silent alarm is going off and no one's answering the phone."

Caitlin shut off the water and slicked her hair away from her face. She pushed the door open and grabbed a towel, smoothing water from her limbs before stepping from the shower. After rubbing on a layer of body lotion, she wandered into the bedroom.

She hadn't been able to go back to sleep. The house was too quiet with Tick gone, the silence pressing in around her. She grabbed panties and wriggled into them, tugged a snug T-shirt over her head and slid into a pair of yoga pants.

No, the house was too damn big. As much as he loved it, it was too much house for just the two of them. They lived in a grand total of four rooms and the idea of the formal rooms up front and the other bedrooms upstairs, closed off, sitting silent and empty, gave her the willies whenever Tick was gone.

He hadn't intended for those rooms to stay empty. He'd planned to fill them with children, a family, with the noise and chaos and love that bloomed in his childhood home, his siblings' homes. She pressed a hand over her flat stomach, the pang of loss sharp and strong.

Instead, he'd ended up with her and a huge, empty house.

She slammed the drawer shut.

Stop it, Caitlin. Right now.

Irritation simmering under her skin, she trailed into the living room to turn on the television. CMT appeared and she shook her head. Didn't Tick get enough of country music in the truck? Tim McGraw strutted on stage in tight jeans, singing about being a real good man.

The problem was she missed her real good man. He'd be tired when he got home, wiped out from lack of sleep and the minutia of investigation. They could take a nap together.

And probably not get a lot of sleep.

"You're pathetic, Falconetti." She laughed at herself.

Tim McGraw segued into a shirtless Kenny Chesney on a Caribbean beach. Her stomach growled and Caitlin tossed the remote on the couch. Microwave pastries and country music. Could her life be more exciting?

With a muffin warming in the microwave and coffee perking, she pulled down the glass pitcher Tick's Aunt Ella had given them as a wedding gift. It was heavy as hell, but perfect for making sangria and lemonade, holding fresh-squeezed orange juice. Humming along with Kenny, she set it aside and rummaged for the juicer. She piled oranges atop it.

The arm came out of nowhere, wrapping across her throat with bruising force, a jacket button digging into her skin.

Oranges bounced away. The juicer hit the floor, exploding into pieces.

Musky male sweat filled her nostrils and panic tried to swamp her. *Oh, God.*

"Agent Falconetti," he said close to her ear. Her stomach pitched. *Schaefer.* He was dead. He was *dead.* He couldn't be here. "How've you been?"

His arm tightened at her throat and clarity returned, icy and strong. Somehow, he was here and one thing was for certain—he wanted her dead.

Caitlin drove the heel of her foot into the arch of his. He yelped, arm loosening as he lost his center of balance. Heart thudding, she threw her weight back into him, shoving her elbow hard into his midsection, her foot sliding on the waxed hardwood. She dug her feet in to keep her balance, a sharp pain shooting through one sole as a plastic shard from the juicer snapped beneath her foot.

"Fucking bitch!" Pain filling his voice, he scrambled to his knees. Caitlin snatched the pitcher from the island, her damp hands sliding on the glass. As he pushed up, she smashed it into his face. The bulbous glass imploded, leaving the curved handle in her hand.

Schaefer dropped, groaning. Blood spurted from his nose, pooling on the floor. Hell if she was going to give him the chance to get up. She flung the handle aside and grabbed the first object at hand—one of the cane-backed island stools.

The cane weaving shattered on the first blow across Schaefer's shoulders. His body jerked. The second blow separated the seat from the legs. A moan shuddered from him. After the third, he was still, silent.

Her chest heaved, raw sobs tearing at her throat. Oh God, she was getting the shakes. She couldn't, not now. Not with Jeff Schaefer in her house. Her gun. She needed her gun and her cuffs.

She sprinted for the bedroom, fire racing from her foot up her calf with each step. Scrambling across the unmade bed, she jerked open her nightstand and grabbed her cuffs first, tucking them into her waistband. She snatched up her holster, hands shaking.

God, Caitlin, hurry. She threw the holster aside, checked the magazine, clicked off the safety and threw the slide, chambering a round. She pushed the safety back on and ran for the kitchen.

Schaefer hadn't moved and she tucked the gun in the small of her back, cringing a little at the violation of her training. She grabbed Schaefer's arm, twisted it behind his back, slapped the cuff on his wrist, repeated the action with the second arm. He never moved.

Had she killed him?

She wasn't touching him to find out. Revulsion pulsed under her skin, her stomach churning, and she dragged in a deep breath.

Hold it together, Falconetti. Just keep it together.

The phone. She needed to call for backup. She grabbed the cordless from its charger. No dial tone. The implication twisted her stomach once more. How long had he been waiting, planning this?

And why wasn't the son of a bitch dead like the GBI said he was?

Cell phone. Where the hell was her cell? She dragged in a breath. Sweet Jesus, she was losing it, couldn't think, and where in hell had she left her cell?

Schaefer moaned, a gurgling sound in his throat, and she jumped. He didn't move.

She backed away, gaze darting around the keeping room, seeking her cell phone. Not that she'd be able to get a signal anyway, since her damn husband insisted on living in the middle of BumFuckEgypt, Georgia. Rubbing a hand down her face, she snagged her keys and headed for the back door. She skirted the island, not looking at the prone man on the floor.

Her shaking fingers fumbled with the deadbolt. Damn it, how had he gotten in the house? Why hadn't the alarm gone off? Finally, she flung the door open and stumbled onto the porch. The blue glow of the mercury light illuminated the back yard. She rattled through her keys on the way down the steps. At the bottom, she froze, staring at the driveway.

Oh hell, where was her car?

Gravel crunched under tires and the *whup-whup* of a siren check broke the silence. She froze, clutching her keys until they bit into her skin, as a Chandler County sheriff's unit slid to a stop, an unmarked unit flying into the driveway as well.

How did they...?

What was going on?

Her pulse pounded in her throat, heart thudding against her ribs, adrenaline pouring through her body. Nausea trembled in her throat and her lungs refused to work as they should—more heaving than breathing.

The unmarked unit screamed to a stop beside the patrol car. A door slammed, and Troy Lee and Deputy Vann Starling ran toward her. Tick and Stanton stepped from the unmarked unit, more doors slamming.

"Cait?" Tick's voice shook. The beginnings of relief shuddered through her, not quite touching the confusion and fear.

"Agent Falconetti?" Troy Lee reached her first, touched her arm with a gentle hand. "Are you all right?"

All right? She'd just had a serial killer, risen from the dead, attack her in her kitchen, and he wanted to know if she was all right? He was insane.

"*Don't touch me.*" She punched him in the jaw, the right hook she tossed into the heavy bag on a regular basis. Pain shot up her arm, reminding her she was alive.

"Son of a bitch!" Bent over, he backed away, holding his jaw.

"Holy hell." His face pale, Tick stopped a step or so away. "Caitlin?"

She closed her eyes. Tick was here. She could trust him to have her back. She could let it go now.

Her eyes snapped open, hands shaking so badly her keys jingled. "Tick, Jeff Schaefer was in my house." She glanced over her shoulder, somehow still expecting him to come out the back door, come after her again. "Correction, he's *still* in my house. And you took my car!"

"I know, precious, I'm sorry. If I'd had a clue—"

"Shut up, Calvert." She pressed her clenched fist to her forehead. Nothing made sense. Tears pushed at her eyes, a sob struggling to free itself from her chest. "What the hell is he doing alive?"

"Troy Lee, Vann, check the house. Cait?" Tick's voice was soft, soothing, cautious. She glanced at him. He watched her, concern in his dark eyes, a frown pulling at his brows.

The sob tore free and the tears spilled. "Oh God, Tick."

She covered her mouth with her hand, trying to stop the frightened, gasping sobs. She took a step forward and shook her head. "*He was in my house!*"

"I know." He tugged her into his arms, the embrace bruising in its intensity. "I know. It's over, I swear, baby. It's over."

Nodding, she buried her face against his chest. His arms around her shaking shoulders, he held on, whispering reassurances while she cried.

Stanton left Falconetti in Tick's arms and bounded up the back steps. The kitchen door stood open, and when he stepped into the large keeping room, Vann and Troy Lee were hauling Schaefer to his feet. His face was nearly unrecognizable, blood rushing from his nose, mouth and eyes already swelling and bruising. He spat, blood and mucous hitting the floor in a slimy trail.

Vann chuckled. "Man, I take back everything I ever said about Calvert being whipped. Look at this guy."

Troy Lee rubbed his jaw. "She's got a hell of a right hook too."

Schaefer spat again, his shoulders hunched, breaths coming in harsh wheezing gasps. Stanton surveyed the scene— blood pooled on the hardwood floor, shattered glass, something that looked like the remains of a small blender, a thinner trail of blood leading to the bedroom and to the back door.

He caught Troy Lee's gaze and jerked his head toward the door. "Go call for an ambulance."

"Yes, sir." Troy Lee slipped out, leaving a stiff and sullen Schaefer in Vann's capable hold.

Stanton folded his arms over his chest. "Well, Jeff, seems like you've had an eventful night. Couple B-and-Es, murder, assault."

Not to mention one royal ass-kicking. An irresistible smile quirked at Stanton's mouth. Schaefer sucked in a breath, a sick gurgling sound.

"I want my attorney," he said, the words garbled and laced with pain.

Stanton froze, his smile dying. Triumph flashed in Schaefer's blue gaze before pain drowned it again. Stanton narrowed his eyes. "Vann, search him and put him in the car until the ambulance gets here. Make damn sure you Mirandize him."

Vann nodded and escorted Schaefer out, using slight pressure on the cuffs to guide him. Stanton rubbed a hand over his face. Schaefer asking for his attorney didn't surprise Stanton at all.

Hell, he had to call Autry.

Chapter Eighteen

Jeff Schaefer alive?

Autry eased up the steps to the emergency room, her entire body aching. The last thing she wanted was to be up at five in the morning, dealing with a man who was supposed to be dead. So much for rethinking her career.

The automatic door slid open and she stepped into the waiting area. For once, it was deserted and she crossed to the admissions desk. "Hey, Louise. I had a call from the sheriff's department that one of my clients was here. Jeff Schaefer?"

Louise pressed a button and a buzzer sounded, followed by a loud click at the door. "Exam three."

So it wasn't a mistake. She hadn't been hearing things when Stanton had called to tell her they'd rearrested Schaefer and he wanted his attorney. Her stomach rolled.

She pulled the door open. No sense in delaying the inevitable. Why did doing the right thing suck so bad?

A couple of scrub-clad nurses leaned against the wall, talking. Farther down the hall, two of Stanton's deputies engaged in a hushed albeit animated conversation, punctuated with exaggerated hand gestures.

Oh, that had to be the one.

Taking a deep breath, she headed that way. Sure enough, a small plaque marked the room as exam three. At her approach, the deputies fell silent. The door stood partially open and Tick's voice, low and taunting, flowed from the room.

"We've got you dead to rights this time, Schaefer. There's no warrant error to save your sorry ass. You won't get out of it."

She pushed the door completely open and stepped into the small room, its air pulsating with anger and tension. Stanton drew her gaze first. His face weary and clothes crumpled, he propped against the sink base, arms folded over his chest. He met her eyes for a moment and glanced away.

Schaefer lay on a narrow gurney, both hands cuffed to the side rails. IV tubing snaked from his left arm to a bag of fluids dangling above him. At least, she thought it was Schaefer. His nose was purplish-black and hugely swollen. His eyes flared when he saw her. Her stomach pitched.

Lord, he really was alive.

At the foot of the gurney, Tick stood, hands at his hips, the entire line of his body rigid and angry.

Autry folded her arms. "Is this how you're doing it now? Taunting and browbeating?"

Eyes narrowed, Tick slanted a glance at her. "Don't worry, he hasn't said anything. His jaw's busted." He grinned at Schaefer, more the baring of his teeth than a smile. "Plus he's been too busy pouting because he got his ass kicked by a girl."

She frowned and turned her attention to Stanton. "What are the charges?"

Stanton's eyebrows lifted over shuttered eyes. "Right now? Breaking and entering. Battery. And we're looking at him for a second B-and-E and a homicide."

"Escaping custody," Tick added, his tone hard. "That's an automatic five years."

Another murder? And battery? "Who...who's dead?"

"Nance Milson. Strangled in her bedroom." Tick's jaw stiffened and he jerked his chin in Schaefer's direction. "We'll have prints from that. DNA from your little midnight snack too. You're toast, Schaefer."

"Tick." Stanton's tone held a distinct warning.

Autry crossed her arms over her aching stomach. "And the battery charge? Who's the alleged victim there?"

Tick scowled. "Cait."

Autry sucked in a breath. Was Schaefer stupid? Going after Caitlin again? He'd better be smart enough to take any deal McMillian offered this time around. "I'd like to speak with him alone."

Stanton nodded and straightened. "McMillian's on his way," he said, voice cool. "I'll let you know when he gets here."

Tick leaned forward, hands wrapped around the side rails, gaze locked on Schaefer's blazing eyes. "If you ever touch my wife again, you stupid son of a bitch, I'll rip off your fucking head and piss down the hole." At the infuriated hiss of Schaefer's indrawn breath, Tick displayed his teeth in another sneer. "If she doesn't do it first."

Autry glared at Stanton. "Would you get him out of here, please?"

Stanton took Tick's arm. "Come on. Let's go."

Not budging, Tick shook him off and pointed at Schaefer. "You go near her again, ever, and I'll kill you."

"*Tick.*" His face rigid, Stanton shoved him toward the door. "Come on. Let's go check on Falconetti."

She waited until they'd cleared the room. Resting a hand on the sink base, she eyed Schaefer. Disgust curled through her. They all would have been better off if he'd died in that explosion. "I hope you at least had the good sense to keep your mouth shut."

"I didn't—"

"Shut up and listen." The obvious pain in his slurred words didn't spark any sympathy within her. If not for him...none of the horrific events of the last ten days would have happened. Anger burned in her. "When Tom gets here, he'll probably make an offer. It won't be generous. You'll take it. You'll allocute and you'll serve your time."

"No deal." He pushed the words out.

"I'm not asking you. I'm telling you how it's going to be."

Rage and hatred sparked in his icy blue eyes. "No."

Her own anger deepened. "I don't think you understand how incredibly stupid you've been. McMillian will bury you."

"No. Deal."

Autry opened her mouth, ready to let fly, but a quick tap at the door made her retreat into silence. She sucked in a deep breath. "Come in."

On crutches, lower leg in plaster, McMillian swung into the

room. "Autry, good to see you."

She slanted a glare at Schaefer. "Talk to me about a deal, Tom."

He chuckled. "A deal? You're kidding, right?"

Far from amused, she pinned him with a look. "You wouldn't have come down here if you didn't plan to offer one. Stop wasting my time and lay it on the table."

A grin quirked at McMillian's mouth. "Sometimes you sound just like your daddy."

A frisson of grief traveled over her. "The offer, Tom?"

"He pleads to all the murders." He glanced at Schaefer. "*All* of them. He allocutes. We'll drop the battery and B-and-E charges."

"Sentencing?"

"Life with the possibility of parole for each murder. I'll even be generous and recommend concurrent sentences."

Autry nodded and turned to Schaefer. "Take it."

He struggled against the cuffs to lever up on the pillow. His gaze flared, hatred spilling into the air. "No."

Gripping the railing, she leaned over, eyes fixed on his. "Take it."

"No." The syllable emerged an enraged whisper.

Oh, she was so through with this. Through with him, with trying to do the right thing and losing everything for it. She wouldn't be a part of his evil anymore. "Then find yourself another lawyer. I quit."

He straightened, a smug expression on his damaged face. "You can't."

She leaned closer and smiled. "Watch me."

Aware of McMillian's shocked gaze, she walked out of the room, her heart lighter than it had been in months. The hallway was nearly empty, the deputies and nurses nowhere in sight. At the other end, Stanton leaned against the wall, deep in conversation with Tick. Stanton looked up, his gaze skittering over her. He turned back to Tick and spoke again, punctuating his words with his hands.

Her heart constricted once more.

When you make up your mind, you know where to find me.

She was on her way to making up her mind about her career. Hell, she'd probably ended it, walking out like that. She could be disbarred, sanctioned at the very least. And the bad thing was, right now, she really didn't care.

She'd sort it out later.

But she still had no clue what to do about Stanton.

Once Louise buzzed her into the waiting room, releasing the door lock, she slipped outside. A damp chill hovered in the air and she shivered, gooseflesh rising on her bare arms.

She met Ray Lewis, the local newspaper editor, coming up the steps and smothered a groan. A predatory smile lit his face. "Ms. Holton, I sure am glad to see you. I understand Jeff Schaefer has been rearrested. Can you tell me anything about that?"

Autry straightened her shoulders. "I have nothing to say about Mr. Schaefer. Now, or ever."

"Tick, it's three stitches. I do not need crutches." Falconetti slid from the exam table and tested the foot in question, a slight wince twisting her mouth. She pushed her hair away from her face. "What I need is to get out of here."

"Come on then." Sticking her discharge instructions in his back pocket, Tick wrapped an arm around her waist so she could lean on him and keep her weight shifted off the injured foot.

Stanton walked with them through the fairly deserted hall to the waiting room. "I'm assuming you need a ride—"

Shit.

He sensed Tick's stiffening at the same moment he spied Ray Lewis waiting, like a damn vulture, by the front door.

Great. Just fucking great and just what he wanted to deal with right now.

"What's wrong?" Falconetti glanced up at Tick's set expression then followed his line of sight. Her low frustrated sigh grated on Stanton's already raw nerve endings. She stepped free of Tick's sheltering arm. "If you're going to work in a political job, you have to learn how to deal with the press.

Although, I'm not really sure *he* counts as a member of the press."

"Cait, please. Not right now." A taut weariness colored Tick's voice, as though this was an oft-repeated discussion, one that held no satisfactory conclusion for either of them.

Lewis met them halfway. "Any comment, Sheriff?"

"Not at this time, but we'll have a prepared statement for you later today—"

"A prepared statement." Lewis made a disgusted sound deep in his throat. "You let the man get away, only to murder a defenseless elderly woman and—"

"Excuse me?" Falconetti narrowed her eyes to glittering slits. Stanton knew that look well enough—he'd been on the receiving end once or twice. "What did you just say? I can't have heard you correctly."

Tick coughed into a clenched fist. "Caitlin."

She pulled in a breath, glanced up at him and exhaled, the line of her mouth drawn and unhappy. "Can we go? Reed, will you take us back for my car, please?"

Obviously unhappy, Lewis retreated. Outside, Falconetti paused at the unmarked patrol unit. "You two must stop giving him the upper hand. As long as you allow him to crucify you in that rag he calls a newspaper, you risk losing everything you've worked to build here."

Tick's shoulders lifted in a painful shrug. "What do you suggest we do? You don't understand—"

"No, I know nothing about politics and the press." Heavy irony laced her words and an unwelcome spurt of humor shot through Stanton. With her family background, she'd probably been immersed in deftly handling reporters before she could read. He frowned.

"Falconetti?" At his voice, she shifted her narrowed gaze from Tick's and focused on him. "What would you do?"

"Hire a department spokesperson, at least part-time." She folded her arms. "As capable and multitalented as the two of you are, that is obviously not your forté or you wouldn't have allowed Lewis to have run you down the way you have. Trust me, with someone like him, strong and silent is not the way to go. You need a person who can be positive and go on the offensive at the same time."

Stanton's frown deepened. Tick was capable of both of those things, which was why he'd always stepped back and let his former partner do the talking for the department...until the Schaefer fiasco, when suddenly Tick, too, had morphed into the strong and silent role Falconetti had just described.

"Right now," Falconetti continued, her voice softening, "you need an outsider, someone who doesn't believe underneath it all that maybe you deserve the things Lewis is printing about you."

Uncomfortable with her directness, Stanton shifted but didn't miss the sharp glance Tick shot her.

"Because you don't." She met Tick's gaze dead on. "Because you did everything you could, from Schaefer's background check to the way you conducted the murder investigations. This bombing came out of nowhere. You had reason to believe Autry might be in danger and you followed protocol in providing security for the courthouse and Schaefer's transfer. It's time to get back in the game. If you don't, Lewis's bad press will bury you and all you've done right. Don't let that happen. What you've achieved with this department...it's valuable, even if not everyone can see that right now."

Tick looked away. Her gaze swung to Stanton's and a genuine smile played about her mouth.

"Like I said, it's valuable, even if you can't see it right now."

A ringing doorbell pulled Autry from a troubled doze. She grabbed her robe and struggled into it while stumbling to the front door. Glimpsing her sister through the peephole, she smothered a sigh and swung the door open.

"Why didn't you call me?" Waving a folded newspaper, Madeline strode into the house and down the hall to the kitchen. She thrust a cardboard cup holder bearing two cups of coffee at Autry.

"Call you about what?" Autry set the tray in the middle of the kitchen table, pulled a foam cup free and popped the lid. She drew an appreciative sniff of the rich brew.

"This." Madeline tossed the newspaper on the table. "Forget *Peyton Place*. This place is like fucking *Days of Our Lives*."

Coffee halfway to her lips, Autry stared at the headline

article in a special Sunday edition of the *Daily Herald*. "Accused Serial Murderer, Thought Dead, Rearrested." Coffee forgotten, she picked up the paper and began reading, stopping when she reached the paragraph listing her as the attorney of record, who refused comment. "Damn."

"You won't be able to get him off." Madeline swung the refrigerator door open and pulled out a can of whipped cream. She sprayed a swirl atop her coffee and offered the can to Autry.

"I don't have to worry about getting him off." Autry glanced at the whipped cream and shook her head. Biting her lip, she dropped her gaze to the article once more. "I quit."

"Oh shit." Madeline stared, mouth open, a dab of cream on her upper lip. "You did?"

Autry sank into a chair. "Yep."

"Just his case or the defender's office?"

"It's pretty much the same thing." Wry humor tugged at Autry. "So I guess I'm out of a job, maybe out of a career."

Madeline made a strangled noise in her throat. "Hell, Autry, when you break bad, you break *bad*, don't you?"

Autry rolled her eyes. "Obviously."

She should care more about the career she'd worked so hard to attain. She should care that her actions would have broken her father's heart. If he were alive, he'd be so disappointed.

But disappointed didn't describe her feelings. Apprehensive, maybe. But mostly...she felt relieved.

"You could always come back to Jacksonville with me." Madeline eyed her with a critical gaze. "A change of scenery might be good for you. Show you there's more to the world than Coney, Georgia."

Autry shot her a look over the edge of her cup. "I have been out of the state, you know. And the country, for that matter."

Madeline matched her stare for stare. "Just think about it. You never know. You might even find Stanton Reed's not the only man in the world."

"You believe this stuff?" With a disgusted sigh, Tick tossed the newspaper on the table. "How does he get this bullshit out that fast?"

Stanton glanced at the headline. At least Ray wasn't calling for his resignation this time around. But he'd be willing to bet tomorrow's regular edition would include an editorial blaming the sheriff's department for somehow bungling the whole affair and leading to Nance Milson's death.

As bad as he hated to admit it, Falconetti was right—he couldn't step back and let that continue. They'd screwed up, yes, and God only knew, Stanton had paid for what had happened at the courthouse...but he couldn't let what had happened undo all the work that had gone into building a good, decent department. He couldn't let it keep them from moving forward.

"I was thinking about what Falconetti had to say earlier."

"Yeah?" Tick lifted a stack of folders from a banker's box.

"She might be on to something with the whole spokesperson idea." Stanton cleared his throat. "And she's right about not letting two incidents, however major they might be, get in the way of the big picture of what we've done."

Tick slanted him a look before twisting to peer out the small window. Stanton shook his head.

"What are you looking at?"

"Seeing if Jesus is coming through the clouds." Tick grinned. "You just said Cait was right about something. That has to be a sign the Second Coming is imminent."

Stanton laughed, the sound rusty and hoarse, but welcome after the last few days. "Smartass."

Tick chuckled.

"What are you doing?" He nodded at Tick, who was spreading files across the white folding table in the makeshift squad room.

Tick grimaced. "Trying to get my stuff organized again. I'm still missing folders, but I need to sort out our open cases, get back to work on those." He lifted a stack of files, tucked a couple under his chin, laid the others on the table. "We have those burglaries in the north end of the county, not to mention Autry's sick pen pal. And some cold cases we inherited from the previous administration."

At his mention of Autry and the stalker, Stanton made sure his face stayed expressionless. Obviously, she'd made a decision about her career—if walking out on Schaefer constituted a resignation from the public defender's office. When he'd called her on the way to the hospital, she'd refused his offer of a ride, and from the way she'd left the hospital without speaking to him at all, he was beginning to think she'd made up her mind about him as well.

Maybe she'd figured she was better off without him and it was time to cut her losses.

One thing was for sure—the waiting and uncertainty were killing him. But he'd promised her time and space and he'd be damned if he broke that promise. Hell, who was he kidding? He was already damned. She didn't want him anymore.

A quick rap at the open door shook him from his reverie. Tick dropped a folder and cursed as papers flitted across the floor. Stanton glanced up. Botine and McMillian stood in the doorway, faces grim. Stanton's gut tightened. Local head of the GBI and the DA, together, looking like that? It couldn't be good.

Botine cleared his throat. "You boys got a minute?"

"Sure." Stanton leaned against the table, arms folded. "What's up?"

"The Evidence Response Team has come up with its initial report." Botine ran a thumb under his collar. "We're going to bring some people in for questioning and we thought, under the circumstances, you might like to observe."

Observe? He wanted to rip the bastard apart, but he could settle for watching the interrogation. "Yeah. I'd like that."

Tick stacked his folders on the table and dusted his hands. "What did the ERT come up with?"

McMillian loosened his tie. "The main thing we're looking at is a truck axle recovered from Durham Street."

"Examining the distance between the recovery spot and the parking lot where we think the explosion originated, plus the condition of the axle, the techs believe it came from the vehicle holding the bomb." Botine hitched his thumbs in his belt.

Stanton and Tick exchanged a look. After the Oklahoma City bombing, an axle from the rental truck carrying the homemade bomb had led to McVeigh's conviction.

"You have a VIN number, don't you?" Tick asked, his voice quiet. The line of his shoulders betrayed a sudden tension. Stanton didn't need to be told what was going through his head. When they found the bomber, to Stanton, it would be the person who'd killed his daughter. To Tick, it would probably be someone he'd known all his life. Stanton would have some modicum of vengeance; Tick would face an arrest tearing yet another hole in the community he loved.

McMillian inclined his head. "We have a VIN. A local farm truck." He held aloft a folded paper. "I have the warrants for the farm. That nitrogen fertilizer came from somewhere. There'll be a record of it."

Botine glanced at Stanton. "I want y'all with my team when we execute it. Your department's taken a lot of heat in the last few months. You should be involved in the arrest and investigation."

A weak grin quirked at Tick's mouth. "As long as you don't let Troy Lee go along, we're fine." He cleared his throat, a painfully rough sound. "What farm?"

"Jim Ingler's."

"Holy hell." His face paling, Tick closed his eyes. Stanton blew out a long breath. Jim Ingler's wife, Erleen, had been one of the first dead pulled from the rubble. His youngest son remained in critical condition in an Atlanta hospital with spinal and head injuries. Tick opened his eyes, his stiff expression pained. "You think it's *Jim*? I can't buy that. He was adamant about letting the system work."

Botine shrugged. "At this point, we'll be looking at anyone with access to that truck. That includes his workers, his family..."

An image flashed in Stanton's brain, Beau Ingler standing in Autry's office doorway, castigating her. And later, blaming the department for his sister's death. He glanced at Tick. "Beau?"

Tick nodded. "Maybe."

McMillian's intense blue gaze sharpened. "What makes you say that?"

Stanton rubbed a hand over his nape. "He...he accosted Autry in her office, and when we went to talk to him about the notes she'd been receiving, he didn't hesitate to let us know he blamed us for Sharon's death. We'd brought Schaefer here."

"Cait said it." Tick's bleak expression matched the tone of his words. "It was never about Schaefer. It was about us."

McMillian glanced at Botine. "Maybe he decided he'd get rid of Schaefer and get his revenge on the system at the same time."

Botine grimaced. "Wish he'd succeeded in taking care of Schaefer."

"Don't worry," McMillian said, a harsh smile tugging at his mouth. "Arrogant dumbass is planning to represent himself this time around. I'll bury him."

Botine quirked an eyebrow at Tick. "Any idea where we'd find Beau Ingler this time of day on a Sunday?"

"Yeah." Tick tugged a hand through his hair. "Same place I'd be if it weren't for that mess with Schaefer last night. Church."

She didn't want to be here. Autry tucked a stray lock of hair behind her ear. If Madeline's expression was anything to judge by, church was the last place she wanted to be right now too. They'd come at their mother's request, but the curious and sympathetic glances made Autry want to scream.

Madeline leaned a shoulder against a column, her posture indifferent. "You did it again."

Autry dragged her gaze away from her mother, accepting condolences from a group of ladies her age. "Did what?"

"Let Mama guilt you into being here."

Autry's brief laugh was a disbelieving puff of sound. "And what's your excuse?"

"I knew better than to try and get out of it." Madeline traced the edge of the church's brick porch with the toe of her shoe. "But I wasn't just released from the hospital."

"You know what Mama's like when she gets on a tear." Autry shrugged. "And it's only an hour. It made her happy and it didn't kill me."

Madeline straightened. "Well, well, wonder what that's all about."

"What?" Autry followed Madeline's gaze and frowned. Two unmarked units pulled to a stop alongside the road, at the end of the church drive. One was a familiar white county car, the other a steel gray. Doors opened, and Will Botine and Tom McMillian stepped from the gray car while Tick and Stanton unfolded themselves from the county unit. All four men bore grim expressions and the small pockets of conversation scattered among the groups on the church lawn died as they moved forward.

Autry watched Stanton, her heart lifting and falling at the sight of him. Focused, he didn't glance her way and she drank in the details of his appearance—his hair a little tousled, his eyes heavy, his face tired and drawn. Her throat tightened and a desire to comfort swept through her. He'd been through so much lately.

Guilt pricked at her. He'd offered her comfort and his strength, and she'd given him nothing in return. She'd pushed him away.

The men stopped at a small group a few feet away, Tom McMillian apparently doing the talking. Autry's gaze swept over the gathering, her breath strangling in her throat. Beau Ingler stood with his wife and daughter, his arm in a sling, and a bandage still covering the stitches he'd received at his hairline after being pulled from the courthouse rubble. He didn't speak, merely glared at Stanton and Tick while McMillian talked. A muscle flicked in his cheek. Malevolence gleamed in his eyes.

McMillian motioned toward the cars, and Beau tensed further but nodded. Bending his head, he spoke to his wife and disentangled himself from her hold. Autry's pulse pounded in her throat. What on earth?

But deep inside, she knew.

Head high, Beau followed McMillian up the drive, flanked by the three law enforcement officers. His wife's face crumpled and she turned away, into comforting arms. Autry sucked in a deep breath. Lenora Calvert's arms. Autry's gaze darted to the men's retreating backs. Stanton and Tick, their bearing erect, proud, despite the tension in their shoulders, followed behind Beau.

Autry's eyes stung. Stanton, keeping his promise to find the person who'd killed their daughter and her father. Tick, performing his duty for the community he loved. Neither of them flinching from what had to be done.

Neither of them running away.

She swallowed. "Madeline," she whispered, "I can't go to Jacksonville with you."

Her face set in grim lines, Madeline looked at her. "Why not?"

Autry watched Stanton slide behind the wheel of the county unit. "Because whether I'm an attorney or not, this is where I belong."

Chapter Nineteen

"Mama, I'll be fine." Autry ran a listless hand through her hair. "I drove over here; I can drive myself home. It's barely ten miles."

And if you're so concerned, why did you insist I come over here after insisting I go to church?

She left the question unsaid. Sometimes, silence was the way to go.

Her mama stood on the steps, fretting with the hem of her sweater. "I just worry, is all."

Eyeing the lines of grief on her mama's face, Autry sighed and went back to hug her. "Don't." She softened her voice. "I'm going straight home, and I'll call when I get there. Okay?"

"All right." Her mother's arms tightened around Autry's neck. "I love you, sweetheart. Be careful."

"I will." Autry disentangled herself. With a wave, she slid behind the steering wheel. She backed down the drive and turned onto the road. Relief washed over her as her mother's home shrank into the distance and she smothered a spurt of guilt at the emotion. Maybe Madeline was right. Maybe she needed to focus more on what she needed, less on what her mother wanted.

But she could do that without hurting her mother, without breaking her heart as Madeline had broken their father's. She clenched the wheel and flexed her fingers. Laying all the blame for that estrangement on Madeline's shoulders wasn't fair. Her father had been harsh, unyielding, when Madeline had wanted to make her own way. They'd all been at fault.

How unyielding have you been, Autry?

She slowed for the stop sign at the Flint crossroads. Had she done that with Stanton? Ignored his needs and focused only on what she wanted? She'd needed time to figure out what she wanted. But what had he needed? Comfort in his grief? Support in the face of Ray Lewis's disparagement? Everything she'd asked for, he'd given her.

In return, she'd given him nothing.

Shame flushed through her. Her face hot, she flipped on the air conditioning with one hand and steered into a right-hand turn with the other. She'd been so unsure of his feelings, had wanted a declaration of love, and he'd given her one, by respecting her wishes, her choices in terms of their relationship. His actions talked loud and clear. She was the one putting out mixed signals.

He deserved better, deserved *more* from her.

She swooped around the double S-curve and fumbled for her cell phone. They needed to talk. Her signal was weak, but she punched his speed dial number. After only one ring, his voice mail picked up.

Frustration flowed through her. More than likely, he'd turned his phone off if he was involved in an interrogation. Or he'd let the battery die, which he was wont to do.

At the tone, she swallowed hard. "Stanton? It's Autry. I really need to talk to you. I'm on my way home. If you have time, would you stop by later?" She paused, feeling awkward and tongue-tied. "Please? It's important."

She ended the call and tossed the phone on the passenger seat. The car sputtered and the engine revved up as if idled too high. Frowning, she glanced at the gauges. A half-tank of gas. Temperature normal.

It faltered again as she slowed to turn left on the access road cut-through. Her oil light flashed, along with the check-engine indicator, and she groaned. "Just make it home. Three miles, okay. Four at the most."

For a moment she thought it would die completely at the stop sign for the Highway 19 intersection, but the little car chugged roughly on, smoothing out a little as she neared town. By the time she reached her own driveway, the warning lights had gone off and the engine ran normally.

Weird.

She scanned the driveway and yard before sliding out of the car and hurrying to the back door. She'd shower and take a nap while she waited for him.

As reliable as he was, she had no doubt he'd come by.

Stanton leaned a shoulder on the wall, the concrete block cool even through his shirt, and stared through the two-way mirror.

Hands folded before him, gaze fixed on his fingers, Beau Ingler sat at the table, Botine and McMillian across from him. The man's expression rarely changed, and he said little.

He wasn't denying it.

He wasn't asking for a lawyer, wasn't adding information.

But he wasn't denying it, and with each second, Stanton's certainty that this was the man who'd killed his daughter deepened.

A cold rage licked through him, seeking a place to dig in and take hold.

"You can't do it, Stan." Tick rested his hands on the thin ledge below the viewing glass. His gaze rested steadily on Ingler's face.

"Can't do what?" Stanton focused on the conversation as a way to keep the fury from eating him alive. This...*bastard* had taken Claire from them, almost killed Autry, had killed so many others. He'd destroyed too many lives to count.

"Let that anger have you." Tick jerked his chin toward the room beyond. "That's what he did. That kind of anger is just a short step away from evil, and once you let it have a foothold, it's too easy to let it take over everything."

"He killed my daughter, Tick."

"I know. You want to tear him apart and I get that." Tick's grip tightened on the window ledge. "But you don't have to let him have any more of your life. That's the mistake he made. He let Schaefer, let his anger at us, have his entire freakin' life. You're stronger than that."

"Yeah." On the other side of the glass, Botine leaned forward with another question. Again, Ingler didn't react.

Stanton stared harder. How could the son of a bitch be so cold? Didn't it bother him at all, what he'd done?

No. Tick was right—somehow, the anger and need for vengeance had destroyed the man's conscience, his soul.

And damn if Stanton would let him have anything else of his.

He'd lost Claire and Autry already.

That was more than enough to lose.

"Hey." Tick tagged his arm. "Weren't you supposed to pick up the boys?"

Shit.

"Yeah." Stanton looked down to check the display on his cell phone, remembering too late he'd left it on the kitchen counter, plugged in. "What time is it?"

"About one-thirty." Tick tilted his head toward the door. "Use the phone at the front desk, call Renee, then get out of here. You need to be with them more than you need to be here, probably." He cast a dark glance at Ingler's stony face. "Son of a bitch isn't going to talk."

"Probably not." Stanton took one last look at Ingler. Yeah. Bastard had taken enough. Stanton wouldn't give him the time with his sons either. He slapped Tick's shoulder. "Let me know what happens."

"Will do." One corner of Tick's mouth quirked up in a crooked grin. "Now get out of here."

Stanton unlocked the back door, and the boys spilled into the house, scattering backpacks, iPods and jackets in the kitchen. Jostling each other amid good-natured ribbing, they went straight for the refrigerator.

A smile tugged at Stanton's mouth. He was glad they were with him, dispelling the house's morose silence and some of his own loneliness. Dropping his keys on the counter, he tried to shrug off the melancholy blanketing him. Schaefer was in custody again, they had a valid suspect in the bombing with an arrest pending and he should be pleased. Cases closed.

But he didn't have Autry. That colored everything.

"Dad, there's nothing here to eat." Hadden peered into the pantry.

John Logan popped the lid from the milk and wrinkled his nose. "Oh man, that's sour."

Stanton chuckled. "We'll order pizza tonight, all right?"

The boys exchanged a look and dove for the drawer by the phone, where he kept the takeout menus. He eyed their dark heads, bent over the menu, and affection pulled at him. Part of him wished he didn't have to return them to Renee after the funeral tomorrow. Since losing Claire, he'd felt a desperate urge to get to know them better, to make amends for prior neglect. He'd talk to Renee tomorrow, talk to the boys, see if he couldn't increase his visitation time with them.

"Pineapple and banana peppers," John Logan said.

Hadden glanced at him with an incredulous expression. "You're whacked. Pepperoni and onions."

Stanton rolled his eyes. "Order two."

John Logan looked at him over his shoulder. "Then what are you going to eat?"

Laughing, Stanton pulled his cell phone from its charger, where he'd forgotten it. "Fine. Order three. One with all meat."

The phone's screen glowed to life. New voice mail. "Guys, I'll be right back." He stepped over John Logan's backpack and exited the door to the deck, phone at his ear.

"Stanton? It's Autry…" Her voice flowed over him, and his heart stuttered. She wanted to talk to him. Hope flared in his chest.

When you make up your mind, you know where to find me.

Had she? Did she want him back?

Stanton folded the phone and clipped it to his belt. He tugged his wallet free and returned to the kitchen. It was empty, and he followed the sounds of male enthusiasm to the living room and found the boys camped in front of a football game.

"Hey guys, I've got to run over to Autry's for a while."

His sons exchanged a knowing look. Ignoring it, Stanton extended a hundred to Hadden. "That's for pizza. If you two can stay out of trouble while I'm gone, you can split the difference."

The boys grinned. Hadden lifted an eyebrow. "You're

bribing us?"

"Yeah. Is it going to work?"

"You gonna make this a regular thing?"

"No. One time only. I've got my cell and I'll be back in a couple hours."

A smile flirted around Hadden's mouth. "Take your time, Dad. We'll be fine."

Autry tugged on a camisole over her pajama pants. Her abdomen ached around the still-healing incision there. She closed her eyes on a burning wave of tears. Hours had passed. Stanton hadn't called. Hadn't come by.

Had she left it too late?

A knock at the back door stopped her heart, then sent it racing. With a last glance in the mirror, she hurried through to the kitchen. Beyond the glass in the door, she could see Stanton on the stoop, his back to her. The porch light glinted off his dark hair. A frisson of nervousness moved over her skin.

Eyes closed on a swift prayer, she stepped forward and opened the door.

He spun, hungry gaze roving over her. They stared at each other, and she took in the strain tightening his face, the tension in his shoulders, the fire leaping to life in his eyes. The weight in her chest lightened.

She reached for him, pulled him into the house, into her, and lifted her mouth to his. He tasted of coffee and warmth, his lips moving over hers in a light caress before his arms closed around her and crushed her to him. The kiss deepened, full of yearning and discovery.

Autry wrapped her arms around his neck and pressed against him. Sweet certainty washed through her. This, *this*, was what she needed—this man, by her side, in her life.

Stanton pulled his mouth from hers, kissing her temple. His hands roamed over her back, down her sides, up her arms, as though he couldn't get enough of touching her. "God, I love you, Autry. I was such a damn fool where you were concerned."

"It doesn't matter." She stroked her fingers along the strong line of his jaw. "Now matters. And I wasn't too smart, myself."

Linda Winfree

He smiled, some of the stress leaving his face. The fine lines by his eyes crinkled. "Does this mean you made up your mind about me?"

She traced his mouth, touched the point of his chin. "I love you."

His lashes dipped, and he swallowed, throat working. "I don't deserve that from you. I failed you in so many ways—"

"No." She laid a finger over his mouth and his lips moved in a tender kiss against her skin. "You did everything I asked, everything I wanted, and I was too blind to see it." She tiptoed up to kiss him again. "I want another chance, Stanton. I want us to try again, to make it work this time."

His eyes opened, the hazel depths golden and fiery with a brightness she'd not seen there before. "To make it forever."

She nodded, a sweet ache in her throat. He pulled her close again, arms firm around her, his chin resting on her hair. Autry laid her hands on his back, fine tremors racing along his muscles beneath her palms. Peace settled in her.

They stood, holding each other, for long moments. Finally, Autry sighed. "Stanton?"

"Hmm?" Pure contentment lingered in his voice.

"I still don't know what I want."

He stepped back, confusion darkening his eyes. "What? You just said—"

"I mean professionally." She smiled and curved her hand along his jaw. "I know I belong here, but I'm not going back to criminal defense."

"Take your time." He turned his mouth into her palm and murmured the words, lips moving against her skin, sending tingles racing up her arm. "Whatever you want to do is fine with me, as long as we're together."

He tightened his embrace, rocking them in a slight side-to-side motion. Autry drank in the soothing sensation of being this close to him, this quiet, this connected.

"I've missed you," she whispered against his chest and squeaked when his arms tightened further.

"Come home with me." Pulling back, he gazed at her, a fierce light in his eyes. "The boys ordered pizza. We'll have

268

dinner, spend some time with them—"

"I don't want to intrude on your time with them." She pressed a finger to his chin, wanting nothing more than to do as he asked. "They need you."

"And they'll have me." He cradled her head, his body close enough that she could feel the fine tremors running through him. "I've been without you enough, Autry. Tomorrow, the funeral...I haven't yet figured out how I'm going to get through that. I need you with me, starting tonight."

She needed that too. Closing her eyes on a wave of tears, she nodded and he caught the small word that left her lips with his mouth.

"Yes."

Small rays of sunlight peered through the overcast sky. Autry stared at the tiny white coffin on the green carpet. A spray of miniature pink roses covered the white wood. Her throat closed, one of the threatening tears spilled over her lashes, and she leaned against the strong chest behind her, grateful for the warm hands rubbing her arms.

The service was over, and yards away, Autry and Stanton's friends and family members gathered at the handful of cars parked beneath the spreading oak trees. The hum of their low voices carried to Autry.

But she and Stanton were alone with their baby. Their little girl, waiting to be buried next to the grandfather she'd never known.

Autry closed her eyes, more of the tears seeping beneath her lashes. A sob tore from her chest, and Stanton tightened his arms about her, holding her close. Autry turned her head, pressing her cheek into the curve of his biceps.

"Stanton, I don't want to leave her here."

"I know." He rested his chin on her head. "I don't either."

She cried harder, clinging to him. "I can't do this." No longer fighting the tears, she turned into his embrace, wrapping her arms about his waist and holding on. "I can't bear it."

"Sshh. You can." He whispered the words close to her ear.

"We can. Together."

Eyes closed, weeping in broken sobs for all they'd lost, she nodded, cheek rubbing against the soft cotton of his shirt. She'd get through this. They'd get through this.

Long minutes later, when she'd finally cried herself out in his arms, he led her away toward the waiting cars, one arm strong about her waist. She rested her head against him.

Back at the courthouse area, she knew the recovery operation was still ongoing, and his departmental duties didn't go away merely because of their personal loss. His presence would be required elsewhere.

"You have to get back, don't you?"

He stopped, spun her to face him, rubbed his thumb over her cheekbone. "Do you think I'd leave you now?"

She gazed up at him, taking his face in her hands. "I think you have an important job and a county that needs you."

"You need me."

"I do," she said simply, letting her fingertips slide over his warm skin. "But I was raised from day one to understand that duty comes first, remember? Besides, I'm sure the boys are ready to get away from here. Go on. I'm going to spend some time with Mama and I know you have a lot to do."

His cheeks puffed a little under a long exhale. "Are you sure?"

She nodded. She wanted something to keep her mind busy; dealing with her mama definitely was one way to do that.

He frowned a minute before he gave in. "All right. I'll meet up with Renee so she can take them home, then head to the courthouse. If I'm on site, Cookie can take some time. He's been over there for nearly two days."

A solemn smile touched her mouth. Oh yes, she knew him better than he realized. One part of his mind was always, *always* focused on his department, his men, his duty.

"How about I run you over to your mom's—"

"No, thank you. You can take me back to my house for my car and I'll drive over there." He opened his mouth to protest and she shook her head. "Stanton, it's one thing to go spend time with my mother. It's another to not have an escape route if she starts."

He looked only marginally convinced—brows lowered in a slight frown, his mouth a taut line. "Fine, but promise me you'll be careful."

She leaned up to kiss him, wanting to wrap him close and not let go, knowing part of loving him was doing exactly that. "I promise."

"Falconetti, what are you doing here?" Four hours later, dusty and dog-tired, Stanton stopped on his way through to his temporary office and eyed her. She stood at the table in the middle of the makeshift squad room, biting her lip in concentration, tapping her designer shoe on the tile floor, rifling through one of Tick's banker boxes. "Don't you ever work?"

"I am working, Reed." She didn't look up, flipping a file open, discarding it, reaching for another.

"You don't work here."

"Thank God." She lifted her head, a rueful smile curving her bottom lip. "Sorry. I shouldn't give you the bitch treatment today of all days."

"Don't do me any favors. Makes me nervous when you're nice to me." He spread his hands, almost grateful for the distraction sparring with her gave him. "Let me reiterate: what are you doing?"

"Tick lifted my personal notes on the Schaefer case and I need them."

"Why? And why not just ask him for them?"

She fixed him with a look. "McMillian wants to see them. And I can't ask him because he's not here. Cookie ran him out to Lawson Automotive to pick up his truck. You know there's no cell service between here and there." She made a frustrated sound, staring down at the box with its alphabetical dividers. "I do not get the way he organizes his things."

Stanton rolled his eyes. "Your notes, right?"

"Yes."

He leaned forward, flipped through two sections and withdrew the folder tucked behind the "P" tab. She took it, opened it, looked up at him with her elegant brows lowered in a small frown. "How did you...never mind."

"You're welcome."

She ran her fingers over the file, her expression troubled. "Reed? I'm truly sorry, about the baby, for your and Autry's loss."

He darted a look at her. She would understand how the aching emptiness felt, had weathered her own version alone for months. The grief grabbed his throat and he swallowed hard. "Me too, but thanks."

"I should get out of here." She dropped her gaze to the folder once more, flipping through the pages within. With a wry twist to her lips, she shook her head. "Unbelievable."

"What?"

"A whole page of notes on Keith Lawson, whether he made a logical suspect in the Schaefer murders or not."

"Not," Tick said, closing the door behind him as he entered. He jerked his chin in Stanton's direction before stopping at Falconetti's side to drop a kiss on her cheek and read over her shoulder. "He's not smart enough."

"Yes, I know that, now." She closed the file. "He's a more logical candidate for my profile on Autry's stalker..." Her voice trailed away and she stiffened, her gaze lifting to Stanton's. "Oh my God."

He stared back, senses going on the alert, instincts starting to scream. "What are you thinking?"

She spun to the table. "Tick, the diary, Amy's diary. Where is it?"

"Right here." Tick leaned over to slide it from the brown paper evidence bag. The hair lifted on Stanton's nape at the urgency crackling off her. "What is it?"

"There's an entry, back in March. Amy had sex with Keith at some party, referred to it as a pity fuck."

"Okay." Tick shrugged. "But why is that important?"

"Because." Stanton ticked it off in his head, a sick feeling settling in his belly. "That's about twelve weeks, isn't it?"

Falconetti flicked a look at him. "Exactly."

Tick's brows lowered. "You think Keith is the father of that baby?"

"It doesn't matter if he is or not." Falconetti turned over several pages. "What matters is whether or not Keith believes he might be. It was in the newspapers, how far advanced Amy's pregnancy was. He may not be the brightest bulb in the socket, but even he's capable of doing the math."

Stanton watched her. "You think it's him?"

"I think if I were you, I'd want to talk to him." She ran her finger down a page and handed the diary off to Tick. "See? And when I interviewed him the day of Amy's funeral, he was insistent they'd been close, wanted my assurance that the person who'd killed her would be found."

"If he figured later, once the word about her pregnancy got out, that he might be the father of that baby, that his baby had been killed too..." Tick's mouth firmed. "Hell, he might just be off kilter enough to want to get back at Autry for defending Schaefer."

"Transference. Displaced revenge," Falconetti said. "He can't get at Schaefer, but he could make Autry afraid."

"So fear is his intent." Stanton tried to still the unease shivering down his back. "You don't think he'd attempt to hurt her."

"Statistically, most stalkers never go beyond the stalking behavior, but..." She shrugged, a small lifting of one shoulder that reeked of frustration. "I can't give you any guarantees, Reed."

"Falconetti, I want you to be the one who interviews him."

"Are you—"

"I'm sure." Stanton swallowed a harsh growl and tugged his keys from his pocket. "Tick, come on, let's run out to Lawson's garage—"

"Won't do you any good," Tick said. "I just came from there, remember? Mike was pitching a bitch because the boy took off in the wrecker and won't answer the radio."

Falconetti shifted her gaze from him to Stanton, and what he saw in her eyes made his veins ice over. The line of her throat moved and she passed the tip of her tongue over her bottom lip. "Reed, I think you should call Autry. Find out where she is."

He was one step ahead of her, cell phone already in hand,

hitting two for Autry's speed dial. It rang repeatedly, stretching his nerves, and finally her voice mail picked up. Phone at his ear, her lyrical voice directing him to leave a message, he shook his head at Tick. "Call her mama's for me, would you? See if she's there." He waited for the tone as Tick pulled his own cell from its clip. "Autry, baby, it's Stan. I need you to call me, ASAP."

He slapped the phone closed. She had to be at her mother's. Had to be.

"How long ago did she leave?" Tick's dark eyes met Stanton's and he shook his head. "Are you sure? Did she say where she was going? Thanks, Miss Miranda. You too. Bye now." He disconnected. "Left her mama's about ten minutes ago. Said she was going back out to the cemetery for a while."

Stanton was already moving toward the door, the unease and his screaming instincts still dogging him. "I'm going out there."

"Want me to ride along?" Tick asked.

"No, I'd rather you two tracked down Keith Lawson. I want to know the little son of a bitch is nowhere near Autry."

Oh, this was unbelievable.

Autry watched the gauges flicker wildly on her dash once more. Ten miles from her mother's, five miles from the cemetery, and her car was acting up again.

The oil light flashed at her, blinked, stayed lit.

Maybe she'd be lucky and the engine would even out like last time.

An ominous knocking filled the car and it lost power once more. Great. It wasn't going to cooperate. Autry muttered a curse, and the engine knocked hard, stuttering, before shuddering to a complete halt. With the power steering gone, she swung the wheel and let the car coast to a stop on the shoulder.

She rested her head on the wheel and let out a frustrated growl. Not today, of all days. Her emotions were still too close to the surface and she regretted sending Stanton back to work. She'd needed him with her, needed his steady presence to stave off the waves of grief buffeting her. Going to her mother's had been a bad idea too—making the jittery feeling inside worse until finally Autry had escaped, going where her baby was, if just for a little while.

After another murmured curse, she lifted her head and sighed. "C'mon, Autry, it could be worse. You're less than a mile from the main highway and you should have a cellular signal. You can call for help."

Grabbing her cell, she flipped it open and hit her mother's speed dial. The little envelope indicating a waiting message swirled next to her signal strength indicator. Obviously she'd missed a call while coming through the cellular black hole between her mama's and the highway. She tapped a finger on the wheel and waited through ten rings. Madeline and Mama must be outside, probably on the back porch. Why wouldn't her mama give in and buy an answering machine? She had to be the last person in Chandler County without one.

Autry blew out a frustrated breath. Now who to call? She really didn't want to pull Stanton away from the recovery site. Nate was out of the question. Was it Tick's scheduled day off? Maybe—

An engine rumbled to a stop behind her and she looked up. In her rearview mirror, yellow lights flashed atop a familiar red wrecker. One of the Lawson men. Exactly what she needed. Still holding her cell phone, she pushed open the door and stepped out.

The wrecker door slammed and Keith Lawson approached, smiling. He removed his cap and scratched the top of his head. "Having a little trouble, Ms. Holton?"

Her abdomen aching and with grief and exhaustion pulling at her, she rested a hand on top of the door. "It shuddered and died."

He tilted his head, studying the car. "She's spilling oil. Might be your oil pump. Tell you what. I'll load her up, take her into the shop and give you a ride."

Autry glanced at the wrecker. Nerves jumped low in her belly, a weird tickling sensation. Something about this was too easy. Something was simply off. She forced her smile to remain in place. "It would be great if you'd run it to the shop, but I don't need a ride. I just called my sister and she's on her way—"

"Is she?" Keith's eyes narrowed, a knowing glint sparking in them. Autry tightened her grip on the door. Something was seriously off here. "Really?"

Autry nodded, not sure why she'd lied. The nervous feeling in her gut intensified by the second. A thick metallic taste filled her mouth and her pulse raced beneath her too-snug skin.

Trust your instincts.

Tick's voice, from the self-defense class he'd bullied her into taking last spring.

Her instincts were awake and screaming.

"She is." Autry flipped the phone open and slipped her thumb over the nine. She made a move to slide into the driver's seat. "I'm just going to see what's keeping her—"

"Don't do that." His voice turned hard, the threat clear.

Trust your instincts.

Autry scrambled into the car and slammed the door. With one hand, she pushed the automatic lock button. Her other hand, shaking wildly, pushed the emergency nine on her cell phone.

Keith slammed both palms against the windshield, fury twisting his features. "Get out!"

Fear curdled in her throat. The cell phone clicked at her ear. Finally, it rang. She clutched it as Keith moved out of sight. Please, let him be leaving.

"Coney 911, how can I help you?"

The window shattered. Glass showered around her. Autry screamed, dodging the hand reaching through the driver's window.

"Ma'am? Ma'am, can you hear me?" Urgency filled the dispatcher's voice.

"Yes!" Autry attempted to scramble over the console, the slim skirt she'd worn to the funeral hampering her. "I'm on Smokehouse Road."

Halfway in the window, Keith grabbed for the phone. Autry clawed at his arms and he snarled a curse. The lock popped. The door opened and he wound a hand in her hair, pulling hard.

Pain shot through her scalp. The healing cut at her hairline gave way. "Help me!"

She was screaming now, trying to free herself from the cruel hand holding her hair, dragging her from the car. She clung to the phone. Adrenaline raced through her. He was enraged. Would he kill her here, before help arrived?

"Shut up," he grated next to her ear.

"Ma'am, we're dispatching units now. Can you hear me?"

She hit the ground, gravel scraping her bare legs. Certainty and determination fired through her, giving sudden clarity to her thoughts.

911 calls were recorded. If nothing else, she could make sure he faced what he was doing. "This is Autry Holton," she yelled into the phone, clinging to it, while trying to claw him, kick him, anything to get away. "Keith Lawson is—"

He tore the phone from her hand, her nails breaking past the quick. He flung it into the woods and pulled her to her feet. Fire flamed along the healing incision on her abdomen. He yanked her toward the wrecker and Autry dug her feet into the gravel.

She wouldn't make this easy for him. God, why was he doing this?

Amy. He'd been infatuated with Amy Gillabeaux. And Schaefer had murdered her.

She pulled in a breath, her lungs heaving. "Keith, listen to me. Don't—"

Her back slammed into the hood of the truck, the air rushing from her body. His arm at her throat cut off any further words. *His arm at her throat.* Dear God above, the way Amy had died. Did he mean to do to her what Schaefer had done to Amy?

Images of the stab wounds on Amy's body flashed in her head. She struggled against him, digging into his arms, kicking at him. The pressure at her throat didn't let up. The edges of her vision wavered.

Sirens.

Desperate, she scratched at his face, gouged an eye. He roared with pain and she twisted away, stumbled, fell. She scrabbled, trying to push to her feet, dry sobs wracking her body. Burning agony twisted through her abdomen, and she fought the weakness. She had to get away, had to run...

He grabbed her hair, tugged her up against him. Tears flooded her eyes.

"You're helping him." His breath, hot and smelling of cigarette smoke, rushed over her cheek. The muscled forearm pressed against her throat. "That son of a bitch killed Amy, killed my baby, and you're *helping* him."

Nausea pushed up, choking her.

The sirens, closer.

Lord, please. Her lungs ached for oxygen. She clawed at his arm, fingers weak.

Tires squealed. Through blurred eyes, she saw the Chandler County unit slide to a stop on the road, followed by a Coney City PD car.

They moved again, Keith sliding them towards the wrecker, yanking her along. His arm loosened, enough to let her draw air into starving lungs.

Doors flew open and she glimpsed a deputy, gun drawn, using the car as cover. Troy Lee. Inappropriate humor spiked in her. Only she would get Chandler County's screwup as a would-be rescuer.

"Let her go." Authority laced Troy Lee's voice. He trained the gun on Keith.

Keith's chest heaved against her back. "You shoot me and you hit her!"

Face set in intense lines, Troy Lee gripped and regripped his gun. "Let her go, Lawson. Walk away."

She felt Keith's hesitation. His arm closed tighter on her chest for a moment.

"Step away."

She was free. With Keith's arm gone, her legs refused to hold her. Her knees gave and she hit the gravel, palms stinging. She dragged in gulps of air, Troy Lee's voice flowing over her with terse commands for Keith.

"Kneel down. Cross your feet. Hands behind your head."

Shaking, she lifted her head, sitting on her haunches, wrapping her arms around her midriff. A familiar white truck screeched to a halt beyond the patrol cars. Behind her came the metallic rasp of handcuffs, followed by Troy Lee's recitation of the Miranda rights. Everything had the weird unreality of a dream or watching a late night television show, half-asleep. This wasn't happening to her.

Her stomach revolted, bile burning her throat, and she moaned. Eyes closed, she focused on breathing through her mouth, keeping the sickness at bay. Her abdomen was on fire.

"Autry?" Concern coated Tick's soft voice.

She opened her eyes, the fuzzy realization he'd been in truck settling in. She looked around—Troy Lee pushed Keith into the back of his patrol car while two city officers watched. With Caitlin behind him, Tick crouched a few feet from Autry, watching her with intense eyes.

The one man she wanted was nowhere to be seen. Fighting off the trembling, she swallowed, her mouth tasting foul and dead. "Where's Stanton?"

"He's on his way, I swear. He'd gone out the back way to the cemetery to meet you and there's a train blocking Broad and Scott streets, so he couldn't come this route, but he's on his way." Tick's gaze roved over her. "Are you hurt?"

"I...I don't think so." She touched a hand to the aching cut at her hairline. Blood stained her fingers. The pain in her abdomen throbbed in time with her pulse.

Tick jerked his head toward the ambulance pulling to a stop behind the patrol cars. Red and blue lights whirled in the dim light of falling dusk. "Let's get you checked out, okay?"

She nodded, tears spilling over her lashes. "I wish..." She sucked in a breath, brushing the tears away. "I wish Stan were here."

"I know. He'll be here." Tick rose and held out a hand, still watching her. "Come on, Buckshot."

Autry placed her hand in his and let him ease her to a standing position. She stumbled, knees still unsteady, and he wrapped a supportive arm about her waist. She turned her face into the familiar solidity of his lean frame, the tears running free again.

He tightened his arm around her. "It's all right, Autry. It's okay now."

She shook her head, sobs tearing at her chest. No. It

wouldn't be okay until Stanton was here.

At the ambulance, he handed her over to the paramedics. He disappeared, his deep voice rising and falling as he talked into a radio and consulted with Troy Lee. Caitlin remained with Autry while the paramedics looked her over.

Doors slammed and an engine purred away.

The trembling of reaction set in, her teeth chattering, wild, disconnected thoughts flying through her head. Caitlin wrapped cool fingers around hers. "Autry, it's okay."

"Y'all have to stop saying that." Autry pushed the high, half-hysterical words through clicking teeth. The paramedic inserted an IV in her hand and she hissed at the prick. "It's not okay. Nothing about this is okay."

Caitlin laughed softly. "You're right. It really is a stupid thing to say in situations like this."

Rubber squealed on blacktop and Caitlin shot a look beyond the wrecker. Her clasp on Autry's hand tightened and she smiled. "Reed's here."

Relief crashed through Autry and she closed her eyes, not even flinching as the paramedic daubed antiseptic over the abrasion at her hairline. Stanton. Thank God.

"Autry?" Footsteps clattered on the metal step at the rear of the ambulance and when she lifted her lids, he crouched before her, broad shoulders hampering the EMT's efforts. He framed her face with shaking hands, his hazel eyes glittering with emotion. "*Autry.* Oh baby, I was so damn scared."

His palms ran over her, down her neck, across her shoulders, along her arms.

The paramedic attempted to nudge him aside. "Sheriff—"

"Back off." Stanton snarled the words, his gaze roaming over her. "Autry, honey, are you all—" His gaze dropped to her abdomen, his eyes darkening with sudden fear. "Shit." He turned on the EMT. "She's bleeding."

The man gave him a look. "Why do you think I'm trying to get you to move, sir?"

Stanton shifted to her side, big hands smoothing her hair, his nose pressed to her temple, while the EMT worked with gentle hands to assess her injuries.

"God, baby," Stanton whispered, his mouth moving against her skin. "I love you so damn much."

She turned her head, his hazel gaze so close she could see the flecks of brown and gold against the mottled green. Emotion curled through her. "I love you too."

He cupped her face, mouth meeting hers, his cheek damp against her. "Marry me, Autry. I'll be whatever you want, whatever you need—"

"You're already everything I want." She kissed him, hissing a little against his lips as the EMT prodded her sore stomach. "Everything I need."

The paramedic leaned back with a frustrated growl. "You two are going to have to do this later. Tell the man you'll marry him so I can finish making sure you're okay."

With obvious reluctance, Stanton moved back, his gaze never leaving her face. "I'm going to talk to Tick, let them finish checking you out. I won't be far."

She nodded as the EMT eased back into position. When Stanton jumped down from the doorway, she swallowed hard against the lump in her throat. "Stanton?"

The medic groaned.

Stanton turned to face her. "What, baby?"

She laced her still-trembling fingers together and smiled at him, a little tremulously. "Yes. I'll marry you."

Epilogue

"Prunella."

"I hope you're kidding." Stanton slanted the paintbrush to finish cutting in the corner.

"Gertrude."

"No."

"Ida."

"Nope."

"Elminor."

He turned and laid his brush aside. "Where the hell did you find that one?"

"Made it up." Sitting cross-legged on the carpet, Autry gave him a cheeky grin. Baby-name book in one hand, the other resting on the bulge of her belly, she eyed the chalk-pink wall. "That looks good."

"You mean I'm not going to have to paint it a fourth time?"

"Not my fault the guy gave you the wrong color three times."

"No, it's not his fault you changed your mind three times."

"Funny." She waved him down to her and he dropped beside her, stretching out to lean on his elbow and look at the list of names. She smiled at him, her hair falling forward to frame her face, and ran her finger along one line. "What about this one?"

"Gabriella. Pretty name." He rolled the name around, trying it on for size. "Gabriella Reed."

"We could call her Gabby." Autry rubbed a hand over the side of her abdomen in an absent circle. Stanton laid his palm over the spot, a flurry of activity vibrating under his touch.

Autry groaned. "There you go, getting her all worked up."

"All I did was touch—"

"That's all you have to do." Autry stretched, arching her spine to relieve the stiffness he knew lingered there daily now. "She's a daddy's girl already."

"So if daddy's little girl is named Gabriella, she needs a middle name."

"Caitlin."

He choked on a laugh. "In your dreams."

"Lynette."

His mother's name. A smile tugged at his mouth. "Your mother would have a fit."

Autry leaned forward to kiss him. "Who cares? I like it."

"So do I." He swirled his hand over the hard roundedness. "What do you think, little girl? Gabriella Lynette Reed, Gabby for short."

The baby kicked at him again and Autry laughed. "She likes it. You don't see any way Tick can turn that into a weird nickname, do you?"

He chuckled. "No, I don't think even he—"

His cell, tossed on the desk earlier, chirped and cut him off. Autry leaned up to grab it and studied the display before handing it over. "Speak of the devil."

Straightening, he lifted it to his ear. "Hello?"

"Hey." Pain and resignation lurked in Tick's voice and Stanton really didn't need him to say anything else. He closed his eyes, listening. Finally, when Tick was done, he cleared his throat. "Take whatever time you need."

"Yeah." Tick's rough sigh traveled over the line. "Thanks."

The phone beeped with the end of the call and Stanton folded it shut. Autry watched him, her eyes full of sad knowledge. "They lost this baby too, didn't they?"

Stanton nodded. Months of hormones, two rounds of artificial insemination, six weeks of bed rest...and now, nothing.

"Lord, I hate this for them." Autry folded protective arms over the swell of their child.

"I know. Me too." Reaching for her, Stanton pulled her against him, into a warm embrace, his hands covering her lower belly, stroking, soothing.

Autry rested her face against his arm. "I can pull that extra lasagna out of the freezer and we should run it over there. They won't—"

"Hush a minute, Autry." He pressed his mouth to her cheek, still rubbing his hands over her in gentle circles.

"Why?"

Eyes closed, he let the love and warmth seep into him. This was everything he needed, everything he wanted right here.

"Stanton, why am I hushing?"

"Because." He brushed another kiss over her jaw. "I'm holding my girls."

About the Author

How does a high school English teacher end up plotting murders? She uses her experiences as a cop's wife to become a writer of romantic suspense! Linda Winfree lives in a quintessential small Georgia town with her husband and two children. By day, she teaches American Literature, advises the student government and coaches the drama team; by night she pens sultry books full of murder and mayhem.

To learn more about Linda and her books, visit her website at www.lindawinfree.com or join her Yahoo newsletter group at http://groups.yahoo.com/group/linda_winfree. Linda loves hearing from readers. Feel free to drop her an email at linda_winfree@yahoo.com

She keeps a secret buried in the past. He wants the truth—now.
But an unknown killer could destroy their future.

Hold On to Me
© 2007 Linda Winfree

For FBI profiler Caitlin Falconetti, immersing herself in her job is the only way to quell the memories of a vicious, near-fatal attack and all it cost her, including the only man she ever loved. Better to let him think she simply rejected him, rather than reveal a painful secret that she's certain would have destroyed his feelings for her.

Investigator Lamar "Tick" Calvert is determined to clean out the corruption-riddled sheriff's department in his hometown. While he understands Caitlin's drive to excel at her job, it doesn't mean he's happy about the prospect of working with his former lover, the one woman he tried and failed to hold onto.

A rash of unsolved murders brings them together to find the murderer before another woman dies. Daily contact re-ignites the lingering attraction between them, but Caitlin won't risk opening herself and revealing her secret. She plans to complete the killer's profile, make an arrest and get out of town for good.

Tick plans to solve this case, too, but now that Caitlin's back in his life, he also plans to finally dig up the truth about why she left him.

But there's an added complication—the killer isn't done, and Caitlin could be the next target.

Available now in ebook and print from Samhain Publishing.

A woman craves. A man wants. Their collision pitches them into the hot zone.

Private Maneuvers
© 2008 Denise A. Agnew

Sometimes a woman craves what she shouldn't want...

Marisa Clyde wants nothing to do with the soldier acting as a temporary bouncer in her uncle's tavern, even though the stoic, six-feet-of-smoldering hunk rescued her during a tour gone bad in Mexico. While those few short moments sent their sexual tension screaming off the charts, a devastating hurt in her past now blocks her willingness to surrender to him. He'll only be in town a month. If she can just wait it out, he'll soon be out of her life.

Sometimes a man wants more than a woman is willing to share...

Jake Sullivan watches Marisa like a hawk, well aware his need to protect is messing with his mind and making him care way more than he should. Priding himself on clinical detachment in the game between man and woman, he figures once he's slept with her, she'll be out of his system for good. But that's before he experiences her at a deeper level—and learns she just might be in danger again.

Available now in ebook from Samhain Publishing.

Printed in the United States
147686LV00003B/80/P